T0114403

BY KEVIN CANTY

A STRANGER IN THIS WORLD

INTO THE GREAT WIDE OPEN

KEVIN CANTY

NINEBELOWZERO

Kevin Canty, author of the short story collection *A Stranger in This World* and the novel *Into the Great Wide Open*, won the Transatlantic Review Award for the opening chapters of *Nine Below Zero*. His work has been published in *Esquire*, *The New Yorker*, *Details*, *Story*, *The New York Times Magazine*, and *Vogue*. He currently lives in Montana with his wife, the photographer Lucy Capehart, and two children and teaches fiction at the University of Montana.

NINEBELOWZERO

A NOVEL

KEVINCANTY

VINTAGE CONTEMPORARIES
VINTAGE BOOKS
A DIVISION OF RANDOM HOUSE, INC.
NEW YORK

The Library of Congress has cataloged the Doubleday edition as follows:
Canty, Kevin.
Nine below zero: a novel / Kevin Canty. —1st ed. in the U.S.A.
p.   cm.
I. Title.
PS3553.A56N56   1999
813'.54—dc21   98-41402
CIP

ISBN: 978-0-375-70799-5

Author photograph © Lucy Capehart
Book design by Jennifer Ann Daddio

www.vintagebooks.com

146694632

FOR LUCY, TURNER, NORA

ACKNOWLEDGMENTS

I'd like to thank the Henfield Foundation for their support of a very early version of this novel. I'd also like to thank the teachers, students and fellow students who kept me company while I was learning to write this, especially Marjorie, Padgett, Harry and Joy; the Bad Persons of Gainesville, Florida; and the women of New York who have given me my professional life, especially Nan, Denise and Deb. Thank you all.

NINEBELOWZERO

He bent to kiss her and found last night's bar in her hair: cigarette smoke, stale beer and pine disinfectant. Lie down with bartenders, he thought, wake up with angels. A sense of fairness. He summoned his courage to kiss her neck. She chased rabbits in her sleep, stirring and mumbling.

Marvin Deernose slipped out of the bedroom in stocking feet and laced up his boots in the kitchen. The philosophical Indian: he liked this hour before daylight, when he could stand outside himself, watching. An inheritance from his father, who never slept past six-thirty in his life. Marvin longed for coffee but Carla was a coffee artist, whole beans and the grinder and Herr Coffee, the German machine. No way to fire it up without waking her. He gave up, rested in her kitchen chair for a moment, enjoying the quiet, the heaviness of his body and the blue edge around every shape. The philosophical Indian finds something to admire even in the depths of a hangover. Nothing is lost on him. Empty beer cans stood along the counter like witnesses. Guilty, they declared, guilty, guilty, guilty.

Quarter to six, half an hour before daylight.

A memory: Marvin and his father sitting around the kitchen

table while the rest of the house slept, his father listening to the radio, the cow and pig news out of Billings.

Cold wind pressed against the windows, a thousand miles of empty sky. It was only November but winter already, with months to come. Marvin hunched down into his good wool coat and stayed a minute longer in the warmth of her house. A longing for marriage, normality. He rubbed his face into his hands and felt the damage that had not been slept away. A moment's glimpse of the soul inside his chest, the pearly whiteness shining through the black of his sins. Like an egg. Curl up inside it. He thought of Carla sleeping, foul naked comfort between the sheets, cursing in her dreams. No, you fuck you, she told him, sound asleep. An empty pack of Marlboro lights lay crumpled on the table. Marvin saw it, felt his head spin slightly, one degree off, and then it was time to go. Temple of his body. The gates of sleep were closed against him. The day, begun, would not go backward.

Outside was zero, plus or minus. The small hairs inside his nose stiffened and froze within ten feet of her door. Petrified dog turds lay in the snow, in little caves of their own making, the action of the sun being stronger upon the darkly colored turds than upon the lightly colored snow. So saith the scientific Indian. The time and place for science, and not for natural comfort or ease, living simply in the world. In the darkness and cold was the need for technology. When his pickup started on the first crank, Marvin reached his bare hand out and petted the cold steel of the dashboard, good dog Ford. The cold was like a gigantic weight, pressing the houses down against the earth. The human skin, like the skin of an orange.

The sun was just under the horizon, rising up out of the plains. The sky was hammered lead. Marvin could see fine but when he turned the headlights on, he was surprised at how bright they were.

King of the world: the only one awake. He drove the sleeping streets downtown, past the Sportsman's Lounge, scene of the crime. The one traffic light was blowing around on its cable, stop, go, I forget. Nine below zero by the Rosebud Farmers and Merchant clock, nowhere close. If the bankers wanted Marvin to trust them, why did they set their clock to lie? A kind of flattery. Colder in the winter, hotter in the summer, the pioneer spirit lives on in our hearts. Indian uprising: try extra value checking. The American suckers were asleep with their wives in their snug little houses, the chainlink yards holding in each private patch of blackening snow. Dogs barked at his pickup. Little box houses with too many things in the yard: boats, trucks, Corvettes, doghouses, decorative concrete, motorcycles, birdbaths, wishing wells, Studebakers, canoes, firewood, anonymous shapes under blue plastic tarps, a plaster Mexican, a painted-plywood rear view of a fat woman planting flowers, snowmobiles, Montegos, Satellite Sebrings, barbecue grills, deer hides, smokers made from dead refrigerators, all covered with a rotting patchwork of snow, all but the satellite dish, swept clean to improve reception.

It felt like breaking free when he passed the last Circle K, the final mobile home lot: trailers lined up along the highway like tin pigs and the American flags and the enormous sign lit up against the morning sky: INSTANT QUALITY LIVING. Out onto the plains with the sun just balanced on the line of the horizon. A break in the clouds along the edge of the world. The first light shined up against the hills and valleys of the clouds, another country, upside down, undiscovered. Lighting out for the cloud territories. Marvin laughed at his own joke, feeling a lightness anyway, the road curving around and then up into the sky in his Ford F-150.

The angel was separating out from the animal.

Marvin the body (the husk, he thinks, the shell, the left-behind) was starting to disintegrate. The morning sunlight was everything he was not: pure, clean, lovely. He remembered Carla pouring bar whiskey out of the gun. The memory made his teeth hurt in the morning light. He kept his mouth shut so the light wouldn't get to his teeth. The empty pack of cigarettes on the kitchen table was not the one he had started out with but a second pack he had bought in the bar. Carla smoked a couple of them but still: why? Death by cigarette, maybe, but that didn't feel like the point either. He held his hand in midair in front of his face, to see if it was trembling, and it was. Marvin was feeling sorry for himself, the expansive alcoholic self-pity, when he saw:

A white horse was bleeding to death in the snow, coming down the hill into the Silver Creek valley. Red snow and the front legs slashing and what? Something was wrong. He couldn't catch up.

Marvin hit the brakes and the Ford went sideways, black ice magic. First he did a straight spin, a 360, wound up somehow going forward again at about forty miles an hour with his brakes locked up tight. He tried to get his brain to let up on the pedal but the brain was paralyzed, too much confusion, too fast. In his eyes he saw the horse, a white horse, brilliant red bleeding, blood coming out of its nose and its asshole, eyes still open, looking at him, intelligent: Why are you doing this to me? Marvin knew it was his fault.

A scorching sound when the tires bit dry pavement again and then the brain started to work a little and he was able to pump the brakes and slow things down.

Down at the bottom of the hill lay a black Cadillac upside down in the snow with its wheels still spinning. Twenty feet off the pavement? Marvin saw the wheel tracks veering off into the borrow pit and then the mess and mud where it flipped. A giddy little voice inside him was shouting accident! accident! which would not shut up when Marvin tried to make it. Accident! There might be blood, there might be gasoline. He couldn't stop the curiosity, the midget sick excitement welling up in his chest. Eyes of the horse still on him.

He flipped the CB on to Channel 9: "There's a wreck out on 191," he told the microphone. "Right by the Silver Creek grade. I don't know if anybody's hurt. There's a dead horse too."

A second of quiet so he wasn't sure anybody heard and Marvin felt like a fool. Then heard the dispatcher's voice: "A dead horse?"

"Well, it's hurt, anyway," Marvin said. "I'm going to take a look."

"There's people, too, right?"

This was Linda Fontanelle, the night dispatcher, a little dim but foxy.

Marvin hadn't seen anybody. He said, "I guess."

"I'll get some help out."

Linda sounded bored with the whole business. The white horse was bleeding to death so that Linda Fontanelle could live, so that Marvin could live. Streams of red blood, curious eyes. Something to think about sometime, not now. This was an *emergency*—but he couldn't get up for it somehow, couldn't make himself focus. People might be dying, he told himself. Bear down. The wheels of the Cadillac were still spinning. Good bearings, Marvin thought. My truck wouldn't do that.

The cold was waiting for him outside. Everything metal was lethal cold, skin-freezing-to-it cold. He had forgotten the cold while he was driving. The snow made squeaking sounds under his boots, especially where the roof of the Cadillac had packed it down, like the track of a giant sled. Fuck O dear, Marvin thought. He could see a body, at least one body, dangling upside down by the seat belt. He looked in the back for a car seat but no babies, not that he could see. A set of golf clubs lay scattered around on the headliner. Nasty thing to have loose. He knelt in the loose snow next to the driver's side and steeled himself and looked inside.

An old man's face stared back at him, upside down. A stream of blood ran downward from his chin and onto the dome of his bald and freckled head, where it dripped. The eyes were blank, mineral.

"You okay?"

Marvin shouted through the window glass, just to see if he could get a rise. The old man didn't flinch, though he was staring straight at Marvin. Dead or deaf or just indifferent. Maybe something was happening with him. Maybe there were more important things than Marvin at that moment.

"I called for help," Marvin shouted. "I've got a CB."

Nothing.

Then, slow and jerky like a run-down carnival attraction, the old head swiveled on its neck to face forward again, and the lips muttered a word that Marvin couldn't catch.

"What?"

The old man said it again, and again Marvin couldn't catch it.

"Roll down the window," Marvin shouted, but the electricity that powered the old man's movement had spent itself, the lights had flickered off again. Puppet, Marvin thought, remembering funhouse Frankensteins, Lincoln at the World's Fair 1964, four score and something years ago. . . . He could not get his brain to work right. Concentrate. He was starting to lock up in the cold. He couldn't think of what to do.

The door was locked or bent, shut solid. Or frozen, Marvin thought. Took his watch cap off and wrapped his hand in it and hit the window hard as he could, trying to break in. But the glass was harder than his hand, and he only hurt his wrist.

He stood, and when he looked around it was quiet morning

everywhere, everywhere but the accident. The sky was a pale delicate gray and the hills were covered with snow, and lighter than the sky. The peace he sought was everywhere but inside him.

Marvin tried the other door and—surprise—it opened, and then he was kneeling on the roof liner of the car.

"Are you okay?" he asked—and his voice was intimate, just the two of them in that little cold space.

Nothing. Then the old man started up again, the power coming intermittently from someplace way inside him, the head turning toward Marvin, the lips fumbling around a familiar word so that Marvin couldn't understand the first time and asked the old man to say it again and again the old man said it: "Blind."

Blind.

Marvin didn't know what to say, where to put himself.

"You could see okay?" he asked.

Then called himself names: stupid, unfeeling. They'd give a blind man a license, sure they would. Idiot.

"Are you okay?" he asked.

And continued to feel like an idiot. Sure I'm okay, just a little blind is all.

"I'm cold," the old man said.

Marvin looked at him, strung from the ceiling by the seat belt like a bird or bat, and wondered if he could move him without damage.

"Make a fist," he said.

The old man tried to do it, the one big liver-spotted hand grasping around an empty circle of air. He couldn't quite close it.

"I don't want to move you," Marvin said. "I could hurt you."

He didn't want to say the word *paralysis* but it hung between them.

"Upside down," the old man said. "A blue . . ."

"What?"

"Nothing."

"We'll get the ambulance here in a minute," Marvin said. "We'll get some help."

This seemed to satisfy the old man. The lights and motors shut themselves off again and it was quiet between them. Fuck O dear, Marvin thought: blind. The last thing in the world, except for paralyzed, and the old man might be both.

"What happened?" Marvin asked.

But it was just to make conversation, and the old man knew it. He didn't answer or respond or even move, and still there was something wrong. It took Marvin a minute to understand that the radio was still going, softly, the Beautiful Music station out of Havre. It was all wrong for this occasion but Marvin couldn't figure out how to shut it off.

"Blind," the old man said again—this time for himself, not for Marvin.

"You'll be okay," Marvin said, useless reassuring noise.

The old man's face was lined and weatherbeaten, left out in the rain. Marvin couldn't tell him he was fine. The old man knew things Marvin didn't.

Then the sirens started, off in the distance.

The old man cleared his throat but his voice wouldn't clear. He took a couple of false starts and then cleared his throat again and Marvin hoped he wasn't drowning in his own blood. He'd seen that in the Navy.

"I don't want to die like this," the old man said. "You understand?"

His voice sounded like somebody tearing a piece of cloth but Marvin could understand him. The old man took one hand off the steering wheel and reached it toward Marvin and Marvin understood that he was supposed to take it.

"I don't want to die like this," the old man said again. "I'll make you a deal."

Reluctant, Marvin took his glove off and held the old man's hand. The skin was cold and stiff as leather.

"What?"

"Anything."

"No, what do you want?"

The old man's face turned, upside down, in the direction of Marvin's voice. Marvin saw how big the head was, how powerful.

"You know what I mean," the old man said. "If it becomes necessary."

"You're going to be fine."

The old man blinked impatiently—*blind*—and Marvin was ashamed of himself. He knew what the old man meant, knew what he wanted. No good pretending he didn't.

"They'll be here in a second," Marvin said. "We'll get you out of here."

"What do you say?" the old man asked. Marvin felt the old eyes boring into him, sightless.

"We'll get you out of here," he said.

"I was almost gone," the old man said. "I wasn't even cold anymore, just sleepy. Then you came along."

Marvin felt the accusation, a little needle in his heart.

"I was just trying to . . ."

"No," the old man said, and for the first time there was a shadow of force in his words.

"I'm sorry," he said more softly. "I don't want you to feel bad."

"No."

"It doesn't seem like I can do much of anything for myself, that's all."

"You'll get better," Marvin said.

"Don't you lie to me."

The old man's head swiveled forward, toward the sound of the sirens, then back toward Marvin.

"A favor, if you want," he said. "I'll make a deal if that's what you want. But I don't want to be at anybody's mercy."

"No."

"I want to know if I can count on you."

Let me out, Marvin thought. He heard the sirens like they were rescuers. But he knew that this would be done and concluded before the sirens ever got there. It was done already, almost: a life for a life. He brought the old man back and now he owed him.

"You'll be all right," Marvin said.

The old man made a small clucking sound with his lips, impatient.

"I want to know if I can count on you," he said.

"You're pushing me around."

"I need to know."

"You'll be all right," Marvin said again.

"It would be a kindness," said the old man. "You understand that, don't you? A kindness. You can't leave me here by the side of the road."

"You can get better."

"All right," the old man said. "I can get better. What if I don't?"

Marvin didn't say anything.

"Can I count on you?"

The ambulance stopped by the roadside. The siren shut off all at once and a silence rushed in to fill the empty place where the sound had been.

"Look, I'll pay you," the old man said. "Whatever language

you understand. But you won't do it—you're afraid to get your hands dirty, right? I'm blind, now. I can't work my hands. Are you a Christian?"

"I'll help you," Marvin said.

He said it without measuring, without meaning to.

"Thank you," the old man said.

"If you need it."

"I understand," the old man said. "I put my hand in front of my face, I can't tell if it's there or not."

"They're coming for you now. It'll just be a minute."

"My name is Henry Neihart," the old man said. "I want you to remember my name. I may not be able to come looking for you."

"I'll find you," Marvin said. "If you need me."

"Thank you," Henry Neihart said. "I can count on you."

He sounded like he was trying to convince himself. Marvin was still holding the old man's hand and it was still cold, cold as ever. It was like his own heart's blood was being drained out toward the cold endless winter, through the old man's body, which was already a part of it.

The old man said, "A kindness."

Then the ambulance crew was prying the door open. Then the seat-belt cutters did their work, and quickly—before Marvin could orient himself—Henry Neihart was out of the Cadillac and strapped to a backboard, a green gas mask over the bottom of his face, eyes open and unseeing. Commotion, cop cars, a wrecker. In the time it took Marvin to pull his glove on again, to take the hat and fold it over his numb ears and wipe the freezing snot from his nose, they got the old man in the ambulance and the doors closed and gone, down the road in silence. There was nobody to use the siren on. Marvin watched it all the way around the curve and gone.

Then a rifle shot. He heard it echo and then looked up and the horse—he'd forgotten about the horse—was dead. A black scare-crow stood next to the nest of blood, holding a rifle. The gunshot split the quiet and then it was gone, the quiet rushing in again.

"That's quite a deal," said Gil Sibbernsen, a county deputy.

Marvin looked at his watch: twenty after seven. He wondered what he had let himself in for.

"Your day to be the hero," Sibbernsen said. "He would have died if you hadn't come along."

"He's going to die anyway," Marvin said.

"So are you," Sibbernsen said. "So am I. What the fuck."

"Have a nice day," Marvin said, walking toward his truck. Walking toward the horse where it lay, dead by the road. The wind whistled in the dry roadside weeds.

Justine was peeling eggs when the call came, an ordinary winter Tuesday, alone in the house and waiting for Neil. She was making deviled eggs for a baby shower the next day. Public Radio was describing the day's events for her, measuring the known world. A cold Oregon rain fell through the bare trees, tapped against the window, nothing that would slow traffic. Neil would be home safe.

Measuring the known world.

Then the telephone rang, and it was Marliss, Henry's cook: *There's been an accident with the Senator . . .* A stroke was what they were calling it. Next of kin. Neurologists, insurance.

She hung the telephone receiver back and carefully measured herself a glass of wine. Neil had decided that they each had an alcohol problem, though he really meant that Justine did, he was just being supportive in his way. Then he decided that they would not treat it as a disease but as a failing, a defect of character. Instead of stopping altogether, they would each drink no more than half a bottle of wine apiece each day, though when they made this decision Justine was buying vodka in cases. This had been going on for two years and so far, with exceptions for New Year's, arguments and parties, they had been able to stick with it.

They drank only good wine, and measured out their halves like chemists.

She was well through her half of the bottle when the phone rang again. She knew who it was before she picked it up: Val, her sister, down in California.

"You heard?" Val asked.

"Marliss called me."

"Jesus, Jess, I'm so sorry."

"It's not happening to *me*," she said. "It's Henry you should feel sorry for."

"That's not what I mean."

"I know," Justine said, and sipped her wine. One good thing about disaster, she thought: it gives you all kinds of permission.

She said, "How bad is it, did they tell you?"

"Not really," Val said. "It's still early."

"One of us ought to go out there."

Justine heard the rush of static on the telephone line in the momentary silence, Val's children in the kitchen behind her, the primary noise of a Disney cartoon. She could hear Val composing her objections on the other end of the line.

"I could go later in the week," Val finally said. "I don't know, I haven't even told Johnny yet, I haven't been able to get ahold of him. He's got some big closing today over in San Mateo, big residential."

"You can't go."

"I could take the kids with me, maybe."

"Take them out of school? And who's going to baby-sit Johnny Boy if you go?"

"Jesus, Jess, leave him alone."

"I'm sorry."

"He's my *husband*."

An expensive silence, the hiss and sizzle of outer space on the line. Justine knew that her sister was thinking up some new disqualification, some new reason why she shouldn't go. And maybe she shouldn't, she knew that, but she wanted to. It came as a surprise, unexamined, but she wanted it.

"I've been okay lately," Justine said.

"I hear."

"Good grades in deportment. Works well with others."

"Don't make fun of this."

"I'm not. I'm trying to tell you."

"How much sadness do you need?"

Val's voice was hard and sharp, the voice she used when one of her children strayed too close to the lighted stove, too near the edge of the overlook: Get back!

Justine sighed.

"It seems like you've been better lately," Val said.

"I don't know. Maybe I'm just getting used to it. Maybe you're getting used to seeing me this way."

"Do you really think you need this? He's old, Jess, almost eighty. If this isn't the last straw, then it isn't far off."

"He was fine last summer."

"That's how it goes sometimes. That's how it was with Johnny's father."

"I don't know."

"What?"

"This is just something I want to do."

"Then I imagine you'll do it."

A pause, to let the message sink in: she was worrying her sister, worrying all of them. She was being selfish.

"Just be careful, Jess. Call me."

"As good as I can be," she said. "I promise."

Then the empty house, waiting for Neil, and the guilty secret excitement of the trip. She started to pack without asking Neil first, without permission, because disaster had allowed her to. She could do whatever she wanted to. She could have another glass of wine.

She took the bottle upstairs with her as she selected which clothes to take.

She gave up packing and wandered the hallways of her own house.

She could see it, the house, which was unusual. Gradually it had become invisible to her, as hard to see as her own face in the mirror, but this evening she could see the artifacts of her first life almost as well as a stranger could, walking in for the first time: the living room without television, the shelves of books, the carefully selected totems of America and childhood, rusty antique Coca-Cola sign, Nehi thermometer, cast-lead fire truck. Archaeology, she thought: lives and artifacts. The ceramic pitcher of dried flowers on the table by the window. It was an old house, a family house. It had a porch and a banister. Evidence of good taste lay all around her, intelligence and good intentions. The table, say: a battered maple wreck out of a farmhouse they had rented when Neil was in graduate school, cleaned and polished but still wearing its nicks and scars. The Rauschenberg poster on the wall. Oh, she was sick of it.

All but the one room. She resisted the idea but at some point she knew that she was going into Will's room.

She opened the door and the stale air rushed out at her, thought it hadn't been long since it was open. Neil went in sometimes. Justine was forbidden.

The toys sat on the shelves and in the plastic crates and hampers: Lego, train set, brio-mech. Will had been four when he died, four in perpetuity. The souls of children who die before they are baptized wait in purgatory for the Second Coming. Innocent, they suffer anyway.

Will was four when he died in a car crash in the rain. Neil had been driving. It was not his fault. She had forgiven him.

She understood why she was not allowed in this room.

Although she'd laundered the sheets and the quilt Val made for him, she could still smell him in the bed: the baby-powder sweetness and the bitter smell of urine. She knew why she shouldn't be doing this, resting her cheek on the flannel pillowcase to take in the smell. A little gift to herself. She understood that this could only lead to more suffering but the suffering didn't seem to go away, no matter what she did. At least she could give herself this small pleasure.

She was well into Neil's half of the bottle by the time he made it home. The eggs lay white and naked on the counter.

"What's going on?" he asked, suspicious.

"It's Henry," she said. "My grandfather. He had a stroke."

Neil's face softened into his usual look of concern. "Is it serious?"

"Jesus, Neil, did you ever hear of a stroke that wasn't?"

"I'm sorry."

"I mean, he's blind, for Christ sake."

"I said I was sorry," Neil said. "Jesus. Blind."

"They don't know. It might be temporary, might not. I guess there's some loss of movement or whatever. I'm going to drive out tomorrow."

Neil stared at her as though this was some new symptom, his face a mix of sorrow and surprise and anger. Why did she refuse to get well, to be happy? Why wouldn't she do him this simple favor?

"You think that's a good idea?" he asked.

"I'm the only one in the family that's still talking to him. You know. He needs somebody's help."

"He's got his people out there."

"*Paid* help, Neil. It's not exactly the same. Besides, those are my spoons that they're stealing."

He was disappointed in her. He's doomed to disappointment, Justine thought. He thought she was running away from things, trying to escape, that's what he would say about her.

"What are you going to do about work?" he asked.

"They can find somebody."

"You haven't talked to them yet?"

"I just got the call an hour ago," she said. "Maybe two hours."

"Did you talk to Dr. Fairweather about this?"

"Jesus, Neil."

She clucked her lips impatiently and then, unable to sit still, rose up out of her seat and circled the living room, coming to rest at the bar that divided the room from the kitchen, where she poured another half glass of wine for herself. She leaned against the bar, looking at Neil, trying to see him: a good-looking curly-headed man in the middle of his life, in jeans and battered holey cashmere sweater and his fancy parka, still dressed for outside. He had his painting shoes on, densely spattered. He looked like what he was: an art professor, a husband. All he wanted was his peace and quiet and his three five-ounce glasses of wine.

I don't care about you, she thought. That's my little secret.

It gave her a lost feeling to know this but also a kind of power.

"This is a family emergency," she said. "The regular, old-fashioned kind. It doesn't really matter whether Dr. Fairweather approves or disapproves or what my feelings are or whatever."

"Why don't you want to call him, then?"

Again, she saw the sheeplike injured look on his face: she was staying sick, staying sad, as an affront. She was doing it *to* him. But she could think of no other way for him to feel. Justine felt the needle of contrition: my fault, my fault, my most grievous fault.

"I'll call him, if you think I should. I mean, I was going to call him anyway in the morning."

Neil shrugged.

"It's after office hours now," she said. "I'd have to call him at home."

"You're going to do whatever you want to," Neil said. "That's okay. I just think you should figure it out before you go rushing off. You need to think this through."

"I'll call him, then," she said.

"Fine," Neil said. "Whatever. I don't mean that."

"What?"

"Oh, you know, whatever. It's not like I don't care."

"I know that."

"I'm just tired, is all. It always seems like there's some new development." He laughed, as a way of underlining his words. "I mean, just when we seem to be getting back on an even keel."

"I didn't do this," Justine said. "I didn't make this happen."

Excuses: Justine was the baby girl and Neil the big bad Daddy. He didn't like this any better than she did. He was just as sick of it—and again, that needle of contrition. She was, in fact, doing this to him. In some small way, this was fine with her.

"Maybe we can go to Florida when I get back," Justine said, in a rush. "Catch a few rays, go to the beach. I mean, it's so gray around here! No wonder I get blue sometimes."

"Don't," he said.

"What?"

"Just don't," he said. "I'm going to get changed."

And left her there, by the kitchen, with the dinner unstarted, her clothes unpacked, everything half under way and botched. Florida: she closed her eyes and tried to force a memory of the smell of the air, which would not come. Sometimes the smell would visit her in a flower shop, or peeling an orange, this sudden memory of sex and perfume. There was this other life, this other shape. Things had been started that never came to fruit.

No: this was her only life. Neil her only husband. She stared at the telephone on the kitchen wall, trying to get the courage up to call Dr. Fairweather, to be scolded by him. Run away, she thought. Run away.

Neil was already in bed and asleep or pretending sleep by the time she finished the hundred small errands and efforts, the laundry, the bills, the late night trip to the ATM and to gas up the Bonneville. They'd had a skirmish over the Bonneville. Neil wanted her to take his car, the Volvo, which besides being safer was almost two decades newer and quieter and got better gas mileage and so on. Of course he was right. He also pointed out that the convertible feature of the big Pontiac was not going to be much use in Montana in December, which he was also correct about.

Because they were married, though, because they had known each other for a dozen years, this fight was not about what they pretended it was about. Justine would take the Volvo gladly except it was *his*. The Bonneville she bought with her own money, and though it had turned out to be a financial bomb (she'd dropped a whole new engine in it, and an exhaust system, tires, a paint job) it was at least her own mistake. Plus it didn't feel like a mistake, driving it. It felt like a beauty.

Neil had come to see almost every aspect of her personality as a symptom, though. Her attachment to this impractical car—it got eighteen miles to the gallon on the highway and had to be tuned up every year to squeak by the emissions test—was evidence of her failure to come through, to reattach herself to adult life.

"What if you were in an accident?" he asked. "That thing would fold up like a Japanese lantern."

"That thing weighs like five thousand pounds."

"But it's a convertible," he said, and so on.

Really it was simple: Neil wanted her to wear the Volvo for all to see, he wanted her to be sane and to be married and Justine did not know what she wanted. This new coldness that she felt—she thought about it in the 7-Eleven at midnight, waiting in the rain while the attendant poured gallon after gallon of gas into the Pontiac: the way she could think about Neil when he was there or when he wasn't and there was just no feeling there, like Novocaine, or like the trick called Dead Man's Hand she used to play with Val when they were children. They'd stack their left hands together and close their eyes and the feel of the two hands together—half her own feeling flesh and the other half her sister's numb skin—was so perfectly and completely creepy that they would do it for hours. The touch of that dead flesh. The only scary trick she knew that actually worked.

She thought of Neil as though he was far away, though he was sleeping or pretending to sleep in their marriage bed ten blocks away. She knew that he was suffering too but it didn't help her feel any closer to him. I could be anywhere, she thought, looking around at the neon, the red-white-and-blue of the Budweiser signs. I could be anyone.

And Henry was ill. Henry lay injured, maybe dying, and she was using him as an excuse for her own self-indulgent sorrows. Justine saw herself plainly, as others would see her: *selfish*. It felt like a needle piercing skin, the good clean pain.

She resolved to take the Volvo, declare allegiance, be a good girl. But when she got home, she packed the trunk of the Pontiac as she had planned to all along. She packed a sleeping bag, and the tire chains, and a little can alleged to seal a flat tire and reinflate it. She packed her jean jacket and her cowboy boots. She packed her diaphragm, wondering if Neil would notice. Would he look? Sure he would. She didn't mean to hurt him, she thought, composing a shopping list in her head: bananas, vodka, diaphragm junk. She packed her watercolor box, her easel, and her pad, and a college Emily Dickinson, the Norton Critical Edition with her idiotic notes in her idiotic college handwriting. *Slip is crash's way*, she thought, heaving the lid shut on the Bonneville trunk.

It was one in the morning by the time she made it to bed. Neil was pretending to be asleep, she was almost sure. He pretended to wake up when she slipped in next to him.

"I love you," he said automatically.

"I love you," she said back, a ritual from the days of marriage, days of family. There were worse things than habits. In the first days after the accident, days and weeks, the little rituals of their lives had been all that held them in place. They made this little shape in time and space—work, television, meals, ways of touching—and they could take shelter inside this shape and wait for their souls to return to them. Except that the boy had worked his way into every corner of their lives. There was no place safe. Neil said it: even when he took the picture off his desk, because he could no longer stand to look at it, he could still see the place on his desk where the picture had been.

Justine felt the emptiness opening up between them again, in the silence and the dark, the deadness returning. She didn't want it. She reached for his cock, felt the soft skin with her fingertips circling him: familiar beast. He smelled faintly of turpentine. She felt him stiffen slowly under the touch, the ritual gestures. He never said a word. This was the way it had been lately. He slipped his fingers inside her, almost rudely, almost a soldier. There in the dark, without any talking, he could have been anyone. That's the way it had been lately: the calculated roughness, the things her body wanted. It was all right if it hurt a little. Neil knew how to give it to her. She gave him back her need, opened up to him, whoever he was, let the noises come out of her mouth into the dark and silence around them. Fucking: he turned himself toward her and then on top of her and inside and she was with him all the way, Neil's surprising big dick inside her, unprotected. She couldn't stand calculation anymore. If she got up to put the diaphragm in, the feeling was gone by the time she made it back (cold lights, running water) and so she let him inside her and they took their chances and hoped that he would remember to pull out but not yet, not yet.

She was with him all the way, she lifted her hips to meet him and rose and let him all the way in, the head of his dick deep inside her, she could feel it and she was with him. Kiss my tits, she thought, and he did without asking. Kiss my neck. Then she felt him start to hold back.

"Don't worry about me," she whispered.

"I'm not worried."

"Just go ahead," she said—but the feeling was already gone, she just lost it someplace and it was two white winter-fat bodies flopping around on the flannel sheets. The dislike she felt for her own body spread to his. She felt her skin cool, though Neil was still inside her, on top of her, working and working, trying to fix her. It's just the drugs, she told herself. I'm clean, not guilty, it's nothing to do with me. He slowed, and started to kiss her tits again: annoyance.

"Don't worry about me," she said again, and he stopped, and looked at her: care, concern, sorrow.

"I'm a million miles away," she said. "It's no good."

Neil stared at her face a moment longer, then started back in, alone.

5:26, 5:27, 5:28: She watched the changing of the red numbers of the clock while the happiness extinguished itself. Repeating dreams, the tiny treadmill of her self. Boy, she thought, remembering Will from dreams, forming the word with her mouth: my boy.

She got up, got dressed, kissed Neil in the air above his forehead, not wanting to wake him. She was heading east on the Banfield before six.

In the drizzle and the unfamiliar morning dark, the headlights and taillights shone and reflected and became part of her dream: the busy bees of everyday life, driving and bustling and making honey. Justine was just another pair of headlights on the highway. She was still full of Will, sharing the space inside herself. Which was fine. She was nobody special, nothing to be guarded and tended and taken care of. A boy was welcome there, in that empty space inside her where he used to live.

Daylight came slow and weak through the clouds. Coffee, mile markers. The traffic thinned when she got out of Portland but it never died out, just got more industrial, purposeful. The rain came down with fresh violence once she got out into the Gorge. The rain blew horizontally across the road, and the tandem-trailer semitrucks shimmied in the wind as she passed them. The driving was difficult, which was better: she could lose herself in the effort. The lightness of speed. The miles, the green shaggy hills passing quickly in the rain. The Columbia sat sullen and metallic to her left, pooled behind dams and plied with barges, more like a highway than a river. She had this feeling, driving, going. Then thought of Henry, her grandfather, blind and hospitalized. He kept getting lost in the excitement of her trip: her fault, she felt the needle of guilt again. Selfish, she called herself. Self-centered. (You wouldn't call a drowning man self-centered, Fairweather said. You wouldn't blame him for not wanting to go under.) But Neil knew her better than anyone, better than she knew herself, and he knew she was selfish, he told her so. Even Val had told her.

By eleven o'clock she'd driven out of the rain and she was low on gas. She stopped in Umatilla, in the shadow of a fifty-foot plywood cowboy, got out. Waiting for her in the air was the perfume of the sagebrush in the air, and the hard sunlight. The smell spun her back in time, homesick, dizzy: she was West again.

She was West again and free. Just to be out there in the open made her happy, remembering the feeling of nineteen years old and careless, the promise of horses, sex adventures with cowboys. To look back on a time half your life ago, a series of summers, and say, *The best time of my life*—what did that mean? It meant it was over, she understood. Unless it wasn't. A rising feeling inside her chest, escape and speed. The middle of her life disappeared, Neil had never happened nor Will, neither the joy of him, the weight of his small body, nor the aftermath, and after that she was nineteen and driving a big fast car. Justine knew it was an illusion, a trick of feeling, but she didn't care.

She picked up a hitchhiker on the two-lane through Richland, a college boy bound for Pullman, just to give him a surprise. Nine feet tall and bulletproof. Nothing could touch her.

"Nice car," the college boy said, running his hand along the chrome expanse of the dashboard. He was blond and clean, a Mormon-looking kid.

"This thing will go a hundred and twenty," Justine said, and the boy looked at her nervously.

She had changed into a sweatshirt and jean jacket at the gas station in Umatilla and now she wished that she had changed into her boots, too. She didn't want any part of her to show the sad housewife.

"I'm going to Rivulet, Montana," she told the boy.

"I've never been there."

"Nobody has," she said. "There's nothing there, and it's not on the way to anything."

He looked at her, expecting more, but this was all she felt like saying. She liked the power she seemed to have over him, liked being slightly dangerous, and she knew that if she revealed herself this power would be gone. I am thirty-eight years old, she thought, I am married, childless, I find it hard to concentrate and I'm taking pills for sadness. She thought of all the names that Dr. Fairweather and Neil had found to call her, and shifted in her seat, restless.

"You don't have any pot, do you?" she asked the boy.

"Sorry," he said, flustered. "I guess I . . ."

"You wouldn't tell me if you did, would you?" she asked. "It seems like such a big deal these days. I used to smoke pot all the time, everybody did."

The college boy was trying to think of something to say.

"It makes the time pass quicker, when you're driving," she said. "What are you majoring in?"

"Forestry."

"God, all the foresters I ever met were serious dope smokers."

The kid looked at her.

"I mean, *raging*," Justine said.

The mile markers ticked by in silence for a while. The road had been upgraded to four-lane in places since the last time Justine drove it, which made her feel disconnected and strange. How long had it been? Years, three or four anyway. The hills didn't change, the dusty yellow-brown, a crust of snow showing white in the shadowy places. And the traffic didn't change, the trucks and pickups, or the construction which had been going on for as long as she could remember. These things stand still, she thought, and I fall apart. It didn't seem fair.

Near Ritzville, though, the road went back to the old two-lane.

"I'll show you why I love this car," she told the boy, heaving the Bonneville into the oncoming lane and flooring it around a truck. Out of the engine compartment came a massive roaring sound and the car hurtled forward, momentum pushing them back into their seats. The hills blurred yellow and then they were around the truck and tucked back into their lane, the turn signal clicking.

"Try that with a Toyota," she said. "Try that in a Volvo."

The boy didn't say anything.

"The thing is," she said, "you start letting chances go by, the next thing you know you're stacked up six cars deep behind a Winnebago, you know what I mean?"

She didn't wait for him to answer but lurched over into the left lane again, ducking back at the last minute when it wasn't clear. The semitruck rushed past them, a millisecond later. The boy was holding on to the dashboard. Calmly Justine eased the Bonneville out again and this time it was clear and the engine roared again, downshifting all the way into second.

"Those Winnebagos," she shouted above the roar. "I tell you, I'd be in jail right now if I carried a pistol."

She eased back into her lane again, safe by half a second. By God, she thought. I really do love this car.

"Are you okay?" the boy asked in a small scared voice.

"Am I making you nervous?"

"I guess."

"You can get out if you want," she said. "I mean, I'm going all the way to Spokane but if you want out."

"Actually," the boy said. "Um, if you don't mind."

Fuck you, she thought, and then she said it: "Fuck you."

She spun the Bonneville into a gravel turnout, dust flying all around them. "What are you? Twenty years old?" she asked him. "You act like somebody's grandmother."

The boy didn't say anything but got his pack out of the back seat, shut the door gently. All the trucks and cars she had passed in the last ten miles rolled past her while she waited for him. She rolled the window down.

"You don't have any nerve," she told him.

He pretended not to pay attention.

"You're not going to have any kind of life unless you get the nerve," she said. "Look inside yourself, maybe join the Marines."

She peeled out in a spray of gravel, cutting off a stock truck so she wouldn't have to smell the shit. Zero-to-sixty, she thought, looking forward at the line of cars and trucks to pass. This is okay, she thought. This is going to be okay.

He wanders through the old house, room after room crowded with lights and people and all the chitter-chatter talk talk talking and all too fast for him to understand! He's looking for a quiet place. He needs to sit alone for a while and collect himself, because as it stands they're all talking too fast for him like a great party with drinks and energy but he can't keep up. It's not quite like a foreign language. Women in dresses, men in beautiful suits, cigarette smoke and cigars and chatter—and down there in the kitchen is his mother and his sister Butte Montana 1921 and all he wants is his peace and quiet, a place to collect himself. All the people he ever knew are there but he can't find the time to talk to them, rushing frantic from room to room, a reception hall or maybe an embassy. It's like a wedding, it's like this, it's like that, chitter-chatter talk talk talk like birds or the first time he ever fucked anybody couldn't remember her name and hadn't been able to ever but she's there, too, Fat Girl Number One but he sees that he wronged her, she's kind at least and not bad-looking and somebody he could have spent some time with but didn't but she isn't accusing him, just looks at him and smiles as he rushes by and it starts with a J—Jenny? Deer meat and rivers, sound of a shot and the clean sound of water over gravel and the cigars and suits in

Washington, the television lights, the smell of makeup, gasoline, wood smoke, perfume, all mixed up and fallen apart. He tries to start the work of putting it together again but it slips away from him, he can't take hold, can't stop moving from room to room and all of them full of surprises: Tom Mix himself, dead drunk at a party, and the one man he had honestly cheated, stolen six hundred thousand dollars from, and now he's here and not even angry, saying, *I just want to talk to you, Senator,* but there isn't time, there isn't time. He has to get clear.

Justine closed her eyes. In the darkness she could still see the snow rushing toward her in the headlights, driving the tunnel of scattered light, she could still feel the road vibration and the steering wheel in her hands. It felt as if she had never gone anywhere, as if she was still asleep in her motel room in Missoula or next to Neil in her Oregon home, safe and warm. Her side of the futon. She couldn't understand how she had lived through the drive, up and over the Continental Divide at Rogers Pass, the coldest spot—she learned this when she stopped for gas in Lincoln—in the history of America.

The tire store in Missoula had been backed up for five hours, the first big snowstorm of the winter and everybody wanted their snow tires on all at once. Justine had a vodka hangover, lonely motel-room drinking. The waiting room smelled strongly of tires. The four big studded radials cost almost five hundred dollars but the Bonneville was hopeless without them, an ice-skating elephant. She didn't get out of town till three-thirty and it went dark a little after four and it never stopped snowing, the little towns— Ovando, Clearwater, Lincoln—disappearing into the thick, feathery flakes, like a storm of goose down. There wasn't even anything on the radio, *nothing* on either band, except a basketball game that flared briefly onto the AM near the top of the Divide and then disappeared again immediately, like a communiqué from outer space. The world ended at the edge of her headlights.

She slowed to forty and then to thirty, twenty-five, as the snow came thicker and harder and drifted onto the road and still there was nobody in front of her, and no other lights behind. For an hour, she saw no traffic coming the other way either. Maybe the pass was closed and maybe she was crazy, the only one to try it, the only one not home and safe in bed. She had a perfectly good home, five hundred miles behind her. A perfectly good life.

And the snow kept coming toward her in the headlights, the endless tunnel and nothing at the end but blackness, empty highway. She barely touched the pedal and the Bonneville slid sideways, slid and then caught. She had no idea what was over the side but she could feel the emptiness there. The road seemed to close in behind her, to seal itself up. Even when she saw that this was a bad idea—that not even the locals were out on the roads, not even the trucks and Greyhounds, only herself—she couldn't see any place to turn around, walls of snow on either bank. Behind felt as dangerous as ahead.

Alone at night, lost, she knew she shouldn't have come this way. She just wanted to stop, to rest, but there was no rest. CHAINS REQUIRED the sign said CHAIN UP AREA but the arrow pointed into a flat filthy wall of snow. Twenty-five miles an hour, twenty, and the snow bated and fluttered and then whirled down through her headlights. Then she thought that she would die there, in this lonely place, they would dig her Bonneville out of the snowbank in spring. Nobody knew she was here. Nobody knew she was coming. There was a lightness to it, a lack of consequence that was almost a pleasure. It was like the feeling she got about Will, driving out of Umatilla: as though he never happened, no more substantial than a dream, the whole middle of her life a dream but with that same false certainty. She could feel the memory of her son's head in the hollow of her chest but neither of them was real, weightless, moving. It doesn't matter, she thought. It doesn't matter what happens to me.

She started to prepare herself.

Then saw a light, somewhere in front of her. A human sign, she thought. She tried to speed up, to catch up to it, and she found that she could hold a little more speed than before. The snow was just as thick but the road seemed better and better and the lights grew closer and she thought, No. Not this time.

It was the plow, ahead of her: a yellow truck the size of a small house, lit and flashing, throwing a column of clean snow out into the darkness and spreading gravel behind. It was going maybe twenty but she had no desire to pass. She slowed obediently into the lane and felt the good new tires grip on the gravel and knew she had been saved. From what? The unreality would not stop. She closed her eyes and saw it, still: the blowing, drifting snow and the darkness outside, waiting for her . . .

Now it was the next morning, although it didn't feel like morning. The night, snow, driving continuing into the day. She'd gone straight to the hospital when she got to Great Falls. Yesterday is yesterday, she told herself, today is today, last night was last night—but the boundaries wouldn't hold up, everything rushed in and mixed together with everything else. She was home, she was here, it was last night, tomorrow.

She opened her eyes into the white hospital room, where her grandfather was lying out. He was still alive. You wouldn't know it to look at him. He lay on his back with his hands folded together on top of the white sheet, the neck—furrowed and sun-cracked—rising out of the white hospital gown. His face was blank and faintly angry, like the face of San Javier in the mud cathedral south of Tucson, the ancient effigy of wood, rubbed dark by hands looking for a miracle. They pinned things to his robes, little miniatures of elbows and knees, little whiskey bottles, car keys, boats.

And the hospital smell, the sounds, always all alike or maybe just that whenever she's been in the hospital—birth, death, stitches, once a tetanus shot—she's been too busy to notice. Will lived for nine days after the accident, although he never came out of the coma. It was bad luck even thinking about him. She looked down at the lifeless hands. She thought: God, I hate this place.

Even in her maternity. Will was a difficult birth, a c-section finally, green gowns and big lights, sharp knives and blood everywhere.

The moment when they'd gotten him out and there was a silent shocked medical rushing around when they saw him, panic and business and she saw that her baby had been born dead and then she heard the tiny cry and her heart opened up all at once.

This shouldn't happen to anybody, she thought.

She went to the panel by the door and started throwing switches at random. By luck, the second one turned off the lights. The half daylight from the windows came down soft and cold, not comforting exactly. Henry's face looked worse if anything, more jagged and angry, further gone and dreamlike—and this was becoming a problem again, the leakage of dream life and dream feeling into what was supposed to be her waking life. The flat white panels of the walls were alive with tiny colorful dots that bubbled and faded. The dark spots that wandered liquidly through were called swimmers, and they were a function or a symptom of aging, her eye doctor had told her on her last visit. There was that word again: symptom.

Justine took a chair by the side of the bed and tried to pry the old man's hands apart, so that she could hold one of them, so that she could at least imagine some purpose for her being there. But the hands were locked tight together. Henry still had his strength, or part of it. She rested her own hand on top of his folded hands, and tried to think of what she should be thinking, what she might do, but her own lack of usefulness was all she could find. Nothing in the world that she could do to help him now. Even if she was, say, a neurosurgeon as opposed to a fuckup, failed housewife. She had all kinds of names to call herself. Even with her eyes open, the snow rushed forward at her, sparkled and faded in the headlights, little tails of light . . .

She should pray, she decided.

She knew exactly how much this would get her—she'd prayed and begged and bargained continuously for the nine days Will was in the hospital, without effect—but Henry was a believer, and this was his world. She was a visitor at his dying.

She hadn't quite forgotten how. Got down onto her knees at the bedside and folded her hands together, not in the pointed praying hands of children but in the clench, the clasp of fist on fist that belonged to old women in black. Dear Heavenly Father, she started, but this was as far as she got. She hadn't been to church in two decades at least, not since before Neil, and besides, this was the way he liked it: Neil would sit on the edge of the bed and she would kneel and take his dick into her mouth, touching the puckered skin of his ball sack with her fingertips, especially in the afternoons or mornings . . . The pressure of her weight on her knees, she had to pretend she didn't feel it either way. At least in church they had those leather kneelers, padded. Still trying to focus herself in prayer, she couldn't stop the joke, the Ideal Christmas Gift, for the Man Who Has Everything and the Women Who Love Them, and the pleasure of knowing this was the wrong thing to think, they couldn't make her think correctly—*they* meaning schools, hospitals, Neil, etc. Blow job, she said to herself, whispering it in the still room: blow job, blow job, blow job.

Spinning out of control, slightly.

Center, she told herself. Focus. At least if she could *remember* all the words to a Hail Mary, at least then she'd prove something—some connection to her own past, maybe, evidence that the little girl in white, studying for her first Communion, was part of the same lifetime as Justine. It felt like stories, something she read somewhere: The Girl, First Kiss, Riding Horses With My Sister, The College Artist, Sorrow. She lost the thread sometimes, the thing that bound her into a single person. She had this history, and then something else, this living hand . . . It would be easy for someone else to know her. Anybody could look at her from outside and see what she'd done and what she was like, her favorite color was crimson, her favorite food was hot and sour soup, her favorite sexual act and partner and the way she parted her hair and so on. It was only from inside that she looked all jumbled up, a yard sale after the event, everything out of place and wadded up and the best things long gone. Fuck me, she said to herself, Me Me Me. She'd made the discovery once again that being sick of yourself didn't mean you got to go away.

Also that she couldn't change history. Things couldn't be undone.

"Okay," she said, "again. We'll try again. Hail Mary, full of grace, the Lord is with thee."

Good, she thought. Not bad. She didn't remember it with her mind but with her body, her mouth shaping itself around the familiar words. She took a running start and tried again, whispering but aloud: "Hail Mary, full of grace, the Lord is with thee. Blessed art thou among women and blessed is the fruit of thy womb fruit of the loom Jesus. Holy mother of God, pray for me, now and at the hour of my death . . ."

Hour of my death.

The old man's hands started to move, as if he were pinching

an imaginary rosary. She could see the invisible beads passing through his fingers.

Henry was alive, moving.

She said the prayer again, aloud and louder this time, and watched the old man's lips move in rhythm to the words, shaping themselves around the words, and a faint hum came out of the center of his body. It was the prayer, but without consonants and without sense—it was just his body remembering, Justine told herself, just his body. But when she reached the end of the prayer he started again. His stiff wooden fingers notched another bead, fingered the imaginary cross: Hail Mary, full of grace, the Lord is with thee . . .

This is fucked, she thought. This is working. What was she supposed to do now, or think, or say? But she knew what to say: the prayer, the rosary. She whispered five Hail Marys with the old man growing stronger with each and then the big bead, the black one that called for an Our Father and at first she couldn't remember, panic. She saw the life breathing back into the old man and needed that prayer, that one deep memory, but it wouldn't come.

"Our Father," she said. "Our Father who art in heaven."

"Our Father who art in heaven, hallowed be Thy name"—the words came all at once, unsuspected. The old man's lips went smoothly over the words like water over a familiar stream course, never pausing or stumbling. Kingdom come, she thought, will be done, Big Daddy up in the sky. Mary didn't have a kingdom. Her son nailed up with railroad spikes and bleeding. She has her precious *suffering*, Justine thought, and I am the bitch because I want, what? Something else. It's very nice suffering, yes, but not what I had in mind. . . .

But the prayer was restoring Henry to life before her eyes, evidence of her own senses, the only thing she trusted, and he was with her, undeniable. His eyes blinked open. His hand woke up from its memory of prayer and then his whole face startled, suddenly awake, and the prayer vanished from his lips and he raised his head off the pillow, as if to look around.

"Who's that?" he whispered urgently. "Who's there?"

"Justine," she said. "It's all right."

"There was a . . ."

"What?"

"I don't know."

He shook his head slowly, stiffly: No. She covered his hands with one of her own, still kneeling by the bed. His hands were cold as the steel of the bed.

"Where exactly am I?" asked the old man.

"Great Falls. The hospital."

"I was gone," he said. It took him a moment to gather himself before he could speak again. He'd seen things that he should not have seen, that was her feeling. Gone places from which he shouldn't have returned.

"Are you all right?" he asked her.

"Jesus, Henry, look at you," she said. "And you're worried about me."

The first hot flush of tears welled up in her chest. For herself but not exactly: sometimes she saw herself from outside, like a stranger, and she saw the awful things that had happened to her, and how sad it had made her, all the people around her. It shouldn't happen to anyone.

It didn't help to know that others had lost their children too. Watching the news, Bosnia, Somalia.

"How did you get here?" he asked.

"I drove from Portland. I just found out two days ago."

"That was good of you."

Piecing himself together. In the silence, Justine found the

rhythms of the prayer circulating inside her, around and around like blood, a different face of the prayer presenting itself each time around: Hail MARY, full of grace, fruit of THY womb, fruit of thy WOMB. Womb and bomb, she thought. Exploding Jesus.

Her brain still wouldn't behave. They couldn't make it.

"I can't see anything," Henry said. "They told you about that?"

Justine nodded, then remembered that he couldn't see her.

"Yes," she said.

"The doctors—what do they tell you?"

"I just got here, this morning. I just drove in."

The lie sat strangely in her mouth. The one doctor, Reilly, had given her the news as he was going off shift at seven that morning: Henry was not going to see again or walk and would be lucky to leave the hospital. But God was in the room or at least Mary, she felt the presence—dream life invading the real.

"Christ," she said. "Look, I talked to them a little, this morning."

"And what?"

"They aren't optimistic."

Henry shook his head, impatient. An angry clicking sound in his mouth.

"About what are they not optimistic?" he asked.

"Okay. You had a stroke and I guess a pretty bad one. There's a lot that they don't know or can't say."

The clicking sound, again. He was not going to let her off the hook until she gave him all of it.

"They don't really know," she said. "You were critical when they brought you in but you're up to satisfactory condition now. Stable and satisfactory is what they say. That means you're not going to get any worse, or something."

"They don't know."

"They guess."

"Your mother," Henry said. "June. Is she okay?"

Justine looked at him, startled: her mother, Henry's daughter, died of ovarian cancer in 1966, when she was eight and Val was ten. She'd learned to say this quickly to strangers, people she was meeting for the first time, but between herself and Henry these words could not be made light. And so they were never said.

"What do you mean?" she asked.

The old man turned his face toward her voice, then realized he had mistaken himself. She could read it in his face, and then he turned away, ashamed.

"I'm sorry."

"No, it's okay," Justine said.

"I just, for a minute I . . ."

"You rest now."

He shook his head.

"It was like I could touch her," Henry whispered. "It felt like she was right there in the room."

"You rest now."

She folded his hands together for him, there in the soft half-light, and let go. Henry rested his head back onto the pillow. His open eyes stared at the ceiling, blank.

"I'm very sorry," he said.

"I don't mind."

"I'm going back to sleep now. Whatever you want to call it. One thing."

"What?"

"I'm not going to die in here," he said. "I won't stand for it."

"Nobody's asking you to."

The smell of frying bacon and of coffee woke her, and for a moment she was home. Not her Oregon home, but the place she was always missing, the absent place. If she could find it, she would be all right. Home: her son's head resting on her chest, breathing in time. The house. She belonged with him, and nowhere else, not anymore.

But this was a kind of trouble she'd finally learned to recognize, the occasion of sin. She steered her mind toward mental health, toward positivity and charm. Slipped from the warm covers and opened the curtains and there, miles away on the horizon, rested the mountains. Beautiful, she thought. She'd almost forgotten. Justine felt her soul lift out of her and out into the empty air, miles of nothing between the window and the horizon. The sky was a mess, scraps and tatters of cloud, and the light that managed to fall was a dull steel gray and cold and the snow was half ice and half melted, filthy. A dense pubic tangle of alder and willow ran along the vein of the creek, and a line of cottonwood trees. The horses stood together at the far end of the home field, huddled together out of the wind, dark shapes against the snow. Again she felt herself lift toward the cold outside, out of the window, out of the cold neutrality of Henry's new house.

This new house still felt strange to her. She couldn't understand why Henry had built it. When she and Val had spent summers here, it was in the old house, the Jacobson place, which still rested down in the valley below. Henry had built the new house up on the hillside to catch the view but the wind blew up here, and it was lonely. The Jacobson house sat abandoned down in the shelter of the valley, a white house with green shutters and trim, the same colors as the old barn and the stable. Trees had grown in around them, old cottonwoods mostly but a pair of hundred-year-old spruce trees framed the front of the house, all lived-in, comfortable, abandoned. Settled, she thought. She would have been more comfortable there, among familiars, ghosts and wood smoke. For a moment she thought of asking Marliss, Henry's cook, if she would ask one of the men to open the old house up again, seal the windows up and light the fires.

But she wasn't there to make a fuss. She reminded herself.

Justine dressed quickly, as if it was cold, but in fact it was perfectly nice and still. A machine for living, this new house was. The windows triple-paned, the furnace sighing quietly somewhere out of sight, discreet as a butler. The theme was Disney Western: the outer walls were made from peeled logs and chinked with something that looked like mud, though she was sure it was polyurethane. Navajo blankets hung on the walls, real ones, and black Hopi pottery, and baskets. Henry had money. There was a wall of photographs from his time in Washington: Henry at the signing of the Medicare bill, Henry with his finger in LBJ's chest, making a point. The furniture was oak and leather, expensive and solid, but an aura of fakery hung over the place. A little too finished, too perfect. It didn't suit him.

"You're up," Marliss said, and glanced at the clock: nine-thirty.

"I was tired."

"You came a long way. Coffee?"

"I can get it."

Marliss always made her feel this way: the princess, there to be waited on. It wasn't her fault, in fact she was perfectly friendly and younger than Justine. But Marliss seemed to belong here, and to know where she belonged. She worked, she went to church. She made Justine feel as if she wasn't getting it at all, as if she'd misunderstood the basics of life: what it was, what it was good for.

"How's Neil?" Marliss asked, when Justine settled at the table.

"The same, I guess. He's fine. He's working with kids these days."

"I thought he always was."

"That was college kids. Lately he's been volunteering to work with these high schoolers."

"Doing what?"

Justine looked up at her. She forgot sometimes that she was not as big a part of Marliss's life as Marliss was of hers. Justine thought about Henry's place all the time, it stood for something in her life, she dreamed about it. But her own life in Oregon must have seemed as insubstantial as a puff of smoke to Marliss, not even a daydream.

"Well, he teaches art at the college," Justine said. "You remember that. With these kids, it's a little of everything—poetry, drawing, anything to reach them. They're what they call at-risk kids."

"High school kids?"

Justine nodded.

"Geez, I thought they were all at risk," Marliss said. "I thought that's what you *did* in high school."

"It's a different world," Justine said, "city kids. He's got kids bringing crack cocaine to class, guns, all kinds of stuff. He told me last week that some kid's little brother was in there, nine years old and he's flashing these hand signs at Neil, you know, gang signs."

"No, thanks."

"It's a different world," Justine said.

She picked up the rumpled paper, the *Great Falls Tribune*, and started to leaf through. Others had already been up, hours ago, had read the paper before her. God bless coffee. Silence for a few minutes, while Marliss fussed and Justine searched the paper for Henry and finally found him, buried in the second section, a follow-up: SENATOR STABLE IN ACCIDENT. She tried to read but felt the pressure of Marliss working: Marliss, a solid brunette with a piano butt, a couple of years younger than Justine but more settled and solid and real than Justine was, world's oldest living adolescent *just ask her husband* but she was finally able to calm herself. Marliss was kind, Marliss accepted her. Justine came slowly into Henry's place, the comfort of it.

"Who's on the place these days?" she finally asked.

Marliss finished with the counter before she came to the table and sat: a visit.

"It's just me and Lex, same as always. My dad?"

"How is Lex doing these days?"

"Well, he had the hip, you know. Did you hear about that? Calving last spring, he got a foot caught under a cow and she rolled right over on him, caught him wrong or something."

"Henry did say something."

"He was in the hospital for a while. You can imagine how he took to that. Then we had him on a rollaway in the dining room for a while. Then he was in jail for a night, of course."

She said it so lightly, almost laughing, that Justine thought she was kidding. But this was no joke.

"What did he end up in jail for?"

"Oh, you know," Marliss said. "He was just being himself. He was down in the Silver Dollar on Saturday night and he got into it with some kid—twenty-year-old kid and Lex almost sixty. Broke his arm, too."

"Broke his arm?"

"Well, he fell against the curb, I guess. My dad says he didn't mean to. You know how these old cowboys are, they like to solve things on the spot."

Justine felt a little suspicion, a little warning prickle: things were being said, things were done here in ways she might not agree with. The Code of the West, she thought. Right and wrong.

"It's just the two of you still?" she asked.

"We get help out from town when we need it," Marliss said.

"They don't like to stay out on the place anymore, not the kind you want, anyway."

"Even back when I was coming out here, they were a little iffy, some of them. Saddle tramps."

"Tramps is right. Were you out here when they came to arrest that one fellow?"

"I don't think so."

"You'd remember. He holed himself up in the pump house and started shooting at anything that moved. He had a little—I think it was a Mini-14."

"Did they get him out?"

"Finally he killed himself."

"I didn't know that."

Justine breathed out, trying to fit this new information into the picture she held of this place. People had died here, people had lost hands in balers or drunk on the road and now Henry, dying. It wasn't all sunshine here. It never was, except in her memory.

"It was a heck of a deal," Marliss said. "They only wanted him for getting drunk and tearing up a bar over in Choteau."

Justine made a small human noise, noncommittal.

"He would have been out in a week," Marliss said. "Probably less. It was a waste."

"I didn't hear about that."

"What do they say about your grandfather?"

"It's pretty bad."

She hesitated, trying to think: who was she saying this to? What could she leave out? Marliss had a husband when she came here, a boy named Dan who died of cancer a couple of years afterward. Justine didn't know her well enough to work out the math of what might hurt and what wouldn't.

"It was a stroke," she said. "Part of the brain gets cut off from the blood supply. I don't know how much you know or want to know. Anyway, it was a blood clot or something, they don't know what caused it exactly, they're going to do some more tests today.''

"Will he see again?"

"They don't know. Talking to them, you get the feeling that they don't think so."

"He won't stand for that."

"I know."

"He couldn't."

Then they were quiet for a moment, each of them retreating into each, the memory of Henry between them and the mystery of what would happen next. She loves him, Justine thought. She's like family. She knows him in ways I don't.

Justine asked, "What was he doing out driving at six in the morning?"

"He doesn't sleep lately. I should have . . ."

"What?"

"I don't know what I should have done. I still don't. I couldn't think of anybody to call but he just wasn't sleeping for a couple of months before the accident. I mean, he'd go to sleep okay but then he'd be right back up. Even when he was asleep . . ."

"What?"

"I'd hear him talking, you know. Shouting sometimes—people's names and so on. I heard him say your name a couple times. Your mom's name."

"He was asleep?"

"He'd wake himself up with it."

"Then he couldn't go back to sleep."

"Well, sometimes he could, I guess—I don't know. You know I'm down in the little house with Lex."

"I thought you were in the big house. Henry's old house."

"It's too much of a chore to heat, with just the two of us. Plus I don't know. It's Henry's place, you know?"

"Why did he move up here, anyway? I liked the old house better."

Marliss shrugged: a mystery.

"Anyway," Marliss said, "I'd see the lights on in his bedroom any hour of the night. I've been worried for him. He'd get so tired, you know, and then he'd get mad or spacy. He'd walk around like he was seeing ghosts."

"You should have called me."

Marliss looked at her, surprised.

"I figured you had trouble enough," she said.

It was a tumor, they found it during the CAT scan under his skull. They found a few others, too, smaller and scattered around. These others meant that it wasn't worth it to saw his skull open, they explained to Justine, the *they* of her bad dreams come to life in the person of a middle-aged doctor with black hair and sweaty hands.

"It's not the news that any of us were hoping for," he said.

Justine drove the sixty miles back out to Rivulet in the ranch truck, thinking all the time of herself. What would become of her. The ranch would be sold, Henry buried, Marliss turned out to find work and she knew this and still her thoughts kept turning in a tight little circle back toward herself. She had been promised a new start. Henry was spoiling things. Oh, she was sick of herself herself herself but she couldn't seem to leave herself behind.

Back at the ranch, she took the dogs out walking before she told anybody. It was a cold bright day and the wind had blown the snow clean off the ridge line behind the house. She was dressed like a hunter, in a red plaid wool jacket, long johns and waterproof felt-lined boots which were the largest and ugliest things she had ever worn on her feet. The tack and feed and fencing wire from Marliss's list of errands stayed in the back of the truck, despite the little idiot city voice that said somebody was going to steal it.

The thin crust on the snow broke lightly with every step, a small satisfying crunch like soda crackers. There was only an inch or two most places, easy walking, but she felt the sloth of an Oregon winter, too much rain, too much time lying around blue in sweatpants. A hundred yards up the slope, she was breathing hard, loosening the buttons of the wool jacket. The dogs raced and tagged each other, making fun of her. They'd been penned up all day and this was fun. Justine was still blue but the walking put her in balance, helped her put things in place, see what was around her—the dogs, for instance. Buck, the malamute, was her one true dog love. Lefty was new. There'd been a black Lab here before, she remembered, always a pair of dogs. She wondered what else she was missing.

Buck raced up to her, stopped cold in the snow and grinned at her: a hundred-and-thirty-pound dog, he could hurt her if he wanted to. He stayed penned up through the fall and winter because he would kill deer, run them down in the snow. He grinned and balanced on his paws, easy. Justine stopped. He waited. Justine feinted left and caught him leaning, darted in with her hand and almost touched him as he raced away, the white flag of his tail waving goodbye.

"Fucker!"

Buck grinned at her, just out of reach.

Then Lefty came running back out of the woods, up behind the unsuspecting Buck—too intent on the game to notice—and shouldered him broadside into the snow. Buck yipped, surprised, then took off after Lefty, who was smaller and faster but clumsy in the snow. Justine found her own body moving to the grace of Buck's, twisting, racing, leaping sideways over Lefty and then knocking him down, standing victorious. The wolf in his eyes. His soul was not contained inside his body but the same thing as his body, his soul was made of bone and teeth and blood. Lefty lay unmoving until Buck got bored and moved on, not that Buck would hurt him. But etiquette must be observed.

I *have* a body, Justine thought. He *is* a body. His singleness and strength. She started up the ridge line again and the dogs resumed their dog business, searching and chasing, ten steps to every one of hers and still they didn't tire. Buck had been here eight years, anyway—older than Justine in dog years, the only kind he had. And these big dogs didn't last, most of them dead by ten. Still she was the one who panted and wobbled and stopped to rest, who measured out her progress up the hill with small slow-paced steps. Fat, she thought, disgusting, the ripple of fat over the waistband of her jeans and the flop of her breasts, fat ass. Thinning hair, crow's-feet and lumpy fingernails, bitten short—she could play this game for hours. While Buck looked to run straight out of the prime of his life and into death, heroic. Even Henry had been alive and vital and full of force when she'd last seen him, the summer before. Henry hung on like the last leaves on the cottonwoods, the needles on the dry branches of broken ponderosa limbs, until now, anyway, two days ago. While Justine was out of season, turned against herself, losing her green before the summer was over.

While Justine was thinking about Justine.

She scolded herself, thought even less of herself. Anyone as selfish as she was *deserved* the failures of her body. A failure of the will, like all the rest, as Neil had told her. Still she felt this small thrill deep down inside her belly when she watched the dogs run, knowing that sometime, in childhood or in dreams, she'd had her own animal body. She'd known what it was like to run, fall, bleed and bite, known it in muscle and blood. Clarity in the cold air and the blood running warm inside her, the body under all these ridiculous clothes wanting to run with them through the deep snow and bring the deer down bleeding, *canine*, she thought, *incisor*.

Here in the dark.

He felt the sunlight with his hands. In the afternoons. He asked Justine to open the curtains and to leave them open after she left until the attendant came and always closed them. The light from the window fell across his bed, he could touch it. His hands lay in the sunlight like sleeping animals, warm and content. It was something they wanted. There was a world inside him Henry didn't know anything about. His hands crept toward the sunlight.

There was a world inside him Henry didn't know anything about. The way his body felt to him. A little dizzy, a high-pitched whining in his ears like television, and the sounds of the corridor outside his room that echoed and reverberated inside the hollow of his body. Now that everything was dark, there was no difference. Inside and outside, dark. There was nothing to keep the world outside, it penetrated him, the tiny sounds and the smells so strong they made his eyes water: disinfectant, shit. Some of this smell must have been him. They came in every morning and sponged him down but he never quite came clean. This heavy meaty thing he was stuck in.

But other times and other matters were resting inside his body.

Quiet, pale, they had been lost in the din of sight, the colors and warnings. Here in the dark, though, he could touch them: vaulting out of bed on a spring morning, seventeen years old, the power coiled in his legs unstretching; or pick-and-shovel work, the way the strength seemed to come out of his belly unending. Swimming, somersaults. The one bad accident, the way his body still cringed around the place where the steering wheel came up into his chest. All these memories were somewhere in his body, living in the cells of some small area, and Henry lived inside them one by one. It felt as though he really was seventeen for a moment—or more than a moment, minutes on end sometimes, he could rest in the memory and it wasn't like a memory at all, it was as though he was there inside it, living it again: the fair, the taste of cotton candy, the ferris wheel, the smell of ozone and burnt sugar and insulation, the rattle and clank of the rickety ride when the music died down and the fear he was intended to feel.

Or the marriage: the music, champagne. Before the invention of sadness or divorce. This was happiness, to sit as king and queen among her relatives—he didn't have any himself, an orphan by then—to marry above his station and still they danced around him and welcomed him, they could see he was a boy on his way somewhere. Coming out of the cathedral in Helena into a sky of perfect blue enamel, hard enough to chip it, and the pigeons flying and later, after the dancing, alone . . . She came into the room with a flannel nightgown on, carrying a taper, like the bear on the motel sign, and he was waiting under the covers. It wasn't his first time, not by a mile. But it hadn't occurred to him to wonder about her, not till that moment. He had speculated. But it never mattered, not until that moment, not until he felt it in his chest and, lying there, he was suddenly angry with her, in advance, just in case she was not a virgin. And nervous and full of tenderness and full of himself, the king for this one day, and she had given this to him. This is the feeling in the dark of his body: this mix of everything and everything, glory and anger, love and arrogance.

Oh, then we carried it off all right, he thinks.

Nothing ever ends. That's the thing he's finding out. That moment, that happiness, there's nothing about the things that happened afterward that will cancel it out. All of the bad times are still there, too: the smell of old telephones, rubber and hair oil, waiting for her to say something, the next thing, waiting for her to make up her mind about him. The courtroom that smelled of cedar, freshly sharpened pencils. But lying there in the dark of his hospital bed, Henry discovers that the old moments are lying there whole inside him, fresh as yesterday or even as today, the colors still bright, the smells unfaded, the touch of Evelyn's skin— the skin of her inner thigh, stippled with goose bumps, soft as anything—he has still felt nothing softer—this moment is lying somewhere inside the darkness of his body, and he can touch it any time he pleases.

Jumping from a railroad bridge into the river, summer, 1916.

The smell of paraffin when she blew out the candle.

This hospital room, this now, he can still find it if he has to but it pleases him less and less. It seems so difficult, like climbing stairs, which he never imagined would be difficult. The ease of his body leaping, two at a time. Everything on the run. Why was he in such a hurry, always? To get here, he thinks. All that running and racing to get here.

"You came on your own," Henry said. "That's something."

"I guess," Justine said.

She was in the hospital room again, it was afternoon again, the dry light from the window, gray skies. Henry was still blind. The attendant, not quite a nurse, came in and flicked the light on to take his data. The attendant was a black man, unusual in Great Falls, Montana. He didn't say anything to either of them or even quite look at their faces, consumed with numbers, but on the way out he shut the light off again. A small kindness.

"Why?" Henry asked, when the attendant had gone. "Why did you come all the way here?"

"What was I supposed to do?"

"You have a life, I suppose."

"Don't," she said.

"I don't understand you," Henry said. He lay back into the pillow again but still: that birdlike tension in his neck, tendons under the wattled skin. He was still angry.

"You were praying over me the other day," he said.

"I was."

"You go to church now?"

"I haven't been since Will died. You know that."

"I don't know that," he said. "I never see you. You remembered the prayers, though. That's good. I remember the whole business in Latin, you know, I have to translate. Do you believe in God?"

"I don't know. You don't ask people that."

"It's a fair question. You were praying. What were you praying to?"

"Jesus, it's good to see you, Henry."

"Don't change the subject."

"But it is," she said—and it is, she thought. The hard bone under the skin. At least he knew what he thought and what he wanted. He didn't wish, he didn't mope.

"I don't know what I believe in," Justine said. "Stop."

"Stop what?"

"We've had this conversation before."

"Maybe I think this is important."

"I'm trying, all right? You don't need to talk me into anything."

"You're thirty-six years old," he said—then raised his one hand toward her in surrender.

"All right," he said. "Okay."

"I'm thirty-eight," she said.

The quiet descended again, the not-quite quiet of the hospital room with the air hushing through the vents and the intercom down the hall, TV next door.

"Do you go to church still?" she asked.

"I always have," he said. "Sometimes if the weather's bad, we watch it on the satellite dish. They have the services, you know. This one time, they had it all the way from Ireland."

He stopped, apparently because he wanted her to think about this. But the force was gone. Justine had the feeling he was somewhere else, someplace besides this room. He hadn't yet made it all the way back into his body, which was not yet completely alive, maybe never again. I have a soul, she thought, trying the idea on for fit, for comfort.

"Can I tell you something?" Henry asked.

"That means a lecture."

"Yes."

"Go ahead."

"I once thought there was an unlimited amount of time," he said. "Most of my life, I thought that a year would be added somewhere for every one I used up. Not that I thought about it much."

Here he attempted a smile, the skull under the papery skin.

"I was in the middle of my life," he said. "I was *engaged*. I didn't have time to think about anything but how to get through the week. Now I have a couple of months left."

"They don't know," she said.

"You know," he said. "I know, I can feel it."

The silence again. The third party making itself felt between them, brush of the wing against her cheek. Justine shivered in her seat, a little.

"That's not what I wanted to talk about," he said.

"I know you want me to be different than I am," she said. "I appreciate that, I mean, I don't think you're trying to put anything over on me or anything. It's just that this is the way I am, Henry, this is what I am and wishing or hoping or getting angry will not change things. I'm trying to change things, Henry, I really am."

"You don't even believe that crap yourself."

"No," she said.

"Spend your whole life getting up to the starting line instead of running the race," he said. "Not even that. Worrying about whether you ought to get up to the starting line or not."

"Guilty," she said. "Okay. You're right, I know you're right. It doesn't help."

"I'm not trying to help."

"Then what?"

"First off, I want you to get me out of here."

She looked at him, the naked bald thing in the white gown, the dead eyes staring at the ceiling, and thought: I'm all alone here, he's really gone. Remembering the ghost of her mother flitting through the room. The IV dangling, the yellow bag of urine slung from the side of the bed, the memory from deepest childhood of her mother smiling, pale. She shivered again, the chill along her spine.

"It's crazy," she said.

"No, it isn't."

"Who's going to take care of you? I mean, I don't . . ."

"I'm not asking you to."

"What, then?"

"I've got money," he said. "You don't bother yourself thinking about money, I know that. I'm not complaining. But you lose sight of what money can do for you. I want you to ask the doctors what I need, nurses, whatever, any kind of equipment, and then see if you can't set that up for me."

"Your place is sixty miles from here. It's ten miles from *Rivulet*, Henry."

"I know that. Why are you telling me things that I already know?"

"It's dangerous."

Henry tried to smile again, and she saw that she was being stupid: dangerous. Why, you could die from that!

He said: "If you don't want to, I'd appreciate it if you would ask Marliss."

"Don't boss me around," she said.

"I trust you to do this. Medical power of attorney, the whole thing, I know it's a lot to ask. I can pay you for your time."

"Jesus, Henry, I don't need money."

"I didn't say that. I know you don't *need* the money but I know you're here, you could be somewhere else, it's an inconvenience for you. That's the way it works: you do a job for somebody and he pays you. You make yourself useful. There's nothing wrong with that."

"What's the job?"

"Somebody needs to run things, Jess."

She looked into his face, the hard, mineral eyes, and saw what he wanted. Then all the small fears she felt came together into one: he meant to have her life, he meant to take her over. My freedom, she thought—what do I want with it anyway? But it's mine, mine, mine . . .

"It's just for now," he said.

"Then what?"

"I don't know. What's next for me? There's a lot of people who would like that information."

"For me, then. What did you have in mind?"

"I don't know that either. I guess I don't care. I like you fine, Jess, you know that. And I appreciate the way you've come all the way out here in the dead of winter and so on, the way you rallied round. But I guess you're going to work things out for yourself, or you're not, and there isn't much of anything I can do about that. I mean, not even now, while I'm here. Do you understand?"

"Yes."

"What hurts," he said, "what hurts is the way things are falling apart and there's nothing I can do about it. I've been alive, I'm not complaining, there's things I've missed out on but not a lot, not that I really wanted. That sounds like crap but I mean it. But you try and you struggle to put a thing together, you know, the ranch, and keep it going. Does that make sense? I never thought I was going to live forever. But to see the thing you built come down to nothing. The thing you worked for."

"What can I do?"

"I'll give it to you if you want it."

"Henry," she said—and then stopped herself. The air in the room was tightening around her, the feeling that she might run out of breath, the fear.

"I don't know anything," she said.

"I know. I couldn't pick a worse person, I do know that. But there isn't anybody else."

"There's Marliss," she said. "Lex."

"They're help."

"There's Rudy."

"You know what I think of your father," he said. "You know what *you* think of him. When was the last time you talked to him?"

An antiseptic silence opened between them, while Justine considered and Henry waited for her. She thought of the others who should be there with them: her mother, more than anyone, a woman of good sense and practicality, beauty, humor, goodness. As beautiful as she was good, as the fairy tale said. Justine had dreamed her into such a perfect shape that she might as well be wishing for the moon.

And who else? Henry's son, her mother's brother, was killed in Korea. A stepson and -daughter from his second marriage—Henry sent them checks in California and they stayed out of his way. She felt the loneliness inside, deep in her belly, down where the child would go: this was why you had children, five children or seven or eleven, so you wouldn't end up lonely like this. She thought of Neil and his endless concern for the world. The world doesn't *need* *more* children, it needs *better* children. I see this all the time at work. These yuppie parents, they love to have children but they don't want to take care of them. You don't want to be sixty years old and still have a kid in high school.

Really it was a kind of cowardice. She knew it, he knew it himself. What were they afraid of?

This was not the business at hand but it really was. What was she afraid of? Henry was offering all he had, and all he wanted was a little of her time, a month or two or even six months.

"I don't care what you do after I go," he said—as if he was tracing her thoughts, and answering them.

"Henry," she said.

"I'm not trying to put anything over on you," Henry said. "I'm asking you for a favor and I know it and I am willing to see that you get something of value in return. Please look at this from my end, Jess. I don't want to see things fall apart now."

"Plus you want to help me."

"I'm not going to lie to you."

"Will you give me a little while to think about it?"

"No," he said. "You help me out of here. Get me back to the place and then you can think all you want."

She didn't say anything.

"It's taking the life out of me, Jess. Please."

On the hillside again, above the house.

A December thaw: the sky was low and silver, the roads were wet, the fields still in tatters of snow. Under her boots, the ground was wet and soft for the top fraction of an inch, still frozen underneath. A false promise of spring hung in the air. The dogs sniffed at newly uncovered skeletons and turds.

She walked until her body loosened. All the time in the hospital, the driving back and forth and worrying, she'd held her shoulders stiff and her lips tight. Her ease returned in the rhythm of walking, the hard work of carrying her body uphill. She'd been in Rivulet a week by then and already felt better, the hills coming easier. A *boy's* body, she thought—boots and wool and blue jeans, the dogs lapping and chasing. Lefty, it turned out (it had taken her a few minutes to worm this out of Marliss), was named for an undescended or missing testicle on one side. It gave him an unbalanced look. Once you started noticing a thing like that, it was hard to stop.

Lefty was a stray, which endeared him to Justine. Lately she found herself rooting for all lost persons and underdogs. He had just walked onto the place one day and started eating dog food out of Buck's bowl, and Buck had seen this and hurt him, ripping the tendon loose from the bend in one rear leg. Henry took him to the vet, had him fixed up and then he was four hundred dollars into the dog and didn't know what to do with him. It didn't make sense to spend that much money and then take him down to the county pound to get gassed. Two years later he was still there.

Justine liked this offhand welcome. We don't quite want to kill you so I guess you're staying. That's me, she thought.

Below her, the valley opened up as she climbed. Two arms of the foothills closed the home place in, a ridge to the north and to the south. The hay ground lay in the valley floor, on either side of the creek. The plains stretched out indefinitely beyond. Like looking down from an airplane, there was more than her eyes could take in, miles of empty rolling land in scraps and flags of snow, the black lines of roads and islands of mountain ranges on the horizon, fifty miles away or a hundred, merging into the snow and the horizon and the eye's ability to distinguish one thing from another. It's beautiful, she thought—then dropped the word, so plainly short of the truth. It was beautiful, it was ugly, it didn't matter one bit what she thought about it. She felt her own soul inside her pull toward the miles of nothing. The emptiness inside her answered to the greater emptiness. The look of all that open space was like a ringing in her ears, a high-pitched insubstantial sound, ghostly.

Behind her, starting at the ridge line, was Forest Service all the way to Glacier Park. Grizzly bears sometimes materialized out of the trees to prey on Henry's cattle. Lex told her and she imagined them: the dark loping shapes, big as buffalo and quick. Two hundred miles of wilderness and rock. She could keep walking, lose the human world completely, until she froze to death. The ever-present small rain of Oregon came back to her, the friendliness of the landscape. This was not that.

And below her in the valley rested the barns and sheds and cottonwood trees of Henry's ranch, nestled down out of the wind. A home, not hers.

What did the Devil say?

He brought Jesus out into the wilderness, she remembered that much—took him out onto a high place and showed him something like this. She hadn't said yes to Henry and she hadn't said no, not yet. She couldn't get clear enough. He wanted an answer.

It's only my life, she thought. Not that I've made all that much out of it—remembering the dead feeling with Neil, the tire store in Missoula. She was still lost, somewhere up on the pass, waiting to come down. She looked out at the end of the valley, where the ranch road crossed the creek and came into the valley, and saw the flashing lights of the ambulance that was bringing Henry home, the little train: ambulance, Marliss in the ranch truck and then the nurse's car. Justine had brought a little flask of vodka with her, one of Henry's souvenirs inscribed *With gratitude*. . . . She opened it and sipped. Not yet, she thought. It was about two-thirty in the afternoon. Not yet but soon.

Driving to work, a couple of weeks after the accident, Marvin Deernose passed the spot where the horse had died. The horse was gone, of course, and so was the Cadillac, but the blood remained. The dark red of the fresh blood had faded into a dirty pink, mixing with the snow, but it wouldn't be gone completely until spring. That was real, he thought—and then in a day, in a minute after it happened, it was nothing more than a memory, nothing you could touch, subject to change by desire.

They were working out at Cookie Cutter this month, two dozen bare-naked houses scattered around a hayfield. Basically they were all made out of cardboard. With his own eyes he had seen this: a length of pressboard siding left out in the rain, then walked across by a laborer in hiking boots, so that the lug pattern of the boots was pressed right into the imitation wood grain of the surface. They nailed it up on the back of a house and painted right over it. Some tourist had bought the house, footprints and all, for $230,000. The abundance of suckers was depressing. And no end in sight, not till California was empty.

The saving grace of carpentry: the hours of straight monotony left his mind free to wander. It was a gray cold day outside but they had lights, 500-watt quartz jobs on yellow industrial stands.

They fumed and smoked, burned anything that came near. The heat was not quite enough to warm the room to human standards. This was a rich man's house they were making, 5500 square feet, fourteen-foot picture windows in the living room that looked out over the back end of seven other Cookie Cutter houses and then the hills and off toward the Rockies, floating up from the horizon like teeth or dreams. Marvin looked out the window and felt his soul rise up toward the barren ice and snow of the mountaintop, and then midair, looking down at the cows in their winter quiet, the trailer houses and corrals scattered like toys into the hollows, the pretty little lights of town. He felt the little flame inside his chest, the candle.

And then subsiding. The mountain romance: it was only stone, only trees, only ice. There was no message, for him or anybody else. Still it was easy to believe otherwise.

He went back to laying tile for the kitchen counters. Forest green and white: at least the archaeologists of the future would know what year this was built. Everything was forest green this year except in Kmart, where it was still pale blue and dusty rose. Bob Champion, the builder, was downstairs cursing at a length of flexible dryer vent pipe. Marvin heard his radio coming up the stairwell, not quite music, not quite noise. Marvin couldn't stop his mind from worrying at it; he recognized a song once in a while anyway: *Big city, turn me loose and set me free* . . . Just the two of them, and Bob was in no hurry to finish. It would be May before he could start to pour foundations again.

A pleasant sense of shelter, anyway, of calm and order and work. Marvin found himself wondering, as he worked, what had happened to the drum solo. When he used to go to concerts, in high school in Tacoma, even the high school drummers would get a solo, and sometimes the bass players did too. Everybody got to express themselves back then. It was bad, always. The bass solos were especially bad. But he missed them anyway, stranded in this new America where everybody had to eat their shit and get along. So what if the bass player didn't get to express himself? Everybody had to be a *team player* now. Get on the bus. You didn't want to get on the bus, they'd find another bass player. The job of the bass player was just to stand in the background and make things happen for the boys up front, and if you didn't like it, learn to play guitar.

Though when he thought about it, the guitar solo seemed to be disappearing too.

America was shrinking.

Or maybe it was better, all this worker-bee stuff. A place for everybody and everybody in their place.

Marvin could argue with himself for hours. He would take one side and work it until he had it pretty convincing, at least until it sounded okay to him, then he would turn it around and start the other way. It could take him all kinds of places, high school dances in the high school gym and so on. The slip and wobble of thought, the way he could end up anywhere after starting almost anywhere else—from kissing a high school Mary Lou in the rain to Ralph Nader, for instance, by way of bands, bass solos, individuality, conformism, and the decline in individual fearlessness in America since 1970—this was what he loved, just the feel of his mind in full-speed topic drift. He read the paper just to keep himself in starting places. There was a seventy-eight-year-old man in New York, for instance, who'd gotten his license lifted for driving drunk and so he drove his riding lawnmower two hundred and eighty miles to visit his brother. There was a woman, on vacation in Florida, who found a human brain in a bait bucket at the end of a fishing pier in St. Augustine.

Sometimes he thought it would be better for him to think about carpentry, which is what Bob Champion did, which was why Bob Champion was the boss and Marvin wasn't. Bob was always meditating on some new or better way to do a thing, always trying out new methods. The joists in this piece-of-shit house, for instance, were these new aligned-fiber I-beam processed-wood two-by-eights that didn't weigh anything. These bugged the hell out of Marvin but Bob loved them. Marvin loved wood and hammering things together with a hammer while Bob was infatuated with nail guns, glue, various forms of cardboard.

And was it better to be Bob or to be Marvin?

Was it better to succeed or to live as Marvin did? A kind of dignified twilight, neither a success nor a failure, a regular working person when he wanted to be romantic about it. *This here's a song for the working man*, said Merle Haggard. Marvin knew this was basically more made-up bullshit, made-for-TV and the Republicans. But even assuming he was to get his little entrepreneurial ass up off the sofa and get busy—even assuming he was suddenly able to start thinking about carpentry with his whole mind—was it better to be himself as he was or himself as he ought to be, according to the Republicans?

He could work this topic over semi-endlessly. On the one hand, Bob had a drift boat, which Marvin coveted. On summer evenings he'd invite Marvin along for an evening float and it was about all Marvin could stand—the generous rich man, sitting in Bob's boat drinking Bob's beer. On the other hand, Bob lived in a cardboard house he built himself, a house that couldn't make anybody happy who was in his right mind. Bob owed enough of himself to the bank so that he had weekly conferences. Sometimes the banker guy, Doug, would come along on the fishing expeditions. Also, Bob's wife was a known whore, his kid was mean and his dog bit the UPS guy every chance he got. Bob's UPS stuff all came to Marvin's house now.

He was kicking this one around for the ten thousandth time and checking his watch and trying to figure out whether he should leave for lunch early and try to beat the crowd at McDonald's or whether he should just get some cheese at the market or just eat the fucking granola bar under the seat of his truck—emergency rations—and then knock off early and see if he could get some firewood in before dark when a dark blue Bonneville convertible, about a '72, came idling smoothly down the road and parked behind his truck.

Majestic, Marvin thought, admiring the weight and gravity of the thing. A woman got out, or a girl, and came walking through the slush and sawdust and mud.

A tall woman, Marvin saw. This girl was six feet tall! He tried to picture her with Bob and laughed: Bob was like five-eight. He must have gotten the picture about his wife and decided to branch out. Maybe now he'd get rid of the dog.

"Is Marvin Deernose here?" she asked.

"What do you want with him?"

"I'm sorry," she said, looking confused. "Look, I . . ."

Marvin's turn to be ashamed of himself.

"I'm him," he said. "Do I know you?"

"I don't think so. I don't see how you could."

"Do you want to come in?"

She looked at him dubiously, and actually there wasn't that much difference between outside and in—table saws and mess and cold. She was somewhere around Marvin's age and almost exactly his height, dressed in the modern teddy-bear clothes, quite a bit too clean for here. But she followed him inside anyway, stood with her arms folded against the cold and looked out the picture windows of the Great Room, that's what Bob called it, the Great Room.

"That's quite a view," she said. "If you take those other houses away."

"Do you want some coffee?"

She blinked at him, like he had changed the subject on her.

"Sure," she said.

"That hill up there?" he said. "That first ridge when you look over toward the mountains. That's all subdivided already, they've got the power in and the roads graded. I don't have any cream or anything, sorry."

"I'm fine."

She sipped from the plastic thermos cup, still looking out. She seemed confused.

"My grandfather asked me to find you," she said. "Henry Neihart."

Marvin put it together right away: the old man, the Cadillac upside down in the snow. He started to be afraid as he remembered the promise that he had made, the blank check. She'd come to collect.

"My name is Justine Gallego," she said.

Held a gloved hand toward him and Marvin took it in his own bare hand and he felt as if he was being held, captured. He remembered the feeling: what had he agreed to do? Things were overtaking him. The soft synthetic of her glove against the hard callus of his palm. She seemed too soft to be the angel of this announcement.

"Marvin Deernose."

"I know," she said. "I mean . . ."

Stupidity. Of course she knew. Marvin offered her an overturned plastic bucket that once held drywall mud, in lieu of a chair, and sat on another bucket himself with his own cup of coffee. She was maybe thirty-five, tall, slender, dark hair almost black, with a worried look that had pressed itself into the lines of her face.

"My grandfather would like to meet you," she said. "To thank you. I guess. I want to thank you myself."

"That's all right."

"He was hoping you could come for dinner, any time next week."

"I did what anybody else would do."

"Please," she said. "He's not well."

"Can he see yet?"

"They don't think he's going to. There's a tumor they found, a few of them actually, they aren't too hopeful. He's actually home now."

"They aren't treating him?"

"Just for the pain, you know."

"What do you think?"

Sad-eyed lady, Marvin thought—she had a slow-moving grace, long neck and a long face. She looked out of place in the bright primaries of Polarfleece she was wearing; she ought to be wearing silks and velvets, Marvin thought, like the Elvis painting. There was something overdramatic about her, self-absorbed. Still she was beautiful. Not some fading high school Mary Lou—she'd never been a Mary Lou at all, never a Betty—but a woman, Marvin thought, just growing into herself. She'd never looked better than she did just then, except for the sadness, Marvin thought, and I could maybe do something about that. If you would let me.

"I think what the doctors tell me to think," she said. "I know he can't stand it, being blind."

Marvin didn't know what to say.

"You don't know him," she said. "He knows what he wants and then he almost always gets it. It's always been that way."

Marvin started to see the outlines of what she was after, the thing that neither one of them could afford to say out loud. Talking around it.

"He doesn't want to be sick," the woman said. "He doesn't want to be weak. He wants to go out on his own terms, that's what I think, not at anybody's mercy. I don't know."

"What?"

"Maybe that's just what I want from him. That bravery."

"Being brave is not that hard. I don't know him."

"No."

"I do know that people give up when they shouldn't. It's harder sometimes to eat your little spoonful of shit and go on with things, you know. Tough it out."

"You're right. You don't know him."

Marvin liked the little rise. Her face, when it was awakened by feeling, became a passionate thing he would like to see more of. Her neck, the swell of her breasts against the parka, her legs in the fuzzy sheathing of her tights. Today's subject was *thighs*.

"I didn't mean anything by it," he said. "I'd be glad to come to dinner, any time."

"Is Tuesday all right?"

She was still a little angry, still looking good.

"My social calendar is a blank, as far as I know," he said. "Tuesday should be fine."

"All right, then."

"What are you doing here, anyway?"

"Here?"

She pointed toward the floor, toward the wreck of the unfinished building.

"No, Montana. You live here?"

"I came to keep him company, I guess. I'm family, you know—you're supposed to come when there's trouble."

"Not everybody does."

"Not in my family either."

"So what are you doing here?"

She looked at him, measuring him. Would she trust him? Did she trust anybody? Marvin didn't think so.

"You've got to get back to work," she finally said.

"It's nothing," he said. "I'll see you on Tuesday."

"On Tuesday."

She took his hand again and this time it was awkward, sideways. Things were trailing off between them, unsettled. We both made small mistakes, Marvin thought.

"I think it's good, what you're doing," he said. "Running his errands, keeping him company. It's no good being lonely at the same time you're sick."

She looked at him—panic, connection—and she squeezed his hand so that the memory of it stayed on his skin, long after she had fled. A woman's hand, he thought, rubbing his hard palms together. A soft thing.

Then it was five o'clock and everybody was fine, down at the Sportsman's Lounge. Bob stopped by for his one customary bottle of Coors and whipped Marvin's ass at eight ball. Carla was pouring, draft beer and peppermint schnapps, and they had the Western Christmas lights strung up behind the bar, little Conestoga wagons and Western boots and cactuses. Santa stared down from half a dozen beer ads.

"Sarcastic Christmas," Marvin said. "I can hardly wait."

Carla looked at him. She was ready to say something but somebody needed a drink down the bar, or maybe she was being careful. Her and Marvin didn't advertise. She lived off tips, for one thing, and Marvin was Indian-looking—not that anybody was being an outright asshole about it these days, most of the time. But it wouldn't take much to make a difference in her take-home.

The other factor was Carla had a kid, a girl of twelve, and she didn't want the rumors flying around. The kid, Rosette, knew about Marvin but she wouldn't like it if the news came back to her in the cafeteria.

So Marvin drifted down the bar, another customer, another evening disappearing into night. Carla was on shift till two, and Marvin had to work in the morning, so they wouldn't see each other that night. He knew he ought to go home, have dinner, be a good dog. He couldn't quite face it.

Somebody had taken a red elf hat and fitted it up on the moose head over the bar. Somebody had strung Christmas lights on the jackalope. They'd already had Sarcastic Thanksgiving, him and Carla and Rosette: they made a couple of turkey pizzas and laid around Carla's house drinking rum and eggnog and watching Jackie Chan videos, him and Carla sneaking out to his truck once in a while to smoke a joint. Rosette looked like she wanted to join them. It was strange how fast the kids in these little towns seemed to grow up, Marvin thought. They were in the bars from baby-hood, driving at thirteen, pregnant and living in a trailer a couple of years after. The bloom and fade was so compressed that it was like the time-lapse flowering on public TV. He watched Carla, thinking how much of her Rosette had already absorbed: thin face, fast talk, the black hair with the bangs too long like Chrissy Hynde. Carla used to do serious speed, once upon a time, but with Rosette it was all attitude.

Another thing he didn't understand.

He had a daughter himself, somewhere.

Marvin had only been back in Rivulet a little over two years. He was held so lightly there. He watched the others from his station by the bar: tables of men and tables of women and others, mixed, smoking cigarettes and drinking gin out of tiny bar glasses while George fucking Strait played on the jukebox and Marvin envied them. He imagined them bound to each other with a thick web of connection: high school romances, cars bought and sold, weddings and divorces, cousinhood. Not only did they know each other, they touched each other. This town was not made out of streets and houses but a huge invisible structure, geometric, that they carried on their shoulders in the air between them.

"Marvin."

He felt the touch on his shoulder, turned and it was Gil Sibbernsen, the deputy, dressed for hunting: orange shirt, green wool coat and pants, pac-boots. He was tall as Marvin but big. On his head he wore a red wool collection of flaps and plaid, topped off with a deedlee ball.

"Do any good?" Marvin asked.

"Didn't expect to. I got my feet nice and cold."

He grinned and took a drink from a cold can of Pabst Blue Ribbon, seventy-five cents a can. It was the cheapest beer they sold here, a point of pride with many regulars, who wouldn't drink anything else.

"That was something, the other week," Sibbernsen said. "I didn't know that was the Senator. I didn't realize."

"Me neither."

"I should have known when I saw the Cadillac."

Marvin felt the little glow of his accomplishment—not that it was anything in particular but a way in, a place for himself. He had even gotten his name in the paper.

"You think he was drunk?" Sibbernsen asked.

"Didn't seem like it."

"Should have popped him on it, though. Should have made him breathe into the tube."

"Why?"

"I don't know," Sibbernsen said. "Get my name in the papers, I guess. Come on, there's somebody I want you to meet."

He led Marvin off toward the back. The room ran all the way through from Front Street to the alley behind, a long rectangle dotted with leaning tables and lit with bright fluorescents. Two thirds of the length of the place was the bar, and behind it dusty bottles along a solid maple mirrored back-bar, made by Brunswick in 1906. The owner had been offered twenty thousand dollars for the back-bar alone and one of these days he was going to take it, Carla said. It was only a matter of him being broke enough.

"I've been waiting to see the two of you both down here at the same time," Sibbernsen said.

Maybe it was personal history or maybe Sibbernsen's attitude but Marvin didn't like him. He didn't like Marvin, either, but they got along when they saw each other. His father and Marvin's father had worked together. Sometimes Marvin saw what it was like to try and live here and knew that he was crazy for trying.

"This is Billy Lefthand," Sibbernsen said. "He was the other Indian that worked for the railroad, back when your dad used to. Billy, this is Frank Deernose's kid."

Billy Lefthand stood up slowly, gravely—an old man, and Marvin was surprised to see it. His father was a young man, still and always, in the way of those who died young. This man was his father's age. Marvin felt the old eyes on him, weighing and judging.

"What do you know," Billy Lefthand said. "I didn't even know if you were alive or whatever."

He reached his hand toward Marvin, a hand crippled up with age and arthritis. Claw, Marvin thought, taking it in his own. The old man sat alone, drinking something-and-Coke, dressed in clean polyester Western clothes—the telltale sheen and blue of the pressed blue jeans and the knife edges of the shirt collar—but his face was used and dirty. He made no move to welcome Marvin. Sibbernsen clapped Marvin on the shoulder, then moved on down toward the crowded end of the bar.

"You were a friend of my father's?" Marvin asked.

"We worked together."

Then there was a silence, a thing he wasn't saying or getting ready to say. The jukebox, a roar of laughter as somebody hit the punch line down at the end of the bar. Marvin lit a cigarette before he could remember not to.

"Your mom," Billy Lefthand said. "She still with us?"

"She lives out in Tacoma now. You know she got married again?"

"I didn't know that."

Lefthand seemed so comfortable in these long silences that it made Marvin's teeth crawl, waiting. He was slow himself but this old man was a miracle.

"You live out in Tacoma too?" Lefthand asked.

"I went to high school there. I've been here and there since then. I'm back up here, now."

"That Tacoma, that's a shithole of a town."

The jukebox twirled and twinkled and the beer signs, strung from the ceiling on gold plastic chains, were frosted with white wispy stuff that looked like Spanish moss. All the pretty little lights, Marvin thought. Sarcastic Christmas. Where was his father?

He tried to look into the face of Billy Lefthand but the old man caught him at it and wouldn't let him.

"You remember your dad much?" Lefthand finally asked.

"A little. You know."

Billy laughed. "I don't know or I wouldn't have asked," he said.

Marvin tried to put it into words: the memory of railroad grease, diesel and hand cleaner, the touch of cold steel school fencing on a cold morning and the chocolate and doughnuts after weekday mass in the school cafeteria. His father was in there somewhere, bound up with the other threads so tight that Marvin couldn't separate him out.

"It's hard to say," Marvin said. "I mean, I remember him but he was just there."

"He was a person with a lot of sides to him."

"What does that mean?"

"He was different, sometimes, when you would see him. I don't know how to explain it. I worked with him fifteen years or so but I never got hold of him, you know? He was a good worker right up to just before the end. That's what I was wondering about, whether he was the same way around the house or what."

"I don't know."

"Did he raise you Indian?"

"No, he didn't."

"Did he ever tell you why not?"

"He never had a chance."

"Didn't you ever ask him about it?"

"I was ten when he died," Marvin said. "A ten-year-old doesn't think to ask a question like that, not from his dad."

"I don't suppose so. What did your mother tell you?"

"Nothing. She didn't like to play it up, changed my name when she got married again. I was Edwards for a long time, till I came back up here again."

"You know where I live?"

Suddenly the old man was leaning forward, right in Marvin's face, talking in a whisper.

"I don't," Marvin said.

"I don't want to talk about this business when I'm drinking and you're drinking. You know where Victor Lane is?"

Marvin nodded.

"Three miles up in the canyon, there's a trailer with a blue stripe down the middle, beat-up-looking thing. That's mine. You come around there, any time you want to talk. I'm retired, you know."

Marvin nodded.

"You try that sometime. You try working with your hands for thirty years and then you just quit one day. See if you like it."

He was still trying to get in Marvin's face. Then he leaned back and grinned.

"I'm getting bad," he said. "Pretty soon I'm going to start calling the radio shows and complaining about the god damn government this and that."

"I'll buy you a drink," Marvin said.

"I've had enough."

Lefthand drained the whatever-and-Coke, ice rattling against his teeth, then got up to put his red plaid coat on.

"You come see me when you feel like it," Lefthand said.

He went out the back door of the bar and Marvin felt the cold rush of wind come through the door around him. Okay, he thought—my father. He was excited but a small voice kept on asking if he really wanted to know. The feel of the cold wind. That was the thing: his father was here everywhere, in the smell of stale beer and the ice on the sidewalks, pressed into the shape of boot prints and frozen. Did he need to know anything more? He sat alone at the table nursing his beer until he saw that Carla was watching him from the end of the bar. Then he went down and stood next to Sibbernsen.

"Thank you," Marvin said.

"The two of you down there," Sibbernsen said, "it looked like Browning on a Saturday night. One more and we would have had an uprising."

He grinned at Marvin. He didn't mean it unkindly. Marvin laughed along to show he didn't mind.

A story about his father:

All his life, Frank Deernose was a big music fan. He even used to play the guitar at parties, though his hands were so messed up with working on the section gang that he was clumsy, and he made a lot of mistakes. This was about half of what Marvin remembered about him, sitting around drinking beer and listening to records or hammering away at the guitar. When they got a baby-sitter, him and Marvin's mom, they would drive down to Great Falls and go to the bars there to hear the bands.

He liked all kinds of music, was the other thing. People would only pick country music and some of them jazz but Frank Deernose would listen to anything. He said it was ignorant of somebody to say, I don't like this kind of music or that. There were two kinds of music, good music and bad, and that was it—good country and bad country, good rock and bad. There was even a good polka out there somewhere, although he hadn't heard it yet.

They'd go to all the different kinds of bars out by the air base, even the black clubs, where Marvin's mother would sometimes be the only white face. She would brag about it afterward. She'd describe the rhythm and blues bands to her friends, the uniforms and the dance steps, with an excitement on her face that Marvin didn't see much.

After he died, she kept his records—in the living room at first, and then in the basement when she remarried. Marvin rescued them before they started to get the basement smell too bad and kept them in his room after that. Some of them were LPs but most of them were 45s—Chuck Berry, Howlin' Wolf, original Hank Williams and Merle Haggard and Johnny Cash on Sun Records. He had a copy of "Sonny Boy's Christmas Blues" and a copy of "Tee-Ni-Nee-Ni-Nu" by Slim Harpo, "The Race Is On" by George Jones. Marvin felt like a rich man, looking at them all, and he would bring them out at parties and play his way through the stack. People would come up to him just to look at the things. They'd take a 45 of "Heartbreak Hotel" or "Matchbox" by Carl Perkins and stare at the old Sun label, the yellow rays radiating out. People just wanted to touch them. Everybody knew they were worth a bunch of money.

The guitar just disappeared, though, which was too bad.

Marvin carried the records around with him in a blue Naugahyde box like old luggage, a box with special dividers to put the 45s in and a little stack of adapters. The LPs he just took around in a cardboard box. They went to San Diego with him and then to Tucson and then, when he got divorced in the Navy, they were the only thing he rescued from the house.

When he got broke down in Tucson, though, when things were really bad for him, he knew it was time to sell the records. He needed the money. Also, it was like they were looking at him. This was when he was doing drugs and he didn't want to be seen by anybody, he just wanted to disappear into the high. He told himself he was going to use the money to clean up, get the hell out of town and make a new start. It was hard to say if this would have happened or not.

Anyway, he took the whole stack, box and all, out to this fancy collector's record store up on Grant or Pima where the punk guy behind the counter looked through them one by one, like he was appraising diamonds, and finally he offered Marvin fifteen dollars for the whole bunch.

Fifteen dollars!

They were partied out, was the problem. The punk guy pointed to scratches, torn labels, cigarette burns. He showed Marvin the descriptions of condition in the collector's blue book, from Mint right down through Fair.

"These aren't even Fair," he said. "These have got more scratches than record."

Marvin told him to fuck himself but the next guy wouldn't give him more than ten and the only other store in town didn't want them. "You might try Phoenix," the guy said. "You might try the Swap Meet. People like these things for decorations."

That was the story of Marvin's record collection. He still had them, still in the same box, in the corner of his living room. He went out and got a turntable with a 45 speed just to play them, which he did late at night sometimes: Muddy Waters and Hank Snow, Ernest Tubb and Louis Armstrong, Bessie Smith, Roy Clark. The trouble was, it made him lonely. He impressed the hell out of Rosette with them, though.

The cow had stumbled, crossing a snow-filled gully, and broken its leg and died there. It wasn't till the vultures started circling in on it that Lex had discovered it missing. The cattle were clustered near the house, most of them, but they could range almost a mile up the hill if they wanted. That was where this one had wandered to.

"Fence that yard in, one of these days," Lex said, looking down at the dead cow. "Keep 'em down on the flats."

"They don't need to graze in the winter?" Justine asked.

Lex started to laugh at her but then he stopped himself. She was supposed to be the new boss lady. She felt pathetic, fraudulent.

"There's no real grazing in the winter anyway," Lex said. "That's why we feed them the hay. Grass for grass, you know. The Senator just likes to let them wander a little. He says it looks too much like a feedlot when you've got them all bunched up in front of the house."

"What do you think?"

"It does smell a bit," Lex admitted. "Still, it keeps them out of trouble."

They both looked down at the corpse of the cow: the gut

section eaten raggedly away, scraps and tatters of fur and meat and clean white bone. The head was intact although the eyes had been pecked out.

"Is that all birds?" she asked.

He almost laughed at her again.

"Take a bird awhile to do that much damage," he said. "That's coyotes right there. Or maybe not."

"What else would it be?"

"Could be a cat but I don't think so—I don't see the tracks." He waved his arm toward the scatter of prints in the snow, a steady dirty bloodstained line between the woods—fifty yards away—and the dead cow.

"Those are dog tracks," Lex said.

"Our dogs?"

Lex laughed, without humor.

"They would if you let 'em," he said. "We put one down the other year, he was coming up and over the ridge from those new houses down at the end of the valley. Big old German shepherd. Somebody's pet." He spat for emphasis. "They just let him run loose."

"What did you do with him?"

"Oh, I had to get rid of him. Everybody's got a lawyer now."

This was just cryptic enough to make Justine curious but she knew better than to ask. Lex had a deliberately blank look on his face. Then, slowly, he clucked his tongue—too bad about that—and turned back to the dead cow.

"No," he said. "This was coyotes, is my guess. Or maybe a wolf."

"There are wolves here?"

"Not so loud," he said. "The Fish and Wildlife hears about it and we'll be in deep."

"How can you tell?"

"I don't know," he said. "I just see these prints sometimes a lot bigger than what a coyote would make. Looks like a damn tiger. Don't tell anybody."

"Why not?"

"The Fish and Wildlife," Lex said, counting on his fingers. "The state Fish and Game, the Environmental Protection Agency, we'd probably get a damn OSHA inspector out here. Making it dangerous for the cows. I'm not kidding."

"Oh, no. Of course you're not."

"You think it's a joke," he said. "Wayne Henderson, you know him? over in Rexville. He got a twenty-thousand-dollar fine and had to give up his hunting license. One damn wolf. You know how many calves a wolf can get through in just one night? I tell you what."

"Look," she said, "I'm not arguing against you."

"No, but you don't agree with me. You think a wolf's a beautiful animal and I would have to agree with you. You think a wolf belongs here and I would say you might be right. The wolf was here a long time before we showed up. But to say that a wolf and a cattle operation can go on side by side—well, that's just living in a fantasy world. Newborn calf is the easiest prey in the world for a wolf. Even a full-grown cow if she's off by herself. I got nothing against the animal, understand."

"Yes, you do."

"No, I don't. You just have to decide: am I going to run a cow operation here? Because if you are, you can't coexist. That's just the fact. You've got to decide."

There was a glint in Lex's eye, the true believer. And maybe he was right, she thought—maybe he knew better.

"Did you talk to Henry about this?" she asked.

"Don't have to," Lex said. "He knows. It's a hard way to make a living. Got to do what you have to."

Everybody's trying to teach me a lesson, she thought. Not like I don't need one.

Lex pried the frozen corpse of the cow out of the ice and snow, using a long steel bar, a tool of some sort that Justine didn't recognize. Frozen stiff, she thought, the legs jutting straight out at an odd angle. Then Lex asked her to hold the bar, holding the weight of the cow off the ground. He knelt and fed a length of chain under the front shoulders of the animal and fastened the ends of the chain together. Then he backed the ranch truck up next to the gully—the big flatbed Ford one-ton bucking and heaving across the broken ground—and laid a pair of planks from the cow to the bed of the truck and fired up a little gas-powered winch. Slowly, almost comically, the stiff-legged corpse was dragged along the ground and up to the planks and then slowly up. The gas-powered winch made a racket, too much to talk. The smell of it reminded her of lawnmowers and outboard motors, it reminded her of summers past and pleasure and warmth, and for a moment she closed her eyes and let herself imagine: a lake, a drink, a lawn chair . . .

Then he shut it off and in the silence was the cold raw December wind.

"Off to feed the minks," Lex said.

Spit-shined and polished, Marvin drove the long gravel road in from the county highway to the Senator's house. It was
a cold clear night. A fat moon hung just under the ridge. It lit the
white hills on the far side of the valley but not the valley floor, not
yet. A little Cessna rested on the ground, snow on its wings.

Uneasy: this was a rich man's place, he didn't belong there.
Down in Tucson, the rich stayed in camps of their own, walled
and guarded. Here you just never saw them.

A couple of horses loitered down at the far end of the field.
The lighted door of an old barn offered some comfort. This was
home to somebody. Plus there were trees, big ones all around. He
drove into the shelter of them, out of the big blank mirror of the
sky, and he felt it again: home.

Not his home, though. The house was dark and empty and he
had come to the wrong place. A pair of dogs circled up around his
pickup and a gaunt white man in a filthy Carhartt coat came out
of the barn and into the yellow of the yard light.

"Can I help you?"

"I was looking for the Senator. He said . . ."

The white man looked at Marvin a second, looked him over
before he answered—that tiny moment, he was almost used to it

but it still made him angry: are you a danger? criminal? You're not like us.

"He's up at the new house," the white man said. "He's expecting you?"

"He invited me."

That moment again, while the white man doubted him, measured his word. Not quite rude but close as he could shave it. Maybe he didn't even know he was doing it. Reluctantly, the white man went along.

"Back down the yard," he said. "There's a split in the driveway back there, go up the hill. You'll see it."

"Thank you."

The white man shrugged, and the words stung in Marvin's mouth, they burned: thank you.

The big house was lit, big-windowed, and he wondered how he'd missed it before. A pair of dogs circled the truck when he shut it off. He tried to get out and they snapped at his legs, barking and growling. Marvin started to laugh. He wasn't even mad anymore.

As he was about to start the engine and go home, the woman Justine came to the doorway and called the dogs in. She must have heard them barking. Marvin sat in his truck and watched her in the light from the doorway behind her: a tall slender shape, long neck. Her hair was long and braided into a tight, unflattering knot. Marvin thought: Once we get past a certain age, our troubles belong to us. There's no one else to blame them on, the tight knot of hair, the tension he remembered around her mouth. Dr. Deernose, the famous psychologist and stamp-collection expert.

"I didn't know they were out," she said. "I'm sorry."

She clutched the dogs by their collars, one per hand, while

Marvin tried to walk up the icy gravel in his best Western boots. The dogs lunged and barked. Marvin started to laugh.

"What?"

"If I was any more welcome, you'd have a shotgun on me."

"Look, I'm sorry."

She didn't laugh with him, she *couldn't* laugh. This was a house of sickness and death, he remembered. Still it was more than that, something in her clockwork.

He said, "I got lost down at the bottom of the hill. I thought I was in the wrong place! That old house, all shut up like that."

"That's the house they built a hundred years ago. Henry got tired of it, I guess. He built this two or three years ago."

"It's nice," Marvin said—though this was exactly like the houses they had been making fun of at Cookie Cutter last week, one hundred percent Western and about an inch deep. He took his good wool coat off and hung it on a fake-antique rack with a wildlife mirror behind, wolves in a winter forest.

"What's in back of you, here?"

"Nothing," she said. "About three hundred miles of nothing, all the way to Canada."

"That's nice."

"Oh, it's beautiful."

She was saying something but he couldn't tell what, the little bitter twist to the corners of her mouth.

"Come on," she said. "Henry wants to meet you."

"We already met."

"To *see* you, then."

She didn't like to be corrected and—in this house, anyway—seemed to be perfectly joke-proof. She led him through the kitchen, which smelled of roast beef, and into the Great Room. Marvin thought of Bob. The windows opened up along the big end, over the valley and the big black sky. Mine, it said: my view, my mountain, my sky.

The grandfather sat in a rocker by the window, arms folded, a blanket over his lap.

"Henry, this is Marvin Deernose."

Marvin was surprised when the grandfather stood to take Marvin's hand in his own strong hand and Marvin remembered the grip.

"Senator," he said.

"Don't bother with that," the grandfather said. "I'm glad you could make it. Do you want something to drink?"

Marvin had a sinking spell—he had been expecting more from this evening, it was hard to say what, but now he saw the formality and stiffness extending out in front of him and he saw this would be a waste of time. He looked at the woman Justine like this was her fault.

"We have beer, wine," she said. "There's some decent Scotch in there, I think."

"Scotch it is," Marvin said. "Full speed ahead."

"What?"

"Nothing. Let me give you a hand."

They were all standing there in the middle of the floor like actors waiting for the play to start.

The theme is Western Hospitality, he thought: cow meat and red wine for dinner, and an anecdote about the history of this place. How long this family has, etc. Cigars on the veranda. And why did the rich love hillsides so much? They liked to see what they owned, they liked to look down on the nonrich and be glad.

"Have you always lived here?" Marvin asked, just to try to roll the ball.

"Near Butte," the grandfather said. "You know Montana?"

"More or less."

"Well, I was born in Rocker. It was a tough little town. We lived there and then up on the hill in Butte before they leveled it. Where are you from?"

"Right here."

"I never heard your name much."

"We moved away when I was ten. I've just been back up here these last couple of years."

"Okay," the grandfather said, satisfied.

King me, Marvin thought: King Me! The old man liked to know who his subjects were, what they were up to. She handed him his drink and her hand touched accidentally, cool skin, and he remembered their last confusing touch when she visited the site. Her long face, worried. She was wearing black and beautiful in the lamplight. She was out of his price range, though—he had known it before but here, in the vault and gloom of the log mansion, he felt it.

"Are you a local too?" he asked her.

"I used to come here, years ago," she said. "I mean, I still do. But my sister and I used to spend every summer up here, all the way through school."

"You didn't live here, though."

"No," she said, embarrassed. "California."

Henry said, "Thirty million people living like pigs down in California and paying a lot of money to do it."

"I live in Oregon now," she said to Marvin.

Henry said, "Oregon's next."

A silence: logs snapping in the fire. This agreement, Marvin didn't like it—this feeling between the rich that they needed to keep the rest of the world out. Never mind that he had been thinking the same thing himself earlier that day.

Marvin said, "They're just looking for something."

"What?"

"You know: a job, a change of scene, people trying to make a fresh start. There's nothing right or wrong with that, it's just going to happen."

She looked at him like he was saying this directly to her, a secret between them. Maybe he was, although not exactly meaning to. The grandfather was genuinely blind, they could have been doing anything in front of him and he wouldn't have known, they could have been kissing, or worse.

"That's what they went to California for in the first place," Marvin said.

"Let them stay there, then," said the grandfather.

"Let's sit," the woman said, and they sat with their drinks in the dim light of the fire and watched the lights of the room reflected in the glass. It started to snow, thick flakes, like insect wings flicking against the windows. Marvin imagined he could hear them.

When dinner came, the servant woman had already cut up the grandfather's dinner on his plate, the roast beef and potatoes in small chunks, swimming along with the peas in a pool of brown gravy. The grandfather ate with a spoon. His big hands were clumsy from the stroke, and he hung his head like he was ashamed. He wanted to be invisible as well as blind.

The body, Marvin thought: why are people embarrassed by the failures of the body? He'd seen it in accident victims. Cover up the body, hide it, hide the blood inside.

The woman ate a cut from the center of the roast beef, blood-rare. She took very little but ate it all so that nothing was wasted. Marvin took too much, it was urged on him, heaped on him, the guest. Watching her eat—her small precise movements—he felt an obligation not to disgust her. Slowly and carefully and neatly he took the pile of food down, though his appetite was gone before the food was gone. American food, he thought, feeling the meat set and harden in his gut. Then coffee and white chocolate.

By then it was safe to look at the grandfather again, his dignity in place again, but by then he was mostly gone. Marvin saw the effort it took him just to stay upright, the tight lines around his mouth, the skin of his upper lip puckered in fine vertical lines like someone had sewn his mouth shut.

The servant woman cleared the dishes and Justine left with her.

"Go ahead and smoke," the grandfather said. "I can smell it on you."

Marvin couldn't tell if he'd been insulted or not but he lit up anyway, then searched for an ashtray.

"Those silver things on the sideboard," the grandfather said. "The ones that look like candy dishes or something. Go ahead and use one of those, that's what they're there for."

"Thank you."

"Ordinary common courtesy. People seem to have forgotten. Besides, I like the smell, I'd smoke myself if the doctors would let me. I still smoke cigarettes in my dreams."

"When did you quit?"

"Nineteen sixty-six."

The grandfather pantomimed the act of smoking, holding the imaginary cigarette in his fingers, blowing air out through pursed lips.

"I'm going to quit myself," Marvin said. "I mean, I already do about once a week, but for good."

"I always thought," the grandfather said. "You know, the smoker's prayer: Dear God, let something really awful happen to me so that I can start smoking again."

A small polite laugh from Marvin.

"And now it has happened."

Marvin looked down at the cigarette between his fingers with a sudden revulsion, knowing that the death he played with, the death he held so lightly, was real. It was there in that room. He knew his own stupidity.

"Would you like a cigarette?" he asked.

The grandfather smiled.

"No, thank you," he said. "At this point, I would just be doing it to offend the Puritans around here."

He meant Justine, Marvin saw. Some separation between the two of them, some difference or lack of understanding. Some disapproval.

"I've lost the desire," the grandfather said. "You don't know what that's like, at least I hope you don't. I knew it would never happen to me, you see?"

He grinned, slightly death-mask.

"I *knew* it. Even though I would look around me and see it in their faces, the other men around me. They'd get older, year by year, and they would be the same and then one day they didn't want anything anymore, they didn't have the desire. They wanted to be comfortable, you know, they wanted to be left alone in peace, that's all they wanted. A good-looking girl walks by you and your dick doesn't get hard anymore. I'm sorry if I'm offending you."

"You're not."

"It's not just physical. It's not just being tired out or worn out although that's part of it, I'm sure. That's what death is."

"What?"

"When you don't want anything anymore. You lose the desire. It doesn't matter whether you're breathing or not at that point, you're dead. I am not there yet."

"No."

The grandfather folded his hands on the table in front of him. He had said what he wanted to. Not now but soon.

The sound of the wind in the corners of the house.

There was a nurse in the house, too. Miss Sterling came in along with Marliss and together they led or carried the grandfather toward the back of the house like a drunk, one to each shoulder. Marvin turned his eyes from the indignity.

Alone in the dining room, he smoked another cigarette before anyone else came to join him. It was a long low room, a little claustrophobic, old expensive furniture and paintings that were too big for the walls: a herd of buffalo in the snow, a hazy sunrise along the Madison. A couple of small Remington bronzes rested on the sideboard. What was it about the West? It needed so much equipment to keep it going, so much reinforcement. Did people in Connecticut need this many souvenirs to remind them of who they were and where they had been? Western art and Western wear and Western movies. Eastern art and Eastern wear and Eastern movies.

Plus there was that sad, defeated Indian slumping on his bronze horse, eight inches tall. It was like childhood, where whoever made up the game got to play all the good parts. Let's play hospital and you be the dead guy and I'm the doctor.

The eight-inch Indian. Marvin was thinking about Billy Lefthand, wondering if there was a message there for him. Ninety percent of what Marvin knew about himself came through Westerns, ninety-nine percent. What was an Indian? An Indian was a noble yet sad creature of the plains, unless it was now. If it was now, the Indian was a noble yet drunk source of trouble. Why was

the Indian noble? Because he lived closer to nature and understood it better. Why was the Indian sad? The Indian was sad because we took his land and buffalo away. I will fight no more
forever. Fierce warlike Comanche, Apache. Them noble savage.
Them wagon burning.

Marvin knew about three true words of his own history:
Browning, Blackfeet, 1956. He wore this thing on his skin, the
color of his skin and his hair and the shape of his nose, and everybody saw him in it and thought they knew who he was.

Justine came in, scowling at the cigarette smoke. She didn't
mean to be unfriendly, it was just some kind of a reflex. Marvin
stubbed the butt out anyway.

"He's down for the night," she said.

"He's tired."

"I thought we could take our coffee in the living room. Unless . . ."

"What?"

"I don't know, I don't know what you feel like doing. I appreciate your coming out to see him. If you need to get going,
though. I mean, I'll be up for a while, so either way."

Marvin tried to sort out the messages and then gave up.

"I don't need any more coffee," he said. "I'm not in any special hurry, though."

"Do you want something to drink?"

"Sure."

She left the room, and Marvin stayed a minute, not sure
whether she meant him to follow or not. A momentary spark of
anger, fuck this place, fuck you, but it passed as quickly as it came
and then he was all right. He went to find her: pouring drinks in
the living room.

She looked up when he came into the room. She startled. Her
face, lit from below by a small lamp, was hard to see but he saw

her and it stayed with him: she turned to him full of longing and then away, disappointed, because it was not him, the one she was waiting for. The one who wasn't coming, could never come, was Marvin's guess. He'd seen the life inside her. What was she waiting for, what did she want? Nothing with a name. He knew that much. He saw himself reflected, his own longing, like the moment when you catch sight of your own face in an unexpected mirror and for a moment you see yourself as others do, a stranger.

He saw himself mirrored.

Then it was over, and she was giving him a glass of Scotch, no ice, the whiskey was too good for ice. She was still drinking wine herself. A gas fire flickered in fake logs. She arranged herself on the leather couch by the window, leaving him the big chair, the Daddy chair. A few feet between them. The lights were off or dimmed down to almost nothing and the snow still came down hard. The world ended a foot outside the window, in a flurry of white.

"It's good of you to come and see him," Justine said. "It's hard for him."

When she spoke the imaginary closeness left, she became again the stranger she was, disappeared inside her body. The mystery was not the disappearance but the closeness of a moment before. Sister, he thought, saying the word in his head. Not sister exactly.

Other people, other planets.

Marvin said, "I was curious to see him anyway, how he came out from the accident. He's stronger than I thought."

She laughed, a little bitter.

"Don't underestimate Henry," she said. "You'll pay for it."

"You're from Oregon?"

"Portland."

"I lived in Portland for a while."

"Where?"

Marvin's turn to laugh.

"Not the part you come from," he said. "This was a few years back when I was having some hard times, I guess you could say fucking up. Pardon my language."

"It's fine."

"It's just that that seems like the only way to say what I was doing, you know?"

"It's fucking fine," she said, and smiled at him—and for that moment she was in the room with him, she was fine with him, they were fine. He remembered that quick glimpse inside her.

"Just ask Henry," she said. "He says I have a garbage mouth."

"I didn't notice."

"Oh, I'm better about it now. We used to spend summers here in high school, my sister and I, back in my wild years. Not that they were all that wild."

"I bet you had fun, anyway."

"Oh, no. I mean, sure it was fun—good to get away from the parents and out West, you know. We had adventures. But I was always, I don't know—I was the one who was playing it safe."

"It doesn't seem like you."

"How would you know?"

Now she was grinning at him, low, wolfish—something feral in the firelight. He didn't know her at all.

"I'm sorry," he said.

"No, I mean, how would you? I don't mean to make fun of you. It's just, I don't know."

"What?"

"I was the kid, when we would go to the fair or to the circus with a bunch of people? Like a birthday party or something. And all the other kids would be dashing around the sideshow, picking up guns at the shooting gallery and bugging my dad for quarters and so on. And I would be the one who would stick close to them, I was always worried that one of us would get lost. I tried to make them stay close."

"Did anybody ever get lost?"

"All the time. We always seemed to find them again, though."

Quiet again, the soft flick of snow against the windowpanes. The talk between them felt set on velvet, like a jeweler's display, against the hush. He could feel the snow absorbing the sound, stealing it into itself—not that there was anything to hear, not this far out in the country. He thought of the cows out in the fields: turning their backs to the wind and waiting it out.

"I lost a child, a few years ago," she said. "Two years ago."

At first he didn't understand and then he did. She didn't lose the child at the fair.

"A boy or a girl?"

"A boy. He was four. Have you got a cigarette?"

He shuffled the pack toward her across the table between them and said, "Henry said you didn't smoke."

"I don't, much. I don't around him."

She lit the cigarette. He watched the red reflection of the coal dance around in the dark window glass.

"It's strange," she said. "I'm so much of an adult, you know? And then I get around my mother or my father or my grandfather and I turn into this punk kid. I just wonder if it ever stops."

"Why did you tell me that, about your child?"

"My *son*," she said. "He had a name, Will. I guess I had too much wine at dinner."

"I'm just asking."

"It's what there is to know about me. It's my *story*."

Her mouth curled around the words, not quite in control.

She said, "I'm sorry if I'm embarrassing you."

"You're not embarrassing me."

She busied herself with the cigarette for half a minute, arranging herself again, the social self she wore over her feelings. Marvin felt the loss. He wanted that glimpse of her naked self again. He wanted the intensity.

"I try to tell people," she said. "Otherwise, if they find out later, it's like I've been hiding it from them. It's like my secret, which I don't want it to be."

"You don't have any other children?"

"No."

"And you're still married?"

She looked up quickly, spooked—he'd said the wrong thing, the deer's head swiveling up at the sound of the broken twig.

"I didn't mean," he said. "I just read somewhere. They said that's the hardest thing, or one of the hardest, when a kid dies on you."

"It's hard enough," she said. "The hardest thing I have ever done. But we are still married."

"I'm sorry I asked."

"It's all right," she said. "You want to die sometimes, at least I did—not so much that you want to be dead in particular but you just want it to be over. I got to a point where I would have done anything."

"I can imagine."

"No, you can't."

She said it without anger, without putting him down.

"You literally can't imagine," she said. "Not till you've gone through it. You wake up every morning and it's still there."

"I'm sorry," he said again.

"Just the fact of it. He's still dead, my son is still dead. The first thing tomorrow morning, that's the first thing I'll think."

She stubbed out the cigarette.

"I'm drunk," she said. "I'm sorry. I don't mean to bother you."

"You're not bothering me."

"Inappropriate personal disclosure," she said. "There's a name for everything."

"Let me tell you something," he said, leaning toward her. "People will find names for you. People will call you this and that but the thing is, you get to say. You get to name the thing yourself. There are about three things in the world that I know but this is one of them."

She blinked at him.

"I don't mean to play the wise man," he said.

"I didn't take it that way."

"Everybody always knows more than you do. Everybody's got a plan."

"Not me."

"Me neither."

She looked at him, not quite a smile but an opening up. Again he felt himself reflected. He saw a confusion inside her that looked like his own, an answering loneliness. It was a question he'd worked over any number of times without coming to any conclusion: what he was looking for in another person, what he wanted. Before, when he had been really lonely, he had known what he wanted—he wanted to be touched and talked to. He let another sailor give him a blow job once, which still worried him once in a while. He remembered the stainless steel of the toilet stall, and the smell. Loneliness drove him to it, or at least that's what he hoped, as opposed to some latent ambivalence. He still felt like a fraud sometimes in the company of men but he believed that they had their secrets too. Being a man was acting like a man. Maybe it came naturally to some people but not to Marvin, who had dropped the ball a few times.

And you, he thought, turning toward her face again. Your secrets.

The carrier had been the loneliest place he'd ever been in his life despite being the most crowded. Just thinking about it made him grateful for the warmth and the company here.

"It's good of you to have me," he said.

"You think a lot, don't you?"

"Why?"

"There are just these leaps between the things that you say. You're just sitting there and then these things come out and I don't get the connection."

"I've been accused of that."

"I don't mean it the wrong way. Please. I just think it's interesting."

"I was thinking about going up to Sleeping Child on Saturday," he said.

She looked at him, puzzled—and then she saw that this was the game, this was how it was played.

"Okay, I give up," she said.

"What?"

"Who or what is Sleeping Child? Why Saturday? Why are you telling me? And so on."

"It's a hot springs," Marvin said. "I was going out to maybe get a load of wood on Saturday morning and I was thinking about going to the hot springs on the way back. It's about sixty miles. You could meet me there if you wanted to. Get out of the house, you know."

"It's an idea."

"You don't have to."

"I know I don't."

She was looking at him again, looking for something, evidence.

"There's a bar," he said.

"I could just drive down with you," she said. "Make a day of it."

"I'm going to get froze out of my place if I don't get some firewood in. I kind of underestimated at the start of the winter."

"I could help. Don't look at me like that."

"What?"

"I'm not some delicate flower," she said.

"I didn't think you were."

"No, but you look at me like that. See, I tell people about my son and they automatically assume I need to be taken care of. I'm sick of it."

"We all need to be taken care of."

"Okay."

"Just bring some gloves, if you're coming. You want me to pick you up?"

She looked around, though nobody was watching, there was nobody to see. Marvin saw with some pride and some pleasure that she meant to keep him secret, and a guilty secret at that.

"I'll meet you someplace in town," she said.

"McDonald's?"

"Do we have to?"

"We could try the Snow White but last time I was in there, it took me an hour to get breakfast."

What Marvin wasn't saying was that he didn't want to advertise either. She looked at him across the firelight, and for a moment he wondered if she would ask him to stay, and wondered if he would, which of course he would. The dog in me, Marvin thought. Tall, attractive and sexually active. But there was something else, too.

Also there was Carla.

"McDonald's it is," she said. "What time?"

"Seven-thirty?"

She scowled.

"Late as you want," he said. "I just want to get it over with and get to the bar, the woodcutting part, you know."

"Seven-thirty it is. Just don't talk to me till nine."

"Deal."

He looked at his watch and sighed.

"I've got to get going pretty soon," he said.

"Me too."

"Six in the morning, the alarm clock goes off. One time down in Tucson I slept from five-thirty till almost noon, hitting the snooze button every ten minutes."

"That's impressive."

"A night like this," he said, "I keep a second alarm clock in the oven. It makes a hell of a racket."

"Thank you for coming," she said, and put her own hand over his to cover it. Her hand was warm bare skin. He remembered the touch of it all the way home, crawling along in the snowstorm. Thank you, she said. The touch of her hand. Trouble reaching out to him again, and he knew it.

"I'll tell you what," Lex said. "To run a place like this, a banker that knows a little bit about cattle will do a hell of a lot better than a cowboy who knows a little bit about money. The cow part is easy."

"It's not easy," Justine said.

They sat at the kitchen table, late on a cold dark morning, with cups of coffee and the ranch books spread out in front of them.

"I'll tell you what," Lex said. "Half of the people who used to run cattle in this valley are out of business and living in Billings or some such. There wasn't one of them couldn't tend to a cow."

"What happened to them?"

"They got in over their heads with the bank, most of 'em. Borrowed money to expand their operations when they thought prices were going up. It works sometimes. You can parlay a little investment into a pile of money if you guess right but you can really get whipsawed if it goes the other way. You only have to be wrong once."

Justine looked at the parade of meaningless numbers on the page in front of her and her heart sank.

"Brains and capital," Lex said. "I never had enough of either. Your grandfather, though . . ."

"I assume he does okay."

"He bought up most of the places that went under, or he did for a while. Lately he's been getting hit with taxes. I guess they reappraised the south end of the valley, down where they're putting that subdivision in, and now he's paying ski-resort taxes on land that he's raising cows on. It's complicated business."

"I'm starting to understand that."

"Tell you what else," Lex said. "You can hire somebody to take care of the cows."

"You can do that."

"If you want."

Lex bobbed his head, thank you, you're welcome, something.

He said, "What you can't hire is a manager, somebody to take care of the big picture. I know a few here who have tried."

"What the hell am I supposed to do then, Lex? I don't know the first thing."

"Study up, I guess. I don't know. You could wait till he passes on and then sell the place."

She looked up, shocked—then tried to figure out if he was testing her.

Lex said, "If you don't think you can do it, then don't try. He wouldn't want you to make a mess of things just to prove a point. He says he doesn't care what happens after he's gone."

"He says."

"Well, he might be telling the truth. I don't know how he would find out, one way or the other. Even if Marliss is right about this religion business, I imagine he'd be down in hell, which would make him too busy to care."

"Why would he end up in hell?"

"Read the fine print," Lex said. "We're all going to hell if Marliss is right."

"Henry's a believer, too."

"No, he's not. He's a Catholic."

Justine looked at him.

"It's not the same thing at all," Lex said. "You can look it up."

She opened her mouth to argue but then she didn't want to waste the time.

She asked, "What would you do, if you were me?"

Lex thought about it for a long minute, then grinned at her.

"I'm sorry," he said. "I can't even *imagine* what it's like to be you."

Then it was Saturday morning.

Justine drove off the ranch at ten after seven, bare light. It felt like an escape. She hadn't left the place except to run chores or visit the hospital since she got there three weeks before, and with the little ropes that Henry'd laid around her, she was starting to feel trapped—like Gulliver in Lilliput, the thousand fine strands.

Marvin waited for her in his big black truck. She felt the rush of sin, looking at him, and at first she wondered if she was going to go through with this.

"We can get takeout, if you want to," he said, standing by the window of her car. His breath streamed out white.

She shrugged her shoulders, either way.

"It's sixty miles," he said. "We may as well get a start on it."

"Where should I park the car?" she asked.

"You can leave it up in the corner of the lot. It doesn't fill up, even on Saturday, I don't think."

The rush of sin: she wondered how much she should trust him—not just his soul but his brains also, and his capacity for carelessness. The car was evidence, the size of a house. It was plainly too late to start worrying about it, though. She was going to act as if she trusted him, whether she ought to or not. In for a dime, in for a dollar.

Inside his truck was battered but clean, red rubber floor mats and a pine tree dangling from the rearview.

"Did you do this for me?" she asked.

"What?"

"I know you don't keep your truck this clean all the time."

"I try to," Marvin said. "I've got a little bug in my head. I try to keep things straight when I can. In honor of the eight million things I have no control over at all."

"You do the dishes after dinner?"

"And I make the bed in the morning."

They went through the window and collected their bag, their steaming coffee vats. Instantly the truck cab filled with the smell of fried grease.

"I live like somebody's grandmother," Marvin said, and they started off out of town.

Justine tried to eat her awful breakfast—something on a bun or biscuit, with something else on top of it, everything yellow and grease-spotted—and they settled into morning quiet, on their way to work. He drove and ate his breakfast out of the paper and sipped his coffee. She stared out the window at the white hills, cows, the rhythm and swoop of telephone lines.

Finally she gave up, crumpled the rest of her biscuit into the paper and back in the bag.

"I always think these things are going to be better than they are," she said. "You know?"

"What?"

"I never eat at these places but I always think it would be really great to. You build these things up until they get a life of their own, I mean, I always imagine McDonald's food to be really sinful and greasy and bad for you and great, you know, all those

American sins like salt and sugar and fat. Then when you actually break down and go to one, it's just crappy."

"Half the kids around here wouldn't know what meat tasted like if it wasn't for Mickey D's."

She felt reproved by him, a lesson here she was missing.

Marvin said, "There's a couple of granola bars in the glove box there. Go ahead if you want them."

She didn't want to give in to him but she was still hungry. After a few miles she reached into the glove box for the granola bars, as unobtrusively as she could, but he noticed anyway and smiled. She burned under his smile.

"I just don't like that fast-food crap," she said.

He didn't say anything. Some obscure point had been won or lost. It isn't fair, she thought: we're not married, not even sleeping together yet, but we're still playing the same stupid game of who's right and who's wrong and maybe it's my fault, maybe I carry it with me.

Also, she realized that she meant to sleep with him, or at least expected to, which came as not quite a surprise.

"I'm married," she said. "Did I tell you that, the other night?"

"You did."

Then the silence between them tipped, turned awkward. She knew too much about her own desires. Better to leave them down in the dark, she thought, the place before words. She found herself imagining the shape of his body under the brown work clothes, the things he would say and the things he might do. A fleeting wish for a drink, a step sideways out of the predicament of herself. She could imagine the burn of vodka in her mouth, even better than she could imagine Marvin. Two feet away from her on the bench seat of the pickup, and still he was going hazy on her, gray.

The bright fire of alcohol.

"How tall are you?" he asked.

Justine felt herself blushing.

"Why?"

"I've got a spare pair of coveralls behind the seat," he said. "You look to be about the same height as I am."

"I guess."

"Keep you from wrecking your good clothes."

Again, she felt reproved. Her good clothes and her fancy eating habits. Her height and her money. Never quite good enough for anybody. She closed her eyes, and Marvin lit a cigarette, and in the close heat of the cab she daydreamed of Florida. She dreamed of light and ease and warmth.

Out in the woods, Marvin was running his chain saw in the middle of a little man-made clearing, an island of mess and noise in the general silence of the winter woods. Man the Maker, Justine thought. He had his coveralls on, and his goggles and ear protection. He looked like some primitive Martian with his weapon. Marvin limbed the fallen pines, then cut them into stove lengths. Her job was to fetch the cut wood to the pickup and stack it there.

At first it was easy, then after half an hour it wasn't. She was still inside her dream of Florida, for one thing: the air as thick as coffee cream, the feel of heavy sunlight on the skin of her arms. A day when they went out to the lake island, she and Mark the Genius—her boyfriend at the time—and two other girls and a poet from Germany. She'd worn a yellow dress from the second-hand store and a straw boater with silk roses on the band. The dress was still closeted somewhere, loved but not worn. It was a fifties relic, an I-love-Lucy special. She could feel the sunlight on her neck when she wore it, on the flat of her chest. The tease and dance of these old dresses: this one was cut low in the front but not past the point of modesty, just far enough to focus attention on her neck. An air of modesty and of virtue, Donna Reed, but when she used to wear this dress she often caught men looking at her, undressing her. It was the unexpected exposure, back and shoulders and the bare arms, which made her walk differently. The air in unexpected places, something. Sexy but deniable. There was some old magic of womanhood which had been lost between her mother's time and her own.

She'd worn the yellow dress, anyway, and the straw hat with roses, and big green Wellingtons for the slog out to the island. They started out trespassing through cows and then across a broad shallow plain of marsh, a river of grass, toward the island. It was hot work, dragging the picnic basket and the checkered tablecloth and the guitar. After a few hundred yards she started the easy everpresent sweat that was part of Florida for her, the fine damp sheen on her arms and forehead. She was twenty or twenty-one. She was still young enough that her sweat didn't smell bad, the way that Will's breath came sweet. The way we sour and rot from experience. Will was dead.

They took a grown-up picnic of foreign cheeses, strawberries and white wine, olives, chocolate, a meal where nothing quite fit together with anything else. She was twenty or twenty-one. The island was a low hummock of tall grass and cattails, rising a few inches out of the duckweed, bound together with the roots of the wild palms that grew there—twenty or thirty of them, rising into the blue sky at their own angles. They bent and dodged. She saw an otter, and an alligator, and a hundred wading egrets, little white exclamation points in the general green.

It's better to be a visitor, she thought. The land around that island had been fought for and fought for—by the Indians first, and then the Spanish and the English and the Confederates. On the grass, though, half drunk on wine with Mark the Genius resting his head on her bare thigh and the slow air moving over her, there she was at ease. It's better not to know sometimes. Who needs a past? The German poet brought a couple of joints along. Erase, erase.

She could have used a joint then: tripping over cut limbs and branches, carrying the wood with sore cold hands. She was taking a beating. Marvin didn't seem to notice.

Then Mark the Genius went off with the other girls to find an alligator nest and the German poet kissed her.

Marvin shut off the chain saw and the sudden quiet filled her ears, relief. She had not realized how much she hated the sound till it was gone. He cracked open a beer, offered it to her. She turned it down.

"Are you okay?" he asked.

She shrugged her shoulders.

"Jesus," she said.

"Welcome to the working world."

She looked up—was he teasing her?—but he didn't seem to mean it unkindly.

"It's like the organ bank," he said. "You put a little bit of your body in, get a little bit of money out. It uses you up after a while."

"That's a gruesome way to look at it."

"I do this every day. Something like this. Some days we get to lift bathtubs."

He held the beer out toward her again and this time she took it: cold in her gloved hand, cold liquid one step away from ice.

"Actually, I will," she said, and sipped at the cold can. "That's not bad."

"Keep that one," he said, and rummaged for another behind the seat of the truck. She listened but there was nothing to hear, the small sounds—her own breathing, the tiny clunk of beer cans—magnified in the still air. She had Marvin's brown duck coveralls over her own good clothes, now wrecked with sweat and steaming in the cold. This is what the body likes, she thought. Her fingers were bleeding inside the American Rose gloves.

"I'm not used to this," she said. "I guess I don't have to tell you that."

"You did fine."

"I'm just so out of shape!"

"You did fine. You saved me half the time. Besides, it's always easier with company along."

"Well, thanks."

"Even if you just sat there, which you didn't. Let me see your hands."

"Why?"

"You're holding that can funny. Let me see your hands."

"I can't even really feel them," she said.

The cold air hit her skin when she peeled the gloves off and then her hands started to hurt. A blister had burst at the heel of each thumb, pink tender skin welling some kind of liquid.

Tears in her eyes from the sudden pain, she said, "It's nothing."

Marvin laughed, not unkindly.

"Don't lie to me," he said. "That hurts. I've done that to myself before."

He took her hand in his own and there it was again, she thought: contact. She was walking into trouble with her eyes wide open. Fine with her.

The air burned at the new skin as he examined her hands. He tried to be easy but his fingers were callused and hard.

"I've got a first aid kit in the truck," he said. "I'm sorry—I didn't know or I forgot."

"Don't," she said.

"Don't what?"

"Don't princess me. I'm not made of glass."

"I didn't say you were. That hurts, is all. I know because I've done it myself."

She looked into his face, watched him to see if he was trying to fake her out, look down at her, but he didn't seem to be. He seemed to be what he was. The word is *condescend*, she told herself. You finished college. Don't pretend you didn't. Don't pretend.

"I'll be fine," she said.

"You don't want a bandage on that? Bacitracin?"

"We're done, right? I'm fine. I feel good, in fact."

"They say wood warms you twice, once when you cut it and once when you burn it."

She looked at him.

"I didn't make it up," Marvin said. "Somebody says that every time we go out to get wood. It's like a law or something. It's like when somebody sneezes and you say, God bless you."

"I don't."

"Well, I don't either, mostly. But the law is still there."

I want you, she thought, but she didn't say it. Not even the right words: she couldn't find the right words, something about desire, about her body wanting things from him, but also something about the way he lived. The simplicity of working with his hands. Justine was jealous of the bare hard facts of his life: cutting wood, pounding nails, drinking beer. Subject-verb-object, she thought. I shot the deer. I built the house.

She was so far away from that!

She felt the distance in the burn of her hands: stigmata. Her soft and brightly colored clothes, under the brown coveralls. She felt her body cool a little in the wind and zipped the opening of the coveralls back up.

"We should get going, then," he said.

"Okay."

Neither of them moved for a minute, though, enjoying the quiet and the rest. Wind sifted through the pine tops, spraying a mist of fine snow over them. The wreckage of the trees.

It felt accidental when he touched her face.

For a moment she was sure he hadn't meant to. Then she saw that he was looking into her eyes, he was asking her. She closed her own eyes and relaxed into his rough hand, cradling her cheek. Sweet touch.

"I don't know," she said.

"We don't have to . . ."

"No," she said. She opened her eyes again, searched his face for the greed or the unkindness that would give him away but she didn't see it.

"It's just confusing," Justine said. "I'm easily confused."

He took his hand from her but she grabbed it back, held it between her own despite the sting and burn of her hands. She saw a rifle in a scabbard behind the seat of the truck. He was the one, she knew it from the signs.

"I just . . ."

"No talking," Justine said.

He pressed her into the fender of the truck with his body and kissed her neck. She was full of sadness. She wanted him to fuck it out of her. Clothes and clothes and the cold wind waiting for any naked skin, she felt the vague outline of his body under the layers of cotton and wool but it was like spacemen and then she saw them as though she was floating up above, two brown-suited woodsmen and their ridiculous kissing and she couldn't stop herself, she started to laugh.

"What?"

"Nothing," she said. "I'm sorry, I just . . ."

"What?"

"Stupid," she said, and shook her head.

His eyes were clouded over with sex, and then she saw them clear. She saw that she was losing him, he didn't trust her. She reached into the front of his coveralls and touched his cock through the thin cloth of his jeans.

"Just not here," she said. "Okay? It's freezing."

"I noticed," he said.

She let him go, zipped him up.

"We've got all day," she said.

Then driving out, she thought: Did I do that? Did that actually happen? She reached across the bench seat of the truck while he was driving and touched him on the outside of his thigh and they wound up wide-open necking on the seat of the truck, off on a side road, motor running and the heater going full blast and the Carhartt coveralls tangled all together. He was eager but considerate. His hands were rough and cold as pig iron but he was good with his hands. Justine opened right up to him. She fell into weightlessness, she couldn't tell what was up or down, what was his or hers in the tangle of clothes except the feel of his skin and lips. Layer after layer of underwear!

"Hold on," she said.

She pressed him back against the seat—somehow she had ended up on the driver's side—and slowly, deliberately, took off the layers of clothes until she was kneeling on the floor of the truck, naked and shivering. Starting with the coveralls, she peeled the layers off Marvin, folding the clothes on the seat. She was kneeling on her own clothes but stray clumps of snow and cold metal sent shivers up her legs. Marvin was small, smaller than Neil anyway—she didn't have that big a base of comparison—but even thinking like that pulled her out of herself, made her an actor in this thing she was watching and this was exactly what she didn't want. Before she could lose it, she crawled up into his embrace and then he was inside her.

"Oh," he said.

It was clumsy, the angles weren't right but she could move a little and she did, moving over him with her eyes closed, trying to lose herself in the touch, trying to forget the comedy: the truck, the tangled, ugly clothes. She wished they had started some other way—she was in control, she was driving him and she didn't want it to be like that. She wanted to be driven herself. She wanted to be fucked—and the old disappointment started to rise up in her, the distance. She was miles from her body, miles from anybody, and she felt like weeping. It was a relief when he started to shudder under her, and then she felt him whisper her name while he was coming, "Justine," the hot damp breath in her ear.

In the quiet, when she should have been holding on to him, she tried but she couldn't rest. She could fuck up anything. No fresh starts, no second chances. She was stuck with herself and herself and herself. She crossed her arms between them.

"What's the matter?" he asked.

"Nothing. I'm cold."

He wrapped a scattering of clothes around them—scratchy

canvas, cold brass zippers—but nothing could pull her toward him, nothing could pull her out of herself.

"Are you okay?" he asked.

"I don't know."

"Nobody's going to know, if that's what you're worried about. Nobody's going to find out from me, anyway."

She shook her head. The tears, which had been inside her for months, started to bubble out of her and she fell back onto the slack skin of her belly against his and she tried to hold herself away but couldn't. She held against him like a drowning woman and wept. She might be hurting him. She didn't care. She had been trying to be good for months and to be well and now this little opening, this little crack of daylight, had undermined her. Her life was going to be sorrow and sadness. She saw this simple thing.

He awakens at some unspecific hour and he is still blind. It comes as a surprise, still: waking into the blackness, day or night. One morning it was the sun, crawling up his arm, that woke him up; and he was frightened at first, not knowing what it was.

He has to piss.

He fumbles for the bar on the bedside clock and the Korean girl inside says, "Three—forty—one A.M." The Korean girl seems surprised by whatever time it turns out to be. A blessing, he reminds himself. He is lucky to live in an age where electronics can tell time for the blind, where no disease or accident is ever quite final. The doctors continue to hold out hope for him, if he can stay alive until the research is finished. The one doctor, Robison, talks about rewiring the brain, about connecting the circuits differently. There's nothing wrong with your eyes, he says. It's all upstairs. The wiring got messed up inside his brain. This isn't comforting. The idea that his eyes are working almost perfectly, but without him—this frightens him, it seems wrong to even know this. In a simpler life he would be blind and that would be that.

And he still has to piss and it's too early to wake Marliss. He hates it when he has to ask a woman to help him piss, anyway. Get it over with. It's soft, sentimental to think that anything good is going to come of what's left to him. What's the best he can hope for? Life as a houseplant, tended to. There's a balance some-where: he knows that someone would have to come in, find the body. He's known men who shot themselves, always for a reason but it was always a cold-blooded hurt to the ones they left behind. An act of violence, there was no way around it. The dead man was never the victim. Still, the comfort of the thought, the promise of rest . . .

A selfish act, and a cowardly one.

Henry will see this through to the end. He will find the strength. These are night thoughts, he knows it, the creep of doubt and fear that grows up like a vine out of the darkness. Except that it is always night. He can't escape the dream life anymore.

He fumbles his way out of bed with his awful hands, leaning against the log wall. The wall is cool and he knows it's winter outside. The wind in the corners of the house. There's a walker somewhere by his bed, never in any particular place. One hand on the blanket—for location—he circles the room, groping for the walker with his outstretched hand, knocking his water glass over. The bedside table is an antique, brought from back East in the last century, and the water will wreck the finish. He could still call Marliss and have her clean it but he doesn't. Instead he clears off the top of the table, lamp, pills, a book, and takes one of his pillows and blots the wood as best he can. The surface of the table is still damp when he is done but no more than damp. Maybe it isn't wrecked.

The walker is on the other side of the bed. He rests for a minute after lifting his body onto it, listening to the house around him: shush of the furnace blower, refrigerator motor, Marliss's faint snoring from the guest bedroom. He feels a faint vestige of lust, listening to her: the memory of a woman's breath, the heat and weight of her sleeping legs. Not Marliss in particular. The smell of a woman's body from between the sheets, sex and sweat and perfume. It's been awhile since Henry's smelled perfume, except for Dexter Varden down at the bank, who wears cologne in quantity. He must be hard of smelling, Henry thinks, and awards himself a smile for his own joke. Hard of smelling.

He makes his way along the walls of his bedroom, still new, still not quite familiar, using one hand to support himself and the one hand stretched out as a guide and rangefinder: here is the light switch, here is the closet. The Master Bath, they called it. Henry told the builders that he didn't need a god damn bathroom bigger than the living room of the house he grew up in but they talked about resale—you couldn't sell a house that didn't have palatial toilets.

This is work, heaving the body forward a foot at a time. His weakness appalls him.

His weakness: even when he was building this house, he was weakening, building for resale. He sits to piss now, and waits and waits for the piss to come.

Inside his chest, something is building: some black storm front.

The piss comes at last in drabs and dribbles. The sound is shameful and he wonders if either of the women is awake to hear his weakness, either Marliss or Jess. He can't tell but it seems that he might have pissed on his own hand. Something wet or cold. Clumsy gloves over his own good hands. He built for resale. A man should build for his own pleasure and his sense of what is right and wrong and this bathroom is dead wrong, a palace of shit. This house.

He goes to stand and the bright stars spiral toward him out of the blackness.

When he comes around again, he is wedged between the toilet and the tile wall. He is breathing, and no worse than before, but in his weakness he cannot stand. He can't move. He struggles to right himself for a moment, squirming over the expensive tile floor like a nightcrawler on a hook. Somehow he turns himself around so that he hits his head on the toilet. Then he gives up, and lets the energy drain out of his body. It is peaceful lying there, the way he's always been told that people go when they're freezing to death. You give up after a while, apparently, and just lie there and a sense of warmth and peace and ease will come over you. Except for the cold places where he touches the tile floor, especially his cheek, Henry feels the ease of knowing there is nothing he can do for himself.

But only for a moment. Behind the easy feeling comes a vision of himself as he must look, huddled on the tile floor with his pants down and piss on his hands: a helpless pitiful thing. Remains, he thinks, remembering when he was respected and even feared. Nixon came to me for advice, he says to himself. The Air Force named a housing complex after me. Out of nothing and now nothing again.

The women, the knives of their pity.

There is nothing else, though—no hidden untapped strength or miracle machine to set him upright again. He needs human help and the women are the only ones near.

"Jess," he calls out. "Jess!"

The bleat of a lamb, barely filling the bathroom. He clears his throat and tries again: "Jess!"

"Jess!"

He hears a stirring in the hallway, footsteps and then the sound of his bedroom door being opened and a woman's sharp intake of breath in the bathroom doorway.

"Jess," he says.

"No, it's me. Marliss. Are you all right?"

"Where's Jess?"

"What do you mean?"

A silence, while he tries to figure out how to answer her question.

"I mean . . ."

"Are you all right?"

Sarcastic answers dance in his head. In this mood, he wants to say anything hurtful, anything harmful. He doesn't want to be kind, or to receive kindness. But Marliss is help.

"I can't seem to get up," he says.

"What's wrong? I mean, is it anything new or . . ."

"I just can't seem to get up," he says. "If you could give me a hand."

She plops the toilet seat down, then he feels her arms gather under him, around his chest.

"I'm going to pull you forward," she says. "Let me know if this hurts."

She drags him out and his head bumps against a sharp edge of something, the base of the toilet, maybe, or the shower stall. He lets out a short, sharp grunt and Marliss stops.

"I'm fine," he says.

"No, we're okay. Feel over here."

She leads his hand up to a cold metal bar, a round grip, textured—the old-man railing they put alongside the toilet.

"I've got it."

"Now one—two—three."

She lifts him and for a moment they embrace, face to face like lovers, and he smells the bitterness of sleep on her breath, bitter almonds. She makes a small sound with the effort and Henry groans, he can't stop himself. Then he is sitting on the closed toilet seat.

"Are you okay? Did I hurt you?"

"No, I . . ."

What he means to say, what he longs to tell her, is that he cried out not from pain—the pain was everywhere, a constant, low-level background noise behind a screen of morphine—but from the pleasure of her embrace, the touch of a woman's body, no matter how accidental. He remembers flying home from Washington once in winter, the week before Thanksgiving or maybe Christmas, and a young woman sat next to him on the plane and fell asleep and slowly her head drooped onto his shoulder so that he couldn't move without waking her. He remembers the hours of sitting still. He remembers the sweet, illicit pleasure of her body, the weight of it in sleep—and how she woke with the weave of his tweed sport coat imprinted in her cheek, pink and white, and how she ran from the jetway to meet her husband or boyfriend, both of them twenty or twenty-one.

Maybe he's always been this lonely. Maybe this is just the end of the same life he's always lived.

"Where's Jess?" he asks again. "What were you doing in the house, anyway? Isn't she supposed to be here?"

"We need to get you to the doc."

He waves his hand, dismissing the idea.

"You're not answering my question," he says.

"I don't know where she is."

Marliss sounds shameful, reluctant—and Henry realizes, as the anger rises inside him, that this is part of it: embarrassing him in front of the help.

"Where did she go off to?"

"She hasn't been around all day," Marliss says. "I saw her take off this morning."

"I know she wasn't there at dinner."

"I don't know where she is now. You want to lie down?"

"Please."

He lifts himself with the strength of her arms and she slips his underwear up again and fastens his pajama bottom around his waist. She leads him to the bed. He feels her strong arms around him, the pleasure of being touched as she lowers him gently into the sheets again. Then he remembers that Jess has betrayed him, that she is leaving him too—that all that's left to him is paid help. His children have all left him and his work is long behind him. He can feel the air in the empty corners of the new house. Jess has betrayed him. She is being unfaithful.

"I'll call the doc," Marliss says.

"Please don't."

"You were lying on the floor, Henry. I don't mean to interfere in your business but that seems serious."

"I don't want to wake up Robison in the middle of the night."

He can tell right away that he's said something wrong but he doesn't know why.

"What?"

"It's seven-fifteen in the morning," Marliss says. "I'm sorry."

Marvin kissed her goodbye in the doorway of his house and watched her get into the Bonneville and listened to the grind of the big starter, the roar of the fan when the big engine turned over. She got out to scrape the windshield—a few ineffectual swipes at the parts she could reach—and again he admired the length of her. Her thighs in their teddy-bear-fur stretch pants.

"You don't want to stay?"

"Is that an invitation?"

"I'll make you breakfast," Marvin said.

"No."

She seemed a little panicky at the question but she smiled as best she could.

"No, thank you," she corrected herself. "I mean, I know they're wondering where I am by now. They've got enough to worry about."

Marvin nodded agreement. It was true, what she said, but it wasn't all of it. The truth, the whole truth and nothing but the truth, he thought, quoting a thousand Perry Mason reruns. Somebody should have told them it was impossible.

There was something else to say but neither of them knew what it was. They stood in the cold morning—her in her down jacket, Marvin in long underwear and jeans and wool socks—while the car idled loudly toward warmth.

"We never made it to the hot springs," Marvin said. "You want to try to go next week?"

"It's almost Christmas."

"Okay, so . . ."

"No, like next Saturday, if that's what you mean—it's only three days before Christmas."

"Four."

"Well, it might be busy, I don't know. I don't even know if I'm still going to be here."

She wouldn't look at him. Marvin got the lost feeling again, cut adrift.

"We can go today, then."

"They're expecting me."

"They can expect you a little longer. I'm not trying to talk you into anything."

She laughed at him, still holding the ice scraper.

"You'd never try to talk me into anything."

She walked across the tundra of his yard and held him close and kissed him. He felt a little of her warmth even through the cold and the clothes. He found the soft sensitive spot at the base of her neck and kissed her there, felt the little shiver run through her.

"Don't do that."

"Why not?"

"I've got to go," she said, but she didn't pull away. He turned his body all the way to meet hers and felt her legs open, just a bit. But this was too far too fast and she did pull away then, looking at his face with blank eyes. Then returning.

"I've got to go," she said again, and kissed him briefly, husband-and-wife, and got in her car to leave. Marvin didn't know what he wanted. It would have been fine with him if she stayed but also he could stand to think about things. Justine happened before he could think it through, before he even knew that he was supposed to be thinking about her. But part of his brain had known all along. It was taking her forever to get the car moving. Part of his brain knew she was there—not the thinking part but down in the deep part of the brain. Thinking and thinking and thinking but she was there all the time underneath, working on him.

Finally she shut the motor off and got out of the car.

"Fuck it," she said. "You don't mind?"

"No."

"We can go to the hot springs if you want to."

"I think you'd like it."

She walked up to where he stood in the screen door, put a finger to his chest, wouldn't meet his eye. It was her turn to think about him.

"Do you have any clothes I can borrow?"

"I have some that'll fit you, I bet. I don't know if I have anything that's exactly your style."

"Let me take a shower, then. You're sure you don't mind?"

"Not at all," he said.

"I didn't start out to do this," she said. "I'm not trying to talk you into anything you don't want to do."

"Take your shower," Marvin said.

She emerged slowly from the mass of winter clothing: giant white puffball boots lined with fake fur, hat gloves scarf down coat. Marvin remembered the touch of her, the soft tired skin, a little loose but soft and scented with mysterious oils and ointments. Marvin was angles and calluses and bones. Let us praise womanhood, he thought, the ancient ways and wiles. Let us praise perfume. It had been awhile. Carla smelled of cigarette smoke and beer. Shelley, his ex-wife down in California, would wear perfume sometimes but only when she was strung out, running high and fast on speed or coke and not wanting to slow down for a shower. And Marvin's own daughter. This is what I want for you, he thought, sending the thought south toward her—the ease and elegance, the feminine secrets. How old was she now? Seven or eight, no, eight next year. She should have been learning. Shelley's mother was taking care of her but she had never taught the secrets to Shelley. How could she teach them to Monica?

Marvin dug out his softest and most faded jeans, old treasures that he rarely wore, paper-thin and fraying. He heard the toilet flushing and blocked it out, wanting to preserve the illusion. Lovely Woman never shits or pisses. Lovely Woman weeps in her beautiful sadness. He felt an answering sadness, thinking about Monica, his deep fuckups. He heard the water running in the shower, and pictured Lovely Woman naked.

No. Something besides sex.

He wouldn't have minded if it was just sex between them, but he knew there was something more. He didn't know exactly what. His feelings were ahead of his mind again.

His softest jeans, anyway, and a deep-green turtleneck that his mother had given him for Christmas one year which he'd never worn. She'd have to fend for herself in the underwear department. He took the clothes into the tiny cramped bathroom where the shower was running, a cold front moving in behind him into the damp steam-heated air.

"Close the door!"

"Behind me or what?"

She looked around the corner of the shower curtain, her hair wet down and a spaniel look on her face. Without the artifice, she looked bedraggled and wan.

"You don't want to see me like this," she said. "Besides, there isn't room. How much hot water have you got?"

"I don't know. I've never run it out."

"I guess I'll be testing for myself. I don't suppose you've got any other shampoo."

"I doubt it."

"Answer me this," she said. "When did all the health food migrate into soap? I mean, wheat germ and honey shampoo."

"It was on special at Buttrey's."

"I bet," she said. "Kiwi-lime conditioner."

"That," he said. "I don't know exactly where that came from. I think maybe it was a sample or something—it's been in there awhile."

"I'm going to smell like dessert."

She gave him one of her slightly pained smiles and pulled the shower curtain closed again. His bathroom, like the rest of his house, was dinky, damp and old. Most of the time he didn't mind but at that moment he wanted it better for her. He tried to think if he had any better shampoo somewhere or better anything— soaps or lotions or other hoodoo—but he couldn't imagine how it would have found its way into the house. No woman had lived here since he moved in.

He let her alone, finally—pulled the bathroom door closed behind him and then the rest of the house seemed cold and unlovely: the vinyl sofa with the cow head on it, wagon-wheel chandelier.

He turned the in-wall heater up to seventy-five and it whooshed to life, somewhere inside. He started some bacon in a cast-iron frying pan and looked out the window over the sink at the cows scattered around the pasture next door. Beyond the cows lay the foothills and then, in the distance, the mountains. The gray of their sides and the white of their peaks was neatly camouflaged that morning by the broken landscape of the clouds. It was impossible to tell where the earth left off and the sky began. Beautiful, he thought. He felt his own smallness, his inadequacy.

The problem with his house, he decided, was sarcasm: the painted saw blade over the couch, for instance, and the posters for the Miles City Bucking Horse Sale, even the 30-30 on the wall, all the emblems of the West and he didn't mean any of them. Actually he half-meant all of it. He wanted to be a part of the project and yet he didn't, there-and-not-there, this-and-not-this. This was the modern poison: this ability to do something and yet not be a part of it, holding yourself above what you did, who you were. All the carpenters down in California who were really rock climbers and international explorers. All of Shelley's junkie friends who were really artists.

All of this would fold up in the face of real emotion: the thing he felt when he looked out at the mountains, the thing that Lovely Woman felt when she was thinking about her son.

Marvin tried to imagine: couldn't. He wasn't going to know what she felt. At least it was something. At least it wasn't the coldness. The coldness scared Marvin, when nothing meant anything and nothing mattered. He tested himself by thinking of Monica and he could still feel—the familiar sadness and his own stupidity and drift. At least he could still feel.

And so could she. What did Justine need? She didn't need a lecture and she didn't need a fuck, he'd gotten that far. She didn't need taking care of. She needed her son back, Marvin thought, the one thing she wasn't going to get. He knew that feeling a little: the blank face of the world, the indifference to what you wanted or needed. It didn't matter how much she wanted a second chance. *It doesn't mean anything,* she told him. *It's not good for anything. It's just suffering.* Maybe she didn't need anything, he thought. Maybe this was just going to be her life, to live and suffer through this.

The slow coming out of herself on the way down the mountain, yesterday afternoon. He had thought he lost her—bundled into the brown coveralls, staring at the forest outside, black and white and green. He had thought that he would take her to her car and she would drive away, his little fantasy of the rich girl done and over with. She thought he was a mistake, that's what it felt like. Incredible shrinking man. Noble Savage. Finally Marvin had gotten pissed, without a word from her.

"I can drop you in town," he said.

She looked at him, surprised.

"I'm sorry," she said. "I'm being selfish. You can drop me off if you want to."

"What do you want to do?"

"Really?"

"Sure."

"I want to get high," she said. "What we used to call fucked up. You don't have any dope, do you?"

"What kind?"

"It doesn't really matter to me."

"I don't have any, no," Marvin said. "I try to stay away from the stuff, to tell you the truth."

She looked at him, a little puzzled.

"It's not that I'm against it," Marvin said. "I didn't used to be, anyway. I knew some people, I don't know—one guy I used to work with, he knocked about forty points off his IQ with cocaine. Used to be a pretty smart guy."

He felt the lecture grating against her, the last thing she wanted.

"Besides," he said, "this is a small town, things get around. It's not a part of what people do here."

"They don't smoke dope?"

"Somebody, I guess. The high school kids."

"They don't lie, cheat or steal either, I suppose?"

"The people of Rivulet are thrifty, reverent, obedient, kind and so on. Don't make me lie to you."

"What?"

"People around here will cheat on their taxes and their wives and so on, a lot of that going around. There's other stuff. But once you're on the outside, you're out—somebody gets caught with dope like that, you might as well move. If you ever get out of jail."

"Or if you got caught, say, sleeping with a man."

Marvin felt tired, talking to her.

"Look," he said. "You know better, I know better, there's nothing wrong with that if it's what you like. People around here, they don't know anything about it. It's just not part of their vocabulary."

"What if you grew up here?"

"I did."

"Let's just get something to drink, then," she said. "I mean, that's okay, isn't it? People do drink around here?"

"Pretty much have to," Marvin said. "At least in the winter."

Now it was Sunday morning and an empty 1.75-liter bottle of Black Jack lay on the counter and a line of pale blue light glowed around everything. A lot of whiskey, Marvin thought. There was a blank place at the end of last night. It seemed like they had tried to have sex again at the end of the whiskey but he couldn't remember how it had gone.

Old snow over ice. Dispiritation and drift.

He pulled on his felt-lined boots and his jean jacket and went out for the paper, across the empty road to the mailbox. It was maybe ten degrees. The ragged snow in his front yard crunched. He stood in the snow for a minute, looking at the red bark of the alders along the stream, the dirty gray foothills and then the mountains. The sky was a little bit darker than the snowy ground, something coming, some kind of weather. The question was whether he had any business with her. It wasn't so much Carla—not that she'd like it, she'd be pissed, but she'd walk away from him without anything permanent wrong with her. *If* she finds out or *when* she finds out?

It didn't matter. What mattered was what he was doing himself, not what other people thought about it. He remembered that he had been going to lighten up on the drinking some and in fact had been doing pretty good. He remembered that he was going to start going to church again after the first of the year, a New Year's resolution, and this was Sunday morning. He remembered what he came back to Rivulet for: to have an idea about his life and then to live it, instead of drifting and drifting. She was danger, he knew it. It wasn't her fault but she was drawing him off course.

It wasn't her fault.

Fractured light of morning. All the frayed ends and burned connections. Last night she had said that there were some things she just couldn't stand to do anymore like go to a park or to a beach or even watch certain channels on the cable TV. Anything with *family* in it or *family life* or *decorating.*

Inside the shower had stopped but she wasn't out yet. Marvin heated the bacon fat to sizzling again and dropped two round venison steaks into the pan. He started the timer of his nerd watch at zero.

"Breakfast!" he called out. "Five minutes!"

"Okay!"

He cleared the kitchen table and noticed that the mountains outside had faded, disappeared into the white of the sky: incoming weather. The water boiled and he poured it through a filter cone into his battered green steel thermos bottle and he laid the

Tribune out on the table, separating out the ads and color supple-
ments into a pile on the floor unread, all but the funnies. He had a
method in all the small things. At three minutes, he turned the
venison steaks, approving of the lovely browned meat color and
smell, the rising bacon-fat aroma. He poured the filter cone full of
water again and started the first two slices of bread in the toaster.
Marvin felt in charge of his life and of the world in these small
things. He felt an affection for a world in which these small rituals
were possible and, in passing, dedicated this breakfast to Jesus,
just in case. I thank you, he said to himself. Whether you are there
or not.

She came out just as he was breaking the eggs into the pan,
careful to keep the yolks whole. The edges whitened and curled in
the hot fat. Marvin dropped a tablespoon of water in, to much
spitting and splattering, then covered the pan tightly to cook them
sunny side up.

"Jesus," Justine said. "Are you sure about this?"

"Cure you or kill you," he said. "Are you okay?"

"I'm fine. More or less. I wish you didn't smoke."

"Sorry."

"Is it okay?" she asked. "That I'm still here, I mean. I can go if
you want."

Marvin saw her standing there uncertain in the middle of the
kitchen floor, alone, and he felt a stab of pity in his chest like a
muscle binding up. She thought so little of herself!

"I know," she said. "You may have plans already."

Marvin didn't say anything but stood behind her and held her
back against his belly and she closed her eyes, like she trusted him.

"We'll be fine," he said. "Come with me today."

She was standing naked, shivering on the cold cement floor of the Ladies' Dressing Room at Sleeping Child. The mirrors were half silvered from age and damp, flecks and bubbles and lines of black rot across her belly. Looking in the mirror as if she could see herself. She was trying not to listen, trying not to move or to be heard.

In the other half, behind a wall of drab green lockers, a woman was trying to hurry her child into her clothes.

"Come on," the mother said. "Hurry up! Your father's waiting for us."

"I can't find my underwear."

"It's right here inside your tights."

"But it's wet."

"It's all you've got. Come on."

The mother didn't speak unkindly. Justine couldn't stand it anyway. Happy family.

"Come on!"

"I'm *trying*."

Justine backed into a corner of the dressing room and slid down to the cold cement floor and folded herself into a ball, as small as she could make herself. She didn't want to be seen or heard. She hoped that the mother and child would not come into this side, which they shouldn't have to. The exit was on their side, and they were done with the showers. She closed her eyes, feeling the cold cement, feeling the cold enter her body and penetrate.

"Your father's waiting. Everybody's waiting."

"I'm getting dressed."

"Look. I had just as many clothes as you and look at me. I'm dressed. Why can't you get dressed?"

"I *am.*"

"I'm just getting tired of this, Julie. Every time we go anywhere."

Justine shrank smaller into herself, wrapping her hands tighter. She hoped, she prayed that they wouldn't come over and see her because she knew that she'd look like a crazy person. She just couldn't think of anything else to do with herself at the moment.

"Where are your shoes?"

"I don't know."

"What do you mean you don't know?"

Drawing tighter and tighter. She didn't move from her corner till they were gone and then for some minutes after, until she was afraid that Marvin would come looking for her or send someone. She didn't want to be seen. She didn't want to move. At last she thought that he was not doing this to her, that he didn't have a plan for her or a reason to harm her. This was just the everyday life of the world. This was just something she was going to have to get used to. It was hard, with her nerves all open and raw from last night's drinking. She was sensitive, was all. She was only slightly broken. He didn't mean it. Finally she got up and put on her bathing suit and went to meet him, cold to the center of her belly.

"Where were you?"

"Look, Henry, I'm sorry."

"I didn't ask about your feelings. I asked where you were."

Henry's room was dark, the curtains almost closed, though once in a while the sun would break through the clouds and draw a crooked cane of sunlight across the floor. She went to the window and looked out through the slit between the curtains: a big and restless sky, every kind of cloud at war. It looked like more of a spring sky than December. And in fact the snow was melting off the roofs, the sound of dripping came faintly through the window. Chinook, she remembered: the warm wind that came sometimes in midwinter. I was out fucking an Indian, she thought—then blushed, ashamed of herself for using Marvin that way, to make it worse for Henry.

"I was out," she said. "You don't want to know more than that."

"This is my house," Henry said. "Still."

"I know. I'm not trying to do anything to you."

"I don't care whether you're trying to or not. This is still my house."

"It's my life."

He made a small dismissive wave of his hand, like the Pope, she thought, or the President.

"I need to know if I can trust you," Henry said. "This makes me think that I can't."

"Well, you can't."

She stood by the window, opened up the curtain and the shaft of sunlight fell across the floor, shifting in and out of focus by the passing hazy clouds. Veiled by clouds. She wished that she had brought her pastels and her pad, or even one soft charcoal pencil. She could feel the gritty bite of the charcoal against the textured paper.

"You can trust me to be what I am," she said. "I'm not like you, Henry. I don't mean to disrespect you or to make your life seem smaller or anything. In a lot of ways I'm jealous of you. I wish I had your power to make things happen."

"It isn't magic."

"No, it's your will. You want things badly enough and you make them happen. I'm not like that."

"There's no other way to be."

Justine said nothing. He had stung her.

"There's no other life," Henry said.

Quiet filled the room, and light.

"One minute," Justine said. "I'll be right back."

She left him there and for a moment she thought that she would just leave, she'd pack her suitcase and the trunk of the Bonneville and just go, she didn't know where. She'd pick up Marvin on the way. They'd drive to Florida. They'd drive to Hawaii.

She stood thinking in the center of the floor of her room, balanced between the past and the future, not quite able to move. There was so much quiet here! She could hear herself think, which was not always good. She could go *this* way. She could go *that* way. It didn't seem to matter where.

She might have been having a nervous breakdown except that she'd already had one—an official one—and it didn't feel like this.

She took a calming swallow of vodka from the bottle in her suitcase, although it was only eleven in the morning. She brushed her teeth.

She went back up to Henry's room at the top of the house with her drawing pad and her charcoal pencil. In the half-light of the morning, she sketched the lines of his hands, which lay like sleeping animals on the blanket. Henry was asleep or ignoring her.

An old man's hands: she wasn't good enough to show them the way they were. She started and started again, turning to the next blank page impatiently, as if the fault was in the paper. Really it was sentiment. She wanted to make them noble and strong and rooted in the earth and really they were just broken. She didn't want to say that about Henry. She wanted to show him in autumnal fullness and ripeness and so on, the orderly creep of season into season and death as the next in a series. She wanted this death to make sense. Looking down at him, though, she couldn't find the sense. It was just defeat and weakness. Incomplete.

She took a pleasure in the work, though—pushing the pencil blindly across the page while her eyes rested on Henry's hands, hoping for the lucky accident, hoping for something beautiful to come out of this. She glanced down, to see where the line was going, and for a moment she could see her own hands, as though they were somebody else's, like a photograph. For a moment they were no longer part of Justine. The empire of myself, she thought. Rebellious provinces. Hands don't lie, was what they said—and there was that *they* again, the nameless faceless . . . Her own hands were wrinkled, the skin over her knuckles collapsed into folds and puckers, the fine hard-looking lines that serrated her fingers. Let's be polite and call them freckles, those small tan splotches that had crept across the back of her hands. She saw herself reflected in the landscape of Henry's hands, the riverous veins and cracked dry valleys. Welcome to age. A death waited for her somewhere, too, and a slow humiliation before. Henry's problem wasn't the nearness of death—he'd flirted with it all his life, drinking and driving and smoking cigars, riding horses and shooting guns—but the weakness of age.

She stopped, and set her own hands out in front of her like a book, first the palms and then the backs. She was thirty-eight years old, no longer young. But she had been exiled from the country of the young when Will died anyway. What, then?

She'd done so little.

She'd taken the safe route and it wasn't safe. Now here she was, stranded in middle age. Part of her just wanted to get the thing over with, declare failure and get out as painlessly as possible—a little drinking, a little sleep, and the next thing you know . . . She'd thought, when she was seventeen, that she would know something by now. She'd thought that at some point she would have enough experience so that the world would become clear to her. Gray hair and zits, wrinkles and confusion. Henry was full of wisdom but it might as well be in Chinese, for all the good it did her. He kept telling her she should be some other kind of person, which was good advice but not really useful. And the experience kept piling on, and piling on. I was fucking an Indian, she thought.

She didn't know the first thing.

She looked at her hands like a book in a foreign language. She should have known *something* by now but she didn't. Little snippets: it was good to change your oil regularly; it was bad to gossip about your friends; algebra was easier than it looked; there was no machine or mind behind the things that happened, there was no reason. She'd done bad enough things, she'd been malicious and mean, she'd stolen small things and even once—once before Marvin—she'd cheated on her husband, but never once in her life had she done anything bad enough to merit the punishment she'd taken. I don't care about me, she thought. This was a dangerous place to get to. She recognized this.

Henry stirred, his blind head waving toward the light like a plant. There was a name for that, a nice-sounding name that had escaped her.

"Hello?"

"I'm here," she said. "I'm still here."

"Asleep," he said. "I was . . ."

"What?"

"They were all here."

"Who?"

He shook his head to clear the cobwebs and only then did he wake up.

"Who is that?"

He looked frightened, his lips drawn back in a kind of sneer. She'd never seen him before like this.

"It's me," she said, "Justine. Jess."

He looked around, like his eyes could see—into the corners of the room, the air above his head. Slowly he returned to himself and to calm.

"I was dreaming," he said.

"About what?"

"You don't know," he said. "You don't want to know. Things happened, a long time ago. It stays with you."

"What does?"

"It doesn't matter," he said—drawing the topic to a close, snip, tuck and stitch. She'd never been able to touch him. She knew what he wanted her to know, nothing more.

"Your husband called, when you were gone."

"Neil?"

"That's his name, yes."

"Don't be sarcastic with me, Henry, please."

"You didn't have to answer the phone. You didn't have to talk to him. Lie to him."

"Neither did you. Marliss did the talking, unless things have changed around here."

He nodded toward the sound of her voice.

"It's true," he said. "It was Marliss that had to lie to him. She said—just so you can keep the story straight—she said you went to the movies down in Great Falls. I don't like this one bit, Jess."

She sat, numb, with her drawing pad in her lap. She looked at the sketch she'd done and the earlier ones, lying around her on the floor, and she saw that they were all shit. She was an amateur, not even a talented one.

"I didn't mean to make trouble for you," she said.

"You didn't think about us, one way or the other. Myself or Marliss or your husband. Where were you?"

"Don't lecture me," she said.

"I'm not trying to lecture you."

"What are you trying to do, then?"

"Look, if you saw a two-year-old child wandering around the middle of a highway, you'd stop to help, wouldn't you?"

She couldn't answer. So *that* was the way he saw her!

"Like your friend," Henry said. "That Indian fellow. He stopped and he saved my life. What's his name?"

"Marvin Deernose," she said. She took comfort in pronouncing his name.

"It isn't him, is it?"

"None of your beeswax."

Henry stopped and started—it was all his business here, every little bit of it. He ran what he could touch.

"Your husband called, anyway," he finally said. "He wants to know what you're planning to do for Christmas."

"Christ."

"He says he's thinking about coming out here, unless you're planning to go back to Oregon. He says he thinks it might make a nice break. Marliss says he asked about the weather, and about some kind of skiing."

"Nordic," Justine said.

"That was it."

"It's, like, cross-country."

"Marliss said she never heard of it but there was plenty of snow. I guess he's looking forward to it. That's what he said, anyway. If I were you . . ."

"What?"

"What?"

"If you were me, what?"

"I don't know," Henry said. "I really couldn't tell you."

Marvin knelt in the empty church, seven-thirty on a Wednesday night, one of the lost hours of the week. Other people were cooking dinner, children were doing their homework. The church smelled of candle wax and dust, flowers and oil heat.

Marvin was praying or trying to pray. He fixed his eyes on the pale plaster body of Jesus and tried to see the holy spirit behind it. He kept getting stuck on the surface, though—on Jesus' nipples, for instance, which were the color of orange Life Savers, or on the smooth girlish curve of his hips into his thighs, not an innocent shape at all. Somebody had been guilty of desire, somebody besides Marvin. The question was whether the man who made the statue was trying to turn Jesus into a girl—not on purpose, Marvin decided, just some memory of a smooth hip, touch of the soft skin—or whether the maker desired this as a man's body. Skin is skin, Marvin thought. Maybe the boundaries between one thing and the other are not as solid as we pretend they are. The sculptor may not have made the distinction between holy desire and unholy. Maybe it didn't matter to him. Sex with God, Marvin thought. Sex versus God.

Maybe the statue was made by a woman, though Marvin didn't think so.

Maybe he had no business here.

Maybe there was a way around the pointlessness of his life that was not here. He heard Dear Abby in his ears: join a club, get out of the house, do some volunteer work. What would it be like to be mentally healthy? The cheering squad of the safe and sane, repeating that theirs was the real life, this was the only.

He tried to focus his mind on prayer: Dear God, what am I doing here? But he remembered the unreality, the shimmer and haze of sun on asphalt, down in Tucson. He had been working as an EMT, on contract to the Fire Department—the one skill he managed to take away from three years in the Navy. It was always summer, it felt like, except that four months out of the year where it felt like some other unexplored season, a hundred degrees for a hundred days in a row one year. Marvin used to keep an oven mitt under the seat of his pickup so that he could touch his steering wheel at the end of the day. The old men, moving down from Ohio and Michigan, planted round green stones in their front yards instead of grass, and spent the brilliant mornings walking the yards in shorts, a spray bottle of Roundup in their hands, searching out the phantom weeds. A spray of water would shine like diamonds in that sunlight, and be gone, evaporated, in ten minutes.

It had all been fine with Marvin at first: the saguaro cactuses and the elf owls, Gila monsters and scorpions. It was beautiful sometimes but always menacing, evil Dr. Seuss. Fire started showing up in his dreams, and traffic accidents—the one fat man who they found sleeping in the middle of Speedway, nestled down into the soft asphalt and muttering in his dreams, all the time Marvin was trying to keep him from dying. He woke up finally for the tracheotomy, but the face that Marvin saw in his dreams was the fat man asleep. The jumble of words coming out of his mouth arranged themselves into messages, which Marvin could never quite remember in the morning, except for their weight and swing—I married Paul, turn me on, dead man. And then the separation between the dream life and the waking life began to break down, the lines that said *this* is one thing and *that* is something else. . . . He'd been on a fire, a night in June where it was a hundred and something at midnight and somebody was smoking in bed or just passed out drunk and set the mattress on fire. Long before Marvin got there, anybody inside was dead. They swept the next-door buildings with water, to keep them from catching, and waited for the fire to settle down while the neighbors stood with their arms folded in front of them, like they were cold, staring. Marvin was smoking cigarettes and thinking about ice skating. Then Collins came up to him and said something about who brought the marshmallows? and Marvin just turned and popped him one. Collins raised up his hands, to defend himself, and then the logic of the fight carried its own way. It ended up with Marvin down on his knees and hurting Collins in the face but he was bleeding himself by then. This was the part that he understood: Collins had punched and spat and made him mad.

This mess in his head.

He kept going back to that first punch and the thing was, he had no idea where it had come from. It ended up feeling like it wasn't even his, the anger. It belonged to the world, it was just another current running through and Marvin got caught up in it.

And if it was just a big current, if Marvin had just gotten caught in waves that were none of his making, why was it his fault? Big Dad up in the sky. I didn't mean to—he heard the echo of his own boy's voice, the times he couldn't help himself. One time he stole a box of chocolate cherries from the Cub Scout drive, he hadn't meant to but he ate a quarter of them without even thinking what he was doing and then he had to hide the box. And of course he got found out, and of course his father scolded him and talked to him and sent him to bed shamed at four-thirty in the afternoon. His father never raised a hand against Marvin but he knew the ways to shame him. And looking back, Marvin thought that it wasn't that bad, what he did. He carried the shame and guilt with him still for stealing the chocolates but it wasn't that bad—and besides, what else was a boy going to do? He was eight or ten years old. Fuck you, he thought, looking up at the bleeding Jesus. I don't want your judgment. I don't deserve it.

He had gotten off on the wrong foot there.

Marvin calmed himself, reminded himself that he had come looking for a message. If there was going to be a right and wrong, then there had to be a wrong—plus there was confession, forgiveness. Still there was something in his chest that resented it. The mercy felt like just another part of the judgment. We pardon thee, We remind thee who has the power to pardon. Mercy, pity, peace and love, he whispered. His lips moved when he said this. Still, there was something down deep, running under the surface, down where Jesus couldn't get to it.

Not tonight, he thought. Maybe never. He got up from his aching knees, hurt from construction work, and he stared up into the blank face of plaster Jesus. No right and wrong meant no nothing, he knew that. This was the part he didn't want to face, where nothing meant anything and nothing mattered and he might as well go ahead and fuck anybody he could, steal from anybody, kill if they got in his way and so on. Part of it was that Marvin didn't want to live like that. He wouldn't be very good at it. But really it was the dream where God came to him and told him what to do and they lived happily ever after. It worked for some people. Why couldn't he get to it? He left the warmth and quiet of the church, knowing he didn't belong there, wishing he did.

Outside was nine degrees below zero. The wind was blowing

the tinsel trees and candy canes sideways on the streetlamps—an animal cold, like a hawk, biting at any unprotected skin, seeking it out, quick and ready. Automatic tears formed in his eyes from the bite of the cold, drying before they froze on his cheeks, turning to salt in the corners of his eyes. The snow creaked under his steps. There was nobody else on the streets, like a town on the moon, like three in the morning or five except that it was still evening. Motherfucker, Marvin said to himself as the fresh tears rose. Motherfucker.

He walked alone through the edges of downtown, only a couple of streets deep: the grain elevator, the Cenex co-op and then a scattering of gas stations, a motel and then the lying clock on the front of the bank and the lights of Wheeler Avenue. Nothing to tempt a sane person here. You could get a steak at the Stockman's Bar or a beer in three or four other places. You could gamble on the video poker machines. When Marvin first got here, there'd been a live poker game at the Diamond Horseshoe but it petered out. People would rather feed the quarters into the machines than face each other, it turned out.

Out on the sidewalk, alone, Marvin wondered what fluke of his brain had brought him here. There was California, Hawaii, Justine had been telling him about Florida—not that these distant places weren't as fucked up as here. But there was money there, and beautiful women. People went there to start their lives and to do things. While half of Rivulet was just hanging on out of habit, and the other half would be lucky to keep their heads above water anywhere, the born-dumb and the whiskey-dumb and the six-generations-of-dumb-and-don't-know-any-different. They ironed their jeans and steamed their cowboy hats. It pissed Marvin off sometimes, like a joke he had played on himself and then fallen for—when they put on "God Bless the USA" at closing time and everybody sang or when he heard Ford-versus-Chevy in a bar for the thousandth time. He stopped at the door of Sportsman's Lounge but it was too cold for a moral crisis. *Man found frozen in doorway, pondering.*

Inside was clinking glassware and life. Marvin was instantly grateful. He took a deep breath of cigarette smoke and beer fumes and everything was fine—this evidence of common life, the common project. Strangers welcome here, he thought. He settled onto an empty bar stool and waited for feeling to return to his face and his fingers, first as a tingle and then as a burn.

"Cold out there?" Carla asked.

"Witch's tit, brass monkey, pick your joke," Marvin said. "The wind is blowing like crazy."

"Where have you been?"

This was one of those moments, little holes in time, where the whole bar stopped talking at once, so that everybody heard. Marvin looked around, then back at Carla.

"I've been working," he said.

"I bet."

She looked up at him—at five foot two or three, she looked up at almost everybody—and Marvin saw that she was pissed. He felt a small, sharp stab of guilt. Not only that he was fucking this rich girl, bad enough, but he was tearing himself down at the same time. When you know a thing isn't right and you do it anyway, pretending. He felt himself thin out.

"I don't know what you're doing," Carla said when she brought him his beer. "I don't know what you're up to but it isn't right."

The hum and rattle of conversation had started up around them again, the noise and laughter.

"I'm not doing anything," Marvin said.

She stared at his face, watching him lie.

"I bet," she said. "This isn't the time nor the place."

"Can I come over later?"

"Can if you want to. It might be a little late."

"What does that mean?"

"It's a small town, Marvin."

"I know that."

"You can't do anything private. It's not even like you can't keep it from me, Marvin. It's like, you're embarrassing me in front of everybody I know that lives here. Everybody *knows*, Marvin."

"I didn't mean . . ."

"I've got to work now," she said. "You can come by later, if you want to."

She set the bottle on the bar in front of him, took the dollar from his hand.

When he turned on the stool to survey the bar, he could feel them watching him—all of them. It didn't matter how badly he wanted to belong there. He did or he didn't.

Then Carla was weeping, four in the morning, drunk.

"But I liked you," she said. "I *liked* you."

"I'm still the same person."

She shook her head, tears on her cheeks.

"I look at you," she said, "I look at you and I feel like I'm seeing three or four of you. I don't know which one of you is real. I don't know which one of you cares for me at all and which one of you doesn't."

"It isn't like that."

"You don't even *know*. You don't even know when you're doing it."

But he did—he knew it when he was inside her, sloppy and drunk, and felt her little round body moving underneath him and thought, Fat girl, you're a fat girl, Justine isn't like this. The thoughts were just going by like they belonged to somebody else, with Marvin there watching them, and then the lonely feeling came over him.

It snowed all day and into the evening. She stood at the window, watching the snow fall, the soft even light filtering through the clouds. Somewhere up there was a moon. Neil was due in tomorrow.

One foot in front of the other, she told herself. One thing at a time.

But Henry was having one of his bad days. Lately they'd been coming together, two or three in a row. This was the third day he had not been able to leave his bed, or speak, except the small soft whisper he used to tell Marliss when he needed to use the toilet or needed a drink of water. Like a hurt dog, she thought: when the pain got bad, he just wanted to be left alone. She could under-stand this. After Will was killed, the kind words grated like sand against her skin. Every sympathy was a reminder that he was dead and continuing to be dead and that she was not—though later, she reminded herself, she'd been grateful for the ones who had the nerve to speak, even though there was nothing to say. There was such a thing as solace. It didn't help but it was better than the loneliness. That's what kept her here: the promise of solace.

That, and Marvin. Who she couldn't think about.

A bad day, anyway, which left her alone and wandering the big new house without design or purpose. Henry's taste in reading material was like an elevated boy's—the collected works of Mark Twain and John Buchan, Horatio Hornblower and Tom Clancy— and she'd run out of the books she brought herself. An hour of satellite TV in the afternoon made her so restless that she tried to take herself for a walk. She dressed for half an hour, from wool socks to mountain parka, but she didn't make it a hundred yards from the house before the soft snow and the wind drove her back indoors. All afternoon she baked Christmas cookies and made a mess of Marliss's kitchen. Henry had a cookie cutter in the shape of the state of Montana. She and Marliss amused themselves by tracing the famous rivers in blue icing, the Yellowstone, the Flat-head, the Bitterroot and the Missouri.

By four-fifteen it was dark.

By six, she was crazy. This was the day she was going to have not a single drink, not even a glass of wine, nothing. The resolve went out the window quickly. Neil would be here tomorrow, the regulator. This might be her last chance. She opened a bottle of Spanish red, eight years old, admiring the color in her glass: dried blood, old roses, faded velvet. What next?

She took her wineglass into the great room and shut off the lights. There was a glow in the air outside, as if the snow itself was lit from inside—like phosphorescence, she remembered, the line of surf outlined in glowing microorganisms, her footprints follow-ing her down the beach. This was nothing so well defined—a gen-eral and soft illumination, neither bright enough for day nor dark enough for night. She knew it was just the reflection of the yard lights and house lights but still: it was inviting, this glowing world, like the fairyland inside a snow bubble, the castle and the red-jacketed soldiers.

She missed them, the soldiers and princesses. She thought: Why teach these things to children, why bring them up in a world of surprise and possibility and then land them in the middle of the known world? It seemed so flat, the world she lived in, so tired and limited and known—why tease children with magic? But she knew, remembered from when Will was alive. She had read him *Rumpelstiltskin* and *Alice*, *The Polar Express* and *Dinotopia*, she had lived through him in worlds of talking animals and friendly policemen and sad, abandoned children who always ended up making their own way—the magic world, where time and good intentions always made things right, where the world did finally bend itself to the shape of our desires. *There once was a princess as beautiful as she was good and her name was Justine . . .* She'd taught these things to Will so she could believe through his belief. She did not get to live in the magic world but she could visit with her son, a citizen.

Again she had the feeling: a home someplace, that she'd forgotten or lost the way to. Justine was homesick for it. One of the stories she remembered best—she couldn't even remember the name of it but the one where the dog stays home to defend the little princess and the wolf comes in while the family's gone. The dog defeats the wolf, the baby is safe. But the nursery is wrecked, and when the king comes home he sees only the overturned cradle and the blood on the wounded dog's mouth. In a rage he kills the faithful dog. Only later does he find the baby safe under the cradle, and the dead wolf next to it. Justine remembered her own tears, thinking about the story—the false accusation, the impetuous act, the regret—and found herself close to tears in her adult self, alone in Henry's living room. This was not a fairy tale at all but a prediction of adult life: the king acts rightly, according to what he knows. And when he finds out, it's too late. The action cannot be taken back. In a real fairy tale, the dog would turn out to be all right after all. There would be justice, mercy, all the big beautiful words.

She poured herself another glass. She'd brought the bottle with her.

It seemed to her that she knew what she was going to do. She was going to call Marvin before this evening was over, she didn't have the will to stop herself, though both of them knew it would be a bad idea with Neil coming. Maybe Marvin would have the backbone to stay away but she doubted it.

She called him anyway, just to save the time of thinking.

"Can you come over?" she asked him. "Tonight?"

"There?"

"In the old house," Justine said. "You can meet me there."

She could feel his reluctance through the telephone line. Come on, she thought. Get the nerve.

"We won't be in anybody's way," she said.

"I guess," he finally said. "I might not make it if the snow gets bad enough. Have you been out?"

"Just walking. I don't know what the driving's like."

"It's slicker than baby shit, as the truck drivers say. Mostly it's just blowing and drifting but there's ice down under it."

"Don't come if you don't want to."

Marvin laughed.

"I wish it was true," he said. "I wish just wanting to was enough."

"Whatever you want."

"I didn't say anything."

"You don't have to say anything. I know what you mean."

"Look, I'll call you if I can't make it. Otherwise I'll look for you in the old house."

"Look, I . . ."

"Never mind," he said. "Call off your dogs, okay? I'll see you."

Justine held the dead handset for a moment before she set it down: connection, disconnection. They'd barely started, and already they'd lost their simplicity: I want you, I want to see you, I want to see you naked, giving way to the machinery of the practical world. She didn't want to be inconvenient. All she wanted was Marvin's voice and Marvin's body, the unexplored . . . The realm of possibility and practicality was no place for Justine. She wanted the fairy tale, she knew it, the laws and the lines of the real world bending to her will. Marvin would be hers and it would be easy. The pink sugar hearts from Valentine's Day: B Mine, All 4 You. She wanted somebody else to drive her life for a while, another life to live through.

Maybe not, she thought. It hurt when he wouldn't come to see her right away. He was supposed to love her without reservation and without care for himself. It might not be reasonable but it was what she wanted.

She remembered his body, though, long and brown in the lamplight. And she remembered that she didn't know anything about him. Don't give up, she told herself. Maybe he's got something for you, something you need, maybe nothing more than being wanted—and here a small thrill of excitement ran along her spine, knowing that he wanted her, he was on his way, Prince Charming or not. . . .

Marliss was in the kitchen, as always.

"I'm going to stay down in the old house tonight," Justine said. "Is there any firewood?"

Marliss stared at her, amazed. She couldn't quite bring herself to reply.

"I just want a change," Justine said.

"I don't know what all is down there. It's been closed up for a couple of years. I guess the propane is still on there, though, I can't think of why it wouldn't be. It would take awhile to heat the place up again.''

"I'm sure.''

"It leaks, you know. Are you sure you want to try this?''

"Don't ask,'' Justine said.

Marliss understood her: she stared at Justine, hurt and angry. Justine had come into her place and she wouldn't play by the rules. Marliss was actually two years younger than Justine but she would always be more settled, more of a grownup.

"Crazy, on a night like this,'' Marliss said.

"I know it is.''

"That's half of why Henry moved out of that place, trying to keep it warm in the wintertime. You might as well try to heat the whole valley.''

"What else?''

"What?''

"What's the other half? Why else did he move out?''

"Oh, it's no particular . . .''

Marliss trailed off, obviously lying.

"What?''

"You can ask Henry,'' Marliss said. "There were some personal reasons but he never . . . I mean, he never said anything to me about it. Maybe if you ask him.''

"I don't mean to hurt your feelings.''

Marliss looked at her again and blinked—a blank, staring face, animal endurance.

"You don't need to worry about that,'' she said.

"No, I appreciate what you do, all the things you do for Henry, to keep the place going . . . I don't know. When I try to explain myself, it sounds like I'm making excuses.''

"You don't have to.''

"No, I know I don't. It's just, I wish I could make sense out of it for you. I'm not doing this to hurt your feelings or Henry's or anybody's. Or my husband."

The word *husband* hung between them in the air of the kitchen. Marliss seemed to come to life, her face suddenly pink and animated.

"I don't know if Henry told you," Marliss said. "I was married when I first came here."

"I did know that."

"And, um, he died."

She ran out of words and Justine couldn't seem to come up with any. Tongue-tied, they turned past each other, looking away.

"That's what I heard," Justine said. "I'm so sorry."

"No, that's all right. I'm just, I mean, I know with you and your boy and all . . ."

"What did he die of?"

"Cancer," Marliss said. "It was in his, you know, his testicles. And then after he died—I was doing all kinds of crazy things, you know, acting like I just didn't care. Because I didn't."

Justine wanted to ask her what kind of crazy things but she didn't. It would pain her to say the words, Marliss the reliable Christian. Her sin, her craziness couldn't be all that bad but words would magnify it.

"Six years," Marliss said. "It doesn't seem like that long."

"I didn't know . . ."

"The thing is," Marliss said with new urgency, "the thing is, I thought that he would still be with me as long as I could feel him, you know? As long as it still hurt and I was alive. There was a kind of hope. It didn't make sense."

"It doesn't have to."

"Anyway, after a while I started to feel it less and less. I mean, you do get better. Whether you want to or not. I still feel like that."

"What?"

"Like he's fading away and it's my fault."

"I'm sorry," Justine said. "I don't know what it's like to feel that way."

They looked at each other. A moment of recognition, two travelers.

"It's just," Marliss said, "it was like I didn't expect to go on living or want to. It wasn't like something was going to kill me, I just *couldn't imagine* going on, you know? And then I woke up one day and it was over, I mean it wasn't over, it's never going to be over. But I had moved on to the next thing. And there was this mess I had made."

"Okay."

"I'm not trying to lecture you," Marliss said. "Really."

"I know that," Justine said, though they both knew that lecturing was exactly what Marliss was doing.

"It took me awhile to put the pieces back together. That's all."

"Thank you," Justine said—and meant it, stretched her hand across the cool of the kitchen table and Marliss took it, briefly, the damp warm skin of her hands. And she'd lost a husband—*lost*, the word echoing strangely around in Justine's head. I seem to have misplaced . . .

"It's hard," Marliss said. "You just wake up one morning and you're still alive and there isn't a darn thing you can do about it."

"Thank you," Justine said again, slowly releasing her hand from Marliss's. Because this still was nothing she could use. Marliss's advice was like Marliss's cooking: well intentioned, hearty, sincere, not quite what she had in mind. It made her feel guilty and alone to think this.

———

She gathered flashlights, candles, bedding. She put her diaphragm in, figuring that they would have drained the plumbing of the old house when they shut it down. They would have *winterized.*

She stuffed the down comforter and the Hudson's Bay blanket into her suitcase, carried the pillows tied into a bundle with the flannel sheets. She packed her pockets with whiskey and matches, good Scotch that she borrowed from Henry's shelf, intending (someday and someday and someday) to repay him. She took her watch off and left it on the dresser at exactly seven-fifteen, without knowing exactly why. Some idea of nakedness, of leaving behind the last vestige, wiping out the traces. There was some revolutionary group down in South America or someplace called the New Peoples Army, just a name that stuck in her head. We will be New People, she declared. We will leave the Old People behind. Let the dead bury their dead.

Marliss's face, telling her.

Lex was down in the yard when she arrived with her bundles, looking at her with some curiosity.

"Never mind," Justine said. "I'm staying in the old house tonight. Camping out."

"Spiders in there, last time I looked. About a million of them. I imagine they're froze out by now."

Plainly he believed that she was crazy. Now or always? She knew that she'd never impressed Lex particularly.

"I'll give it a try anyway," she said. "I've got a case of cabin fever."

"You could just go to the movies."

"In this?"

She waved her arm toward the snow, which was falling all around them—slower now, in big thick flakes that circled downward like the whirlybird things from a maple tree. There was a foot or more of new snow over the old ice crust, swirled by the wind into deeps and hollows, a little bark showing at the base of the big trees.

"The other thing is," Justine said, "I've got a friend coming. Don't run him off, okay? You set the dogs on him last time."

"You mean that Indian fellow."

"He has a name," she said. "He's welcome here."

"Is that what the senator says?"

"I'd ask you not to bother him with it."

"It is his house."

"I'm not doing anything to hurt Henry," Justine said. "I know you want to protect him but this doesn't have anything to do with him. It's my business, Lex, okay?"

This was not okay. Nevertheless Lex gave in. He bobbed his head deferentially toward her, then backed away.

"Good luck," Lex said.

"Thanks," said Justine. "And the horse you rode in on."

"What?"

"Nothing," she said. "I'll see you tomorrow."

Inside the house was the same cold as outside but it felt sharper, the old wood and furniture holding the cold inside. She set her bags and bundles down in the old hallway and tested the lights, which didn't work. Candles, then. That was the way she wanted it anyway, strictly nineteenth century. She'd brought a dozen votive candles down from the main house with her, and some little tin pie plates to burn them on. She set two to burning in the hallway and another two in the living room. Then, before she started to settle in, she went out into the snow again to fetch an evening's worth of wood. How much was that? She brought in two trips' worth, the wood stacked chin deep in her suffering arms, then went back out and got a third for insurance.

When she got back she closed the door, which had a finality to it. Now she was *inside* and the rest of the world was out. The house had a dream familiarity, a place she used to come to years ago, a place she'd spent her summers but never a place that belonged to her. The living room, for instance, had always been Henry's or her parents' own, and never a place for girls.

Now she'd claim it for herself. She lit a fire with the kindling in the copper basket next to the mantel and the newspapers from two years before. Henry hadn't moved out of this house but abandoned it—the furniture sat where it always did, the usual paintings flickered in the candlelight. The paper was damp and hard to light, but the kindling caught right away, and within ten minutes she had an actual blaze going. The lengths of lodgepole were no thicker than her arm and caught easily, flaring brightly. But the fire had no more than a superficial warmth. Winter still owned this house. When she'd built the fire as high as she thought she should—not quite wanting to burn the place down—she took her flashlight and went exploring, trying to find the thermostat.

Then decided to take her chances on the fire instead. She remembered summer nights, coming in after the last cool of the evening at ten at night and finding a small fire going in the fireplace and Henry reading beside it. He'd always been a reader and a reflector. She realized that she had not been kind to him, that she should have been reading to him, buying him books on tape, talking with him. She felt her own selfishness again. Would you call a drowning man selfish for wanting to save himself? But this time Fairweather's question didn't do any good. There was no other word for it than selfishness. Maybe there was a reason for it but that didn't make it into anything else.

She lit a second fire, as big as the first, in the dining-room fireplace, then went into the kitchen and started up the black-and-chrome cookstove, the old original. She could feel the cold radiating out of the cast iron, a winter's worth of cold stored inside.

How long would it take to chase the cold out of the bones of this house? It felt strange to be here, now—it was a dead place, abandoned. She'd known it in life. There was an electric range in addition to the old cookstove, and a refrigerator with its door gaping open. House, she thought. A place for cooking, sleeping, raising children. A way to keep the rain out.

Marvin was coming or he wasn't.

The cold lifted slowly, layers of hot air that drifted out of the fire and inserted themselves into the cold, flavoring the air with wood smoke. She'd lit candles in every room, and found an old oil lamp with an inch of lamp oil still in it. By some further miracle, she had found the gallon of lamp oil in the pantry, and two more railroad lanterns. The living room was lit for an old luxurious winter party, the small flames of the lamps and the hot light of the fire and the old paintings and photographs flickering in the light. She walked the edges of the living room—it was too cold and too nervous to sit still—and realized, for the first time, that the family portraits and souvenirs were not from Henry's family, and not from hers.

They belonged to the Sorenson family, who she remembered were the people Henry bought the place from. A photograph of Colonel Andrew Sorenson in the mud of Fort Stephens, 1887; an oil of a Sorenson child, a hand-woven Indian basket, a collection of The World's Great Books from the Harvard Library, bound in matching maroon leather—somebody else's family, somebody else's history bought ready made. It was impressive what money could do. All the time she had been coming here, all the summers with her and Val, she had assumed that this display was her own, the arrowheads and Bibles—this was her past, the souvenir cups and velvet curtains. Now that she was actually thinking about it, of course it couldn't be. Henry had been born outside of Butte, worked in the mines at thirteen. He was a bootstrapper all the way.

It gave her a chill, though, to think that she'd mistaken somebody else's past for her own. What really belonged to her? This little inch of earth she was standing on. This little, temporary . . .

She was standing at the fireplace when Marvin came in, leaning against the smoke-stained oak of the mantel and staring into the flames. It was a nineteenth-century pose, except for the down parka and Polarfleece ear band. She wished she had the Gibson-girl waist to go with the pose, the Coke-bottle waist.

"You made it," she said.

"I do know orders when I hear them."

"You didn't have to."

"I wanted to," he said.

"Honest to God," she said. "I don't want to argue."

"I wanted to shovel that snow. I wanted to drive on ice. I need my character built."

She looked into his face and she saw that she had not been wrong about him. They could talk, they could touch. It was easy to forget when he wasn't around, easy to lose him between fantasy and doubt.

"Is it getting warm in here yet? I can't tell."

"It's better than outside," he said dubiously. "Of course, it was six degrees when I passed the bank clock. It isn't hard to do better than that."

"Is this an idiotic venture?"

"What?"

"Trying to make this place habitable. I just didn't want to go to your house, and we can't go to Henry's house."

"I thought you meant the whole thing," he said.

She felt a little chill, waiting for the next thing to come out of his mouth, *This just isn't making sense for me*, or *You've got a husband already*. Didn't he want to fall down on his knees in front of her? Didn't he want to tell her that he loved her? She had something here for him, he knew it, something good, something he needed. She recognized the little drunken wanderings and longings, and wished, maybe, that she had eased up a little before he came. But she knew what was true, and this was true: she did have something for him, something nobody else in the world could give him. She felt it down deep inside her belly, beneath the layers and layers of clothes.

"I'm glad you made it, anyway," she said.

"I am too."

"Are we going to freeze?"

"We'll figure it out somehow."

"Do you want anything to drink?"

"In a minute," he said. He walked over to where she stood by the fire and he laced his hands, still in gloves, around her waist. She turned her body toward his, opened up toward him. He kissed the small of her neck, and then he kissed her lips. His cheeks were cold from the night outside, and his hair wet with melted snow.

"I've been thinking about you," he said.

"Any conclusions?"

"No."

"Anything I should know about?"

He pulled away, far enough to see her eyes. He examined her, took her measure.

"I withdraw the question," she said.

"Good enough."

"We can save it for later," she said. "Or never. We can just not talk about it."

"What are *you* thinking about lately?"

"World peace," she said, wriggling out of his embrace. She

poured herself another glass of wine and, without asking, poured him half a glass of Henry's good Scotch. She sat on the floor, staring into the fire. He took his place on the couch behind her, where she could rest against him; took his gloves off, and rested his bare hand against her neck. She could feel the cold skin of his hand, the winter outside, the storm, the wolves.

"I'll tell you what I was thinking about," she said. "I was waiting for you to show up, wondering if you were coming or not."

"I said I was."

"You didn't make it clear," she said. "That's all right. I'm glad you made it. But what I was thinking about was how unlikely it was. I mean, out of all the world, to end up here."

"I was born here," Marvin said.

"No, but still you choose to be here, out of all the places in the world. You could be anywhere, you could be doing anything, you know? And here you are, and here I am. It just seems so unlikely, doesn't it? I don't just mean the romance movie."

"The what?"

"Oh, you know—out of the burning plains of Africa they met."

"Lost me."

"Never mind. It's just a feeling that I've got. A little thing in my pocket, a little secret, that's what you are. You know exactly what I mean."

She turned her neck up toward him, and now she was testing him, turning tables.

"I can say what I want around you," she said. "You understand me."

"Not all of it," he said.

"I don't understand it all myself. But it's the luxury of seeing you, you know? I don't have to explain myself. That, and other things."

She reached back to run a hand along the inside seam of his jeans, felt him shift and settle under her touch—the live hand, the living flesh under the cloth. Luxury, the warmth of the fire and the wine and the soft light. Beneath the surface ran a constant small turbulence, anxiety, Neil was coming, Henry dying, Marliss didn't like her, Justine's job had disappeared by then and here was that frantic voice again like the sound of mouse feet scrabbling across a floor or the squeaking wheel of a rat in a cage running and running on its little wheel. . . . She could feel it but tonight she could let it settle, down out of the main part of her brain, down into the background. Delicious kisses, she thought. Chocolates. No yesterday and no tomorrow.

"It just seems accidental," she said.

"Maybe it is," he said. He lit a cigarette and the smoke mixed with the wood smoke and the damp, which was slowly coming out of the house in the new warmth. The shelves of books.

He said, "I used to think that there was one person out there for everybody, you know, a soul-mate. You either found them or you didn't. Or you found them and fucked things up and that was that."

"I don't agree."

"I don't agree myself, anymore."

She said, "I think there are a hundred people you could be, or a thousand, depending on what kind of chances you get, and then maybe a hundred or a thousand perfect lovers."

"A million," Marvin said.

"I don't know," she said. "And then the little ball starts going down through the maze, and some things get cut off, you know?—some possibilities, and then a few more get cut off, you make a few more choices or have a few more accidents and then after a while it's just the one life that you've got. That's what I don't get."

"What?"

"How you're supposed to live just one life. How you could be content."

"You've got the gift, though."

"What?"

"You could be discontented with just about anything," Marvin said. "You're so restless. I don't mean that as an insult."

"I know."

"It's just that I feel like I've been starting over about once a week since I was ten years old," Marvin said. "You know—who am I this time? That's how I ended up back here."

"What?"

"It's just the last place where I knew who I was," he said.

Then they were screwing, making love, she didn't stop to figure out the word for it, on the primitive bed she had made out of sleeping bags and comforters in front of the fire, down on the floor with the dust and sofa legs, and the comedy threatening to overtake them, the air—still freezing cold—invading the covers whenever they turned and Justine reaching around him to rearrange, to keep the cold and the laughter out, and then at some point she was just with him and the rest was forgotten, body to body down on the floor. She was with him, moving with him, she could feel him inside her and all kinds of things were stirring up inside her, what she loved and what she was afraid of— not just any one feeling but all of them mixed up, the rising flush and hurry of sex and then the sadness and the disappointment, knowing she'd never come, never amount to anything, it was the Zoloft or the dead child or this live, strong man on top of her, this man who seemed to be interested in her. She felt him quicken and tried to hurry, tried to shut off the voices she didn't want, tried to make herself feel what she ought to feel, and for a moment it worked. For a moment and more than that she was into the sex and just the sex, just the good thing. Fuck me, she thought, then whispered it. Right there. The two of them were clumsy, inexperienced with each other's bodies but still—he was kind, considerate, he was getting there and at least he was trying . . .

And just in that moment she fell out of it. What had been working before was now just mechanical: a body, another body, a blanket. She saw them from above, from the air above them, her own fat white body and Marvin. Who was beautiful but not at all hers. Who was working inside her, operating on her. All it took was a moment of kindness, of charity. What? She didn't have the hunger to keep it up. She didn't have the greed.

He tried to kiss her and she turned her face away, lifted her hips to him as though nothing was wrong, but she couldn't feel it anymore, didn't want his kindness or his charity.

He slowed inside her.

"Don't stop," she said.

"I lost you," Marvin said.

"Don't stop."

"You're crying," he said.

It was true, she could feel the tears standing in her eyes, running down her cheeks, but she couldn't find a name for the feeling behind them—*everything*, she thought, it was all mixed up. Marvin slowed and stopped, raised himself onto his elbows and looked down into her face, the exact wrong thing to do.

"Are you okay?" he asked.

"I'm fucking fine."

She rolled out from under him, lay on her side in the filthy nest of their bed and stared into the fire: cities of fire, faces and animals.

"It isn't you," she said.

"What?"

"I'm on these pills, these antidepressants."

This was a lie, she knew it as she said it but it was at least factually true. It was easier than trying to explain herself.

"It's like Prozac, you know," she said. "Prozac's the joke one, the one that everybody's heard of but this is the same kind of thing. A selective serotonin reuptake inhibitor. They make it so you can't feel anything, you can't come."

"What are you taking that shit for?"

"It's not for fun," she said. "You see this stuff in the magazines, you think it's going to make you happy and relaxed and so on."

She turned toward him again, clutching the comforter against her chest. She felt as if she was naked enough, as if he was watching her, safe.

"I was having a hard time getting out of bed," she said. "I was fucking up at work, I mean, what? weeping and so on. I'd go into the bathroom and not come out. I can still feel it."

"What?"

"The impulse, you know, the . . . It's not like I want to actively kill myself or anything, I don't want you to worry, it's just sometimes I want to just stop moving and just, I don't know. Wait for it to be over."

"You still feel that?"

"Sometimes," she said. "Less and less. The pills do help."

Then she saw that she had given him her alibi, her perfectly good explanation, and now she was a patient and a victim and he could safely pity her.

"You don't know what I'm talking about, do you?" she asked.

"Don't get on your high horse."

He leaned back against the sofa, bare-chested in the cold but covered in blankets from the waist down. He lit a cigarette, looked from the fire to her face to the fire again. His brown body in the lamplight: she felt a vivid stab of sorrow when she remembered what she was missing. Body to body, they could be fucking now, they could be making love, she could not be worrying about which words to put herself in. That other country.

"I used to be married to a crazy woman," he said. "She's bringing up my daughter, okay? but I mean really crazy, I came home one night and found her on the living-room floor, lying down with the speakers on either side of her head and the radio loud as it would go, blasting out rock and roll. She said the only way she could quit listening to the voices in her head was to drown them out, okay?"

She shrugged.

"I'm not trying to take anything away from you," he said. "I'm not saying that you're pretending or that everything's all right or anything. I'm just saying you're not crazy. You're sad as shit, maybe—which I think you are. But you aren't crazy."

She stared at him, angry—she didn't like to be named, not by anybody—and yet there was this other feeling underneath the anger, a kind of release. What if he was right?

"The other thing that you have to remember," Marvin said, "is that I'm full of shit."

"You're okay," she said.

She waited until he was done with his cigarette—watching him, his face in the firelight, his eyes on the cities and hillsides of fire—and then she nestled toward him and started to stroke him with her hand, gently. He didn't want to, some residue of bad feeling from before. But he started to stiffen anyway, the thing the body wanted, divided against himself, and when he was hard again she guided him down under the covers again and inside her. She could feel his reluctance, he didn't want to make it all right, but it was good to feel him inside her even if nothing was going to happen. Slippery skin and, after a while, kisses—on her neck, her breasts; she kissed him back anywhere she could touch. Animal movement, desire and touch, she remembered loving this and wished that she could feel it all the way but still it was good to have him inside her. He didn't hurry and he didn't slow for her, just stayed in his rhythm until it quickened and he came and then he lay on top of her, supporting his own weight but close, he stayed with her. Good boy, Justine thought. Just like that. Good man.

They lay still for a few minutes, breathing, feeling the cold and warm air sift around them. Justine wondered what he was thinking. She wondered if he was waiting to get out of there but she didn't think so. She was much too inconvenient for a simple fuck. She knew that much about herself, especially lately, maybe always.

"We could go to Florida," she said.

"What's that?"

"I was just thinking," she said. "Have you ever been there?"

"No."

"I went to college there, I don't know why. My parents were in California and it was three thousand miles away, maybe."

She shrugged him off her body; he sat against the couch again, and lit a cigarette, as she'd known he would. It was cold and warm in layers and fits but, mysteriously, not uncomfortable.

She said, "I'd like to go somewhere with you, someplace warm. I'd like to lie around on the beach. I'd like to sit around all night in the screen porch and talk. Do you know what a screen porch is?"

"I know what it is. I've never lived in a place where they had them."

"I just think sometimes—it's beautiful here but it's hard. I mean, Florida's a wreck and so is California but you can see why. Life is easy, you know, it's not going to kill you to go outside. You can swim in the ocean at three in the morning."

"Not in California, you can't. You'd freeze."

"Okay," she said. "I just remember, we used to get stoned and go to the Krispy Kreme donut shop at three in the morning and get these fresh glazed donuts right out of the oven. I remember riding my bicycle home in the middle of the night and the air was so soft and it smelled like oranges. I miss that, Marvin. Is that crazy?"

"Well, yeah, maybe. I don't know. I tell you what—you could just buy yourself an airplane ticket, get a hotel room on the beach. I could find you some dope. Go see how you like it."

"You want to come with me?"

"I don't think so," he said.

He sipped his whiskey, stubbed out his cigarette. Justine looked at her watch and it wasn't even eleven o'clock. It felt like three in the morning. It felt like being nineteen again, naked in a strange house.

He said, "I'd go with you for a visit, I mean, I bet it would be fine. I'd like to see an alligator. You can really see them, right? I mean, outside of a zoo."

"You bet. Lots of places."

"I've tried that solution myself a few times," Marvin said. "You know, fuck things up in a place or you get tired of it and you move on. I guess it works for some people, I don't know."

"I just want life to be *easy* for a while," she said. "It's never easy. Except it's easy to be with you, for reasons I can't figure out."

He looked at her a little sideways, irritated, and he was right: it wasn't the time yet to put a name to what was happening between them. It was time to let it take its own shape and form and find names for it afterward, an affair, true love, an escapade.

"I'm having an *escapade*," she whispered, trying out the word.

"What's that?"

"Nothing."

"You think a lot, don't you?"

"The same as you," she said. "The same as anybody. There's no escape."

This struck him silent for a minute, and she watched him while his brain worked. She leaned over, put another couple of lengths of firewood onto the coals. She uncovered herself in doing this, not just naked but lewd, her ass in his face.

"You want to hear my theory?" he asked.

"What's that?"

"Everybody lives inside their head," he said. "Not everybody likes it, though. I mean, the guys I work with, they fill their heads up with all kinds of shit, I mean TV and country songs. They think what they're supposed to think—I mean they don't really. Down deep everybody's got a personality. But most people, they don't want to have anything to do with it. They don't want to think, don't want to stand out. You want to know my other theory?"

"Fire away."

"Thinking doesn't do you a bit of good."

"Sure it does."

"Like what?"

"It can keep you out of trouble, if you stop to think."

"No, it doesn't," Marvin said. "It *feels* like you stayed out of trouble because you stopped to think and then decided not to, but what really happened was, you didn't want it enough. If you wanted it bad enough you'd go ahead and get it, try to get it."

"If I wanted what?"

He smiled at her, sleepy, and didn't say anything. Instead he reached down and touched her warm, wet cunt with his hand. His hand was cold, a little thrill of metallic cold that ran through her and left a taste of copper pennies in her mouth. Maybe he didn't mean well after all. Maybe she was wrong about him. She'd been wrong before.

"If either one of us was thinking, we wouldn't be here," Marvin said.

Mincemeat pie, Henry thinks—cinnamon and suet, disgust-ing if you stop to think. So many things are. The thick aroma of baking pie drifts down from the kitchen, the cloves and butter, and it's the morning of Christmas Eve. Henry waits like a boy for the celebration to start. In the dark of his blindness, he can smell so much better—like when he was well, and he'd be driving on ice, and turn the radio down so that he could see better. No more of that.

It isn't just that he can pick up the smells more easily in the dark. It's the way they penetrate, the way they spin him around inside. The Ivory soap that Marliss is addicted to is the same soap his mother washed in, the same she washed little Henry in, little Hankums, baby boy . . . and then the smell of horses that comes off Lex sometimes, the smell of sweat and leather and work, of manliness, the life that Henry has always loved without quite liv-ing. The real smell of his working life is the dust and paper of an old book, a book that hasn't been opened for decades. He takes them off the shelves of the library sometimes just to open them, to feel the dry paper with the tips of his fingers and smell the law library at the university in Missoula, the touch of a contract, the rough and tumble of wanting and striving and acquiring: Henry at twenty-six, sitting in the library and realizing that he could do this one thing better than the others could. The touch of money, the crisp edges of new bills and the velour softness of the old ones. I won, he thinks, and awards himself a small bitter smile: alone in a bed and blind. But that was how the score was kept, in tens and twenties, acres and Cadillacs.

I won, he thinks.

I'm never going to sleep with a black woman, he thinks. He always meant to investigate the dark nipples. Henry had dozens of these, things left undone: athletic feats, expeditions, regrets. His father had died unreconciled to him, for instance, a fight of two or three years' standing. He had never seen Trudy again, his original sweetheart, after she broke off the engagement. She married a railroad man. He had to content himself with knowing that she read about him in the newspapers: a rich man, a Senator.

Not that it makes any difference. Henry can still feel the spot in his chest where she left him, the sore that never quite healed over. All the tea in China, Henry thinks, all the money in New York City, and still she left him and his mother died. It feels like nothing, this life. He's going to die a rich man, apparently, and still his life feels like a suit that used to fit him and doesn't anymore, as if he's shrunken inside it—a thing, a history, a story. And the other thing, time, the way it's supposed to be moving forward all the time like water under a bridge. Instead it feels like water being poured into a pitcher, each new day mingling and mixing with the ones that have come before so that he is an old man and a boy all at once, the days from this week seeming no more real or present than the days from 1952 or Pearl Harbor or the winter night he spent on a train speeding across North Dakota, snow whipping at the windows of the dome car while Henry and a beautiful woman, whom he never saw again, tried to find a place to fuck. The taste of bourbon whiskey over ice, the stiff ache of a hard-on in a good wool suit. There may be something wrong with his brain—there's certainly something wrong—but these moments, journeys, events come swimming up to him out of the past and he can feel them on his skin, taste them in his mouth as certainly as the pills Marliss feeds him. The North Coast Hiawatha was the name of the train. The woman's name is gone, if he ever knew it, but her face floats in the darkness, small and dark. This was in the Kennedy administration. She looked French, though she was actually from St. Paul. There's a way to understand this— Henry in his money and his good suit, though he never gave her all his name, never gave her the weight of the name *Senator*, he didn't need it, she felt the force of him and she was full of needs, a married woman, on her way home from two weeks of tending to her mother, who was dying of cancer in Seattle. Okay: big man and lonely woman. But Henry still carries her inside him, another path he didn't take, he remembers watching her off the train in the cold Minnesota night (delayed for hours by the snow, the single taxi with snow in the headlights) and thinking, There she goes, I should be going with her. . . . All lies, of course, imagination. He knows by now that there aren't any mistakes in life. You do one thing and then another and that becomes the life you have.

Still he remembers the small dark face, the faded-roses scent of her perfume that couldn't quite conceal the sweat of two full days on the train, the restless sleeping in the Pullman car. They started in the bar, of course, talking about Jackie Kennedy; he remembers the pull, the desire. He wanted to tell her that he had been to the White House, that he had shaken the white-gloved hand, but he didn't want to reveal himself—or maybe it was simply that he didn't need it, the connection was there and it would have falsified things to have a reason.

To hell with it, Henry thinks. He's tired of things falling apart on him—the why, the reason. Things happened, that was all you could say. They happened because they happened, and even then he can't tell the memory from the imagination. Was there a woman? Was there a train? He can remember things that never took place, he's proven it too often. What's left is the tangible: the taste of bourbon whiskey over ice, the ache of a hard-on in a good wool suit.

And then the boy inside him, the longing, he wants the kitchen warmth of childhood, the smell of mincemeat pies and turkey, the black grease of an old Ford motor on his father's hands . . . He wants, he wants, he wants everything, here at the end of his life as always.

Henry rises gingerly out of the bed and grips the aluminum walker. Soon even this will be beyond him.

The woman from the train, her name was Adrian. The name didn't suit her, didn't match her face.

One slow step at a time, easing the legs of the walker out in front of him, he fumbles toward the doorway and out into the hallway, Indian country, undiscovered. This is a kind of bravery too. This is what was left to him—although he knows himself well enough to call it by its right name, restlessness or boredom or loneliness. Bravery is for others. This is simple endurance, disregard for the body. He rams the doorframe with his cheek, no idea it is there. His false teeth rattle in his mouth. The aluminum creaks under his weight, inch by inch down the carpeted length of the hall.

Nothing matches.

His body hurts, it is sick, defeated. But in his chest he feels a boy's excitement for Christmas, the urgency, knowing that it's all about to start and he will miss it if he doesn't hurry and all the rest of it, tiny reindeer and toy trains and Mexican wedding cakes in wax paper.

Marliss stops whatever she is doing when he comes through the kitchen door.

"What are you doing out of bed?" she asks.

"I don't know."

"You ought to be resting."

This is soothing, Henry thinks—a woman's voice to order him around, pick him up and bundle him, little Hankums. It's undignified, the things he wants.

"Resting up for what?" he asks.

She resumes her chopping and bustling; he hears it as permission to stay in her kitchen.

"It's not likely that I'll run the marathon soon," he says.

"No."

Quiet, her hands at work, the faint grinding noise of the clock in the stove, which has always needed to be fixed.

"I was listening to the radio," he says, "then the music came on. Classical music. Why don't they have a different station for it?"

"What have you got against music?"

"I just like the news is all. Everybody's got an opinion."

"There's time for that."

A moment's quiet, again—a sadness trickling slowly into his chest, a feeling like rain. The two of them sitting there and the life slipping away between them.

Marliss says, "What I like is that noon show with the BBC. I love to listen to those English accents. It makes them sound more intelligent, I think."

"Everybody's the same."

"Well, you know more than I do, as usual. They just sound

different to me. And plus I get the feeling of what a big place the world is, with Africa and Hong Kong and all. You tend to forget around here."

"Have you ever been out of the country?"

"Texas," Marliss says. "I don't suppose that counts."

"Almost."

"Dan always said he wanted to go to Argentina."

"Do you think he meant to?"

"We would have done it sometime or another," she says. "He was pretty good about that, a little bit of a bulldog, you know. A lot of little plans and projects."

"He was going to try and train poodles for gun dogs. I remember that."

"He got laughed out of that one."

"I miss him," Henry says.

"I don't even want to think about it."

Henry can't tell if he's put his foot in it or not—trespassing, walking on somebody else's feelings. It wouldn't be the first time, not with Marliss, whom he can't quite read. There is a little locked box inside her that nobody is ever going to get.

"I think sometimes . . ." she says.

"What?"

"Oh, I just think things would have been different if he was around," she says. "When I can stand to think about him. My dad isn't bad at all."

"He keeps the place going."

"But Dan would have had some ideas, you know? Would have kept the whole thing moving forward. You would have ended up running an emu ranch or something."

"I would have made money at it, anyway. More than I can say lately."

Kitchen work, the radio playing in the background.

"What time is it?" Henry asks.

She doesn't answer for a minute, and he wonders if he's managed to hurt her feelings. Then she comes and sits beside him and kisses him—kisses him!—on the bald crown of his head.

"You didn't mean it," she says, and Henry can hear that she's been crying. "I just, you know," she says, "with Christmas and all. It's a hard time to think about him."

"I'm sorry," Henry says.

"You didn't mean anything by it. It's worse when nobody talks about him—like he was never here at all. Like he was something I made up."

"I'm sorry," Henry says again.

"Don't be sorry!" Marliss says. "You've got a right to your memories, just like I've got a right to mine."

He opens his mouth to speak, but there is nothing to say. She is sitting next to him, he can feel her breath, her sweater against the skin of his hand, and it's been weeks since he's been touched, except professionally. She lowers her head onto his sleeve, rests there, a thing she's never done before. Henry doesn't want to move. He didn't know it till she touched him but every inch of his body is tired, ready to sleep.

A bustle and clunk of boot heels in the hallway: Justine.

"I'm going to get Neil," she says.

Marliss pulls her head away abruptly, caught, and Henry's angry to feel her go. Justine's voice is loud and present, somewhere in the room. A moment's peace, a little quiet. It doesn't seem like a lot to ask. Justine and her unhappiness, too—he is tired of it, like an unwelcome pet she drags around with her, look at me, look at my dissatisfaction! Things aren't working out for me!

"What's the weather like?" Henry asks.

"It's okay, for now," Justine says.

"They said something about snow this morning."

"Not for Neil. They'll figure out a way to land that plane."

"Well, be careful."

"Oh, you too!" she says—and Henry hears in her voice that she's caught them resting together, that she will find a way to use it. She's jealous of him, of Marliss, of anybody who's got anything. And yet Henry believes in her, still, against all evidence. There's a person in there somewhere.

The storm door opens, letting the cold wind into the kitchen, then clatters shut again and she is gone.

The grinding of the clock in the stove again, and the radio in the background, Marliss clattering pots and dishes.

"I'm sorry," she says after a minute. "I don't see how anything good can come of this."

"This what?" he asks.

"I don't know."

"I know what you mean," he says. "We'll have to see."

"You ever have that dream, where something's happening, something bad, and you go to stop it and you can't move your body? You know what I mean?"

"It isn't a dream," Henry says. "Not for me, not lately."

"But you still like her," Marliss says. "That's the thing. You still talk about her and you still like her."

"The technical term for what you are," Carla said, "is *asshole.*"

"I know it," Marvin said.

"Christmas Eve and you haven't even gotten a present for your own daughter. How are you going to mail it to her?"

Christmas Eve in the big mall in Great Falls, sitting in a little wrought-iron cookie shop and watching the crowds stream by, crying children and parents who looked like they might start to cry, too, any minute now. Christmas music, plastic Santas. This is not my tribe, he thought. Not that I exactly know where my tribe is. Not that I have lifted a finger. He felt this restlessness inside him, working at him.

"How are you going to mail it to her?" Carla asked again.

"I don't know," he said. "Express Mail."

"What about the guy from the post office? He's got to get up Christmas morning to make his deliveries, because of people like you."

"He's going to have to get up anyway," Marvin said. "There are plenty of people like me. Ready?"

"Not yet," Carla said. "I want to finish my delicious cappuccino."

"Don't be sarcastic."

"Christmas brings it out in me. Christmas and you."

She smiled sarcastically, fake-nice, then turned back to watch the passersby. There was real unhappiness in each of them, in the air between them, Marvin could feel it. The things they were not going to get from each other.

"Tell me about her," Carla said, without turning to face him.

Marvin watched her face, the dull eyes.

"What do you want to know?"

"I don't know, Marvin. I don't know anything about rich girls."

She turned to face him, mean and smiling.

"I mean, we had a couple of rich kids in Ellensburg when I was growing up, but they were just country-rich, you know? I mean, they got to have horses and all and their dads drove real big pickup trucks. But a Senator's daughter, that's the real thing."

"Granddaughter."

"Close enough."

"I don't know what you want," he said softly.

She didn't seem to hear at first, staring off into the blur of the crowd, and then she turned to him and focused on his face.

"I'm disappointed in you," she said.

"What did I do now?"

"You're supposed to be my friend, but you won't play with me. I'm supposed to sit around while you mope all over the place. It's no fun, Marvin. It's not even healthy."

"What do you want to know?"

"Oh, Christ," Carla said. "You're a *moper*, Marvin. I always knew that but lately it's out of hand."

Marvin looked at her, blank.

"I mean, I can't even tease you," Carla said. "You get your feelings hurt."

"You're right," he said. "I'm an asshole. Let's go."

"See what I mean?" she said. "Now you went and got your feelings hurt. Now what am I supposed to do?"

"I'm sorry," Marvin said.

"*A moper!* Let's go on out to your truck and smoke some dope, what do you say?"

Marvin looked at her—but he was the one who'd asked her to come along, he was the one who wanted company, she had a legitimate complaint. Plus then he could ditch the presents he'd already gotten, the tragic little bags: a wool plaid hat for Bob Champion, his boss, a book of poetry for his ex-wife (he couldn't quite send her nothing, though it had been a decade since he'd gotten anything from her) and a green satin sex outfit for Carla that he had bought from Victoria's Secret while she was in Sears. He could feel it, hiding in the hunter's pocket in the back of his plaid wool jacket—a dangerous little joke, a probable mistake. Carla *liked* them, was the thing. She had a couple of these rigs already, teddies and thongs, she'd squeeze her doughy, dimply little body into satin and lace and show off and the other thing was, it worked. It worked on Marvin, anyway.

Streams of shoppers, screaming children, worried faces, they parted the walking crowd and down a long lonely cinder-block hallway and out into the blowing snow. The sky and the air were the same indefinite pale gray. The cars were lined up all the way out to the highway.

Carla said, "I wish I invented Christmas. I'd be making some money about now."

"I don't think you can invent a holiday."

"Did you ever read about Mother's Day? I mean, Hallmark cards just flat made that one up."

"So which one do you want to start?"

"I don't know."

We don't have the edge for this, Marvin thought, the intensity. They nearly got run over by a Toyota in a hurry, stashed their packages in the camper shell, huddled in the pearly light of the snow. Their breath frosted the windshield, like a beer glass, Marvin thought. Carla dug her little brass pipe out of her bag, broke off a piece of green bud. Marvin took a hit.

Carla exhaled and said: "I'd start a holiday for single people, I think."

"Like what?"

"I don't know. How about Single Mother's Day?"

"What about Single Fathers?"

"I don't know any, do you?"

"Okay," he said.

"I'm not trying to get on your back," she said. "It's just a fact."

"Okay," he said.

The dope was not the right thing to do. It was spacing him out, turning him contemplative, easy, and Marvin needed his edge. He could feel the whole thing slipping away from him, holidays and presents and Justine. Her husband was landing about then. There was more there than Marvin could think about: what she would tell him, what she would do. A little thrill of jealousy as he pictured another man's hand on her, her husband's tongue in her mouth, his fingers up inside her. And Marvin with no rights in this at all.

"You're thinking about the rich girl again," Carla said.

"She isn't just a rich girl," Marvin said.

"Bingo," Carla said. "I'm psychic."

"I'm not going to try to explain her to you."

"That's right, you're not. I'm not planning to sit here and listen to it."

"I'm sorry," Marvin said.

"*Moping!*" Carla said, and took another hit.

Marvin slumped back into the seat, feeling the chemical ease of the dope running through his head. He contemplated the gray sky. He was lonely, even with Carla there, the thing she was supposed to protect him from. He touched Carla on the leg of her jeans, the tight blue denim.

"I'm starting to think you're promiscuous," she said.

"I don't know."

"I don't think I can stand to go back in there," she said.

"I don't have anything for Monica yet."

"She can probably stand one more disappointment out of you," Carla said. "She's probably pretty used to it by now. Where is she, anyway?"

"Down in California. Down in Riverside."

"So what are you doing here?"

She'd never asked him before, never quite had permission. Something was different now, something had changed—Marvin tried to piece it out, and realized that she'd gone away from him. Whatever they had been before—and he'd never quite stopped to think about it, put a name to it—whatever had been between them before was gone now. Some possibility had ended.

Carla said, "Let's just go to a motel, right now, you want to?"

Marvin couldn't think of any way to answer this. After a minute, his silence had answered for him.

"You're afraid," she said. "That's the thing I don't understand. I mean, I've got it too. There's that good squishy feeling, all safe and warm and cuddled up against somebody. See, I'm scaring you just talking about it."

"I'm all right."

"Sure, but it scares you, doesn't it? What if you just had to love somebody? What if you could just lay there and feel it and love the feeling and not worry about anything?"

"I don't know," he said.

"I don't know either."

He sat there trying to find a way around what she was saying but he couldn't. He leaned against the satin teddy in his back pocket.

"Let's go," she said. "Let's just drive. Rosette's going to be getting off work pretty soon."

"You need anything else for her?"

"I don't think so. I don't know."

"What?"

"Nothing. Never mind. Let's go."

Now it was Carla's turn to mope, Carla's bad mood filling the truck cab. Marvin started the pickup and wheeled out into the stalled stream of cars, feeling one last pull toward the mall, one more instance of him letting his daughter down. What I *ought* to do, he thought. Everybody knows but me.

Red tinsel sleigh bells and green tinsel trees dangled from the light poles, shivering in the wind. A flat gray sky. The Air National Guard landed over their heads as they waited in traffic. These drivers wouldn't last five minutes in California, Marvin thought— too slow, too indecisive. The light turned yellow and everybody just stopped. An old lady trying to make a left turn from the wrong lane could tie up traffic for fifteen minutes. The big time, Marvin thought, the big fast modern life. It hadn't been good to him but he still felt the pull. This right here was the end of the earth, the place where people stayed when they were too slow or stupid to get out, the place where people came to when they got afraid of the big wide world. Half the houses in Cookie Cutter were getting bought up by Californians, and all they wanted to talk about—Bob Champion told him; they wouldn't even look at Marvin—all they wanted to talk about was what a paradise California was before the Japs and Mexicans came in and wrecked it.

Maybe it was the dope or maybe it was the weather but Marvin started to get the big blue feeling where it was all a mistake, all this getting and making and building and going. California was a mistake and Montana was a mistake and Chevrolet and Pepsi. The world was a dead thing made out of metal. This had been where he started, this was Tucson: when there wasn't any point to any of it, and nothing that he did mattered. Nobody cared what Marvin did.

He shivered a little, remembering: that was not a good way to feel, to believe in nothing. It had led him into bad consequences. You had to pick something and believe in it. This struck Marvin as a supremely stupid way to live but he couldn't figure out a way around it. He had to find something to believe in before he died of general carelessness. But nothing he tried on seemed to fit. Stoned, he could see the humor in it: Marvin on his knees in front of a plaster Jesus, Marvin on top of Scapegoat Mountain, listening for signs, hearing nothing but the wind in the trees. He spent two days there. By the end, he was trying to decide if the world had really stopped speaking or whether he just didn't know how to listen anymore. He read about his Bone ancestors and the living world around them with pure jealousy but he could not get there.

He had tried to live by his work: the gods of carpentry, gods of the fifteenth forest-green tile job in a row.

He had tried to live by kindness.

He had tried to live by simply doing the right thing every time a choice presented itself; until the day he was in Home Depot and absent-mindedly stuck an answering machine tape in his pocket and walked out of the store without paying for it and didn't get caught and didn't go back to pay for it. That was that.

So far, Marvin had noticed, his capacity for self-forgiveness was unlimited. He could do about anything he wanted to and still live with himself. Whatever Marvin wanted, it was all fine with Marvin. Knowing this was wrong was not the same as finding a way out of it. Knowing that he couldn't live without believing in something didn't mean that there was anything to believe in, so far. He was still looking.

"I wasn't going to tell you," Carla said.

"What?"

"Christ! I sound like such a fucking girl. I used to hate the girls in my high school because they all sounded so much like *girls*, you know? It used to drive me crazy."

Marvin mumbled some kind of agreement, though he had no idea what Carla was talking about. She was upset about something, he could hear it in her voice.

"You should go down to California and you should find your little girl and you should take care of her," Carla said. "That's all."

"You were going to tell me something."

"I changed my mind."

"What?"

"You're not even listening to me! I'm trying to tell you the only thing I know that's worth knowing, and you're not even listening."

"What?" he said, and she clammed up. "What?"

Carla wouldn't say anything.

They were just getting clear of the town traffic, past the last convenience stores, tire outlets, the road narrowing down to two lanes and starting to curve and lift with the land around it. Marvin drove, feeling her silence next to him. There was something there. He felt a little terror, fear of contact, racing the pickup a little faster than he should have been, trying to get home before Carla spilled over on him. What did she call it? That squishy feeling, that thing he was afraid of. He didn't trust feeling, it was true. But he owed her and he knew it.

Marvin pulled the pickup over to the side of the road, a little curved clearing for a ranch gate. Semi-trucks and big pickups zoomed by on the highway, making the pickup shiver.

"What?" he asked.

"Nothing," Carla said. "I told you what I think."

Staring off at the sky and fields the same color, the fence posts rolling toward the horizon like a line of stitches.

"I don't care what you do," Carla said. "I just think about that girl who doesn't know you. It isn't right, Marvin."

"I'm on a fucking court order!" he said. "Her mother got a court order against either one of us. She'd call the cops in a minute if I showed up."

"No, she wouldn't."

"You don't even know her."

"She wouldn't."

Marvin thought: She's right. Ruth wouldn't mind if he showed up, not if he seemed clean. It was really her own daughter that Ruth was scared of, Shelley and the needles. He tried to picture it: standing on the front doorstep, ringing the bell. She would be seven now. The last time he had seen her, she was four. The fear rose up inside him. Easier to stay away, let things happen as they happen, not try to interfere. He knew this was wrong.

"I was pregnant," Carla said.

It took Marvin a minute to hear her, and when he did, he couldn't quite make sense of it.

"What do you mean?" he asked.

Carla laughed at him, though she was close to crying.

"What do you think I mean?" she asked. "It's just regular English, Marvin. Fuck! I sound exactly like a high school girl."

"No," he said. "What do you mean, you *were* pregnant? What did you do?"

"I didn't do anything."

"What?"

"It ended by itself," she said. "I had a miscarriage, Marvin."

He looked at her body, the belly somewhere under her big jacket, looking for the secrets there: a child, his child. A flicker of doubt ran through his mind—who else was Carla fucking?—but he knew it for cowardice, and dismissed it. His child and hers.

"You were going to tell me?" Marvin said.

"It wasn't that far along," she said. "I just found out and then it was over, a couple of weeks later."

"I'm so sorry," Marvin said, and took her hand in both his own.

She started to shy away but then, tentatively, stayed.

He looked at her body again and let himself feel the sorrow, running out of her but also out of him, surprising himself. Of all the things in the world he needed, another child was the last one—and not with Carla, either. They weren't going to go anywhere, both of them knew it right from the start. But still. Marvin thought of the small life starting under the skin, the darkness inside Carla, little flicker of hope. They could have kept it, taken care of it.

"I'm sorry," Marvin said again.

"It wasn't your fault," she said. "I mean, it was but it wasn't. I don't know what I would have done."

"It doesn't matter."

"It does to me, Marvin. That's like saying what kind of person you are doesn't matter."

She sat up, took her hand from his.

"It matters to me," she said again.

She fumbled in her purse and dug out her lighter and Marvin remembered, three or four weeks before, a brief attempt by Carla to quit smoking; remembered how he called her a bitch—which she had been, pretty much—and made jokes about how she should start smoking again so she could quit being a bitch and then she did start smoking again, he now understood, on the day that the baby died.

They watched the smoke curl along the windshield, blown and dissipated by the defroster fan. They felt the pickup shake as the big trucks passed by.

"I wasn't going to tell you," Carla said. "I mean, I don't know what I was going to do, really. But you were in the middle of something else."

"Thank you," Marvin said. "Thank you for telling me."

"I don't know."

And just the way she looked, so lost and lonely and staring off at the white pastures and the hills, made Marvin understand a little of how she felt, made his heart suddenly open toward her, his friend, his something, now that she was gone. He leaned toward her and kissed her hair and she didn't turn toward him.

"I'm sorry," he said again.

"No," she said, and turned toward him. "That isn't what I meant," she said. "I just wanted you to understand, all this *means* something. It's not like, you know, we go along and we're just playing with things. I mean, me as much as you, I'm not blaming anything on you. But I just ended up feeling like things were so much more serious than we knew. Life and death, Marvin, the real thing."

"I know."

"No, you *don't*. You don't understand or you wouldn't be here. That's what I'm trying to tell you."

He sat there thinking, not knowing what to say.

"Go to her," Carla said. "Go find her."

Carry-ons and crying children and big shopping bags of brightly wrapped packages: Justine watched the passengers clot and hurry, coming out of the jetway and into the arms of lovers, husbands, children, grandparents, a festival of tears and kisses and arm's-length second looks and still Neil didn't come out.

I bet he's getting irritated by now, she thought, watching the travelers slow and curl around embraces, the business travelers all edgy and hurried, expensive haircuts, trailing their little rolling suitcases like pets. Maybe he wasn't coming.

Maybe all this love has scared him off, she thought. I'm being unkind.

But all this sentiment, it was the kind of thing he hated: presents and candy and ritual kisses, expected and safe. Sugar-coated love. And the small-townishness, the bad clothes and vinyl luggage and the high-school-cafeteria smell of the airport restaurant—she could hear him making fun of it already. She was almost looking forward to it. Everyone here was so nice to one another! A little sarcasm wouldn't hurt.

She scanned the passengers again, and then she started to really wonder whether he was coming or not. A disappointment,

if he wasn't. Justine wanted to see him. She didn't know why
except she wanted to know what she would feel when she was
looking at him. In the weeks she'd been gone, he'd turned into a
ghost of himself, a little puppet of her desire—he was who she
wanted him to be, nothing more. But in the flesh.

The last passengers dribbled off, and then the first flight attendant, and he wasn't here.

Then she saw him, looking smaller than she remembered him,
wandering up the jetway looking ragged and confused, as though
this was all strange to him, confusing, frightening. He was so much
smaller than she remembered him! Her heart leaped toward him,
her husband, a private joy—a mistake, she knew it, she saw the
confusion she was starting herself toward but she couldn't help
the way that she felt. She loved him.

She hurried to embrace him. He kissed her on the lips, then on
the neck, a private place.

"I fell asleep," he said.

"I didn't know you could do that."

"I was up all night."

"What for?"

"Oh, I was working," he said. "I had an idea and I wanted to
work it out before I left to come see you."

To come see you: Justine felt the distance in his words, the
betrayal, how far she'd gotten away from him.

"It's nice and restful here," she said.

"No, I'm fine. I just need to sleep. It's good to see you."

"You too," she said, linking her arm through his for the stroll
to the baggage claim, holding him closer to smell the turpentine
and sweat. He was wearing his painterly shoes, black wingtips
he'd inherited from his father, splattered with the colors he'd
been using lately, green and brown and rust. Apart from that, he
looked fairly respectable, clean jeans and a plaid sport shirt.

"You're showing off?" she asked.

"I couldn't find my sneakers this morning, I don't know what the hell happened to them."

"I hope you brought your hiking boots."

"Why? Are we hiking?"

"For warmth, sweetie—it's about zero out there now, and there's a foot of snow on the ground. Your little feet will freeze in those."

"What do the natives wear?"

"These kind of mukluk things."

She spotted a pair of Sorel felt-lined boots shuffling along the hallway ahead of them, a tall pair in camouflage with a fake fur ruff along the top, and pointed them out to Neil.

"Those *are* attractive," he said.

"They're really warm."

"Jeez, I hope so. I guess I'll have to get a pair. What else do I need? I found a parka, I guess it's mine. Maybe somebody left it over at the house. Did you know that *parka* is one of a very few loaner words from Eskimo? Parka, kayak, anorak, a couple of others I forget."

"Kodak," Justine said.

He laughed, and kissed her again.

"I missed you," he said.

His *lightness*, Justine thought—lightness and intensity, all at once. What the fuck am I going to do now? Too many ideas at one time. Can you feel a thing and a contradictory thing at the same time?

Apparently she could.

"I missed you too," she said.

———

Then they were driving back up to Rivulet through the winter moonscape, four-fifteen in the afternoon, a dull cloudy day sliding into darkness. Neil was letting her drive. Usually or always, Neil drove when they were together in the car, but now he was on her territory and she was behind the wheel. Whatever had come before, they could start fresh here.

Off in the distance, the yard lights started to become visible around the farms and ranches, yellow eyes, horses huddled by the roadside. Neil kept looking down at his new pac-boots, rubber-smelling, bought from Quality Supply on the way out of town.

"These things are damn handsome," he said.

"They're warm, right?"

"I'm not complaining. I haven't been in winter for a while."

He stared out the window at the snow, wind-whipped into little ridges, a thin veil of white that hugged the ground. She couldn't see his face but she knew the look: the hungry, consuming, judging eye, watching always for something he could use.

"People voluntarily live here," Neil said.

"They say the winter keeps the riffraff out. It *is* nice here in the summer."

"Both weeks," Neil said. "Are those cows over there?"

"Probably."

"They just leave them outside all winter? How come they don't freeze to death?"

"I don't know. They don't seem to, though."

"I always thought they had barns for them," Neil said. "I brought you treats."

"What?"

He opened his carry-on, a white canvas plumber's bag, and retrieved a slender eighteen-inch purple eggplant.

"You brought me a dick!"

"The Vietnamese kind," he said.

"No kidding. It's a beauty."

"I stopped at the oriental market on Sandy on the way to the airport," he said. "I brought you some lime pickle and some Delicious Hot Chili Garlic Sauce, what else? A can of litchis, I guess. Oh yeah, and a couple of things of curry paste and coconut milk. I thought you might need them."

Justine found herself going all soft inside, wide open—not just toward Neil but toward the whole lost continent of their beginnings, when they had known how to talk to each other, when they were interesting, when they were light. It felt like two other people and yet there he was, Neil. Stripped of his familiarity. They had been fine at first, once upon a time—now she remembered. Then something happened. (And there was Marvin, off in some small compartment of her brain. . . .) Somebody was going to get hurt, she thought. Somebody had already been hurt. Just the feeling of seeing Neil, seeing her husband and being glad. It was a simple thing but they had not been able to keep it going.

"Where have you been?" she asked him.

"I've been home," he said.

"And?"

"It's all right. I've been busy, you know—teaching and painting. Fending for myself. I've been practically living at Dale and Nancy's, you can ask them. I eat in the kitchen with them and the kids, now. I actually had Spaghetti-Os the other night."

"How were they?"

"Inedible."

But the thought of children's food was all it took to raise the dead. The silence fell over the two of them again, each of them disappearing into the distance, the memory of their own lost boy. I remember, Justine thought: this is what happened, I remember now.

"It's like they trust me," Neil said.

"What?"

"It used to be that they would only have us over for dining-room dinners, you know? No family life for us. But now I've worn them down."

"How does it feel?"

"It's hard," Neil said. "You know."

The silence fell between them again, miles of snowy fields slipping into gray light. The cars faded into the windblown snow, leaving their headlights. Snowing and blowing, she heard a trucker say. It was a way of dismissing the weather: It's just snowing and blowing.

"What?" Neil asked.

"Did I say something?"

"You were talking to yourself."

"A thing I heard a truck driver say," Justine said. "I like to listen to people in the cafes around here, the things that they say. I heard this truck driver say to a friend of his, talking about the pass over to Missoula? He said, 'It's slicker than baby shit up there.' "

Neil laughed, but the good feeling was gone. The easiness.

He said, "It's just like living in a country song, isn't it? Pickup trucks and hound dogs."

And cheating, she thought, but she didn't say it.

"Maybe I'll go native myself," Neil said. "Get a horse and a double-wide trailer, join the Republican Party. You like it out here, though, don't you?"

"Everything but the food and the weather."

"Jesus," Neil said, peering into the drifting snow. "There isn't anything here *but* weather, that I can see."

"You just don't understand it."

"I'm sorry," he said. "I mean, you're right—I don't get it."

"It doesn't matter."

"I should just shut up about it."

Justine felt them trailing off into—what? Not indifference but fear, a polite fade. There was too much scar tissue now, too many hurt places. She saw herself and Neil together as if she was looking down from a great distance—miles of empty space between them. I don't care if we go or not, she thought. I just don't want to go like this.

Halfway home by then, the dashboard light of the Bonneville bright in the fading day, Christmas Eve, she remembered—presents and toys, assembling a Big Wheel in the kitchen after he was asleep. This was intolerable. He was still dead. She felt the old jitter and shake, the swirl of her thoughts going around themselves and returning, and wondered if she should still be taking the pills.

"Neil," she said.

"What?"

"Nothing. Who was that guy, you know?"

Another pleasure of married life, she thought: somebody to finish my sentences for me.

"Which guy?"

"With the orgone boxes and all."

"Wilhelm Reich."

"That's right," she said. "Do you know what he believed?"

"All kinds of crap," Neil said. "Sorry."

"Don't be sorry," Justine said. She could have used a cigarette, something. Maybe a drink.

She said, "Reich thought that when you got hit or something, anything that made you flinch, that you carried that hurt place around with you for the rest of your life unless you did something about it. You had to find a way to get rid of it or you wandered around all bent up."

Neil didn't say anything but she knew he understood.

She said, "He used to go around punching people in the stomach, even his children. I forget what that was supposed to prove."

"Are you okay?" he asked.

"I don't know."

All he had to do was look at her like that, with kindness, concern, and she was instantly a million miles away and running. Resentful. Judgment is the enemy of love, she thought.

"I was trying to say something," she said.

"I'm sorry," he said. "It's just, I don't know."

"What?"

"Something about your face. It just looked, I don't know. It was an expression I hadn't seen before. It just made me wonder."

"What?"

"If you're doing okay."

There it is, she thought: the secret's out. She could lie or she could not lie. Either way she didn't want it. She tried to kill time but only made things worse.

"I'm better sometimes and I'm worse, I think, sometimes. I get a little skittery . . ."

Neil was looking at her. Where had her beautiful husband gone? She couldn't figure a way to turn the cycle back, to get relaxed again with him—and then the distance opened up again, and she saw them from far away, saw them breaking apart, and it was sad. Nothing would be gained by this, nobody would be helped. It was just suffering. It was good for nothing. It was the waste that bothered her the most.

"Are you in a hurry?" she asked him.

"To get to your grandfather's house? I don't think so. Why?"

She didn't answer but swerved the big Pontiac into the parking lot of the Diamond Horseshoe Bar and Motel, a place she'd passed a couple of dozen times and never without wondering how they stayed in business—all alone on a wind-whipped, empty section of two-lane highway, a little beacon of neon. Now she knew: it was there for her. They'd been waiting for her.

"Wait here," she said, and left the engine running, the heater blasting.

The Diamond Horseshoe was almost empty. A single cowboy spun on his bar stool to watch her come in. He didn't say anything and didn't look as if he was about to. The room was dim and hot and smelled like fried onions, lit up pink with the poker machines and the Christmas tree twinkling in the corner.

Then, after another half a minute, a curtain parted behind the bar and a heavy white woman came out of the kitchen behind. Justine felt as if the two of them were married, the heavy woman and the cowboy, that this was how they stayed at home together.

"Can I help you?" the woman asked.

"Have you got a room?"

The woman peered out the side window at the idling Bonneville, then back at Justine: whore.

"We've got one that's got the heat on. We don't heat the others unless we have a reservation."

"Is that one available?"

"One night?"

"Not even that," Justine said.

The woman blinked at her. Apparently she didn't like whores. Justine thought to tell her that the man in the car was her husband but she didn't. She wanted to feel illicit, renting a room for sex.

"Twenty-two dollars," the woman said. "We do ask that you pay for the room in advance."

"A pint of Jim Beam, too, please."

She felt shameless. She liked the feeling. Even the cowpoke was watching her—though it was impossible to be much in the way of sexy in a down expedition parka. Maybe he imagined that she was naked under it.

"Twenty-six fifty," the woman said, wrapping the pint in a brown bag and then twisting the neck, so the world would know it was a whiskey bottle and nothing innocent. How had a moralist like her ended up running a bar and motel? Justine would never know.

"Merry Christmas," she said, collecting her change.

"Merry Christmas," said the woman, and the cowboy too. It was automatic, they didn't have a choice. Have a good one! Take it easy!

Then the breath of winter, waiting outside the door, a bracing sobriety—the cold on her neck, illness and death—that she decided to ignore. She dangled the keys in front of Neil's side of the windshield. Sex, she whispered, though he couldn't hear her through the windshield and the heater's roar. Neil slid over into the driver's seat and followed her down the row of motel-room doors, looking for the number that matched the key. A sudden lunar feeling: what was she doing there? It seemed so unlikely. And Neil besides. There must be a place for them somewhere.

Displaced, misplaced: the feeling persisted as she opened the door into the dim-lit calm of the motel room. She closed the door, to keep the heat in, but hovered next to it, waiting for Neil. She took her parka off. The room was nicer and newer than she had expected, a little slice of Anywhere in the middle of the plains, clock radio and all. A painting of the Champs-Élysées in the rain.

She kissed him quickly when he came in, pressed her hips against his. She wouldn't let him go. Complexity all around her, trying to distract her—Marvin, sadness, pills and blisters—but in *this one moment* she loved her husband. Not even her husband but this man, Neil, with his dick rising toward her.

"Can I take my jacket off?" he whispered.

"If you're quick about it."

But even then she wouldn't let him go. She kept touch as he struggled out of one sleeve, then the other, as he slipped his feet out of the new rubber-smelling boots, and comedy trying to slip in. He turned his back to her for a moment as he tried to get out of his boots and Justine embraced him from behind, unbuttoned the waist of his jeans and slipped her hand in. She felt piratical and wanton, bold. He turned to kiss her and she didn't let go. This was what she wanted. She pushed him down onto the edge of the bed and slipped his jeans down around his ankles, kissing the tip of his dick, listening for the soft sound that never quite made it out of his throat, and then hearing it. Familiar, unfamiliar. She thought of Marvin's body and then she took the whole of Neil's dick in her mouth to shut the thought out. This is where I am, she thought, this is what I'm doing.

Neil parted her legs, put his fingers inside her. Their clothes came off each other in shreds and tatters, little piles in the corners of the room. The nylon brocade of the motel bedspread was scratchy, rough against her skin. She whipped the covers back to the sheets, impatient.

"Do you have a thing?" he whispered.

"Never mind," she said.

"What?"

"Come on," she said. "Come on."

She pulled him down on top of her and felt him slip inside, a little rough, a little too big for her but that was what she wanted. She didn't want to be thinking about any of this and then she wasn't thinking at all, just rocking with him, working her hips. She was *full*, there was nothing empty inside her now, and she wanted him to fuck her and fuck her and fuck her until there was nothing left to think or worry and she whispered the word *fuck*, urging him into her. She could feel her own hot breath in his ear, feel him driving inside her.

Then Neil shivered, pulled out of her—a sudden coldness, cold blue light—and came on her belly. It was shocking. Back in the cold awkward world with sticky come all over her skin. All that movement just to get nowhere.

"What was that?" she asked, after a minute.

"I didn't want to . . ."

"What?"

"I didn't want to take a chance," he said.

"I wanted you to."

He didn't say anything, and she could tell—she could always tell—that she had turned from lover to wife to patient again. Neil was trying to understand her, Neil was safe and smart and able to judge while she was sadly out of control.

No, she told herself. Resentment won't work.

But there he was, contained in his body, regarding her. She wasn't going to stand for that.

"It's good to see you," Neil whispered.

She got up—a bare white butt in the big mirror, sag and dimple of her skin—to fetch the pint of whiskey from her coat pocket. She cracked the top and took a drink while Neil disapproved.

She offered it to him, just so he could refuse.

Instead he took it, surprising her. He padded off to the bathroom (the naked-man walk, he knew he was being watched, just like Marvin) and returned with two little plastic-wrapped plastic glasses, and a warm washcloth. He used the cloth to wipe the come from her skin, then tossed it into the bathroom sink. A moment to wrestle the glasses open, then he poured them each a civilized two fingers of bourbon.

"Merry Christmas, baby," Neil said.

They ticked their plastic glasses together, then sipped. Justine could feel the warm line of the bourbon tracing down her throat.

"You're different," Neil said.

"What do you mean?"

"Just the time here has changed you."

"Better or worse?"

"I didn't dislike you before," Neil said. He was trying to hold her eyes, trying to tell her.

"Testify," she said.

"What?"

"Nothing."

"It was a hard time, is all," he said. "I don't have to tell you. But I just wake up sometimes and wonder how we got through it at all."

"You think we did?"

Neil let the question dangle, looking at her—and suddenly she was naked, sagging, all her thirty-eight years showing. Judgment is the enemy of love, she thought. She pulled the sheet up over her.

"Don't," he said, and pulled the sheet down again.

"I'm cold."

"I want to look at you," he said. "It's been awhile. I forget sometimes, how much I like your body. I can't even see it sometimes, it gets so familiar."

"No."

"Like my own face in the mirror. Then I don't see you for a while and bingo."

"Bingo?"

"Okay, no bingo."

"Neil," she said—and again she felt the fear, the taste of a cold, wet rock in her mouth, that she was the one to fuck this up. That draining feeling, seeing what she was losing while she was losing it. She wanted to call him back to her, wanted to start over.

"You're different," he said again.

"I can't see it."

"You seem stronger, I think."

That's Marvin, she thought—Marvin and Neil both. She felt stronger from being able to hold them both inside her like this. Good and bad, faithful and unfaithful. She could contain her own contradictions.

"Stronger," she said. "Thanks, I guess. Is that good or bad?"

"No, it's good. You look good, too."

"This hardy pioneer life," she said and sipped her whiskey—contemplating the distance between her inside and her outside. She was naked, on the bed, and being stared at by the man who ought to know her best, and he had *no idea* what was going on in her head. She took pride in it, she felt bigger. She looked him in the eye and thought, I'm fucking Marvin, too. He couldn't tell. A simple thickness of skull and skin concealed her.

But everybody knew at Henry's place. Everybody knew.

"What do you want to do?" she asked.

"What?"

"We could stay here. Go down to Great Falls and have a turkey dinner at the 4-Bs."

"Isn't he expecting us? Your grandfather?"

"He is."

She sipped her whiskey, looked at the two of them reflected in the big mirror over the desk. Bodies and bodies, white and brown.

"You know why I like it here?" she asked.

"Because I'm not here," he said. "That's been my idea. You needed a break."

"It isn't you!" she said—the words cutting a little close to the truth, she needed to deny it.

"It's just," she said, "I just needed a break, just from the regular part of my life. Not just you, it isn't you. But the patterns that we made, the way we were living . . ."

"It isn't any different."

"You said yourself, you thought I looked better."

"I said *stronger*, but okay. What do you do now? You can't exactly stay on vacation."

She felt the balance start to shift against her, Neil slipping from lover to parent, Justine the baby child.

"Don't lecture me," she said.

"I didn't mean to," Neil said. "But what are we going to do? We can't stay in a motel room forever. Your grandfather's expecting us."

"I just want to do *something*," she said.

And Neil looked at her then as if he knew, as if he could see right through her and he knew, and she felt the words starting to take shape in her mouth: There's something I need to tell you, she would say, I haven't exactly been exactly faithful. . . . She felt a little surge of power, just thinking about it. She had the power to wound him, whether she used it or not—though she herself would be destroyed, she understood that. Nuclear logic, Justine thought. Mutually assured destruction.

"You can't change the past," Neil said. "You can't put the toothpaste back in the tube."

"Fuck you," she whispered.

"What?"

"Nothing."

But he'd heard her, Justine was fairly sure—and she almost said it again, just to make sure. Don't Ben Franklin me, she thought. Neil's little recipes for a safe and sane life.

"I didn't mean it that way," Neil said.

"What way?"

"I don't want to fight with you," he said—quiet, like he was talking to himself. "I just want things to be different. Better. I want the same things you want."

Justine closed her eyes, saw herself riding across the dry hillsides of August on one of Henry's black horses, with Marvin or without him, she couldn't quite see.

"Maybe," she said.

Marvin was medium drunk, dressed up in an elf hat. Christmas Eve at the Sportsman's Lounge: Carla was bartending, Rosette was home alone, seven or eight assorted customers were clustered around the bar. Other nights they might have been scattered among the tables and poker machines but tonight they banded together. They needed the warmth, the touch of one another's shoulders. Marvin was afraid that one of them might start singing. Then what?

The air, the cigarette smoke and spilled beer and urinal pucks. Stranded at the end of the world, he thought.

He was the only one not white, the only one who hadn't known the others since elementary school, when they had all been bad boys and girls together. Carla was paying no particular attention to him as always—they had to be careful, didn't want to be known—but tonight she was paying extra no-attention to him, ignoring him completely between calls for more beer. She was pissed. She should be pissed, Marvin thought. I'm enough of an idiot. But this calling himself names, it didn't make any difference.

"You fucker!" a woman yelled happily. "Say that again and I'll put you in the hospital, Christmas or no Christmas!"

The knot of faces around her bloomed into laughter, her grinning face in the middle, petals and sepals and stamens, Marvin thought. Even the red-faced cowboy she was yelling at laughed.

"I didn't mean . . ." the cowboy said.

"Damn right you didn't mean," the woman said, pointing her lit cigarette at his face. "You'd of meant it, you'd be in the hospital right now!"

But this fell short, brought only regular rude grins, nothing real. The sign, Marvin thought, the monkey face: we're all together here, no aggression. Maybe pick some nits off each other, a little grooming behavior. But feeling superior was just another way of feeling left out. He knew their names and knew their faces: the laughing woman was named Margaret, married twice but not lately, bred Alsatians, liked to dance. Her friends were Peggy and Dan McKinnon who had a daughter at college in Massachusetts, who wasn't coming home that year, who they bitched about and bragged about like she was made out of fairy-dust. She was in Paris now! It was like she had been accidentally switched at birth with a princess somewhere. Peggy and Dan drove forty miles one way from their place to come here, weekends, holidays, any excuse they could find since Candace left home. They smoked, they drank, Peggy told jokes in a hoarse crow's voice. They could be careless with themselves, Marvin thought—they'd had their lives. If Dan put it into the ditch tonight on the way home, people would remember them, cry at the funeral and so on. Marvin caught sight of his own face in the back-bar mirror: morbid little fucker.

It was maybe eight-thirty.

The evening stretched away like an expanse of sand—not that Marvin had ever been in the desert but he'd seen the movies. Trackless waste, he thought. A waste of what? A waste of time, maybe. His head was spinning around in circles like a hamster in a cage—the place where dope used to come in, to stop the useless movement. He remembered the slow movement like walking in water, the ease and rest of it, and for the moment he longed for heroin. Plus it would give him somebody to talk to, something to talk about. The funny thing was, it solved a lot of problems. But that wasn't why. What he longed for was the rush. The memory of it filled him with homesickness, a beautiful place he could never go back to, a lover who had died—that feeling when it all came over you and your limbs dropped heavy and there was nothing, nothing outside the feeling. The problem was (he lectured himself) you ended up dead. Yeah, yeah, yeah.

He didn't quite have the personality for it, was what it came down to. The ones who didn't get out, they didn't want to. Bo Diddley: *Got a tombstone hand, a graveyard mind, I'm just twenty-two and I don't mind dyin'* . . . It was bullshit and he knew it and they knew it but there was truth in there somewhere. Some people were made for it, Marvin wasn't, not quite. If he was one of those people, he'd still be there. One little gene somewhere.

The feeling was still there, though, or the empty place where the feeling had been. He couldn't quite remember the rush, couldn't quite touch it with his mind, but he could remember how good it felt, the way it used to organize his time. The rest of it fell away: job, politics, God, even sex felt like a joke that everybody else had been tricked into believing in. He knew the real thing, the thing you could touch, and the rest was unreal. Now he was back. The hard part was making the rest of it feel real again. He remembered firing up on Christmas morning, wished he could again. Right now, he thought. If it was here in front of me, I'd do it. . . .

But if that was what he really wanted, he would have been there right now: California, maybe, or Tucson, living the life. Marvin closed his eyes, saw palm tree branches whipping around in a hot wind, black clouds pushing their way across the sky. He remembered an old man dying on Speedway: heart attack at the wheel, he had jumped the median strip and plowed into a pickup truck. When Marvin got there he was lying on the street in a white T-shirt hiked up over his belly, old-man skin and World War II tattoos gone blurry and blue. What? The way he looked so peaceful, sleeping there on the street. The sun was so hot that the asphalt was soft. Waves, heat mirages. Marvin was jealous of the old man's quiet. Then he woke up in a panic and the pain was all over him but that was a different story, the usual emergency.

"You need anything?" Carla asked.

Marvin looked at her. It took him a minute to surface out of his thoughts.

"I ought to get out of here," he said.

"Where are you going to go?"

"Midnight mass," he said—without even thinking about it. The words just popped out of his mouth. She raised one eyebrow, a little secret question: really?

"You mind if I take Rosette?" he asked quietly, so the others wouldn't overhear.

"Fine with me, if she wants to."

"It's actually at ten o'clock," he said. "People were showing up drunk when they had it at midnight."

But Carla was already backing away, indifferent, afraid to get caught. White pride, Marvin thought. Purity of essence. Another gust of laughter from the far end of the bar, the hoarse cawing of crows. Messenger, he thought: magpie. Where was the messenger?

Cold clear night, out in the parking lot. He leaned against his truck and watched the stars.

———

Rosette looked at him like he was crazy.

"I'm watching a movie," she said.

"Which one?"

"*Hellcats of the Navy*," she said. "It's the one with Nancy Reagan."

"You haven't seen that?"

"A couple of times," she admitted. "Come on in, anyway."

She was doing her fingernails red and green, the tiny bottles laid out on the coffee table, a Coke beside her. Twelve going on thirty-two.

"It's a sucky movie," Rosette said. "It's either this or *Mission: Impossible.*"

"The movie?"

"No, the TV show."

"I kind of hated that movie," Marvin said.

"Get out of here," she said. "Tom Cruise?"

"He's a Scientologist, did you know that?"

"So what?"

"He's also about five-two or something."

"I'm not picking him for a basketball team. He's *cute.*"

"Cuter than me?"

"Um, yeah. I would say definitely."

"Why don't you come to mass with me?"

"I don't really get it," she said, intent on the tiny green Christmas tree she was painting on her thumbnail. "The church thing. I mean, you don't go to church."

"Once in a while."

"How come you want to go on Christmas all of a sudden? It's the same Jesus the other three hundred and sixty-four days a year. You think he's going to quit being mad at you because you show up on Christmas?"

"Who said he's mad at me?"

"I was a Christian for a while," Rosette said, moving on to the next hand. "Right when I got to junior high, it was cowboys, jocks, Christians and stoners. And nobodies. So I was a Christian for a while."

She held her hand at arm's length, inspected it: a girl's hand, perfect and unlined.

"That was what we had on everybody else," Rosette said. "We were going to heaven and everybody else was going to hell. God was mad at them but God liked us. It was pretty gross. So yeah, I'm sorry, Marvin, but God is pissed at you."

"Come on with me," he said to Rosette.

"Trees or stars or jingle bells?"

"You've got all trees on the one hand."

"Maybe I'll do red trees on a green background for this hand. How much time have I got?"

"You're coming, then?"

"I guess."

"Forty-five minutes," he said—trying to conceal his happiness, trying not to let it show. And why did it matter? It shouldn't, it didn't, but it made Marvin glad anyway. Maybe she could find something there to make a childhood out of. Maybe Marvin could find something.

"Maybe jingle bells," Rosette said. "What does mistletoe look like?"

The smell of Christmas dinner: turkey and gravy, boiled on-ions, frozen peas overcooked into army-green mush. Justine closed her eyes and imagined herself in her grandfather's blindness, tak-ing it all in through her nose.

Opened her eyes and Neil was still there.

Question: was there a way out of there? Trap door, parachute, the helicopter landing in the prison yard. Fuck me, she thought.

Marliss said, "I'm just going to apologize in advance for the turkey. I left it in till the little red dealie popped out and that's always too long."

Neil, carving: "Don't believe her for a moment!"

"No, really."

"This turkey is fine!" he said. "Done to golden perfection!"

"I can smell it," Henry said. "It smells just fine."

"It always smells good," Marliss said. "Even if it's still bleeding in the middle, it smells good. Even if you cook it so long it turns black. I don't know why they put those little pop-up thingies in there anyway if they can't get them right."

"Call a lawyer," Lex said.

"I just might!"

Nobody was laughing. There was this little glimmer of extra

brightness around the edges of everybody, they were all trying a little too hard to present the illusion of Christmas cheer, stir-fried Happy Family, Justine thought, remembering the enigmatic Chinese restaurant in Southwest Portland. Chicken with Delicious Sauce. Five Flavor Eggplant. Lex was looking at her funny.

Oregon was only one of several places she would rather be.

Plus she was ruining Henry's last Christmas. She stole a glance at him, as if he could see back: the big head staring forward. A fire was flickering in the grate, and the cast-iron sconces around the edge of the dining room were dimmed down to a yellowish glow. The dome of Henry's forehead shone like an antique ivory cue ball, discolored by time, splotched and splattered. He was wearing a new plaid flannel shirt with the sleeves neatly buttoned, tan woodsman's pants, suspenders. He looked as if his mother had dressed him, Justine thought—then looked at Marliss, mother to them all, though she was the youngest one there. Taking care, Justine thought, the satisfactions of. Give the self away to find the self. She knew it could be done, she had been a mother once herself and a good one. She remembered the days of longing, wanting to get her mind back and her body back and her life back while this little needy self came at her again and again, wanting her to change his clothes, change his diapers, make him a sandwich, turn the TV channel, bare her breasts and give him suck and Justine remembered with pain and with some self-approval that she had done it. She had given her life to him—sometimes half-heartedly, absentmindedly, sometimes she'd been filled with a longing to be elsewhere but she did it. There was no small corner of her life that Will hadn't wanted and he got all of it, all there was of her.

A feeling inside her like a length of cloth ripping. Still dead, still dead, the little voices said.

Rubber bullets.

Sticks and stones *will* break my bones, she thought—then looked around the table, a sudden moment of silence, and saw that *everybody was staring* at her. Had she said her thoughts out loud? Was something printed on her forehead? Adulteress, perhaps, or the simpler Whore.

"What?"

"Nothing," Neil said, and went back to carving the thigh of the turkey, the long knife slipping under the brown skin, separating flesh from bone, the living bird into neat slices. She had no appetite for any of it. She wanted . . . What did she want? All the things she couldn't have, that was the problem, that's what Dr. Fairweather used to tell her. She wanted her son back, she wanted Neil back the way he used to be. She wanted him to trust her. She wanted to trust the world. She would give five dollars to hear Neil say, Don't worry, Justine can take care of it.

"I'll tell you something," Henry said. "I'm glad you all could be here this evening. I want to thank you for coming."

"I was already here," Justine said. "Everybody but Neil."

"For being here, then," Henry said. "For keeping me company. Thank you."

"Where else would we be?" Marliss asked—and the question stayed in the air above the table as she cut Henry's dinner into children's bites. Where would she and Lex be? Neil and Justine? Where would Henry be, for that matter—Marliss knew he was going to hell but Justine wasn't so sure. The snow batted and flicked at the big black windows. The warmth, the firelight.

I could have saved him, Justine thought. I could have done something. He could be sitting right here with us.

"What matters is this," Henry said.

"What?"

"This right here," he said. "All of us. That's what I've come to realize."

The others nodded, solemn agreement. But this was bullshit, Justine thought: what about the others, the ex-wives, missing husbands, baby boys? What about the person she used to be, and Neil? The dead crowded out the living in this room. She couldn't help laughing.

The others stared, Neil especially.

"I . . ." she started, then couldn't think of what should come next.

"What?"

"Well, I quit taking my pills," she said brightly.

Marliss stopped in midair, holding Henry's plate above the table. Neil was holding a spoon of gravy above his potatoes.

"It's not a big deal," Justine said.

"What pills?" said Henry.

"It's nothing."

"Antidepressants," Neil said. "She didn't tell you?"

"There's nothing to tell, really," Justine said.

Marliss looked at her, and Lex, and Henry swiveled his big head, his blank sockets toward her.

"Tell us what?" he asked.

"It's no big secret," Justine said. "I've been having a little problem lately, since, since Will. I'm better."

They looked at her—Marliss, Lex, Henry—then quickly away, and Justine saw that she'd been unfair to them. She'd played a trick.

"How long?" asked Neil.

"How long what?"

"Since you quit taking them. How long?"

"Just a couple of days."

"You have the rest of them with you?"

"I threw them away," she said—a lie, a little white lie, she could picture them lying at the bottom of her bottom drawer, placid buff and green. But she didn't want to leave any doors open for Neil, any little cracks for him to squirm through. Slither.

"You're taking a risk. You know that."

"Yep."

She grinned, to prove to him that all his worries were unfounded, that she was fine, really, a little shaky but fine. She saw instead that she had confirmed the worst. My crazy Valentine, Santa's little self-destructive elf.

"He said a year," Neil said, talking as though the others weren't in the room. "You know that. Dr. Fairweather said a year, minimum. And that was if things were going well. Do you think things have been going well?"

"Sure," she said.

The others looked at her again, they knew she'd been sleeping with somebody. They hadn't known she was actually crazy till Neil named it for them but they suspected, and now they knew.

Marliss passed the plates out. The silence, as they sat and started to eat, was raw, half naked, full of bare patches and open sores like a dilapidated calf. Plenty of things unsaid. Neil had lowered her in the eyes of the others, which made her angry. He had exposed her. Naked at the Christmas table, she thought briefly of the one thing that would confirm her as the crazy daughter, the grand gesture. Why not? She couldn't be worse than she was.

"This is damn good," Lex said.

"Thank you," said Marliss.

"Wonderful," said Neil. "I tell you what."

"What?" Justine said.

"I'm going to try to raise Fairweather, before it's too late. Unless you want to talk to him?"

The others, avid, listened to the unfolding. Only Henry seemed distant.

"Why?" she asked. "Why bother him on Christmas Eve?"

"Don't get on your high horse," Neil said. "He's a Jew."

"This is America. Jewish people celebrate Christmas. I mean, anybody can go to Wal-Mart."

"I'm worried about you."

"Oh, I know."

Stalemate: Justine could see the disappointment on the faces of the others. They say they come for the races, said the Indy-car driver on the radio, but really they come for the wrecks. Christmas dinner was restored, for now. The father sat at the head of the table.

The children, now that they've stopped squabbling . . . No. Nothing that easy. Not even a temporary truce.

"There's a drugstore around here somewhere, right?" Neil said.

Bad dog: they stared at him. Maybe they were on her side after all.

"In Rivulet," Marliss said.

"Twelve miles of bad road," Justine said.

"They won't be open till day after tomorrow, not now," Marliss said. "Not with Christmas and all. You might be able to find someplace in Great Falls open but that's a good long ways away."

"And there's no need," Justine said.

Now they stared at her, and she saw that they just wanted the argument to be over. They didn't know and they didn't care who was right and who was wrong. Neil was a stranger there, and now Justine was a stranger there as well. My little secret, she thought. My several . . . And she saw how she had cut herself off from them, how she'd separated herself with lies, and she saw that there was no place for her, not here, not with Neil, and she saw— like looking through the rearview mirror, leaving a familiar city for the last time—she saw how much she had loved being among them, belonging. She wanted to be loved by them again. She wanted to be welcomed.

"I'm not crazy," she said to Marliss.

Neil looked at her, annoyed, and Marliss turned her head in embarrassment.

"I've made mistakes," Justine said. "Mainly, though, I'm sad. You understand that. I just don't know what to do with myself. You understand that."

"Please stop it," said the Senator. He was sitting upright, at last, with as much of the old force as he could summon.

"I don't feel this is a fit topic of conversation," he said. "Marliss has worked all day on this dinner and I will not see it wrecked."

"I'm sorry," Neil said.

But Henry had not been talking to Neil, the big head and its empty sockets fastened on Justine. Yes, she thought—I have brought trouble to your house. But it's *my* trouble, it's part of me. There's no way I could have left it behind. You see, she thought, willing them to look at Neil instead of her. You see what I'm up against.

Not that it was Neil's fault either.

She said, "It's supposed to snow all night—I heard it on the radio."

The others blinked and nodded, turned slowly back to their dinners. The fight was over, or at least suspended.

"There's a Canadian air mass and a Pacific one all coming together," Marliss said. "It's supposed to snow and snow and snow."

"A good old-fashioned Christmas," Neil said—and they all looked over at him, suspicious, wondering if he was trying to start things up again. But apparently he wasn't being sarcastic.

"I grew up in Pittsburgh," Neil explained, "where the snow came out of the sky dirty. The only way for a white Christmas was if it fell the night before. Even then, it would turn into these disgusting lumps."

"I hear it's better now," said Marliss.

Henry said, "They have cleaned Pittsburgh up by moving all the industry out. Those steel mills are all in Japan now."

"The air is better," Marliss said.

"But he's right," Neil said. "The old city is gone. It was what it was, dirty and so on, but it was a real *place.* You knew where you were from, Pittsburgh, Pennsylvania, and even if people made a little face when you said it—which they did—at least you knew where you were from. Now it's J. Crew and insurance offices and the same radio stations as everybody else. Back then, you know, the god damn Steelers! Sorry."

"That's all right," Marliss said—the only one of them it was possible to offend with language.

"There's something about snow," Justine said. "It always seems to take you back in time. There was always one great snowstorm, one real winter back at the edge of what you can remember. After that, it's all just a copy of that one real winter. It never seems to measure up."

"It isn't true, though," Henry said. "Winter is the same as it ever was."

He stopped, and Justine thought to resent him. But he was impervious, his senatorial authority on his shoulders.

"I don't like the idea that the old times were the good times," Henry said. "I dislike the idea that we're living in some kind of fallen world. *This* is the time to be alive. There has never been more opportunity. The world has never seen better health, or longer lives, or more freedom. These new people that come up here to hide out—they're just scared of the world, scared of the rough and tumble. You don't think it was tough in Anaconda?"

"Opportunity for who?" Justine asked.

"Anybody," Henry said. "Anybody that wants to go looking for it."

"I don't know," said Neil. "The best of all possible worlds."

"I didn't say that," Henry said. "It's just, all this mooning after the good old days and the dear departed and so on. I just don't care for it. The average person now lives better than a millionaire used to, if you take everything into account, health care and so on. I can't stand a Honda but it's a better car than a Packard ever was."

Lex chimed in: "People now, they don't know what a hard life is. They don't have a concept."

He's right, Justine thought. They're both right. But something in her resisted—despite the warmth, the wine, the fire flickering in the grate, all evidence of luxury.

"Something's lost, though," Neil said—and for this moment, he was her champion.

"There's that connection," Neil said. "You take music, for example—it used to be a thing where people played on each other's porches, where there was a different kind of music everywhere, church music and blues and Appalachian folk and so on. Then they gathered it all up and put it out on records, which was fine, you know, give everybody a chance to hear it. And then it got all mixed up together, which was fine, again. But now it's like they make it in New York and L.A. and Nashville and it's the same everywhere you go. And people aren't sitting out there on their porches anymore."

"And they don't get polio anymore either," Lex said.

"That's true," Neil said.

"And they don't know what horse shit smells like either anymore," Justine said.

They all turned to stare at her again and she started to feel the blood running hot under her face.

"I mean that literally," she said. "I mean, you don't know! People living where we live, they don't know anything. It's all been filtered through the TV. You tell them beef comes from cows and they look at you nicely and walk away—because they know it comes in a nice package from the supermarket, all wrapped up in plastic."

"People used to know not to curse at Christmas dinner," Henry said.

"I'm sorry," Justine said, "but it's true."

"No, it isn't," Neil said.

There it is, she thought: the bone of marriage, contention. They weren't going to make it, everybody knew that now.

"That's what we see of them," Neil said, "the parts we have in common, watching TV and going to Wal-Mart. People have these private lives when you talk to them—birth and death and falling in love, all the old things in new clothes."

"I thought you were on the other side a minute ago," Henry said.

"Whatever side I'm on," Justine said, "whatever I say, he's against it. That's the key. Watch him."

"Oh, Christ," said Henry.

"*In excelsis Deo,*" sang the congregation, the old Latin stirring memory in Marvin's heart, the child's Christmas, the faces of his aunts and great-aunts, the faces of cousins—lost now in the wide world someplace, adult strangers—and the face of his father. He felt the beginnings of tears for that lost world. He held them back for Rosette's sake, who sat beside him fidgeting, waiting for something to happen—or maybe she was just restless, the way that Marvin himself had been at twelve. The way the world had already announced itself, shown itself in little tantalizing glimpses of sex and money and freedom and weight. He remembered waiting like a bride, for the world to take him. The little virgin, he thought, the one who couldn't wait.

And then God, who had seemed ready to take him. At twelve, he could feel God, feel the tidal pull toward Him, then toward the world, then back to God, then toward the world again. The life I didn't live, he thought: Father Marvin, St. Marvin among the lepers on the streets of Bangladesh. The glory was the easy part, the neon halo. But the life of service: at least then you would know what your life was for, it was for others and for God, and if you never understood yourself or what you were supposed to be doing, at least you would be doing no harm. He could have been *helping*, even now. St. Marvin. Maybe it's a little late.

The other thing: there was this high-pitched keening sound like a coyote at the top edge of the hymns. A quarter of the congregation here was Bone Indian and sometimes the sound of it crept in. It felt like leaving the window open: the sound of the whistling wind, the cold bracing wild air slipping into the stuffy steam heat of the church. *Wild*, he thought: the flavors of his childhood, incense and wild rose, hot chocolate and venison. His father had taken him out to dig camas once, just so Marvin would know what it tasted like, where it came from. His father had taken him into the fall woods and killed a deer in the dry leaves down by the river. It was sunny and cold and the gutpile steamed in the air for a long time after.

He was wide open, the feelings running through him, beyond his control.

He felt like he was pointed someplace, but didn't know where.

The dry leaves, and the blue sky, October sunlight full and heavy on his skin. Marvin was maybe ten, carrying a rifle for practice but really there so his father could teach him to be silent, to walk quietly, to hunt. They waded across a riffle to an island. The cottonwoods were spaced far apart, like a park, still standing with their fall leaves on, yellow and gold and brown. The branches of the willows along the river were naked and red. The sunlight slanted down through the trees, onto the cobble of streamside rocks. They walked in felt soles, slowly, quietly. The deer was browsing near the head of the island. It felt like it was waiting for them, which maybe it had been, Marvin thought. What would his father say about that? But his father was gone, beyond asking. He had pointed to the deer, then to Marvin: did he want to take the shot? The boy shook his head, no, and the father was neither disappointed nor glad. This was business. He raised the rifle to his own cheek and for a moment Marvin wanted to stop him. The deer grazed unaware, head down. It felt wrong: the deer belonged there, held in the light, in the stillness of the air. Midges flew crazy lines through the sunlight, dust, bits of cottonwood fluff floated by like underwater. The deer was part of this, sleeping inside this still world, unaware. But they were hunters, and hunters killed deer. Right or wrong, it didn't matter.

The rifle cracked and Marvin jumped, and the deer jumped, startled. Then fell into its own footprints.

His father wasn't smiling. There was no celebration.

It was the kind of fall day when the houses hold the cold inside, when the heat of the sun comes unexpected in the middle of the day. Marvin sweated in his waders, helping his father hoist the deer by its heels, to bleed her out. The deer weighed as much as the boy did. Marvin waited while his father went back to the truck for a saw and pack frames. Two miles each way, maybe, an hour and a half. The day's warmth was gone by the time he got back. Working quickly, Marvin's father skinned and quartered the deer and lashed the meat and hide to the two pack frames with nylon cord. He gave himself the heavier load but still the boy staggered when he lifted his pack onto his shoulders. It didn't seem likely that he would make it back to the truck with that load—he saw himself down and drowning in the riffle, breaking an ankle—but when his father started off, Marvin kept up. There were two parts to this: one was simple, wanting to stay close to help if he needed it. The other part was complicated, wanting to be the boy his father wanted him to be, carry the load, don't complain, don't hurt yourself. . . . Nothing was spoken. There was the father's back, half disappeared under the weight of meat, and Marvin behind with the deer's eyes staring back at him. One foot in front of the other. The dark came on quickly and they crossed the river channel by flashlight. The cold came on with the darkness. The air felt cold as the river water then, the drops splashing up from his father's wader boots, the wind blowing downcanyon and the feeling of trying to keep up with his father. He had to hurry, every step, to keep from getting left behind. The wind froze the sweat onto his skin. He could feel his own breath, hot on his face, and still his father never slowed down or stopped to look back and see if Marvin was there. He just kept walking, carrying the load. He never stopped until he got to the truck, and then it was too dark to see what was on his face when he looked back and saw Marvin there behind him.

"You made it," his father had said, and he had not sounded surprised.

That was what Marvin heard in the high-pitched Indian sound of the choir. He needed to change his life.

Midnight: now it was Christmas. Neil was asleep, Marliss asleep and Henry, the dogs lay sleeping on the floor between her feet and the fire. She touched the coarse guard hairs on Buck's back and he stirred a little in his sleep. Lefty woke up and stared at her, jealous: You never do that to me! Then settled his yellow head back onto the rug and closed his eyes again. Outside the window was a thousand miles of snow, nowhere to go, nowhere to run. The snow fell slowly, no hurry, in swirls and gusts and sudden stops. She had the lights off in the big room, all she could see was the firelight and sometimes the yellow glow of the yard light, reflected in the swirling snow. Her husband was in bed, her *lover* (she turned the word over in her mind, tried to fit it to Marvin, not quite) was somewhere out in the swirling snow, in the tide and flux of the world, invisible.

She couldn't quite gauge how much she'd had to drink. She knew she'd had a glass in her hand since four in the afternoon, that she'd started with whiskey and moved to wine and by all rights she should have been asleep by now or raving. Instead she felt a little lightheaded but lucid, fine.

She was waiting, she couldn't have said for what.

She put another split length of pine on the fire, dry wood, the flame gathered quickly around it. That afternoon with Marvin, cutting firewood: her hands were still rough with healed blisters. It felt strange how quickly the past became the past. Last night with Marvin, she thought, this afternoon with Neil: bang bang bang and it was gone.

She lay down on the floor with Buck, waking him momentarily, provoking another jealous glance from Lefty. Oh, my dog friends, she thought. I could just be a body, eat and sleep and fuck and run. I could live my life in single syllables.

Neil was waiting for her but she couldn't imagine going in to him. Outside the snow was curling and clotting. She remembered the drive over from Missoula—it seemed like years ago but it was only weeks—the road disappearing behind her, driving alone through empty space, no past, no future, nothing in front of her and nothing behind. I could do *this* or I could do *that*. She stroked the throat of the big malamute, the thick soft fur filling her hand, a luxurious touch. She tried to imagine where she would go, what she would do, but this was all there was, this moment: the touch of the dog's fur, the warmth of the fire. This felt like trouble. She didn't know what else to do.

A faint clattery sound. She couldn't tell what it was or where it was coming from and for a moment, the first moment, she was scared of what it might be—the roof collapsing, Neil coming for her. She just didn't want to talk to him.

Then Justine recognized the sound: Henry walking, pushing the aluminum frame before him. At first the sound was faint and far away and then, step by step, it grew closer and she wondered what Henry was doing up but she knew: he was coming for her. She sat up on the floor and brushed the dog hair from her black turtleneck. She was ashamed of herself, as she knew she should have been: the night before Christmas, the blind old man, coming to put her to bed. Go back to sleep, she thought. Go to your bed and rest and be easy. I'll be all right.

The footsteps, slow as a broken clock: he would heave the walker forward, then carefully place one foot between the metal legs, shift his weight onto his arms, drag the other foot up and rest for a moment, before he started in again.

She was scared of him, she realized—scared of what might bring him out of bed on a winter night, what made him come looking for her. He wanted something. Go away, she thought. Go back to bed. The footsteps dragged down the hallway but they didn't seem to get any closer. Halfway and then halfway and halfway again, she thought, never getting anywhere. She wanted to be alone, a wounded animal. Two kinds of people, she thought: the ones who wanted to be touched when they were hurt and the ones who wanted to be left alone. She was fucked up, she knew it.

Then Henry was there with her in the room, the blind head searching back and forth.

"Justine?" he whispered. "Jess?"

"I'm here."

"What are you doing on the floor?"

"I was sitting here . . ."

"I understand that," Henry said. "I just don't understand why. But that's all right."

"I was down here with the dogs," she said. "Just in front of the fire."

Henry felt his way to the couch, touching the back, the arms, touching the seat to make sure it was clear. Then he transferred his weight slowly from the walker to the arm of the sofa, his big body swinging, out of control for a moment and then landing safely. He couldn't get up without help. Not without suffering, anyway, without a little war of the will against the body.

"I couldn't sleep," she said. "Maybe the coffee, I don't know."

"You don't need to explain yourself," Henry said. "I didn't come to lecture you. Get me a small glass of Scotch, no ice, would you? The good stuff."

"You think you ought to?"

Henry laughed, without happiness.

"There's nothing I ought to do now," he said, "except go quietly and not be a trouble to the nurse. I'll tell you this—if I live long enough to die from drinking, I'll be a lucky man."

"The pills," she said.

"I know. I don't know how to sort it all out, what works with what and so on. So I'll start from the other end, a little experiment. If it doesn't knock me on my keister, I'll increase the dose until it does."

She felt a little chill around her shoulders: this recklessness wasn't like him, not the usual Henry. But she went to the sideboard anyway, poured a small dose into one of his heavy crystal glasses. One of the things she'd come to notice about Henry's life: he wouldn't have anything cheap or fake or disappointing in his house. Everything was heavier than she expected it to be, nothing plastic, nothing made in China. The good shotguns rested in a rack on the wall, heavy with oil. A momentary chill, then, at the weight of his work: there was no place for children here, this was no place she belonged. A man's world, precise.

She handed him the glass and he took a small sip, and thought about what he was tasting. He let the whiskey stay in his mouth for a moment before he swallowed.

"Explanations," Henry said. He set the glass down on the table beside his arm. "I've never quite believed in explanations. They always seem after the fact, if you know what I mean."

"Not exactly."

"People want what they want," he said. "They do what they

can to get what they want. It isn't any more complicated than that. The explanations come later, when you decide it's time to try to patch things up."

"Marvin says the same thing too."

"Marvin?"

"The one who saved your life," she said.

She sat across the couch from him and watched the news cross his face, the trickle of understanding. She hadn't meant to let the cat out of the bag but now she had. And this was fine with her, really. She felt a lightness. It was the lies that had kept them apart.

"He's Indian," Henry said finally.

"Half Indian."

"Why the hell did you have to pick him? I liked him."

"I didn't pick anybody," she said.

"What the hell does that mean?"

"Don't be angry."

"I *liked* him," Henry said. He sipped his whiskey, and this time swallowed, grimacing with the heat of it.

"You think this is going to go easy for him?" Henry asked. "You think people around here are going to like it? This isn't San Francisco."

"I didn't sit down and plot this out," she said. "I didn't mean for anything like this. . . . It's just, I don't know—what you were saying a minute ago. It happened, is all. And then you have to go around afterward and try to pick up the mess."

"Or let somebody else pick up after you."

"I didn't mean . . ."

"I know what you meant and what you didn't."

The old authority was back in his voice, the spine of anger. He was right, she was wrong. It was simple.

"It's late," she said. "I don't want to have this argument now. I just want you to know, I didn't set out to do this, I didn't come here meaning to start anything. And I never meant to land you in the middle of this. You and Marliss, everybody. It's the one thing I feel bad about.''

"You never mean to," Henry said.

"Believe me."

"Then why in the hell . . .''

He trailed off, running slowly out of steam, the anger dissipating, formless, aimless. (And some small guilty part of her was disappointed—she wanted to be scolded, wanted to be the bad girl, wanted a father to tell her right from wrong, wanted somebody to know the difference, somebody to care.)

Then rose out of himself again.

"One thing," he said. "Not in my house."

Christmas morning: Marvin opened his eyes at six, still dark, still cold, still winter. The light of the Christ child had not dawned here, apparently. He closed his eyes and willed them to stay closed, waited for sleep to come again but it was no use. Carla's hot breath on his neck: he tried to reconstruct the end of the evening out of the clues available to him. They'd closed the bar early when the last customer went home. Carla brought a bottle of Jim Beam with her. And what else? Mayhem, Marvin thinks. Foolishness. The Sonny and Cher Christmas Special on Channel 47.

He swung his legs over the side of the bed and sat up. Little stars danced through his vision. His head bloomed into pain, nothing serious. He wasn't going to die from this.

But still, the open question: why? Marvin in the evening wanted different things from Marvin in the morning. In the morning he wanted clarity, wholeness, he wanted to be sane and sensible. In the evening it was another story. And this other person stood inside him, this referee, stood back and looked at Marvin with a cold judgmental eye: why, look, he seems to be drinking whiskey again. He knew, though. He saw himself well enough to know better.

Dread, he thought. The usual morning after. A dry mouth and unspecified terror.

The question was whether to stay for Christmas morning or whether to bolt for home. He had not quite meant to stay here last night; Carla hadn't quite meant to have him stay. But she was there with her bottle when they got back from midnight mass and things went on from there. The warm glow of religion, Marvin thought. All he had to do was one right thing. Rosette had said thank you and seemed to mean it and Marvin felt the distance from his childhood to where he was now. The same question every Christmas: how did I get here?

But Carla liked him for taking her. And Marvin liked the warmth of Carla's house, the comfort, and then it had been too late, really, and he'd managed to drink enough more than enough so it was either stay on the sofa or in Carla's bed and they shouldn't have, they both knew it. There was the problem again, walking in eyes open.

Now it was Christmas morning. Should he stay or should he go?

No false promises, he thought. Carla would be fine but Rosette . . . He liked Rosette, he wanted her to be all right. Maybe that was the problem, he thought. Maybe he was just afraid. And then there was all that cold morning outside, the miles of snow. He thought of Justine, off safe with her husband, and knew there was no place out in the cold world for him; knew that if he didn't stay here he didn't have any place to go but home.

Except he didn't love Carla.

The word did mean something: love. It was the only strong force he could touch, gravity, magnetism, electricity. And she lay next to him sleeping and he knew. The only language he could come up with was from high school: I love her like a friend but I don't *really* love her. My pimply little heart, he thought. I get older but I don't get smarter or better at the things that matter. But still there was a thing called love and he knew it, knew it when he thought of Justine fucking her husband and got this deep sorrow in the small of his belly and anger and jealousy all mixed up. It didn't mean it was a good thing. It wasn't going to make him happy or healthy or whole. It was just something he could touch, a point to steer by.

He knew what he wanted for once. She was out there somewhere, somewhere else.

It was no good pretending.

He swung himself upright—another small head-rush, a pain behind the eyes—and slipped on his jeans, wondering if he'd even make it out the driveway. Water, aspirin, pissing. He stopped outside Rosette's room and sent a thought through the closed door: Merry Christmas, you're all right, I wish . . . But he came up short again. Wished for what? He laced his boots on in the kitchen and slipped out the kitchen door, feeling like a thief. She'd wake up expecting him beside her. Rosette would wonder.

The storm door was piled shut with snow, the stoop was buried: a foot or more. He plowed toward his truck, buried to the knees. He checked the corona of light under the streetlamp to see if the snow was still falling but there was nothing, now—only the stillness of the morning, all sound buried under the deadening snow.

It's better this way, he told himself, starting the Ford—better not to pretend, that way can only lead to more hurt later on. Dr. Deernose, Ph.D., noted expert on daytime radio advice. I know and you don't. This was the wrong thing to do, he knew it and did it anyway, he was leaving the only warm house behind and heading off for nowhere, home. It would have been pretending to stay, and he knew that pretending was perfectly all right. Nobody would be hurt if he stayed. He knew it and he left anyway. He brushed the snow from the windshield, scraped the hard crust of ice beneath it. I know what's good for you. This may hurt a little bit. Nothing easier in the world than somebody else's pain.

The technical term for what you are, she said, is *asshole*.

One last minute, left behind. He leaned into the open door of his truck—the heavy breath of the exhaust pouring out into the cold morning, white—and stared at Carla's house: alone and dark, the windows lifeless, marooned in snow. His one set of footprints, leading out. What was wrong with comfort? There was so much that wasn't comforting, wasn't comfortable. *May call me crazy*, Fred McDowell said. *Baby, I know right from wrong. . . .*

Then he was gone, this time in four-wheel drive, slipping and sliding through the deep and drifting streets. He beat the newspaper boy this morning: no other tracks or even footprints in these side streets, none that he could see. He made his way to the arterial at a sedate fifteen miles an hour. Marvin was the King of Christmas Morning, the only one awake except the restless boy in his upstairs bedroom, waiting, watching the clock until he can wake his parents, maybe slipping downstairs in stocking feet to catch a quick peek at the tree. To see if the sled is there. The new dirt bike in the garage. This passion for *things*, Marvin thought— wanting and longing for and imagining. If I only had a new BB gun I could . . . Did women feel the same? It didn't seem like it. Marvin saw himself, driving away from the warm house in his big lovable truck, latest descendant of the G. I. Joe armored personnel carrier he once longed for.

The main street and a half of Rivulet was plowed and sanded, the highway out was fine. He was grateful for this, technically, but at the same time bothered: this forced return of normalcy, practicality. He wanted the snow to stay where it was, the people to stay in their houses. He wanted a holiday. I want, I want, I want, Marvin thought, and then I get what I get. His new theory was that this was all right, because so many things had happened to him, good and bad, that he would never have thought to ask for. Justine, for instance, a case of pure accident. And now he knew her, and he wanted her back from her husband, but he also knew that this might not be for the best. Getting what you wanted, answered prayers, always a difficulty. And when she left—not *if* but *when*, a matter of time, she might have been already gone— he'd want her back, but who could tell if Marvin should even have wanted her in the first place?

Sometimes he didn't quite want what he wanted. He longed for a surprise instead, an opening into the world. Christmas morning.

A possibility, he thought. He felt it in the white countryside, the trees and fence tops at the edge of his headlights—unbroken white and virginal, a world made new, and clean.

A lie, though. Under the snow was the same dry grass and barbwire as ever. More of the same. The illusion of hope was manufactured by the depth of his need for it: there *must* be a way out. . . .

So when he pulled into his driveway and saw dusted-over tire tracks, he was excited—then drove around to the back and saw her big blue Bonneville under two inches of snow and Marvin didn't know what to feel. She'd been here all night, or most of it, while he'd been out fucking somebody else. He had managed to wreck this thing too—not that it was built to last in the first place. But fuck, he thought, fuck me. I am an idiot. Name calling, he knew it; he retained his good impression of himself despite. But this time he was genuinely sick of his own stupidity.

He shut the engine off and sat.

Dim early light. A faint gray smoke flagged from the chimney: good firewood, clean-burning, the insect-killed lodgepole they had gathered together. The man's world of pickups, firewood and rifles—Marvin was suddenly sick of it. A way of not letting your-self be touched. And then the alcoholic regret surged up in him again and he felt that he was no use to anybody, he wanted to apologize. He closed his eyes and wished that he would be else-where when he opened them, anywhere.

He opened his eyes and she was still waiting for him, inside.

He couldn't quite bring himself . . .

But there was nowhere else to go, no way around it, he felt his life narrowing like a river channeling over rocks, down into the rapids, there was no way through but the fast water. He got out of the truck, cheeks stinging in the sharp air. It wasn't seven yet, still gray, still dim. The day was not quite formed out of the darkness, *the gray area*, Marvin thought. Where I've been.

Inside the wood stove was ticking, glowing hot. The air was hot and dry as a sauna and the lights were off. His eyes opened slowly to the dim light and she was not there: not in his kitchen, not in his living room. His father's records were scattered across the carpet, Sonny Boy Williamson and Jimmy Reed, the black faces staring up at him from the Chess record jackets. Muddy Waters looked especially sharp this morning, a process hairdo from about 1961, a jacket with no lapels. Marvin thought: What have you got for me today? *Can't spend what you ain't got. Can't lose what you ain't never had.*

Justine was sleeping in the bedroom, on top of the covers, still dressed in jeans, her wool socks pulled over the cuffs.

She heard him, though he wasn't making any noise—that mys-terious radar that women had when they were interested in you, she just knew he was there. She opened her eyes, almost.

"Hey," she said.

"Merry Christmas," Marvin said.

"Merry Christmas yourself."

"I didn't expect you," he started to say. "I didn't . . ."

"Quiet," she said. "I don't want to talk right now."

"How long have you been here?"

"I don't know," she said. "It was late. I was waiting for you."

"I'm sorry."

"I don't want to talk," she said. "I want to sleep. Come to bed."

"I can't . . ."

"You can pretend," she said. "Just close your eyes and pretend. That's what my mother used to tell me when I couldn't take a nap, you know, four or five years old. Just lie down and pretend. A rest with your eyes closed is almost as good as sleep. Did your mother tell you that?"

"I don't remember," Marvin said.

"You do somewhere," Justine said. "It's all locked away in there somewhere, everything that ever happened to you."

She sighed, and turned her back to him, stretching her full length on the little bed and then curling again. She was done.

"I'm tired," she said.

"What does that mean?"

"Just what I'm saying," she said. "For once. Come to bed."

Alert—like he was being watched—he took his boots off and his coat and then walked into the next room in his stocking feet and dropped another couple of lengths of firewood into the stove, choking the damper down to make it last. My house, he thought. It seemed transformed with her in it. There was a lot to think about.

The voice from the next room: "No thinking! Come to bed!"

She knows me, Marvin thought. Lucky girl.

He took his pants off, stood over her in T-shirt, socks and underwear, undignified. Tugged at the covers until she helped him, rolling them down. He lay down next to her and then pulled the covers over her shoulders and his. She was still wearing her fuzzy-bunny sweater. He reached his hand under it to feel the soft hot skin of her belly and she pressed her own hand over his, outside of the clothes, keeping him there against the naked skin.

"Good night," she whispered. "No thinking."

It didn't stop. It wasn't that easy. He tried to make his mind a blank and nothing happened and tried to close his eyes and remembered, yes, his mother had said that: A rest with your eyes closed is almost as good. It felt unnatural, the day—already started—coming to rest next to her. He was restless, unwilling. He did what she asked him, though, there in his own small bed with his eyes closed and the great world spinning outside. *Poor boy, I'm a long way from home,* Wolf sang. From a long way off, Marvin saw how tired he really was, how he had been keeping himself going on coffee and nerves. Sleep, he thought, sleep—but part of him didn't want to, afraid to surrender, afraid to miss the action. *Sleep.* It was strange, how deep and bone-tired he was, without seeing it, without knowing it. "Oh," Justine said. "Oh!" and it was in her dreams, in her sleep, and then he was asleep himself.

In the Christmas dream, he's with his father again, deer hunting in the fall sunlight. The touch of the heavy sun on his skin: it's a pleasure, he knows he's dreaming but he doesn't want to stop. His father talks to him, in a language Marvin can't understand. An Indian tongue. Sunlight.

Sunlight spilled across the sheets, across his bare arm. It was eleven or twelve or even one in the afternoon and he was alone in his bed and he wondered if she had ever been there at all. A pillow next to his, indented. He buried his face in the pillow and smelled her perfume: yes.

In his dreams, he wanted something different.

He had no desire to get out of the bed.

He could hear her in the next room: small movements, a coffee cup set gently down on a table, stocking feet across the floor. She was trying not to wake him. Marvin felt a sudden blaze of tenderness toward her, she might be real after all, she might be trying . . . He didn't know, didn't even know what she was doing there. He couldn't tell. Still, the sunlight, quiet morning, the small domestic sounds all filled him with peace, and he rested in the bed for a few minutes longer: domestic bliss, homegrown.

"What time is it?" he finally called.

He heard her stir, then watched her face, half her body, appear around the doorframe.

"You're up," she said.

"I'm not up yet."

"You want coffee? Or are you going to go straight to beer?"

"What does that mean?"

"Well, it's one in the afternoon. You were tired, I guess."

Marvin found this shocking: one in the afternoon! Another dead Puritan. She went to get him coffee, and Marvin thought: what if this was all there was of life? Simple enjoyment, sleeping in, sunlight on skin, perfume. He'd been missing so much. He'd been looking for something else—there, in his little Puritan bed, his Puritan underwear. Maybe I should be wearing silk, he thought. My life as a man. He sat up, propped against the pillows, and saw the sun on the snow all the way down to the bank of the creek, white as a headache, brilliant and cold.

"How long have you been up?"

Justine, curled next to him on the bed, handed him the steaming cup. She looked at his face, interrogative. What did she think of him? Then kissed him the same way, as if she was trying to find something out.

"I don't know," she said.

"What?"

"It didn't feel like I ever slept. I was surprised when you woke me up. And I don't know where any of the clocks are here."

"Where's your watch?"

"I gave it back to him," she said. "I left it on the table beside his bed. I didn't want to take anything of his with me."

"Neil," he said.

She shrugged: who else?

"Runaway housewife," Justine said. "She's out of control!"

Marvin felt a little roller-coaster lurch inside him: she'd left her husband and come to him. Not exactly that this was a bad idea but it was a *big* idea, bigger than he could really get around, and he felt her weight dropping onto him. Now she was *his* problem. Again she saw what he was thinking.

"No no no," she said. "I just came here because it was the only place to go. I mean, the motels aren't even open."

"It doesn't matter."

"Gee, thanks."

"You know what I mean."

"No, I don't. You don't know what you mean yourself. Look."

"What?"

"There's plenty to think about," she said. "Maybe we could start later on. Maybe we could have a little peace and quiet for a little while. It's been a rugged couple of days."

"How is your husband?"

"That's what I mean. None of that."

"What's for breakfast?"

"Better," she said. "Much better."

She laced her fingers into his short black hair and left them there, entwined. She was looking out the window at the brilliant white of the day, sun on new snow, and she was thinking; though

Marvin wasn't going to know what she was thinking about. Justine was presenting herself as simple fact: here I am. Now what are you going to do about me?

Tromping down through the snow toward Silver Creek: Marvin first in line, breaking trail in his knee-high Sorels, Justine following in his footsteps. Squaw, Marvin thought—Algonkian for pussy, according to recent news accounts. But still there was that wistful feeling, the whole twentieth century erased and just the two of them in nature. Man the hunter, woman the helper and gatherer.

The sun was already lowering in the sky, three-thirty. The shadows of the creek willows were lengthening over the banks, basketworks of shadow. Still it was beautiful, sunny and ten degrees and no footprints but their own. Here in the Garden, Marvin thought. What would it take to live here? He thought of firelight on the tipi walls, romantic; thought of the suffering children in February and March, after the food ran out. You wouldn't need to be in love, you wouldn't need to worry about it. You could worry about killing a buffalo with stone tools.

"Where are you from?" he asked her.

"I told you," she said. "Oregon."

"No, your people. What country do you come from?"

"Gallego is Spanish," she said. "My father's name. Then Neihart is German, you know, Henry's name—my mother's side of the family. There's some English in there and some Irish."

"You don't know, in other words."

"Okay," she said. "You're better than I am."

"That isn't what I meant."

"You hear what you say," she said. "You don't hear what it sounds like to me. You've got the tribe, you know where you're from. I'm a mutt, right? Heinz 57."

"I don't know any more than you do."

"You own this place," she said. "It belongs to you."

Marvin cracked up.

"That's me," he said. "King of the hill. I've never even owned a new car, much less a house."

"That's not what I meant."

"Look!"

A yearling moose scattered out of the brush, stared at the two of them for a long angry moment. Tatters of coarse hair hung from its shoulders. Skinny, it was hungry. It wasn't going to make it through the winter, Marvin thought. If he'd had his rifle along, he might have taken a shot. Justine clutched his arm through the thick wool of his jacket.

The yearling turned, finally, and walked away from them. They watched, then watched the place where he had disappeared for a minute after he was gone.

"I thought he was going to come after us," she said.

"He might have," Marvin said. "That's a dumb animal, a moose."

"Compared to what?"

"Compared to you, say. Or a length of concrete curb."

She picked up a double handful of snow, trying to compress it into a hard snowball to throw at him—but the snow was too new and too cold, it wouldn't stick together. When she hurled it at his head, the snowball exploded harmlessly into white fluff.

"You are so mean to me," she said.

"Not yet," Marvin said.

"What does that mean?"

"We haven't gotten to the hard part yet."

He started off again through the snow, leaving them both to wonder what he had meant. Things were stirring up inside him, currents of fear and feeling. Something was about to happen and he had a feeling of danger about it.

The air was hard with the cold but still the winter sunlight had a little power—he could feel it on his cheeks. The sound of Justine's boots sifting through the snow, not the crunch of wet snow and not the creak of below zero but a soft compacting noise. The stream was down to their right, a weed-choked bench, but Marvin knew where the trail was, down under the snow.

He led her to the edge of Silver Creek. It was the inside part of a bend in the creek, almost an island, with a big dark fir in the middle of the bend. One side of the tree was open, a few feet up. He led her out of the wind and into the darkness, the dry ground next to the trunk of the tree. All around them were the deep green skirts of the tree. It was dark at first inside, with the brilliant white of the sunlit snow all around and the sunlight on the water. The ground was almost dry here, littered with dry needles and windblown floury snow. The creek ran between ice banks, ten feet away. Small birds raced along the ice banks, then stopped and stared into the water.

"Look," he said, and Justine looked.

A small bird turned its head halfway around in each direction, to make sure nobody was watching, then walked down the bank and into the water itself. A chill ran down Marvin's back just thinking about it.

"What was that?" she asked.

"Dipper," Marvin said. "They walk along the bottom and catch bugs."

"They don't die?"

"They don't seem to."

"I'd die in a minute."

"You bet you would," he said. "You aren't built for it. It's weird, though."

"What?"

"What if that's what you were made for? You ever think of that? Walking around under the ice and eating bugs. I don't know."

"Have you been smoking dope again?"

"A little. Not since last night. But it's a real question—what you're made for."

"Man is born to trouble as the sparks fly upward," Justine said.

Marvin looked at her.

"It's the Bible, I think," she said. "Henry says that all the time. At least, he says it to me."

"He thinks you're in trouble."

"Oh, I am."

They stopped, stared out of the darkness of their little safe place, out at the fading light of day and the water rushing by. He put his arm around her like a high school lover, clumsy. Their coats rubbed up against each other. What was he going to say to her? Because now she was there with him and she was going to want an answer. Marvin thought: I'm so *bad* at this.

"You are in trouble," Marvin said.

"I don't want to talk about it," she said. "Not yet. Just give me a day, twenty-four hours of peace and quiet, can you do that? It's just, you know, the roller-coaster ride."

"No, that's okay."

"I just want you to know one thing," she said.

She turned to him in the dim light, caught his eyes and held them, solemn: a witness.

"You're the one thing I'm sure of," she said. "Not sure of what will happen, I mean, nothing like that. It's just, when I'm not with you, I think it'll make me happy to see you—and then I think I'm making it up, you know, it isn't really happening. And then I do see you and it does make me happy, every time. It works."

Marvin felt glad and trapped all at once. It was good to hear her say she loved him, which was what she meant, it seemed like, and at the same time it felt like he'd bought into something he couldn't quite tell the size of. He was scared of feeling anyway, he knew this. Carla had told him this. He was scared.

"I don't mean anything by that," Justine said. "I just wanted you to know."

Marvin leaned toward her and kissed her, first on the lips, then on the neck. He couldn't think of anything to say. He didn't need to say anything.

A long, still moment, the creek rushing by.

The dipper emerged on the far bank, shivered the water off his feathers. It walked up and down the bank, gossiping with an invisible companion. The water and the ice were the same color, the same brilliant gray, sunlight shining tiny diamonds. Here, he thought. Right here. Why did he always want more? Why couldn't he take the moment and be grateful for it while it lasted? But he was always escaping himself, always leaping forward. Stop, he told himself. Right here, right now, nowhere else. There is no other life.

There is no other life.

"I love you too," he said.

"Don't start," she said.

Then it was dusk, four-fifteen. The winter light slipped away quickly. The sky turned a transparent blue and then, just for a moment, a soft watercolor pink, and then the day was gone.

The snow seemed to hold the light, though, and it was easy to make their way back, following in their own footsteps. The difference was that now the night had closed around them. Nobody in the world knew where Marvin and Jess had gone, that was part of the charm, but he was back to feeling small. Marvin and his woman against the winter, against hunger. Four generations ago, he thought, maybe five. The old people were strong, they had a place.

But it was harder to wish for the end of civilization now, or an exchange of civilizations, with the night wind picking up in their ears. This was the time for propane heaters, for radios and refrigerators and indoor plumbing. The fact that Marvin's great-great-grandfather could survive this, without guns or horses or iron, proved nothing in Marvin's case. Still, the genes are the same, he thought—his father's half at least. What had been lost? Where had it gone? The ten thousand things to know, small differences between life and death. Marvin knew a hundred words for money, a hundred words for car, one name for snow. Buffalo hump, he thought. Folsom points. It was still all technology, still the clever monkey, the impulse was no different. It just seemed sad when it worked: millions and hundreds of millions of people lived without effort while the rest of it died. I'm antilife and I vote, he thought.

They came up on the house and Henry's Cadillac was parked, idling in the yard.

"Fuck," said Marvin. "Stay down."

"What?"

"Your fucking husband, is my guess."

"What?"

"He's in my house," Marvin said—watching the silhouette cross his window, the shape of a person. It was just dark, the sky past gray, the snow still light enough to walk by but the light shone from his window bright and strong. He felt busted, caught, but at the same time angry. Get off my land.

"I'm going to go throw him out," Marvin said.

"Hold on," Justine said.

"What?"

"I just don't want to talk to him. I don't want to see him."

"He knows you're here."

"Maybe not."

"Your fucking car is parked out front!" Marvin said. "Right next to my pickup. What is he doing in my house?"

"He's waiting for me."

"What for?"

"I couldn't tell you."

The wind, on cue, picked up, and sifted a fine handful of snow down the collar of his jacket. Night and cold and hiding.

"I don't like this," Marvin said.

"Give him a minute," Justine said. "He won't stay long."

"How do you know?"

"I don't," she said. "This just seems so unlike him. He's usually . . ."

"What?"

"Not *polite*, exactly," she said. "He went to prep school, you know? He thinks there's a right way and a wrong way to everything. So I don't think he's just in there raging around."

"What's he doing, then?"

"He's *worried* about me," she said.

Pursed lips, the little bitter child. Marvin was suddenly angry, her and her prep school husband and her psychological problems, and it was too late to tear himself away. Stuck to her. He was supposed to take her seriously.

"So why's he taking my house apart?"

"For some good reason," Justine said. "He's always got a good reason. I don't know what it is."

The ancient grudge, Marvin thought. The dead conductor, the

bus they couldn't stop riding. He saw himself as scenery. He saw that he was a backdrop, nothing more, for the ancient drama of man and wife.

"Why don't you go to him?" Marvin asked.

She looked at him, surprised and hurt, and Marvin felt like a bastard.

"Because *I am done* with him," she said.

They watched the lamplit shade of Neil, crossing and recrossing the living room. What was he looking for? She was next to Marvin but miles away.

She said, "I don't expect anything from you, Marvin. I told you that. I hoped that you would believe me."

"I . . ."

"What?"

"Nothing."

Tongue-tied: not that he couldn't find the words, he just didn't know what he might say with them. She was there with him. She had come to him. She expected something from him and she was within her rights.

"Just stay with me until he goes," she said.

He looked at her: thought about the thousand things swimming all around him, staying and going, home and comfort and fucking and being free. The rock songs all used to talk about being free but now they didn't anymore. That's it! he thought. Too much fucking crap! I have a brain full of crap! He couldn't even muster enough of himself to know what to feel.

Finally he could touch her, that was all. He knew he wanted that much. He touched the bare skin of her neck with his cold hand, and she let him.

"I'm all messed up," he said.

"You're okay."

"No, I just . . . I want things, you know? This and this and this. If you want one thing, it doesn't keep you from wanting another."

"What does that mean?"

"I'm not trying to tell you anything," he said.

"Just stay with me until he's gone," she said. "Keep me company. After that, you can do whatever you want."

"I know."

And still it rankled him to sit in the dark and the cold while another man was in his house. Maybe it was the right thing to do but it didn't feel right.

"You don't want me to root him out?" Marvin said.

"Just sit tight. He'll go in a minute."

"I don't like to look at it, is all."

"You're going to get Western with him? I thought your gun was in the house."

"I got one in the truck."

She looked at him: and in her eyes she was measuring him, what he was capable of.

"I wouldn't shoot him anyway," he said.

"Oh, *that's* comforting."

"You know what I mean."

"Better than you do," Justine said. "Boys are *born* knowing how to make that machine-gun noise with their mouths, you know that? I didn't realize until I had one. You go in there guns a-blazing and Neil will call the cops on you, put you in a world of trouble."

"Not in Montana," Marvin said. "Not while he's in my house."

"There you go," she said. "Let's make everything so big and bright that any second grader can understand."

"Nothing wrong with that."

"A country full of second graders."

"You didn't have to come here," Marvin said. "You don't have to stay, if you don't like it."

"Fuck you."

"What's that for?"

"Fuck *you*," she said.

"I didn't say anything."

"This is my land," she said. "This is my country. Big he-man country. I mean, don't you get sick of it yourself? You don't think they're talking about Indians when they say that. This is the big white-man country, Marvin, that's what it's all about—tough guys being brave and big. No place for me here. No place for you here, either."

"You've been thinking again," he said.

"Fuck you."

"Oh," he said. "No, thanks. Let's go."

"What do you mean?"

"Get in your car and go. I'm tired of this. I'm going to go in there after him in a minute."

"Don't do that."

"That's what I mean. Let's get out of here."

She tried to look at him, in the dark and the cold, but the light was behind him, coming from the house. He could just see her face: sharp wondering, confusion. She really didn't know which way to go, and neither did Marvin. It was time for leadership.

"We can come back later," he said, "if that's what you want to do. Otherwise . . ."

"Otherwise what?"

"I don't know," he said. "I mean, I really don't have any idea. I just want to get out of here now, okay?"

"Or do you just want me to get out of here?"

Okay, he thought: I've been called. Because part of him answered when she said it, Sure, why don't you get out of here?

Take your grandfather and your husband and your mental problems and fuck off. How easy it would be. How uncomplicated. He looked down into her dim-lit face—the yard light thirty yards away and blue—and saw how genuinely fucked up she was and how little she knew and Marvin knew how much trouble she had already cost him. Asking for more. Asking for trouble.

But if he let her go, she was gone for good.

It was a simple thing. He could let her go only if he wanted to live without her, which he didn't, not just then.

"Come on," he said, "let's go."

And she looked at him, trying to read his face. He was eclipsed in darkness. Maybe he didn't mean right by her. And then she took his hand and kissed it and stood and then they were running toward the light, running toward the Bonneville, the loose snow flying around them, like children on a dare. "*Hurry*," she said, fumbling for her keys, "*hurry*," and then they were in and the engine caught and they were gone, history, they were out of there, they were free, Marvin thought, free. . . .

Now concentrate: one foot in front of the other. We will walk the straight and narrow. We will somehow redeem ourselves.

"This is not right," Henry says.

"This is somebody else's house," says Marliss.

"I'm sorry but I'm worried about her," says Neil.

Oh, it is all a lie: possession. This is Henry's secret, the thing he knows. Somebody stole his wife. Now everybody will laugh at him. He wants to pretend it is something else but they always do, the ones on the short end. The strikeout kid tells everybody, I wasn't really trying.

"She's got to come back here sooner or later," the husband says.

I used to like him, Henry thinks.

"We could wait outside, in the car," says Marliss.

"I don't think Henry would like the cold," Neil says.

"Nothing for you?"

"What?"

"Nothing," Henry says.

But it is true: everything he does is pretending to be for somebody else. He is worried about his wife, worried about his grandfather-in-law, probably—if you put him to the test somehow—he'd tell you he was worried about the Indian fellow too. Nothing for me, thanks. But everybody knows, everybody sees, you want what you want and you do what you can to get it. He wants us not to laugh at him, Henry thinks. We will not laugh at him but we will think less of him: he let somebody else make off with his wife. Maybe it is better this way. Better than shooting people, anyway. Maybe there is progress after all. But really it makes the old man sick: this pretending.

"It's not the end of the world," Henry says.

The husband stops pacing for a minute.

"Meaning what?" he asks.

"She'll come back in her own time," Henry says. "She took one suitcase, is that what you told me?"

Silence, which he takes for assent.

"One suitcase," Henry says. "How long do you think that'll last her? She has more than that in shoes."

"There was some stuff," Marliss says. "You know, some things in the back of the car."

"What kind of things?" the husband says.

"Oh, you know. Some winter clothes, and then some other stuff. I saw her putting them in the other day, I don't know what-all."

"Christ," the husband says.

And Henry wonders: What if she turns out to be the villain in the piece? What if she really doesn't mean well, isn't good at heart, doesn't hope for the best for all? A bit of a bitch anyway. Moody.

"You think she was planning this all along," the husband says.

"Oh, no," Marliss says—though her voice gives the lie away. Not quite a lie but a groundless optimism, the next best thing. Nixon never really lied much either, except to himself. The mark of the world-class liar: convince yourself first, and the rest of the world will fall in line.

Lying, cheating, stealing, Henry thinks. All for love.

Not even for love, in Neil's case, but for pride. Though maybe this is his version of love. It never is all one thing.

"I wish I knew what the hell she was doing," Neil says.

"Perhaps we should go back to my house," Henry says. "We could wait for her there."

"If she's coming back."

"Even if she's not . . ."

"Which she isn't," Neil says. "Not any time soon. That's the whole point. I just want to see her and talk to her, I was going to say to see if she's all right but I know she's not all right."

"She's not all that bad off," says Marliss.

"No," Neil says. "She's like a broken watch, you know, one or two teeth missing off a gear in there somewhere. The hands go around and around just like normal."

He leaves them all to contemplate his ability to say, to name things, to judge. Then adds: "I'm sorry I dragged you all out this way. I should have come by myself."

"You shouldn't have come at all," Henry says.

"I can run my own life, thanks."

"I believe you," Henry says. "If you would stop trying to run everybody else's life for a moment, I believe you could."

"Leave it alone," Neil says.

"I don't see why I should."

"Because you don't know half of it," Neil says. "Because you weren't there for the bad part. Believe it or not, this is what she's like when she's *better*. I just don't want to lose it again. She could slip back just like that!"

He snaps his fingers.

Marliss says, "The car is gone."

"Which car?" asks Neil.

"Her car."

He runs to the window—Henry hears the footsteps, then hears him throw the window open, as if the car was hiding behind the glass? Something. Henry is losing sympathy. One thing to have somebody make a fool of you, another thing to act like a fool, which Neil is doing. Hurray for you, he thinks, sending the thought toward Justine and the Indian fellow. Godspeed and good luck, wherever you're going.

Immediately he feels guilty about feeling this. Feeling about feeling. Christ, he thinks: where is my simplicity? My good right arm?

And then he thinks: what if they went back to the house? It wouldn't make sense, he thinks. But not a lot of what Justine did made sense, lately.

And he is worried about Lex. What would happen if she went back for her clothes, say, or if she'd forgotten something? Lex was like a Rottweiler, Henry thinks. He always thinks he's on your side. There was no telling what he might do.

Henry says, "I guess we can go back to the house now."

"I still want to find her," Neil says.

"I'm sure you do," Henry says. "By now she could be any-where."

"She hasn't been gone more than ten minutes."

"South or north?" Henry asks. "Did they head toward Can-ada? North Dakota? Did they take the interstate or the two-lane?"

"They're probably in the ditch by now," Neil says.

"Oh, no," says Marliss. "She's got studded snows all around. She'll be okay."

Henry can hear Neil staring at her: a cool silence. He's still worried about Lex. Henry sighs—then hears the sigh, the noise coming from his body, and realizes again that he's become old. The fact keeps coming at him in different ways, it will not leave him alone. For instance: Henry knows what is right here, what they ought to do, and yet Neil will not defer to him. Nixon paid attention to him! Hubert Humphrey showed up on his doorstep at eleven-thirty one night to ask advice. Little faded pictures in an album, Henry knows this, the past is the past. But still. This little fuck, he thinks. An *artist* . . .

"We can go now," Henry says. "There's nothing more to do here."

A crash—broken glass?—and then he hears Marliss breathe out a soft "Oh, my."

"What was that?" Henry says.

"Nothing," Neil says.

"What was it?"

"Nothing," Neil says again. "A lamp."

"A what?"

"A lamp," says Marliss.

"It was just a dime store lamp," Neil says. "I'll leave him twenty dollars and he can buy three more of them."

"Control yourself," Henry says.

"You don't care. You're the one who likes him, right? You're the one who introduced them."

Bad company, Henry thinks. I have let myself in with bad company, and I am going to pay for this. He starts to let his mind drift back, wondering exactly where he went wrong, what exactly he had done that was wrong that led him into this situation.

"He did no such thing," Marliss says. "The Indian fellow saved his life, is all. What happened after that is strictly between the two of them."

"I shouldn't have said that," Neil says. "I'm upset, I guess."

"We're all upset," Marliss says.

"I wasn't expecting this," Neil said.

He's falling apart, Henry thinks. He's letting himself go. Buck up! Next thing you know, he'll be crying in public. Put on your poker face. Stop, think, act. Nothing good can come of this, this new permission to show your feelings—you give away your authority, your dignity and what was left? No woman wants to kiss a blubbering wreck, or a bully. They can find that in themselves, any of us, is Henry's theory. This weakness is the thing we dislike about ourselves. Power or the illusion of power is all we start with, all we have. He can prove this. Seventy years of experience.

"It's time to go," says Henry.

"I'm going to go find her," Neil says.

"You can drop us at home," Henry says. "Then you can do whatever you want. You can use the car if you want."

"I just don't want her out there, drifting."

"It's fine with me," Henry says. "It's all fine with me."

The air goes out of Neil, out of the room. Henry can hear Marliss on the floor, picking up pieces of the broken lamp. Disconsolate, Henry thinks. We're all disconsolate. She's left us all and now we're stuck with each other. Everybody else has gone to the fair, everybody except us. We don't get to. What? A summer's day, 1925, in the old university library in Missoula when everybody but little Henry was at the river. How long can one person carry a grudge? It isn't clear.

Everybody else was at the river on a summer day with beer and girls.

When did everything become bad for you? Drinking a little used to be fine, even getting drunk now and again. Smoking. You never got the girls. Mary Ellen Pridgeon was her name.

Imagine waking up in the morning and saying that: *I'm an artist.*

"Henry?"

Marliss's voice comes from a long way off.

He tries to explain: the little black and white shoes she wore, no, black shoes and little white socks, she meant to get him, there was no other explanation. They called her Pigeontoes when she wasn't there. An afternoon by the river. You think you invented sex! The little meteor, there in the corner of his eye. She left her shoes and socks on, that was all. August, the heat and blaze of midafternoon and the cool inside the streamside trees where the sun did not reach. Take your clothes off, Henry said. The white on white of her skin and the black patch of cunt hair, she was a whore as the rumor said but that was one thing in public and another thing here. Your turn, she said. They would call her fat now, with the big round ass she had, but they don't know: the pleasure of the curve of her ass in his soft university hands, he knelt in the dirt and kissed each cheek in turn, the meteor growing larger, a little circle of black with a glowing edge and then the sight of her undressed in the little clearing. Maybe she was fat but she wasn't embarrassed, wasn't apologizing for anything, and they could hear the other picnickers a few hundred feet away, shouts and laughter across the water. This was what he wanted, this and more of this and more: the ease and comfort of warm weather and the touch of soft skin, he'd spent his life searching in the wrong places, in libraries and offices, suits and dresses, cocktails and Senate receptions and the smell of the big birdhouse in the Washington zoo, tropical damp and rot and the meteor drawing closer now and Henry sees that it is going to swallow him, bright edges and the plumage flying by, plumage . . .

"Gun it," Marvin said.

"What?"

"Gun it! Now!"

She stomped the accelerator pedal and the big Pontiac leaped forward, graceless and huge, the tires spinning slush and mud into the wheel wells.

"Go!" he said.

Across the little dip in the road, she could feel the big car sledding along on the deep snow, and then they were clear and the momentum carried them forward and forward and then—moment by moment—she could feel the tires losing their grip on the snow and starting to slip and slipping. Then the big car sat with its wheels grinding.

"Rock it," Marvin said.

She tried it forward, then reverse: the car shuddered and shook but didn't stir.

"That's all right," he said. "Shut it off."

Justine shut the engine off and then the headlights and the night closed in around them: cold, maybe ten degrees and dropping fast. And now the car didn't work anymore. She could think of no connection, no safe way home.

"What do we do now?"

"It isn't more than half a mile up from here, if I remember right," Marvin said. "A mile, tops. We can walk it."

"What about the car?"

"What about it?"

"We can't just leave it here."

"Why not? Nobody's going to be crazy enough to try this road."

"Nobody but us."

She couldn't see him but she could feel him looking at her, that strange deadpan that was almost a smile.

"That's right," he said. "Nobody but us. And if somebody comes along in a Humvee or a half-track, there's room to get around you."

"But what are we going to do about the car?"

"Not tonight," he said. "Tomorrow we can come back down and move it. You've got chains, you said?"

"In the trunk somewhere."

"Chains and a jack and a shovel, we'll get you out of there somehow. You might have to go down backward, unless we can figure a way to turn it around—back to the bridge or so."

"That sounds like hell."

"Oh, it will be," Marvin said. "No doubt about it. But that's tomorrow."

They gathered the equipment from the back of the Bonneville by flashlight: the two sleeping bags, the blankets, the bag of groceries that they had managed to forage from the Food Farm before it closed. They looked like refugees setting out, draped and dragging. Justine didn't want to leave the car behind.

"It isn't far," Marvin said, reading her thoughts again. "It'll still be there in the morning."

He stopped and watched her, pointing the flashlight at the

snow between them so the light scattered up into their faces, blinding her to the dark beyond. Just the two of them, shadowy faces. Dead of winter, she thought: lifeless. Where are we going?

"It doesn't feel right, is all," she said.

"We can go back if you want. We can probably get the car dug out somehow, get back down the hill. We can go wherever you want."

His face, in the half-light, was calm but hard and it scared her. Daddy, she thought. Everybody's right but me. Of course he was right, she knew it, there was no place to go (not Henry's, not home, not Marvin's place) but it didn't stop the feeling. She wanted to be in the right for once.

"This is all my fault, isn't it?"

"What's your fault?"

"Getting us stuck out here."

"We aren't stuck," Marvin said. "We're here, is all. The cabin's just a little ways up but we're going to freeze if we stand here."

"Okay," she said, and Marvin started up and she started up in his footsteps. Chastened, she thought. When do I get to be right? When is it going to be my turn?

A hundred thousand stars came out as they trudged and stumbled up the hill, Marvin breaking trail. A gift. She was lightened, heartened. These diamonds are for me, she thought, though they didn't light her way.

The cabin, though: a pathetic tumble-down plywood box, it leaned and sagged, it smelled of damp wood and rot from the first time she saw it, in spite of the cold air. This was where she had gotten herself.

"Jesus," she said.

"What?"

"Nothing," she said. "Who does this belong to, anyway?"

"I don't know," he said. "I mean, it's in my dad's family someplace. We used to come here when I was a kid."

"You don't know who it belongs to?"

"It's all right," Marvin said. "Nobody's going to mind. Nobody's going to chase us off."

"It's locked," she said, seeing the big grim padlock and hasp in the flashlight circle.

The light traveled up the doorframe, around to the top. Marvin fumbled with his bare hand and came up with a key. The key fit the lock, like a lock in a dream. She still felt like a trespasser.

"You're sure this is okay?"

"It's fine," Marvin said.

(The orange and black KEEP OUT signs, tacked to the trees and fence posts on the way in. NO HUNTING OR TRESPASSING. PRIVATE PROPERTY.)

The inside smelled of damp and rot and sulphur but it was warm, almost hot. Marvin shut the door behind her and the last cool air disappeared. She was sweaty already from the walk up the hill, overdressed. The air inside felt heavy and liquid. She couldn't quite breathe.

"Where are we?" she asked him.

"That's the water," Marvin said.

The flashlight circled and darted around the room—bed, shelves, table, cookstove—till it came to rest on a hurricane lamp. He let the flashlight rest sideways on the table while he fumbled for a match, the accidental light shining down one damp board wall, and in the light she saw that there had once been yellow wallpaper with blue roses, now gray and brown and blooming with damp. She wished she had never seen it. It felt as if the walls themselves were alive, teeming.

Then Marvin got a match lit and then the hurricane lantern and the room lit up with the small steady flame. After the dark of the night outside, the light felt warm. She started to peel the layers and layers of clothes off, though she couldn't quite believe it wasn't a trick.

"How does it stay so warm?" she asked him.

"I told you—it's a hot spring. That's what the radiators are for."

Sure enough, when she bothered to look in the corners of the room, she saw the old iron radiators, just like New York, she thought. City things.

"It comes out of the mountain through a pipe," he said.

"Comes out of where?"

Marvin shrugged.

"It was here before I was," he said. "It's been going a long time. My father said it was from the old times but I don't know. He said the people used to winter here in the old days."

"Which people?"

"I don't know, you know—his people."

She was trespassing, she knew it. Ghosts of dead Indians surrounded her.

"We shouldn't have come here," she said.

"We didn't have much of any place else to go."

"I know," she said. "It's my fault, isn't it?"

"Don't be like that."

"Like what?"

"Like that," he said. "Exactly like that."

A moment's cease-fire, there in the lantern light. She could feel herself in the wrong but she couldn't seem to stop.

"Look," Marvin said, "I ain't mad with you. And as far as I know, I haven't done anything to make you mad with me. Let's just take it easy for a while, okay? It's been a long day. You might not mind this place when you get used to it."

"It gives me the willies, is all."

"You get used to it," he said. "Or maybe you don't, I don't know. We aren't going any place else tonight."

He was right, again. Justine could feel the friction: he's right, I'm wrong, I'm turned cross-grained to the whole fucking world. And yes, this is the way I am with Neil and, yes, I'm making the same mistakes with Marvin and, yes, this is a thing I carry around with me. It was all so clearly her fault and she knew it was her fault and Marvin was in the clear again, exonerated. Which only made her feel angry again. She knew this was not the right thing for her to feel but that didn't stop her from feeling it.

Marvin sat on the edge of the old iron bed and started to unlace his pac-boots.

"Take your coat off," he suggested. "You'll feel better."

"I'm all right."

Marvin laughed at this, laughed right in her face.

"I'm sorry," he said. "Don't get your feelings hurt."

"I'm trying not to."

"It just seems like anything I do or anything I say is going to get you going. No matter what. I mean, I'm open to suggestions."

"I didn't get much sleep last night," she said.

"You don't have to make excuses."

"No, I'm just trying to . . ."

"It doesn't matter."

"Maybe I am."

"What?"

"Trying to make excuses," she said. "It's always my fault! I just get so tired of it sometimes."

He wasn't looking at her, he wouldn't. She sat on the opposite bed and started to unsnap unzip unbutton unlace herself, layer after protective layer. Marvin didn't seem to be stopping. He got his boots off and his jacket and his wool overshirt, and then he stripped off his socks and then his pants and then he was sitting on the edge of the bed in Jockey shorts and a T-shirt, looking at her. She was down to tights and a turtleneck herself.

"What?" she asked.

"I'm just trying to figure you out."

"You and everybody else," she said. "I get tired of it."

"You want a glass of wine?"

"Much better," she said. "I'm getting drowsy."

"It's just the heat."

She watched him in the dim lamplight: his long brown legs and arms, his sinewy neck, shock of black hair. His animal body. Men in underwear. He got one of the bottles out of the backpack—she had bought four, just in case—and found his Swiss Army knife in his pants and turned the tiny corkscrew in. Useful, she thought. Practical.

"I don't mean to be weird," she said.

"I know it."

"Things start to go fast and I'm not good at keeping up. I can't keep a lot of things going at once so I sort of shut down, I get all resentful and strange and you know—you've seen me."

"Don't worry about it," Marvin said.

He poured the wine into two jelly glasses: Justine got Bam-Bam, Marvin got Wilma. They drank without ceremony: decent red wine, nothing special.

"You don't have to apologize," Marvin said. "Things are going to happen or they're not going to happen, things are going to feel right or not. You know? It's all written down someplace already. Whatever is going to happen."

"You believe that."

"I don't know," he said.

"I couldn't live like that, thinking that."

"Sure you could," Marvin said. Suddenly he was cheerful, in that sinister way of his.

"It isn't anything you would pick out to think," he said. "But you go along for a while and you see things. You see somebody making a mess out of their lives with drugs or something, you see a couple of people get together and they don't even *like* each other, you know? and they stay together anyway, making each other miserable. I don't know. I just start to wonder after a while if it's really any of our doing. We feel like we're making these choices but, really, we're just along for the ride."

"I don't like that one bit," Justine said.

"I'm not crazy about the idea myself."

"Who's in charge, then?"

"Nobody."

She sipped her wine and contemplated: the million leaves of the rain forest, Charlie Parker, Japan.

"That doesn't seem likely," she said.

"Look at it this way," Marvin said. "You know those things? You put a penny in the top and it rolls down through all these little nails, I forget what they're called. You know what I'm talking about. It's a simple thing, right? The penny's got to go left or right, one way or the other, off or on. So it hits the first one and then there are four ways to go and then sixteen and so on. The thing is, you can never tell where it's going to end up at the bottom. Some little thing comes along and shifts the penny off course by a millionth of an inch and it comes out completely different. That's what I'm talking about."

"What?"

"It looks complicated but really it's a simple thing."

Justine felt a trickle of fear running down her neck. This seemed like a criminal thing to believe, it seemed like permission to do anything. There had to be a right and wrong someplace.

She asked him, "How could you get through the day, believing that?"

"It's no big trick. You wake up in the morning and you go to work and so on. I'm not trying to talk you into anything."

"No."

"That's the way it looks, is all. I'm not about to shoot myself."

He grinned at her again. And Justine was aware, all of a sudden, that she was miles from nowhere, that nobody on earth knew where she was, that if the roof collapsed or the water turned cold they would die here and nobody would know till spring. Not that she was afraid of Marvin, exactly. This faint sinister edge.

"You could kill somebody," she said. "You could kill somebody and it wouldn't matter, because it was all on schedule to happen anyway. It's just another event, like a walk in the park."

"You think you could never hurt somebody?"

"I don't know," she said; then realized that she was being the conventional good girl, finding the right answers. She raised her head and said, "Yes, I mean I *do* believe that. I have made some mistakes sometimes but I don't think I could ever really hurt somebody."

"Never?"

"I hope not."

"You never picked up your child at three in the morning when he was crying, keeping you awake, and thought about what it would take to let you sleep? You never had one bad thought?"

She felt caught, under the x-ray. There are things we don't say.

"Don't," she said. "Leave Will out of this."

"I'm not talking about him, I'm talking about you. I had a child once myself."

"All right," she said. "Everybody's had a thought sometimes. That's different from doing anything about it."

"That's right," he said. "You never crossed that line."

"How do you know?"

"I can see it in you. I used to race motorcycles, did I ever tell you that?"

"I don't think so."

"Motocross, when I was in high school down in California. And the thing they said was that you could tell the riders who had gone down from the ones who hadn't yet just by looking in their eyes. The ones who never crashed, they were fearless! They had *no idea* of the shit that could happen if they made one little mistake. And the thing that was funny was that they almost never made mistakes, because they weren't scared."

"I've made a couple of mistakes," she said. "Big ones."

"Everybody has. But you never crossed that line, the one where you don't recognize yourself in the mirror anymore."

She felt the fear run cold again along her spine, her neck.

"You sound like you know what you're talking about," she said.

"I do."

"Anything I should know about?"

He laughed softly, a sound which Justine did not find reassuring.

"You know everything you need to know about me," he said. "The same with me and you. I don't know every little thing about you but I know enough. You're all right."

"I'm all right."

Marvin shrugged: sure.

"What does that mean?"

He had to think for a minute before he answered.

"You're here, with me," he finally said. "That's what counts for me. The thing I hate is when you're going along with some-body, doing something with them, and then they start to act somehow and you realize this has got *nothing to do* with you, you know? They're playing out some old game with their ex-husband or their mom or they're trying to undo something they did when they were fourteen. You're just an actor."

They looked at each other and they both realized: this was her, this was Justine.

"I think we'd better stop talking," she said.

"I didn't mean anything by it. I mean, I wasn't trying to send you any special message."

"You're talking about anybody," she said. "You're talking about anybody but a newborn baby. Everybody carries their shit around with them, I mean it's sad but so what? You can't help it."

"It isn't how clean you are," he said. "Everybody starts out dirty."

"What?"

"It's just, whether you can get around it or not. Whether you can get on top of it."

"Well," she said. "I can't."

After that, there was nothing to say, apparently. She sat on one of the filthy mattresses and drew her legs tight against her body, wrapped her arms around them, made an egg of herself. He touched her but there was nothing to touch. She was all outside, all hard surface. Dim light and damp heat. It had been a mistake to come here. It was a mistake to be anywhere. She was sweating in her clothes but she did not want him to see her naked, not now.

It was as though he heard her thoughts.

It felt as if he wanted to open her up, tear at the delicate tissues inside.

He knelt behind her on the mattress and she could feel, with-out turning and looking, that he was naked himself. He eased the lower hem of her turtleneck up and over her breasts, then accurately unhooked the back of her bra. Justine did nothing. She felt his callused hands on the fine skin of her breasts and this could be happening to somebody else—that game, again, of Dead Man's Hand, the cold unfeeling flesh. Go ahead, she thought. Whatever you want.

It was as if he heard her thoughts: he raised her arms above her head and she obediently left them there while he slipped the shirt off, draping it over a chair along with her bra, neat, polite, then came around in front of her and she'd been right: he was naked after all. He tugged her legs out in front of her and she felt the soft, damp, weathered wood of the floor with her bare feet. He rocked her gently, side to side, to slip the tights from her legs, rolling them toward her feet and then off. Her panties were stuck on her thighs, a little scrap of pink, and then he rolled them off, too, and set them neatly on the chair. Whatever he wanted. Justine was neither warm nor cool in the damp air. She was drowsy, the wet wooden rot of the room in her nose. Miles and miles of cold black night against the windows.

Marvin led her to her feet. When she stood, she was suddenly naked in a way she had not been before. His eyes were taking her. He watched her without bothering to pretend that he wasn't. Tit cunt ass fuck, she thought, feeling his eyes on her. Go ahead. Whatever you want.

Marvin carried the hurricane lantern in his other hand. He led her through a doorway, into what she had assumed was a bedroom but turned out to be full of water instead. A room full of water, cedar walls, damp and dripping. The smell of wet pencils. The floor of the room was black impenetrable water, she couldn't tell how deep. Step by step, he led her down. The water was hot on her skin, painful, but Marvin didn't seem to notice. He didn't care if he burned her or not, she didn't care herself. The water steamed and curled around her, a soft, slippery heat, she felt as if her head was full of little twinkling Christmas lights and for a minute she thought she was going to pass out.

"It's too *hot*," she said.

"You'll get used to it."

He grinned at her again, then sank himself into the water, up to his neck. She didn't see how this was possible: the grimace on his face was hardly enough. Then drew her body down into the water, inch by inch. At first she tried to hold herself back but then she stopped resisting. This way as well as any other. Death by fire, death by water.

"It's too *hot*," she said again.

"You'll get used to it," he said, and drew her down into the black water. Heat pressed the oxygen out of her lungs. Tiny rockets fired in the corners of her eyes. Burning, she thought, the naked, flayed . . . What do you want from me? she thought.

Then she said it: "What do you want from me?"

"I don't know," he said. He continued to draw her down into the water, too fast, too hot.

"I never exactly had a plan," he said. "I still don't."

"What are you doing to me, then?"

"Whatever I feel like," Marvin said. "Whatever feels right, I don't know."

"Let me go."

"Not right now. Give it a minute."

"I don't like this."

"You will in a minute. Trust me."

That's it, she thought: I don't. I don't trust anybody. Still she let herself be drawn down, she let herself be led. She was into the water all the way to her neck by then. Her hands floated in front of her, pale fish in the dark water, her shameful body (too big too fat too tall too dark) rested on a wooden bench, barely touching, buoyant. Steam rose in her eyes.

"Just relax," he said.

"I can't . . ."

"What?"

"I can't let myself," she said. "You know."

"You can try."

"What do you want from me?"

"You keep asking me that," he said. "I don't have any big plan. I don't have anything in mind for you."

Justine closed her eyes, and in the blackness felt how tired her body really was, how she'd been holding herself upright with nervousness and will, nothing more. She saw herself from a distance, sad: the girl who once could dance all night, now strung together with strong coffee and fear of dreams. How had she gotten here? An image came to her with sudden scary clarity, the picture of her son's stuffed bear (Will called him Ted, no points for originality, no one to care) lying across the small bed he would never sleep in again, the room like a shrine, everything but the candles. But *it is sad*, she thought, I am not wrong to be sad. This was the worst thing.

"Do you feel better?" Marvin asked.

"I'm all right. There's nothing wrong with me."

She saw the hurt in his eyes: he only wanted her to meet him halfway, she could see that, and she also knew that she was wrong to deny him. But he would never understand. This was also clear to her.

"I'm only thinking," Justine said.

He laughed at her again.

"I know," he said. "I can see it in your face. You look like you're all balled up."

"Why wouldn't I be?"

"Don't get your feelings hurt."

"Let's just quit talking about me," she said. "Let's let the patient off the couch for a while, okay? You can stop trying to figure out what's wrong with me and what exercises I need to do to get better and so on. I'm just sick of it."

"I know."

"Then why do you do it?"

"I can't seem to help it," Marvin said, and grinned. "Nobody can. People get stuck on you, you know that?"

"I never asked for that."

"You never had to."

"It's my life," she said. "It's my life. Why does everybody think they've got a right to tell me what I ought to do? Why can't you run your own business?"

"You came to me," he said.

He was right. It swam into focus, in front of her eyes: that she'd been talking *as if* she were in the right when she knew she wasn't. She was wrong, she was wrong again, and still she was sick of being wrong.

"I'm not sorry you did," he said. "I wanted you to."

He was talking softly, as though he was talking to himself, as though she wasn't even there—the water, she thought, the heat and steam and sleeplessness. His eyes were closed. Nothing was quite real.

"Any time you want to," Marvin said. "Any time you need to come running to me, I hope you will. And I don't mean anything by it, you know, you can get along for yourself. I just want to keep things straight. It's too hard to keep track if you get off into the other."

"The what?"

"Oh, you know," he said vaguely, and waved his hand vaguely.

"You say it's purple and I know it's green. Next thing you know, I'm going along with you just to get along. I say it's purple, just like you, but I still know it's green. It just gets too mixed up."

"What's purple?"

"I don't know."

He roused himself out of his watery torpor, opened his eyes a slit to look at her.

"It was an example," he said. "You know?"

"Sure," she said. Then after a minute: "Are we actually talking about something? I can't remember."

She saw the stoned grin spread slowly across his face—and again it didn't seem quite innocent; he might have been laughing at her expense. At her expense: the words seemed strange to her, now that she didn't have a husband anymore, a house or any money. Despite the heat, she felt a little shivery something.

"Somebody's walking on my grave," she said.

"What's that?"

"Oh, just that feeling . . ."

"What?"

But she didn't want to explain it to him: that first dim recognition that she had actually managed to fuck things up beyond the reparable. The guilty part was the pleasure she took in it. *Now* the storm would come, the winds would blow it all away. It seemed as though it had taken forever to get this far. The doctor's explanation: there's a lot of life in a person, life is a tough tenacious thing, it doesn't let go easily. This trying to explain to her why her son hadn't just died at the scene, why he had lived on and on for nearly a week with every fucking machine in the hospital wired into him somewhere. Life did not like to give up. It was a kind of victory, then, when she could bring things to an end.

Which apparently she had.

"What are you thinking about?" asked Marvin.

"Oh," she said. "You don't, you don't, you don't want to know."

"What if I do?"

"Trust me."

He looked at her: that human concern. I don't want your sympathy, she thought. I don't mean to make trouble. That skittery, leaf-blown feeling, the wind blowing the dead leaves down the gutters and the empty noise and feeling, the emptiness and, underneath, the big world turning slowly under her feet, indifferent. That was where she stood: riding the dirt. Pushed and pulled along by things outside her, and her own feelings going this way and that, right and wrong, happy and sad, she was just so completely *tired* of it by now.

She looked at Marvin and felt the pull in her belly, always when she looked at him.

He wasn't looking toward her but staring off into the middle distance, unfocused, living in his body. He was halfway out of the water and still sweating. His damp skin shone in the lantern light. His black hair was matted down on his head, a little fringe of bangs like a Roman emperor. I'm going to hurt you, Justine thought. You're going to miss me when I'm gone. . . .

She never knew what she was going to feel until she felt it.

Things loomed and swirled like a funhouse ride, shimmering up out of the darkness in front of her. This: the sudden certainty that she was going, gone, already halfway there.

She looked at Marvin like the last glimpse of a city in the distance, a visitor, leaving, looking back. . . . She felt the big fake tears starting up again. Poor me, she thought, poor everybody. She thought of her kitchen in Oregon, remembering the care she had taken with it, the hours of planning when they remodeled, sketching plan after plan on sheets of newsprint. I loved that place, she thought. It had her fingerprints. The apple tree outside the kitchen window, she used to watch it while she was doing dishes, through the seasons. Her grandmother's salt and pepper set on the windowsill. The quilt, neatly folded at the bottom of the child's bed.

Say goodbye, she thought.

Let it go, she told herself—but this meant letting go of everything, of Neil and Will and the old house at Henry's place. Even Marvin was slipping past her, faster and faster, more than she could comprehend. A green place at the bottom of a garden, a child's place. Live Oak Park, she remembered: the dank and mossy bottom where the creek flowed through, next to an old disused shed or court or something, the wet light through the trees and the deep park-green paint peeling off the building, the insect hum of the live world surrounding her, the sunlight on her skin. She had been there by herself, watching the little creek. She had not known she was lost. The little girl lay in the grass and turned her hand over and over again in a patch of sunlight, feeling the warm light on the back of her hand and then her palm. The world was made for her pleasure, and all the things in it. The tickle of green grass on the little lost girl's skin, the whisper and gossip of the breeze through the leaves of the oaks, she was there because she was meant to be there, because it was her home. A place for little Justine. She shivered in the heat, remembering.

"What is it?" Marvin asked.

And she was going to keep it from him but she thought, Why bother? No reason to keep a secret. And her own secrets weren't worth much anyway.

"It's nothing," she said. "I was just thinking."

He looked at her, impatient.

"Remembering," she said. "I must have been six or seven, maybe younger. We were on a picnic and I guess I slipped away when nobody was watching me. It's a scary thing, you know, thinking back, but it felt like a big adventure to me then. It was exciting."

"How long were you gone for?"

"I don't know," she said. "I never got a chance to ask my mother, and my father doesn't remember a thing. Maybe it never happened."

"What do you remember?"

"Oh," she said, "just this place, down at the back of a park. I went back a couple of years ago and tried to find it but I couldn't, or maybe they changed it, I don't know. I'm not explaining very well, am I?"

"Nope."

"It's just, I've been about three places in my life, maybe ten, I don't know—places where I felt alive, where something happened to me. I don't know what happened that day. I wasn't scared or anything but I just felt so at home there, like I belonged, I don't know. I can still remember it so well."

"I remember an ice storm like that," Marvin said. "Right after my brother died."

She looked at him—the dark damp skin of his face and his impermeable eyes—and wondered if he might know her better than she gave him credit for.

"Just all the little things," he said. "It's weird the way they stick with you. We didn't have any power for three days."

"The things that belong to you," she said.

"What does that mean?"

"It just feels strange to me," she said. "How little I've got. I always got through clean."

The heat and haze of the tiny dark room, black water and the flame of the hurricane lantern darting and tickling on the surface of the waves. She ended at the waist, Marvin ended. The cut-off people. It might have been anywhere from ten at night till seven in the morning, she couldn't tell.

"You didn't get all the way through," Marvin said. "You're in plenty of trouble now, for instance."

She searched his face but he didn't mean it unkindly. Gentle man, she thought: gentleman. She could trust him.

It was hard to focus.

Then she remembered: when they left the next day, they would leave together or separately. This had not been decided yet. The tableau through Marvin's window: Marliss looking out, seeing her, not saying anything; Henry sightless on the couch and her husband pacing through the familiar rooms. He had no right.

"What do you want to know about me?" she said. "Anything. I'll tell you."

"I know what I need to know about you."

He blinked at her; and once again she realized that she was miles from home, miles from anywhere, and what if she was wrong about him? What if he wasn't kind, didn't care, what if he was just here to take what he could get? Or worse, she thought: a picture of her own body bleeding in the snow, discarded. It was all okay with her. Whatever happened. Sometimes his eyes looked like a snake.

"Tell me a story," she said.

"No. It's your turn."

"All right," she said. "Once upon a time there was a young girl as beautiful as she was good, and her name was Justine."

"Go ahead."

"Oh," she said, "there isn't any more. It starts and it goes along for a while and then it just stops."

He looked at her.

She said, "I'm being a little overdramatic for a naked person. That's what you're thinking, isn't it?"

"No."

"What?"

He shook his head: nothing. There was nothing for him to say, no magic words that would suddenly make sense of things. Stumbling forward, blunderers. It was strictly accidental that they were here at all. She reached through the water to touch his cock, resting just below the surface but—to her surprise—he turned away from her, denied her.

"What?" she asked.

He shook his head.

"What?"

"I don't know."

"That was supposed to be *funny*," she said. "A little joke. I don't want you to be mad at me."

He looked at her, and she found herself under the lens again, the examinee. She found herself judged.

"Judgment is the enemy of love," she said.

"What does that mean?"

"It means fuck you," she said. "We fight like married people and we don't even know each other. I mean, I don't know what I'm doing and it's true, I don't. But I'll find something. I'm not some basket case."

"I didn't say you were."

"That's just it," she said. "That's just like a husband."

"I don't mean to be."

She looked at his body and her anger dissipated all at once like the air leaking from a balloon and in its place came sadness: she'd managed to wreck this thing too. It wasn't Marvin's fault. She had been born broken.

"I'm sorry," she said.

"Don't apologize."

He looked at her, looked right down under her skin and saw her small and scared and weary inside. She felt his eyes inside her.

"Look," he said. "Let's just quit talking, okay? It seems like we only get into trouble."

"What does that mean?"

"*That*," he said. "That's what I mean. Let's just leave it alone for now, okay?"

"And then what?"

"After that I don't know. You don't know either. It's just whatever happens."

"That's reassuring."

"Please," he said. "We could talk all night and nothing's going to change. You know that. You're tired, I'm tired."

He meant to leave her. Justine looked at him and saw it in his face. He was tired of her, the way she was tired of herself— whether he loved her or not, whether it mattered or not. He was tired of trying to keep her up off the ground, the way she was tired herself. She should have been different, she should have been better. She should have been somebody else.

She looked up at him and Marvin had his finger to his lips, quiet.

She looked down again at where the lantern flame was flickering across the surface of the water and his dick floated just under the surface, the brown of his skin all soft and warm in the lantern light.

"Okay," she said. "Okay."

She lay back into the water, a little shock of heat, it was too much for her but she made herself stay, floating amniotic on her back. She let her legs float open, thinking, *There*, that's all of me. Anything you want to see. Anything you want from me. Everything was going fuzzy around the edges, it was getting hard to care. Just the warmth and the water. It didn't matter. She knew that he was leaving her, but in this slow moment she couldn't think about it. Everything was the same as everything else. Her skin seemed like the accidental surface that it was, between water and other water, blood and air. Erased. What she thought about herself or what she felt, it was all the same and it didn't matter. Electrons moving around in her brain. The biggest feeling in the world and still it could never make it out to the surface of her skin, all the operas and tragedies and it was only one extra life in three billion. That was the thing. Say that it didn't work out and stop there. It was going to take so much energy to start again and she didn't have it anymore—she wasn't twenty-three anymore. There weren't that many hours in the day.

He was looking at her.

He was trying to read her again or maybe not. It didn't matter. He was inches from her but what she felt was the miles of empty space between them, the interplanetary vacuum. He was nowhere she could get to, nowhere she could touch. She was alone and Will was the only one who had ever been inside her and now he was gone. She was just broken, was all. She was just fucked up.

He touched her, the inside of her thigh where it floated next to him. She didn't move to let him, didn't move away. His hand was brown on the white flesh of her leg—somebody else's leg, some-body else's hand. This disembodied . . . She closed her eyes and then she felt him move, his fingers up inside her in the heat of the water and it felt all right. She reached for his cock and found him hard already. And it was just one more thing to do, another plea-sure or complication, whatever it turned out to be. It didn't really matter what she wanted, not now—though she didn't trust her body anymore. She knew this sweetness wasn't going anywhere, they could make love all night, all week, and she wouldn't come, she couldn't, she had failures all over her, big and small—and then she felt him slip into the water between her legs, felt his head surface between her legs and he started to work on her with his mouth and it wasn't what she wanted at all. He was so far away down there! And it was useless to start, she'd tried to explain. She did know what she wanted: she wanted to stop thinking for a minute, please, she was sick of herself and tired and wanted to part company with herself and not all this thinking, *please:* the little endless voice inside her watching, talking, the little commentator (you're never going to come this way, you're only going to waste his time, make his fucking tongue tired, what do I smell like what do I look like where are we going) and just to shut her up, Justine would do anything.

She pulled him up and into her and he didn't want to, not at first, but she couldn't stand it anymore, the way he was working on her as if her body was a broken radio. It didn't matter but she couldn't make him understand. She just wanted to feel something. Even him inside her (skin to skin, no protection) seemed to get lost in the drowsy heat. This layer of dead skin all around her. She couldn't feel anything, couldn't feel it all the way.

She pulled away from him—the little spark of anger in his eyes, she was fucking with him, it didn't matter—and led him out of the hot pool still dripping with water and into the cool of the next room and then out naked into the night.

"What's this?" he said.

She didn't say anything but closed the door, led him out into the snow in front of the house. A hundred million stars in the sky and nobody's footprints but their own. A citizen of the Milky Way, she thought.

He was looking at her and maybe he was right, maybe she was crazy. It was a little late for that to matter. She dropped on her knees into the snow in front of him and took him into her mouth and he was still hard, it didn't take much.

She pulled him down on top of her and inside and this was where she wanted to be. She could feel this. She could feel his cock pressing inside her and his weight pressing her down into the snow along the ridge of her spine, the cold starting to touch her, this is it, she thought, just all the way. She was still hot from the water and her belly was hot where he pressed down into it but the cold was growing inside her, up out of her spine. This is it, she thought. This is it. She started to slip away and this was exactly where she wanted to be, nowhere, it didn't matter what happened to her and she could feel it when she started to let go of herself.

"Come on," she said. "Come on."

But he didn't need her urging—he was driving inside her and then it started to fade, she could feel it, the cold grain of the snow melting a little along her back and the red flesh (she could see herself as if she was outside, the flushing skin where the blood was rising) and Marvin was driving and then it started to fade, little stars in her eyes and the stars overhead receding from her, drawing away as though she was falling and then he started to hurry and she said, "Wait!" but he didn't slow.

"Wait for me!"

And then he was done.

Neither here nor there. She had not quite gotten there and now she couldn't seem to make it back.

He rested inside her for a moment, driving her deeper into the snow with his dead weight. Then stood, and stood around naked as though he was waiting for a bus. He didn't seem to know what to do with himself. She was lying there naked, legs open. She couldn't quite remember. He reached his hand down to help her up but she didn't want it. She got up, backing away from him with her eyes on him as if he had wounded her. At the edge of the woods she looked back.

Then slipped into the trees and she was gone, the darkness of the forest closing in around her.

"Wait," he said.

But it was like a voice on television, nothing real. She walked from tree to tree, the crusted ice making brittle noises under her bare feet, and now at last her feet were cold. The heat of the water was starting to wear off. She could feel it coming for her, the cold inside her, the cold outside. She could hear his footsteps far away. She should have run but she was suddenly tired. She was so easily confused. She saw this plainly about herself. She saw a small hollow inside the branches of a tree, a little clearing soft with fallen pine needles, and she crawled inside it and leaned against the trunk of the tree and rested, waiting for the cold, waiting for it to come and take her. She listened and there was nothing. The only thing wrong was that she couldn't see the stars.

Then he was there in front of her.

"I didn't hear you," Justine said.

"Old Indian trick," he said. "Come on with me."

"I don't want to."

"I want you to."

"Why?"

She couldn't see his face. He didn't say anything but reached in and took her wrist and led her out, out of the forest and through the little clearing and back to the cabin. She let herself be led. All the way, though, she was looking back, and twice she stopped and had to decide: whether to go with him, whether to go back out.

Standing there naked, she saw a pale shape tumbling out of

one of the trees, then taking flight: an owl out hunting. It must have been watching them the whole time. She felt it in her belly, the hunter's freedom. I'm going out killing, she thought. I'll keep you company. It felt like prison when she let herself be led inside.

Love changes nothing. A feeling, nothing more, intangible as smoke or steam. Even the word felt like an exaggeration: I love you, I want your love.

But here it was, the feeling. He watched her sleeping.

It was early, first light.

The light looked clean and quiet, out of a gray sky and through a dirty window. It rested on the contours of her face. Her shoulders, in a thin T-shirt, rose and fell with her breath and her mouth was open a little, like she was about to say something. What? Some message out of her dreams. Some direction. He thought of her the night before: the way she pulled away from him, wanting to go back into the forest. More drama, said the Indian psychiatrist: manipulation, high school theatrics. But she wasn't faking, whatever else she was or wasn't. An admiration. Beyond that a kind of lust, not the regular kind. It was like he wanted to crawl inside her, under her skin, to live inside her like a baby. None of this brain work, thinking: he wanted body to body, transubstantiation. This is my body, he thought, and this is my blood. It was strange the things he wanted sometimes.

Tenderness, exhaustion. The end of something.

Well, he thought: now what?

Still he looked down at her and the gray light on her face was soft, like a touch, and he thought that he might run his hand down under the blankets just to feel the warm skin underneath. In the end he didn't. It was time for him to do something but he didn't know what. It would be hours before she was awake and he knew he ought to let her sleep—the wild look on her face the night before, the way she kept on staring at the windows after he had managed to coax her inside and calm her down with wine. Something had been calling her. He thought about the owl outside the window and shivered. Bad luck, that's all his father had ever told him. The magpie was the messenger and the owl was bad luck. But something about the way he said it made the owl seem worse than simple bad luck. Marvin wondered whether the smell of death still stuck to her, from her boy dying—he wondered if that was what drew the owl here. When he thought about Justine, part of her was dead anyway: somebody you loved on the other side, somebody you weren't finished with, somebody who wasn't finished with you. One foot on either side of the line.

He didn't want to wake her, anyway. He wanted to let her body rest, let her body have a little more say. The body is conservative, he thought. It likes itself, wants to keep on being itself.

Hours before she'd be awake, and Marvin was awake and restless and full of bad thoughts: the owl staring down out of the tree, death by drowning, death by fire. The Christ child, born to die.

He sat by the window and smoked a cigarette, watching the first light sharpen into definition: road, fence, tree. Wondering where he would go from there. Back into his life. Down to California. It all seemed the same to him, it all seemed weightless, and in that moment he was angry with her, feeling like she'd stolen from him. I used to know where I was, he thought. I had an idea, anyway.

But when he looked at the bed and saw her sleeping, he loved her.

He slipped his socks off and his pants and slipped in beside her, trying not to wake her. He tried to rest but there wasn't any rest. He waited for her.

"I'm sorry," Justine said. "That was stupid. I didn't mean . . ."

"What?"

"It's embarrassing," she said. "You know."

"I guess I don't."

She looked at him across the rude plank table. Her hair was strung in greasy lines across her face, a bird's-nest face. She was somebody else now that she was awake, none of his business. She said, "Let's just go."

"Go where?"

"I don't know," she said. "We can't stay here."

"There's coffee," Marvin said.

She looked at him.

"All right," he said. "That's the stupidest thing in the world. I agree."

"I don't mean that. I just . . ."

"What?"

"I don't know."

She looked at him: she was unhappy, she was always unhappy.

"I had too much to drink last night and started doing stupid things," she said. "And it's the day after Christmas. All that business with Neil, I don't know. You don't want to hear about what I'm thinking."

"Maybe I do."

"It's just a mess, is all. I'm not trying to keep anything from you. You've seen more than you need to know already."

"I don't know," he said.

"Me acting foolish."

Little messy bird's nest of a face, he thought. Anger without dignity. She wasn't beautiful in this light. The feeling was still there but he couldn't find it for a moment; so when he made himself touch her (a palm cupped around the curve of her cheek) she knew he was faking, and shrugged his hand away.

"Don't," she said.

"Why not?"

But Justine opened her face to him, and he saw that she didn't want the polite anything, didn't want the cushion, didn't want anything from anybody.

"I'm sorry," Justine said.

"Don't be."

"What do you mean? I got you all the way up here. I got you all wrapped up in this stuff."

"I don't mind."

"It doesn't matter," she said. "It's a mess, is all. And I'm sorry."

Marvin made coffee anyway, instant. It was only eight-thirty and it didn't seem like there was anything else to do. Back in the land of the watches. Now it was time to read the newspaper, now it was time for lunch, this was not where he wanted to be. Last night was where he wanted to be, in the country of last things. The last supper, the last kiss, the last conversation. He didn't recognize this feeling as his own. Usually he was the one who wanted to settle things down, usually he was the one who was trying for the ordinary—but he didn't want this to be over. And there didn't seem to be any way to get her safely home. It was either drive on, drive all night, over the edge and gone, or it was this: this slow deterioration. Her face was gray and set against him.

He put a cup of coffee in front of her without asking.

She looked at it but didn't touch it.

Marvin searched his brain for the words that would bring her around but there weren't any words. His brain made a dry rustling sound in his head.

"I made a fool of myself," she said. "You can't just wish it away."

An hour of shoveling snow, digging out, rooting around in coveralls trying to get the chains around the back wheels of the Bonneville and Marvin knew he should have been miserable but he wasn't. He was the one in Carhartt coveralls, making himself useful. She was the one who was standing around semi-helpless in her fancy baby clothes, teddy-bear fur and down. She had scraped the snow and ice off the windshield and the back window and then she had run out of things to do.

While Marvin dug and rooted and cursed and suffered. He busted a knuckle trying to fasten the inside link of the chains, pulled it out from behind the tire bleeding. "Motherfucker!" he shouted cheerfully. "God damn motherfucker."

"What?"

"Fucked up my hand," he said, holding it in front of his face, watching it bleed. Some weird combination of pain and cold and numb ran through the whole hand; the knuckle didn't hurt any worse than the rest of it. He said, "Like trying to undo a fucking bra strap. You can't see a fucking thing."

"You want me to give it a try?" she asked.

"I'll get it."

"You're bleeding," she said.

Marvin grinned at her. Dirty grease from the underside of her car bled into his knuckle. His hand felt kind of ostensible. My so-called hand, he thought.

"I'll get the motherfucker," he said.

He dove back happy into the undercarriage, hands around the wheel, snow worming its way up the sleeves of his dirty coveralls. *Happy*, he thought: I don't even make sense to myself. But making the body behave, that's one thing; doing work, useful work, that's another. They wouldn't die up there and this was his doing. Maybe she would have died and maybe she wouldn't, if she'd been up here alone. Maybe Marvin got to be a hero out of this deal. But really, it was feeling useful. I'm helping, he thought. I'm not wasting my time.

"Okay," he finally said, and surveyed the work: dug out, chained up, ready to go. "You want to drive or you want to push?"

"Drive," she said. "I guess."

"Drive it is. Don't gun it. When I say go, okay?"

"I *know*," she said.

"People from Oregon," he said. "None of them know how to drive. It's nothing personal."

"Thanks."

Marvin gave up, stationed himself behind the bumper and planted his boots into the snow, searching for dirt, rock, solid purchase. A cloud of toxic vapor spewed from the tailpipe.

"You need new rings," he said. "You ready?"

"I need some more advice," she said.

"Fuck you," he said cheerfully, and felt the transmission lurch into drive, the first spin of the wheels. The chains dug in, slipped, caught, slipped again but by then the big car was moving back-ward.

"Easy," Marvin said.

But Justine knew: she didn't punch it but eased the speed up to a walk, slipping sideways on the snow and then back into the tire tracks and accelerating. Down the hill and once she made it past the bridge, he thought, she'd be home free. He watched the big car slip and lurch and then she was over the bridge and turned around onto the flat and clear sailing all the way to Rivulet and she just kept going.

It took Marvin a moment to understand this.

He stood there in his pac-boots and coveralls in the snow, a little cocoon of warmth in a cold world, and watched her brake lights flash on as she came up to the first turn and the car slowed and then the brake lights went off again and the car kept right on going around the bend and she was gone.

Gone.

It was barely afternoon but the light felt like evening, the bright red of her brake lights shining brightly against the general gray. I'm fucked, he thought. He did a quick check of his situation, then, and decided it could have been worse. It wouldn't get cold for hours, and he ought to be fine for the walk out, which was how far? Six or seven miles out to the road but less than that to a telephone, he couldn't remember how far. A scatter of ranches and cabins down at the bottom of the road. And who was he going to call? A prick of loneliness when he thought of Carla, a needle in the heart. Yes, she would come if he asked her. Yes, he would ask her.

The technical term for you, she said, is *asshole*.

He just accepted it, the way Justine left him. He watched the turn in the road, thinking that she might reappear but not really expecting her. Gone away and left me, Marvin thought, just like that. Like she'd never really been there; then remembered forcibly the several ways that he had managed to fuck up his life because of her, Carla, work, social life in general. Still he wanted her back. For her to just ditch him, here in the middle of nowhere, this was what preyed on his heart. Because he couldn't forgive her for this, not without making himself even more of a fool than he already was.

He waited, a minute and then a minute more, and she didn't reappear. Marvin saw that he was going to have to walk out, which wasn't going to kill him. Also that Justine had succeeded in doing something unforgivable.

Talented girl, he thought. She'd found the spot where it hurt. He wasn't going to beg her, wasn't going to kneel; but then, as he gathered himself and started on down the road, he saw that he wasn't about to start drawing lines. It was only pride, and pride was not much compared to the ache in his chest, the hole where she had ripped herself out of him. This is bad, he thought. She wanted to leave and didn't want to. She wanted to hurt him to keep herself from coming back. Marvin could see everything so clearly! And he knew that seeing and understanding and knowing weren't going to do him any good. This is fucked, he thought. The technical term for it.

The sky cleared in one corner and the winter sun broke through: cold, clear, weak. The one thing he knew was that he wanted her back. Although he'd never had her: not quite. There was no wind and no warmth either. A magpie landed in a top branch of a pine tree, shaking off a load of snow that cascaded down to the ground next to him, a heavy sound like a body falling. It was either get moving or stand there and freeze. Marvin didn't want to. Whatever was going to happen next, he didn't want to find out.

Now the snow is falling, drifting. Now the bison are standing with their backs to the wind, pale brown ghosts in the distance, fading to nothing in the drifting white. The snow sticks and freezes into their matted fur. Their breath hangs in icicles around their mouths. This is no place for you.

Watching from the dome-car window, the girl asleep against his arm, Henry feels the world turning under him. The world is a body! It's like he's always known: the curve of the plains falling away to white nothing, all around them. He's just a visitor here. The train is only passing through. The tracks will heal behind them, like the wake of a boat closing the water behind, the tall-grass prairie rising over the right of way, the wind and rain and chinook bearing down on the earthworks until the sea of grasses rises and falls to its own rhythm again. *Vanity* is the word the Bible uses but Henry doesn't feel it. It isn't vain to try, even if you fail. In some ways the failure is reassuring. He doesn't want to look at his own face in the mirror every morning. He doesn't want to live in a world of his own making.

And this, this world is beautiful. This place right here, where nothing has happened. He feels himself lightening, lifting. There's a stirring in his chest like a box of live bees. The difference between outside and inside is getting smaller. Whatever is inside of him—this *light*—belongs to the world around him, and not to him alone. He belongs here.

The snow drifting, the train car safe and warm and the phantom buffalo outside. He sees them fading into the snow, receding into the distance, into memory where they belong. He can't tell if he ever really saw them or if he made them up; their country is the past, the place where they belong. Now Henry sees that this is his own country. He's gone, all but the memory of him, which is fine with him. It used to be a better world—bigger, anyway. There was room to move. He's had this sense for years now that the world was lurching toward some new kind of life, more organized but not in any way he liked. Like a beehive. The individual bee does not count for much, and when he steps out of line he's dead.

This is Henry's way of keeping time.

I'm late, he thinks: the buffalo fading into the windblown snow. They turn transparent as they recede into the distance, and then your eyes are not sure they ever saw them, pale shapes in a white landscape. The diesel-electric locomotives pushing on through the snow, the effortless comfort of the North Coast Hiawatha, bud vases in the dining cars, grinning Negro porters and bartenders, Henry feels the distant rumble and clatter of steel on cold steel—violence is being done somewhere—but his comfort goes on undisturbed, across the plains at eighty-five. The girl is sleeping on his arm, the afternoon light is fading into twilight, turning blue. The snow is whipping by outside. The bison stand and stare and Henry stands with them, outside, in the wind and the snow, watching the lights of the speeding train until they are gone, gone, gone.

I could do this, she thought. I could do that. Justine took a drink from the plastic cup of whiskey. She was in the same bedroom of the same motel where she'd been with Neil. She was in the same bed, in fact, the same blankets, probably the same sheets. The Diamond Horseshoe only kept the one room heated in the wintertime. The same bartender, sitting in judgment, the same lone customer. There was a telephone on the table beside the bed, a television bolted to the wall, a window to look out from, but she sat quietly on the edge of the bed. She wanted to touch her son.

She wanted to hold his body in her arms, to bathe him in the kitchen sink again. She wanted the smell of baby shampoo and baby powder, the rough and tumble. He had already started to tear holes in his jeans when he left, already started to wear out shoes and bring home scrapes and scabs. The things she would find in his pants pockets doing laundry: pennies, pretty rocks, plastic dinosaurs. Plastic army soldiers which had turned—sometime between her own childhood and Will's—from olive drab into the dirty beige of the Iraqi war. Still they were frozen into their same positions, the hand-grenader getting ready to throw, the lieutenant or sergeant shouting, "Follow me!" Will made the same sound for *pistol* and *machine gun* that the boys made in 1958. Will

learned the same songs in preschool, so that listening to him or
overhearing him, singing to himself, would send her spinning: out
came the sun and it dried up all the rain . . . Okay, she thought.
Where was I?

Somewhere there was a part of her which was not damaged.
There must be. She'd make a list.

She sat down at the knotty pine table; or, as the local classi-
fieds had it, naughty pine. Nobody in this whole state knew where
the apostrophe went. On the way into Missoula it said UNIVER-
SITY OF MONTANA VIETNAM VET'S MEMORIAL in two-
foot highway letters. She shouldn't have felt superior, she didn't
have a reason. But these faces, Marliss's face or Lex's face, built
for turning into the wind at ten below zero, plain practical faces
made for endurance—these faces had nothing to teach her. Simple
survival didn't seem like enough anymore. She'd survived herself,
and it wasn't nearly enough. Survivors: the names in the obituar-
ies, the next of kin and the long lost sisters. Justine wanted something more.

She sat at the desk, rummaged in the kneehole drawer for
writing paper, came up with stationery from 1953, it looked like,
MODERN HEATED CABINS with a little fraudulent drawing of
the motel, pines whispering in the background and snow on the
ground. There was a souvenir pencil in the drawer, too; they must
have ordered a lifetime supply during the Eisenhower administration, and never run out. This thing will outlast me, Justine
thought. This place, this room will be here when I am gone.

She had the plastic bag, the painkiller pills she'd stolen from
Henry—forty of them, more than enough. She'd memorized the
drill by now. Dear Henry, she thought, taking up the pencil. Dear
Marliss, Dear Neil, Dear Marvin. I have more or less had enough.
Sorry. Love. She'd been carrying the pills for a month now, Jess's
little secret, her little secret friends like a pack of cigarettes, forty

of them. Though it still seemed a little hazy to her, that moment when she knew she'd had enough. When the pills kicked in enough to make her drowsy she was supposed to pull the plastic bag on. This seemed unlikely: if she was awake enough to pull the bag on, she would almost have to be awake enough to pull it off again. It seemed as though there must have been some part of the instructions that she missed. On the other hand, maybe it would be clearer when she was in the middle of it, step by step, like a recipe. . . .

She laid the pills out on the desk top, lined them up like little soldiers, four ranks of ten in their blue and gold uniforms. Poor little Jess, she thought. Poor me! But being sick of yourself didn't mean you went away.

Unless it did.

Okay, she thought: this is playacting, and time to stop. She went to the window, pulled the curtain aside and saw that it was snowing again, snowing hard, the big flakes driving down through the lights of the parking lot. The lights looked almost like palm trees on their stands, big frilly circles of white at the tops. Beyond these small circles of light was nothing and more nothing and more, the sound swallowed up by the soft new snow, the light—what there was of it—held down close to the earth. Right here the light was neon pink and jaundiced yellow, the evil light of sodium vapor. This little place, this *here*, she thought, and all that nothing out beyond.

She let the curtain flop down closed again but the memory of the snow stayed with her. She remembered in her hands, which were trembling a little, the drive over from Missoula when she first came here, and she wondered if any of the last few months had actually happened. She wondered if she'd ever made it down off that pass or whether she was still there sleeping, drowning in carbon monoxide, somewhere off the side of the road. This seemed as plausible as anything else: the girl, the gift, the guardian. She was tired, and she couldn't figure a way back out.

Florida, she thought. But that had been a long time before, long enough to be somebody else entirely.

Never mind.

She decided she would get up in the morning and drive to Cedar Key or Apalachicola or Port St. Joe, someplace on the Gulf of Mexico, and she would use the money that Henry meant to leave her to buy a little cinder-block house with slatted windows, palmettos in the yard and a skink in the carport. She would get some small job someplace or maybe, if Henry left her enough, a volunteer position helping others. She'd be a receptionist in an abortion clinic. She'd feed the Negro children, the ones who lived—still—in shacks perched up on cinder blocks, the ones she used to see at eleven-thirty on a school morning pushing empty shopping carts down the streets. . . . She knew that she would always be a stranger there, always an outsider. But this was Florida, after all. Not even the natives would claim superiority. The real inventors of the place were speculators from New York and driftings and leavings from the rest of the South.

She saw herself as she was, but older, alone and self-reliant. She would drive a Toyota and bake her own bread; she would be best friends with the gay best man from the local amateur theater group. Flowers in the flowerpots. Twice a year, some timid flirtation.

No. She shivered at the thought.

But what if she could be somebody else? Some leather-skinned aging bimbo at poolside. Some do-gooder. A thousand awful possibilities. Really she wanted to be twenty-two again. She wanted to start over. And it wasn't going to happen. She remembered the tenderness and tightness of her skin, the energy she'd dissipated in long hung-over mornings, the hopes she'd given herself that were never really hers. She remembered smoking dope and riding her bicycle in search of doughnuts down long, clean suburban streets, streets that smelled of orange blossoms from the groves between them, and she remembered the strange synthetic optimism that came from living in a place where nothing was over five years old, the weather was never bad, it was never busy or crowded or dirty.

She sipped at her whiskey and then poured another, a big one: straight on till morning.

She remembered walking into a Publix at eleven in the morning on some fall day, walking out of the damp and heat of the parking lot and into the cool of the deserted supermarket and it was perfectly cool and quiet, except for the thousand and one strings that swelled out of the invisible speakers, and there had been nothing special, nothing in particular, about that day but she remembered it still: how cool it was, how perfect, how still. She remembered the pock, pock, pock of tennis balls being hit, one after the other, in the cool of the lazy morning, the sound of wind in palmetto leaves, the plinking sound of the college baseball team, taking batting practice with their aluminum bats. Now here she was: drunk, fat, close to forty and alone.

Where is my sister? Justine thought. Where are the people that are supposed to help me?

Then remembered that she had sent them all away. Driven them away; though they'd take her back if she asked, any of them, even Neil, even Marvin. It was as though it didn't even matter what she thought, what she felt. It was as though they didn't even care. . . .

She felt herself starting to spin off course, starting to wobble, her mind spiraling back on itself imperfectly so that the same thoughts recurred again and again but subtly different each time, subtly distorted: I am alone, unloved, nobody loves me, I won't let anybody love me, they ought to love me anyway, they love me anyway but they shouldn't, I'm not worth it, I'm not kind and I don't feel real love anyway, I don't know what love is, I'm love-blind the way some people are color-blind, tone deaf, I don't know what other people are talking about when they talk about love except, except for Will, when I did know love and they can't tell me I didn't!

Will: the one place where she touched ground, the one thing she actually knew how to feel.

She didn't work right no more.

She closed her eyes and the room disappeared and everything holding her to earth disappeared. . . .

Then stood up, shivering a little in the back of her neck, and put the pills back in their yellow plastic bottle. A little closer than she wanted to be.

Then the voice came up inside her: Come on, let's go, what is there to be afraid of? And besides, there was nowhere else for her to go, nobody to run to. No place left to hide. She held the bottle of pills in her left hand. Her life was tapering to this room, this night or the next day or sometime soon, sometime soon, if she could find the nerve. Of course she couldn't find the nerve. If she'd had the courage to end it, she could find the courage to live. She saw herself between, beaten. She took another drink of whiskey and another, flipped the television on, knowing that in five minutes she'd be too drunk. Her teeth ached already.

Jay Leno was talking about the President and Justine's mind wouldn't stick to it. Instead she noticed: the faint sticky yellow varnish of cigarette smoke on the walls, the curtains, the black unsilvered corners of the mirror. Dead moths slept in the overhead light fixture and the room, the rug, her bed and her skin all were covered with a faint fine powder of cigarette ash, whiskey and dried come. Travelers caught out in winter, when the sun falls out of the sky at four-fifteen or when the big arctic weather would come down out of Canada, the wind blowing the boxcars around on the tracks. *Shelter*, Justine thought: a place to hide, a place to run to.

It's come to this: this room, this one night. She couldn't imagine anything forward from here.

Later, she thought, looking at her own face in the bathroom mirror. She wobbled back to the bed, the blue glow of the TV, and finished the glass of whiskey there and poured another into the half-melted ice. There's always later.

Justine was drunk. She knew she should be sleeping. Justine was weeping.

Some man that she remembered vaguely from a long time ago was talking on the television and then she realized that it was William Shatner, talking about a persistent ringing in his ears. William Shatner, she thought, William Shatner. The man, the pajamas. And fuck you too. It was as though television was heaven, as though once you're taken there you never grow up or grow older or die. Shatner would always be with us and Mary Tyler Moore and the way some things went on and on and other things just stopped.

Marvin was out walking under the million stars, alone. The lights of his little house blinked and glittered through the falling snow, a quarter mile away, but after that it was all the way God left it: the snow, the quiet, the scurry of footsteps and wings off in the darkness.

A cold night, a few degrees above zero. If it had been any colder, it would have quit snowing and just froze. The snow made squealing and crunching sounds under his footsteps, the individual crystals sliding across each other. Marvin was wearing a union suit, a flannel shirt, two pairs of socks, a pair of Carhartt insulated bib overalls, a sweatshirt, a quilted canvas vest and an insulated chore coat over the rest, everything worked in and sweated in so that a smell of sweat and wet concrete and lumber rose with the exertion of his walking. He was wearing a wool hat with the flaps down and insulated mittens and a scarf and, despite these layers and layers of clothes, he knew this was no place for him, outside.

He belonged inside, he knew, stoking the fire or sleeping. But he couldn't stay inside, he couldn't rest. It was like his own small house had turned on him, his house wouldn't let him rest anymore. The house was full of memories of her: the smell of her perfume on a shirt she'd borrowed, the ridiculous shampoo that nobody else had ever used, a half-finished bottle of red wine. Not so much Justine herself, he thought—just one more fuckup in a long series. But he knew it wasn't true, even when he said it. This woman was the reason he couldn't get comfortable in his own home, the thing in his mind that had driven him out of doors on a cold night. The snow swirled and whipped in his eyes, his face.

He walked across the open fields, pasture buried under ice, and down along the swale to where Silver Creek ran in the dark. The ground came and went, white on white. He looked up, looked around, and then he was struck by a sharp momentary terror: he couldn't see the lights of his house anymore.

He couldn't see anything, in fact—a sudden swirl of snow that blocked out every sight but the ground beneath his feet, and even that was gray on gray, a faint suspicion. Night and cold and dark. There was nothing to steer by, no direction he could see that was better than any other. This is how you get lost, he thought. You start out familiar. You don't know it's happening till it's too late.

But the creek was there, the familiar sound right next to him. He'd be all right. All the newspaper stories, people loved them, about how the body had been found a few feet from shelter, if they only knew, if they could have seen . . . But Marvin understood, now, it didn't matter how close or distant help was. If you couldn't find it, you couldn't find it.

The snow would clear up sometime soon, at least enough to show the lights from his window. Either that or it wouldn't—it'd just keep right on snowing till the end of time, till all the houses and all the cities and all the animals of the earth were buried under it. The birds would fly through the cold air till they dropped from starvation, exhaustion, the trees themselves buried deep under the weight of snow and no place to land.

The cold wasn't going to kill him. He just had to wait it out.

He stayed down by the creek, the one place where he knew

where he was, and to keep himself heartened he started to sing, softly at first and then out loud so his voice split the silence: "Got a hot-rod Ford and a two-dollar bill, and I know a place right over the hill, the liquor is good and the dancin' is free so if you want to have fun come along with me, I said, Hey, good-lookin' . . ."

She's floating in a warm blue sea, floating under a thick liquid sun that pours down on her shoulders, bobbing with the small waves of the inlet. The water is the same exact temperature as she is, so the line of her skin—what's inside, what's outside—seems arbitrary and vague, the water of her body meeting the salt water somewhere under her skin, the saline blood running warm down her spine. She's limp, contented. She cracks her eyes a little and the sun races through her parted lashes, breaking in cracks and streaks of light, not so much seeing as playing with light—though the blue of the ocean and the blue of the sky appear there, too, but crazy and distorted. She doesn't want to see, doesn't want to open her eyes. She's content to lie there but she can feel her eyes starting to open. She doesn't want them to but they seem to anyway, acting on their own, the big world rushing into her again and her eyes are opening . . .

Her eyes were opening into the dark of the motel room and there was a pounding at the door and a foul, rank taste in her mouth. It was still dark. She took stock: found herself naked on top of the covers, her feet were freezing cold, she had a terrific headache.

"What?" she shouted.

"Justine Gallego?"

A man's voice, a rube. He pronounced it Guh-leg-oh.

"What do you want?"

"It's the Senator."

Still she didn't recognize the voice. She got up in a flurry of spins and rockets, and saw that it was still dark outside. This would be bad news.

"Hold on," she said, searching for some costume. What would a sane woman wear to sleep in? She thought back to herself with Will, motherly nightgowns, hearing his cries in the night and going to him, any time, eager to take his small fears into her body and extinguish them. Will was still dead.

"Hold on," she said again, then slipped into jeans and a sweat-shirt. The face in the mirror was worn and scary. My Halloween face, she thought.

Outside the door, a state trooper in his big hat, a young face, a teenager, almost.

"We were looking for your car," he said.

An inch of snow lay on his hat, his shoulders. It was coming down furiously.

"Is he dead?" Justine asked.

The trooper looked at her with disgust: a whore, a drunk. Or maybe it was simpler than that. Maybe she just didn't know how to act anymore.

"I couldn't tell you, ma'am," he said. "They asked us to keep an eye out for your car, is all. They said you were wanted at the house."

"You don't know anything?"

The trooper was lying, edging sideways.

"I guess he isn't long," he said shyly, not willing to look at her. "They didn't give us details."

Now this, she thought: a soaring feeling in her chest, a feeling that at long last she fit in, the key of her life inserting itself into the empty place. This at least was something she knew how to do. She'd know what to wear and what to feel. This simple sorrow was all she was good at anymore. It came as a relief and she knew she was all screwed up for thinking so but that didn't stop it. She felt a simple sorrowful dignity descend over her, like turning to salt she thought, like looking back and turning to salt . . .

"Give me a minute," she said, and shut the door on his face. She dressed quickly, warmly, layer after layer of polypropylene and wool, heavy boots and socks, protecting the soft warm soul inside her, still floating, still drifting. My *carapace*, she thought, snapping the parka shut. She packed the bathroom last, brushed her teeth and saw—with a sudden guilty knowledge, and no memory at all—that she'd had the pills out again last night. A couple of them had spilled across the counter, as if she had taken them out and then was a little too wobbly to get them all back into the bottle. One of these days, she wasn't going to wake up at all. Better that way, better that way, the little voice inside her cried.

It was five forty-five in the morning, December.

They drove into the first suggestion of light. Everything had something opposite at its heart: night held the day inside it, and inside every life was a death, growing toward the surface, like the green fuse of spring. Someday, not even that long from now, it wouldn't be winter anymore. She said it to herself but she didn't believe it.

"Feels like it's too cold to snow," the trooper said. "I guess it's not, though."

"It's been going all night?"

"All night," he said, wrestling the car in and out of the ruts in the road, going maybe thirty-five on the wide-open highway. "Sometimes it just settles in," the trooper said. "You can feel it. It's just going to keep on snowing."

The first light of morning, deep inside the blanket of clouds. The taste of last night's whiskey in her mouth, the stale smell of the cop cruiser and the little iron flavor in her mouth, like blood, that meant she was going to die soon. Will was still dead, waiting for her. Henry was crossing over soon. The world was resting under the blanket of snow, the world was sleeping. Her limbs fell to her sides, without any will to sustain them.

"It won't be long, though," the trooper said.

"What's that?"

"Oh," he said. He looked surprised, as if he hadn't meant to say it out loud. "Oh, it just seems like when you think winter's never going to be over, next thing you know it's spring. Don't you think?"

"I'm from Oregon," she said. "It's always spring there."

The trooper took this rebuke in silence, which shamed her.

"It's a nice thought," she said, by way of apology.

"You've got to think something," the trooper said. "Otherwise, it feels like this is just going to last forever, you know?"

"I know," she said.

And then the road to Henry's house materialized out of the darkness and the snow, and time started again. A cold cloud settled over her heart. It's time, she thought, now is the time. They're waiting for me.

"Looks like I can make it," the trooper said.

"What?"

"Looks like somebody's got a plow down here this morning," he said. "Looks like they're expecting you."

She didn't say anything, just settled back and waited for the next thing to happen, watching out the window.

Lex sat in the pickup cab and watched her in turn—the old three-quarter-ton Ford with the plow on the front, a beast of a truck, battered and worn. She could just see the hatchet outline of his face but she could tell he was watching her. The cop car glided forward, slow as a parade.

Faces in the windows: Marliss, then Neil. They were waiting for her.

She shut her eyes, and in the darkness saw the little house in Florida that was waiting for her, the new life—modest, reasonable—that she'd set out for herself and then spurned. She was turned away from herself, always. She wanted only the things that she could not have. Even here, she felt herself turning away, away from Henry and from Marliss, away from the places and the people she loved. She had been born broken or she had let herself become broken, careless. Useless.

The cop car glided to a stop and Marliss opened the house door for her.

"We were worried about you," Marliss said.

"How is he?"

Marliss blinked, looking for the words, preparing. Then Neil appeared at her elbow, angry and staring.

"We were looking all over for you," he said. "Where were you?"

"I was gone," Justine said. "The other side of the door. It's none of your business, Neil."

She watched the complicated weather cross his face, the first flush of anger and then the slow rise of his resentment and then the full flood of his certainty. Captive, Justine thought. He knows he's got me. He's used my grandfather as a snare.

"As long as you're back," Neil said.

"As long as you're all right," said Marliss.

"How is he?"

Before Marliss could answer, though, they were all struck silent by a noise from inside the house: a human noise, at least it came from a human body, but it was like nothing Justine had heard before—like childbirth, she thought, like the sound of the wounded in some war movie, but this wasn't acting. It sounded like a man with his insides cut open, a loud foul groaning that swelled into shouting.

"Oh," said Justine. The sound escaped her involuntarily, drawn out by this awful shouting, and the trooper glanced at her with quick instinctive sympathy.

"That's your grandfather," Neil said angrily—as if it were her doing, her fault.

"When did this start?"

"Yesterday," Marliss said. "When they got him home from the hospital, or a little after."

The groaning had subsided a little but now it rose again, louder, echoing from face to face.

"Can't they give him something?"

"They're doing what they can," Marliss said. "It helps at first and then it seems to wear off."

"Can you talk to him?" Justine asked.

"Oh, no," Marliss said. "He's well past that."

"Don't talk about the Senator like that!"

This was Lex, down from the cab of the plow and steaming toward his daughter, angry, red-faced.

"It isn't even him," Lex said. "It's the disease."

They all stood still and silent in the cold morning, listening to the shouting, the groaning and bellowing, all of it sounding as if it was torn live from his belly.

"Oh, no," Justine said. "That's him all right. That's Henry."

Forty-foot Indian Jesus comes rolling down the alley-way, careful not to step on the cars, garages, leaving footprints big as fishing boats behind him. A little tipsy, a little trouble. A sudden attack of tenderness, a feeling welling up in his chest of loss and sorrow and love for the tiny people asleep in their tiny houses, snug in their beds with Jesus watching over them outside, trying not to crush the carport. My people, Jesus thinks, my little people.

But he is not one of them.

Tiny people in their tiny beds, tiny cocks in tiny cunts, the forty-foot Indian Jesus has no place to sleep but the snowy fields and no company but the stars. He stands above his people, taking care. There's no one to take care of him. He's stood alone too long, he's gotten too big, he doesn't fit anymore. He squats in the one city park, a triangle of rotted snow and brown grass marooned among three busy streets, and he kneels among the picnic tables and trees to finger the swing set. Is this the same one? He can feel the cold of the steel triangles holding it up, the incipient ice cream headache, touching the cold smooth tubing with his bare hand. Once he was smaller. Once he had Jackie and Johnny and Judy to keep him company, birthday parties and sledding trips—although he wonders now, alone, whether he was simply making this up out of scraps of TV life. Jesus collects the TV through his finger-tips! He doesn't need a set! June Lockhart speaks to him by short-wave, Burns and Allen, Lucy and Ricky, Barbara Eden—not to mention Eastwood Palance Cliff Robertson John Wayne. God always wanted to be a cowboy growing up, wanted to ride the range and fire a six-shooter at a genuine evil person. A horse to love me and a thousand cattle to tend. Stampede! Indians! The school-marm!

Fuck me, Jesus thinks. The dream of freedom and the dream of loneliness are the same dream.

Down the business route, past the cafe and the grain elevators, the houses sleeping and the snow piled into piers and berms and levees along the highway side; out past the outskirts and into the fields, away from the sleeping houses, out past the railroad over-pass where his father plowed into the abutment in a Volkswagen bug and died, with the steering wheel through his chest, before the motor even quit running. It was still chugging along when the emergency crews got there. That's what they told him, anyway, twenty years after the fact, a fire department legend.

Out where nobody's going to follow him.

Out in the fields he can see the Rocky Mountains hovering in the moonlight, weightless as clouds. Jesus stands facing them, closes his eyes and arches his head back and holds his arms out-stretched, palms up to catch the holiness that radiates from the silent mountains and the night sky. Holiness like sunlight radiating down out of the sky, out of Old Man, the invisible sun, disappear-ing . . . He opens his eyes and searches the stars and the land and the line where they meet, the jagged wound of granite, and the thing he is searching for is nowhere to be seen. God is every-where and nowhere. God is not here. God is elsewhere. But I knew him once, he thinks. He can't remember but he feels it in his bones.

The moaning might begin any time, three in the morning or eight in the morning, four in the afternoon, evening. The regular patterns of life—the morning coffee, the afternoon dishes and sweeping and shopping—didn't stand a chance against these sudden uprisings of pain. And once Henry started, he could go for an hour or two, one night he went for six hours, three in the morning till nine in the morning, so that no one had slept or even rested and they walked the hallways of the big house as though they had been sentenced to it.

None of his doctors understood what was keeping him alive. He couldn't eat, and the water he took was fed to him in slow small sips by Marliss, through a tube she slipped between his lips. He was never conscious. His eyes were closed, except sometimes when he was yelling and groaning, when they would flap abruptly open like the eyes of a scared animal.

"We might as well be strangers," Marliss said.

"I tried to talk to him," Justine said. "It's like we've come to hurt him. It's like he thinks we're the enemy."

They were in the kitchen, afternoon. Henry was going at it upstairs and Neil was wherever he was, watching.

"Then there's the cows," Marliss said.

"What about them?"

"My dad said they're starting to drop their calves," she said. "Dead of winter, right out in the fields. He said he found two frozen this morning."

"They can't hear it."

"My dad said he can hear it all the way out to the road," Marliss said. "When there's nobody driving by, of course. But still."

Henry fell silent for a moment, and neither of them broke it. Please, Justine thought: let it be this time. One of these days he was going to fall silent and then nothing but silence after that. One of these days he was going to be dead. On the other hand: as long as he was alive she didn't have to do whatever came next. She had no ideas for herself but she was sure Neil had something planned for her.

"I keep wondering," Justine said.

"What?"

"You know," she said. "If this is going to be the time."

"It's something that you learn," Marliss said. "There's so much life in a body, you know that life wants to hold on. When you swear to God there isn't anything left and there isn't any point in the fight anymore and then they find something inside them. My husband was like that. He gave himself two months of hell, right there at the end."

"This is something different," Justine said.

"What do you think it is?"

It's just his ego, she thought, his self, his soul. It's his soul and not his body that's doing this. But she didn't want to say this to Marliss—she didn't want to talk about souls with Marliss—and so she closed her eyes and shook her head. In the dark of her eyelids, in the unaccustomed quiet, she felt the weight of her body. She was tired of holding it up.

"I'm just so tired," she said, without opening her eyes.

Marliss made a small sympathetic noise.

"You must be tired too," Justine said.

"I was born tired."

Justine opened her eyes and Marliss was smiling—smiling!—and then she saw that this smile had nothing to do with humor and everything to do with survival. She couldn't fight it so she might as well laugh at it. Justine felt a surge of admiration, almost of love for Marliss—and then she knew that it was love, nothing complicated but just a sisterly love, and again she saw that when this was over she would never see Marliss again. She would never be welcome back. This was where it ended.

She reached out, just because she wanted to, and she picked up Marliss's hand from the table where it rested and she held it in her own, not like a lover but a sister, like the next person over in her row at church. Marliss looked a little surprised but she wasn't worried about it.

"I just wanted you to know," Justine said.

"What's that?"

She searched her mind for the words to say but all she found was a big hot molten ball of feeling, hot and acid, resting in her throat. She was way before words, way before any kind of orderly feeling.

"Just this waiting," Justine said.

And Marliss said nothing, just took her hand and squeezed it in sympathy and smiled again and Justine smiled, although it made her face hurt, the unaccustomed muscles.

"I don't know what I would do without you," Justine said.

"That sounds like the kind of thing you're supposed to say."

"No."

"You know what I mean."

"I do?"

Marliss took her hand away and stood and went to the counter next to the sink and wiped it down with a damp dishrag, bustling. Justine had found the magic word again.

"What?" she asked.

But Marliss wouldn't turn now, wouldn't give her face.

"What?"

"Oh," Marliss said, "it's just, I don't know. You and me, we aren't the same. I like you just fine, it isn't that."

"What?"

Marliss turned, and Justine saw how close to the edge she was, the edge of something, like a cracked china plate.

"You're going to walk out of here," Marliss said. "When this is over, you're going to go back home. You've got a home to go to. Me and my dad, it's not the same."

"You're always welcome here, you know that. I hope you do."

"It's like being a guest," Marliss said. "This felt like home. I know it never was."

"You can have it," Justine said.

Marliss looked at her, sharp and angry.

"That sounds like a joke to you," Justine said. "I didn't mean it that way. It just seems like you and Lex, you've got more of a right here than anybody. There's more of your sweat on this place than mine."

"That's not what I'm talking about," Marliss said. "Look, let's just skip it."

"What?"

But this time Marliss held her hand up between them, palm facing Justine, like a traffic cop calling a halt. A cloud of feeling, a wave, welled up inside Justine but now it couldn't come out. She felt the longing, like a spurned lover: if she could only find the right words, she could make everything perfect again. If they could only talk. Marliss went back to her bustling, closed up inside herself again, her back to the table. Justine felt the start of tears in her eyes, a sharp sandpaper feeling. This was not going to work out. This was not going to be fine.

A brief, uncertain quiet.

Then Henry stirred: a soft sound at first, so she wasn't sure she was really hearing it, Oh! and then the gathering noise, the sounds coming closer together and then running together and the voice of his death building in his chest and then spilling out, all at once, over the sound of the dishwasher, over the sound of the house and filling the rooms and the two women stopped in their meaningless movements and looked up and there was only one master in this house.

Seven days, then, since Henry came home from the hospital and no sign of this abating, the sound welling up and out of his chest and filling the house, filling the valley that the ranch sat in. None of the persons and none of the cattle slept easily. Lex had already found a dozen frozen calves lying on the hard ground, half drifted-in with snow. The birds would fly in during the intervals of silence, same as always, but when Henry started up again they would fly away. Justine had seen this with her own eyes.

Twice, now, she'd found herself standing at the head of Henry's bed while he was peaceful, holding a pillow in her hands and praying for the nerve to use it, just slip it over the blank face and hold on and ride him down until he was dead. She didn't have the nerve, though. She didn't have it in her. Those arms of his, those big hands that rested like sleeping animals on the coverlet— she could see the strength still in them. And she knew that Marliss was right, the doctors were right, that there was more life in a body than anybody would guess and that life would hold on to life. She could imagine, easily, those big hands coming to life while she was trying to put him down. I'm only trying to help, she thought. I'm innocent.

Four in the afternoon, the flat gray light of winter. She was alone with Henry in his bedroom, curtains drawn, a single slit of daylight showing through. He was quiet for now and the house was quiet. Neil was somewhere downstairs, waiting for her. They were in separate bedrooms by then, and nobody in the world knew what would happen after this. She suspected Neil had a plan for her. Daddy and daddy and daddy, she thought. I want to marry Marliss. I want to marry Marvin—and realized, as she thought this, that she didn't strictly think of him as male, or as female. A friend, companion. The thing that was calling to her, a soul looking out the window on a clear night.

She had put him out of her mind as an impossibility but just the thought of him awakened her. Where was he? Why wouldn't he come and rescue her? But she knew why: she wouldn't let him. The look on his face when she drove away that last time, not quite surprised. Whatever happened next, she was going to deserve it. Still she carried the image of Marvin deep inside her like a present she was saving for later. It didn't have to make sense to bring her happiness. She wasn't a reasonable woman.

Henry stirred in his sleep and she jumped, startled. Her nerves were sanded, naked and raw after days of sleeplessness.

"The blue," he said.

And she said "What?" but he wouldn't talk anymore. He had not been talking to her in the first place. He was nowhere close to her; or so she thought.

Then she saw him struggling to move his lips and maybe it was Henry and maybe it was the disease but it wasn't the shouting this time. It seemed like he was trying to talk. Justine knelt next to the bed and tried to pray, remembering that it had worked before or seemed to work, in the hospital room when she first got here. She felt how much farther she was from God now. He had turned His back on her. He had decided to let her live in a place where nothing added up and nothing made sense, just so she could see what it felt like.

She tried to pray anyway.

She tried to pray by the old rote and rosary: Bless me, Father, for I have sinned. You moved the beads along and your sins were gone. Hail Mary, full of grace. She watched Henry's face for signs but it was the old blotched and mottled carved wood of his head, still on the pillow. His eyes were moving behind his closed eyelids, she could see this. Blind.

"Your friend," he said.

"What?"

She couldn't understand him. She saw him flick one of his hands dismissively, a little papal wave shrunk to a quarter inch's movement.

"You mean Marvin," she said, suddenly understanding.

He closed his eyes even harder, agreeing. He meant Marvin.

"It's time," Henry whispered.

A delicate thrill ran up her spine as she came to understand the words. She couldn't even tell if the words came out of his mouth but she had read them plainly on his lips: It's time. She watched his face, and knew that this was the last of Henry.

The thing that would be missing from the world when he was gone.

As she watched his face, she saw Henry himself recede from his face for the last time and the tendons in his neck tightened and his head nearly lifted off the pillow. She hadn't seen this before and she wasn't prepared for it. The neck tightened and the head lifted and the first small cry started down in his belly, moving into his throat, a small clearing of his throat and then "Oh!" he said.

She flinched away but it didn't stop. "Oh!" he said, and then the next was the same syllable but long, drawn out, the suffering inside him coming out as sound, escaping. She couldn't stand it. She stood, and found that she was still holding a pillow in her hands, and took the pillow and held it in both hands but she couldn't. She stood next to the bed, calling herself names: weak and stupid and shy. This was a simple thing that he asked her and she knew which way was right and still she couldn't bring herself to do it.

A simple thing.

She dropped the pillow and left the room, closing the door behind her, but the sound was not stopped by the door. She stood in the hallway. She closed her eyes. Something needs to be done, she thought. Somebody needs to do something.

The telephone rang and rang in the empty house. Marvin heard it from outside, chopping wood, and thought to answer it. He set the splitting maul down in the splinters and bark.

But there was nobody he particularly wanted to talk to except Justine, and it wasn't likely to be her.

The blood coursed hot through his arms and back as he rested. It was a cold clear day but he was alive and strong and at home in his body. He picked the splitting maul out of the mess and addressed himself to the lodgepole round on the splitting block. In a single easy movement he raised the maul above his head, then let it fall, guiding the heavy head with his shoulders and arms, letting the weight do the work. The wedge-shaped head drove into the soft wood, hard, not hard enough. It stuck there, the round of wood dangling from the head. Marvin swung the maul again, log and all, and drove it into the splitting block again and this time the wood split cleanly, flying into the corners of the yard with a clean musical sound. It was like hitting a baseball, Marvin thought: the satisfying solid contact, the crack of the bat. It was like catching a fish. It was like this, it was like that—the mind idling while the body worked, which was exactly how Marvin wanted it lately. It was like a codfish. It was like a tampon. Wood heat warms you twice, once when you cut it and once when you burn it.

A Benny shaved is a Benny urned.

Stacking the wood against the outside wall of his house, under the eaves and next to the door, he thought it might have been Justine after all. Justine on the phone. She was calling him to say she loved him. They would fly to Florida. Coconut, pineapple, banana, Marvin thought. A good long ways from here. Lately, the trailing end of winter, he was sick of it: sick of gray skies and indoor living, sick of the scouring wind, on the rare clear days, that blew down the valley like an arctic locomotive. I vote for sunlight and for warmth, he thought, remembering the shape of the words in her mouth. Cut-off jeans and cheap beer, poolside, seaside. Wish in one hand, shit in the other, see which one fills up first.

His father had said that to him. At least, Marvin thought he remembered it.

The grass was always greener.

A long splinter jutted up under the heel of his glove and into his palm. When he lifted the glove to look, there was blood. He finished anyway, the last few bolts of stove wood.

Inside, the heat was sudden, unexpected. He was down to long johns and insulated overalls already, the jacket stripped off in the heat of work, and now the overalls came off, too, and he was hobbling around the house in wool socks and a red union suit. The splinter was deep, jagged, a tear rather than a needle. The skin was ripped away from itself. In the old Navy, *Old Ironsides*, more died of splinters than of cannonballs—one of those facts that wouldn't go away, good for nothing, it surfaced every time he got a splinter and then receded into his brain again, lurking, biding its time. The shit that's in my head, he thought—like the sweepings in the corners of the living room, little dust bunnies of fact, opinion, image. The Vietnamese colonel shooting the Vietcong suspect in the head, on the TV, 1968. The volume of a cylinder: $2\pi r$. Kennedy's secretary was named Lincoln, Lincoln's secretary was named Kennedy.

The telephone started to ring again as he was washing the wound with yellow soap, stinging tears in his eyes. Stigmata, Marvin thought. He couldn't quite rid himself of the feeling that it was her. He let it ring five or six times. Bob Champion wanted him to get an answering machine but Marvin wouldn't, on principle. The soap stung deep within his bloodstream, the curing poison.

Then rushed from the bathroom, before it was too late, and snatched up the telephone and it was a woman, not—it took him a moment to understand—not Justine.

"Marvin?"

"Can I help you?"

"This is Marliss McLeod. From the Senator's place?"

He was angry, for no reason he could justify. Nothing was her fault.

"Can I help you?" he asked again.

"I was asked to call you," she said.

"She can call me herself if she wants to talk."

"She doesn't want to talk," Marliss said. Now she was angry too.

She said, "She just wanted me to give you the message."

"What's that?"

"She said he needs your help."

"Who?"

"She said you'd know."

And he did, and Marliss did, and the secret hung between them on the telephone line: the Senator, the promise. What exactly would happen next? And even as he thought it, a hot, unreasonable spill of anger rose up in his throat, betrayed: I'm not even one of you anymore. I'm not like you. I'm just a servant, same as the servant girl, same as always.

"I'm sorry to bother you," Marliss said. "She asked me to call."

"Tell her if she wants anything, she can call me herself. She knows where I am. She can come find me."

"Please," Marliss said.

And there was a note of worry and of sorrow in her voice that stopped him for a moment.

"He needs your help," she said.

Marvin stopped, thought, breathed in and breathed out. But the anger wouldn't dispel so quickly, and the words came twisting out of his mouth.

"Tell Justine," he said, "if she wants a favor out of me, she's going to have to come find me."

"I don't see how she can do that."

"She's going to have to ask me herself," Marvin said. "You tell her that. All right?"

"I'll tell her but I don't see how . . ."

"You think she likes you?" Marvin said.

A silence, a shock.

"You think it keeps her up at night, worrying about how you're doing? You think she knows your middle name? You're just a way for her to get what she wants, the same as I am. You know that, don't you?"

"You don't know anything about her."

"Maybe I don't," Marvin said.

He took the telephone handset from his ear and held it in the air in front of him. Her tiny insect voice chirped from the speaker: Hello? hello? He slipped the handset down onto the telephone again, slowly, gently, like he was afraid of hurting her, and then he felt the acid backwash spill into his mouth. The momentary pleasure of insulting her and now the long-lasting regret. Nobody's fault but mine, he thought. Nobody's fault but mine.

But the pleasure came back to him. That's what I am, he thought: I'm angry. He stood up, sat down again, lit a cigarette and saw that his hands were still trembling. Oh, but he liked the feeling of being angry. It felt like something, instead of nothing. It's what I've got, he thought: the injured party, the justified man. She'd left him standing by the side of the road and now she wanted him back for a favor. Fucking bitch, Marvin thought—and the words unlocked the things he was feeling, the things that had been hidden from him. Not that it was going to do any good but still there was a joy in the words: Fuck you, rich girl.

Not that any good was going to come of it.

The house was too small to hold him in this mood. He quickly finished dressing the splinter wound, the welcome sting of Mercurochrome, the smell of adhesive tape—another smell of mother, comfort, grade school, afternoons—then pulled on jeans and a denim shirt. Fuck you to the people who didn't love me enough, who died when I didn't want them to. It was good the way this made him feel, all wound up and energized and ready to pop somebody, a feeling the color of good sharp steel. At the same time knowing there was nobody out there to blame it on.

Nobody's fault but mine, he thought.

Out, he thought, the other side of the door, remembering when he had been a teenager and anger had been enough to get him through a day, a week, a school year. On behalf of the injured, abandoned child, Marvin was pissed. On behalf of the scared teenager, the sailor boy in the shit-smelling steel toilet, the grown man ditched by the roadside, Marvin was pissed. He stared in the mirror, full of grievances. He ran cold water over his face. Nothing changed.

This anger filled him with memory; half his life he'd been

angry, the angry child, four years of high school, three in the
Navy, it was something he'd learned to live without but it had
taken him years. Now here it was, back again. Marvin made himself sit at his own kitchen table. He made himself remember
where this anger had gotten him to in the past, fights and jails and
whiskey. Fuck you, he thought. I don't need this again. He saw
her face in the air in front of him and thought, Thanks for starting
this up again.

Out of the house, then. Out into the cold afternoon. The
pickup started first try and he drove back toward town, toward the
Mini-Mart, where he filled the truck with regular and bought two
packs of Marlboros and a half case of Budweiser. Being angry gave
him the right to do anything. He thought about driving by the
state store for a pint but not in winter. If it had been summer he
would have. Too many people dead by the road, frozen in their
cars. One little mistake. Still he felt the longing, he just wanted
the blackness at the end of the night, the only cure he knew for
this. A cure for myself! Marvin thought. The patented . . .

He started off thinking he was driving aimlessly, anywhere
away from town, a cold beer open in his lap and the rest of it
handy. A lead-gray afternoon, the cows like ants at the far end of
the fields, black on white. Cars and pickups passed by, and stock
trucks piled high with bales of hay, big green wedding cakes. All
this earnest work and Marvin wasn't doing any of it. The only time
he didn't feel like a tourist here was when he was at work. This
life went on all around him and he didn't have any part of it—the
people who bought and sold, traded cars, started garage sales and
raised cows, the ones who wore the red vests at the hardware store
in town and helped each other find the right size screws out of the
rows of drawers, the ones who knew how an automatic transmission worked and how to keep a stock tank from freezing up and
how to sew up a hand caught on barbwire, this common life with

each of them holding up a tiny corner of it so nobody had to bear the whole weight—this was what Marvin was jealous of. Fry cook, railroad dispatcher, nurse, truck driver, bartender. They recognized each other in the afternoon and waved and sometimes stopped in the middle of the road, even in the sixty-five-mile-an-hour parts, and rolled down the windows of their pickup trucks and talked for a while. They met each other in bars, at high school basketball games and zoning meetings, they sold each other real estate, they slept with each other's wives and married off their kids to one another. Marvin felt this enormous fake nostalgia for this world, fake because he had never once belonged inside it, because he wasn't even sure it existed. But he suspected it—a common hand-held world, tiny and secure. While he himself was stuck in the big world. Get out on the interstate and never look back, any time he wanted to. Where he could be: California, Arizona, Tacoma, Washington. He could be pounding nails in Portland. He could be dead. Nobody would notice for a while.

Before he knew it, he was out in Silver Creek Canyon again, where he had seen the Senator first. He stopped at the top of the hill, remembering the white horse, and he saw some small discoloration under the snow that might be blood or just old dirt, churned into mud and refrozen and snowed on. Even if it was blood, what would it prove? Marvin had been there, written in water. He was here and then he was gone, the memory thin as air, insubstantial as the peaks that hovered in a gray haze on the horizon. Still, a life had been lost here—the puzzled eyes of the horse on him and Marvin knowing he was guilty. The horse had not done anything wrong. He was just in the way. And then it seemed to Marvin that maybe it had been the horse's doing after all, that the Senator wouldn't ever have had his accident and his attack if he hadn't hit the horse in the first place. One of those ideas that seemed to turn the thing on its head but it didn't matter. Whose fault was the accident? Whose fault was the horse? Things happened was all.

Marvin opened the sliding window behind his head and tossed the empty beer can into the bed. The air on the back of his neck was cold, wet, bracing. It was maybe twenty. There was snow somewhere near.

He left the horse's deathbed behind him, drove right by the place of the accident, opened another beer for himself and started up the Silver Creek grade, a snaky three miles of bad road.

It wasn't till he was halfway up that he realized what he was after: this was the road to Victor Lane, the canyon where Billy Lefthand had his trailer. My father's friend, he thought. There was something worrisome about it. He wondered if he was really going to visit Billy and, as he did, he wished that he had not opened this second beer, that he had not drunk the first one.

Another time, he thought. Sometime better.

But he still drove out the canyon. There was noplace to turn around anyway till Victor Lane and when he turned off he kept going. He didn't stop.

What's he going to tell me? Marvin wondered. What has he got for me? But it didn't matter. He knew there was something there. Besides, this time of year, the road up to Billy's place was enough to keep him full-time busy, rock and ruts and ice and no time to think about anything else. He turned the hubs at the bottom of the hill, shifted into four-hi and ground up the grade in his granny first. Twice he nearly put it into the creek. The canyon closed in tight around him, dark woods and rock and two tire tracks and, after the first mile, no tire tracks.

Billy wasn't there, he couldn't be.

Marvin couldn't quite believe this. He charged on anyway, slipping and sliding and breaking loose little patches of gravel that rattled in the wheel wells. He was wide awake now, the beer forgotten in his lap, a rock wall on one side and a twenty-foot drop to the creek on the other. Coming down was going to be worse. He could feel the dread settle into a ball in his stomach. Shuttered summer cabins rested under the snow, hunting places, shacks. Marvin was the only one up here, he could feel it. He felt the natural world closing on him like a glove on a hand, the big indifferent thing. If he spun the truck into the ditch, he would die here. If he just ran out of gas he could maybe walk out. Inside and inside and inside as the track wound up the canyon.

Finally he came over the lip of a hill and onto a small clear flat, a little park of big-bodied ponderosa pines, and there, in a circle of its own junk, sat Billy Lefthand's trailer. The blue stripe Billy described was nearly invisible under layers of rust and pine sap and dirt. There was a Studebaker pickup, a wringer-type washer, firewood, dog pens, flat tires and wheels and several rusty mufflers welded together to make a man. The muffler-man was waving at Marvin, at anyone who came into the yard.

What he didn't see was smoke in the chimney or any sign of a running car. No way that Billy had been here for at least a month. Marvin felt the disappointment in his chest, harder than he expected. What was he looking for here?

Nobody home. Marvin shut the truck off anyway and the quiet surrounded him, intense and immediate. The cold, the forest, the afternoon slowly fading. He held his face in his hands, suddenly aware of how tired he really was. He felt like he'd been carrying himself for days, trying to keep himself moving to keep from slipping under. The anger was dissipated, gone, but this sadness was no better. I'm depressed, he thought. The word changed nothing.

Marvin got out, looked around. Despite the evidence, he felt like he was being watched; a feeling that took a minute to resolve itself into the idea that Billy Lefthand was dead.

There was no particular reason to think this, no body, no

blood. And none of the cars in the yard looked like they could run. Therefore: Billy was someplace with his good car, and Marvin was here alone. Billy was in Mexico, California. Billy was sipping rum out of half a coconut shell. Marvin couldn't shake the feeling, though. He walked through the unbroken snow of the yard and saw that it hadn't been walked on for months. The old footprints between the woodpile and the door were softened, rounded with the months of snow. There was nothing else to read—a crow in the trees, a wind somewhere above him in the branches of the fir trees.

Marvin had no business here, he knew it. He was trespassing. There was something here for him, though—a broken promise, anyway. Maybe nothing more. He circled the trailer, finding only more junk, no signs of life.

He found himself at the front door again and—before he could stop to think, like diving into cold water—he put his hand on the doorknob and turned it and the door swung open in his hand, no resistance at all, like a door in a dream. It was that easy.

Inside was dark and it took his eyes a moment to adjust. Meanwhile there was the smell of the place to work on, a complex pungent stink of wood smoke, sweat, onions and wet newspaper. It smelled more like a cave than a house.

"Hello?" he called out. "Hello?"

Nothing answered, as he knew it would. Still, he knew he was trespassing, knew he was leaving signs of himself all over for Billy to read. If in fact Billy was alive to read them. Dead man, Marvin thought. Dead man, come and help me out. The things he wanted and the things he needed were always in places he couldn't get to—somewhere behind the mysteries of the Church, somewhere in Billy's life.

His eyes cleared into the darkness and it was a disappointment—an ordinary trailer, ordinary table, chairs and a refrigerator.

What had he been expecting? But it wasn't this, this old man's life. The walls were soiled wherever Billy had touched them, over the years, the oils and sweat built up to a complex pattern of where he had lived and where he had touched—behind the one chair at the table, for instance, where he always sat, where his head would brush the wall as he was getting up. Above the wood stove was a dense plume of black on the wall, a generation of smoke and soot. The chrome handle of the refrigerator was clean but around it was black. Strange, Marvin thought, the feeling he had. It felt like somebody had hollowed out Billy's life and made a mold of where it used to be, and now Marvin was standing inside the hollow place. The only thing missing was Billy himself.

Marvin went to the bedroom, the bathroom, the spare room out back with no sign of Billy—no sign of the body, that is, and no sign of the living man. But Billy was everywhere in this trailer. Everything he had touched bore his mark, the bathroom sink and the bedroom doorknob, the rifles lined up on the spare bed: a .22, a 30–30 and a 30–06. Part of the overpowering wolverine stench of the place was from a bag of deer skulls in the corner of the spare room. There was no decoration anyplace. A kerosene lamp stood on the main table but Marvin guessed that this was for times when the power went out. This was a life whittled down to the bone, what Billy needed to stay alive and nothing more.

There was something here for him, some message. Marvin couldn't help feeling it. He sat at the table, exactly where Billy would sit, and tried to fit himself into the socket of Billy's life. He wanted to know what Billy knew.

But the house was mute, the secrets all kept.

Marvin sat at the table until the silence gathered and surrounded him. He was prepared to wait it out but then the silence came and nothing came after it. Billy was sick or dead, he was staying with relatives, he was gone for the winter. Marvin was home, with nothing to show for it. The thing he was looking for was not here, or else it wouldn't reveal itself.

And he saw, then, that it had been foolish to come to Rivulet in the first place. Nothing more than a suspicion to drive him and now he was here and now he knew: there was no secret, after all. No wisdom waiting for him. The evidence of Billy's life had nothing to say to him.

He'd been cheated again.

The anger started to rise inside him again and this time it was general: he was angry at himself for being a fool, more than that for being a fool again, he was angry at Billy for disappearing, he was angry for the silence all around him and the same stupid questions and the same nonanswers. Just that same concrete wall, always—and then the one thing, the hope of love, and this was maybe the first time he had thought to use the word *love* about her but, standing in Billy's kitchen, he realized that this was the word for what he felt. And she should have loved him and in his heart Marvin knew that she did.

She loved him and she was cheating him out of it—not her, exactly, and not her husband either but the dead boy. Marvin saw them all suddenly from above. It was like looking down from a balcony or an office-building window at the tiny people down below and Marvin could see, for once, what the people down below couldn't: the way they were driven by forces beyond them, the way they chanced, collided, coupled and separated and they thought it was their doing. They thought it was what they wanted but it never was. It was just the big blind machinery of the world driving them along. *Blind:* the old man dangling, the helpless hands and none of his money and none of his power could do anything about it. It was only chance that had brought Marvin along and whether it was good luck or bad, it was hard to say.

There was no mind out there to tell him. There was nobody keeping score.

Marvin saw this all at once and it felt like a cold wind that had come to scour him out. The emptiness inside him rang. His anger came back to him and this time it was even better, even hotter, because he saw that there was no reason to feel ashamed of it. He wanted her and he ought to have her and there was nobody to tell him not to. He pushed himself back from Billy's table and went outside. He knew what he was going to do.

But first he opened another can of beer and rested, in the quiet of the forest. Everything he could have had. The question was still with him: had the world stopped talking? Or had he just forgotten how to listen, or never known? The things a father should have taught him. And now there he was, inside the empty space, inside the shell of his father's life, but he would never grow into it. He listened to the forest but there was only silence, the same as ever.

Justine looked out the second-story window and saw Marvin's truck coming up the drive, and her heart leaped up inside her chest, alive. He was hers. He had come for her.

She stood at the window, watching, when she knew she should be going down to him. She was afraid for him. Her husband was here, her grandfather, Lex, all the men had brought her back here. Recaptured, she thought. She hadn't been sleeping well.

Still there he was, Marvin!

A moment's sadness came over her, sadness inseparable from the sight of him. Love had come for her at last and found her overripe and damaged, full of water. She couldn't love him as she should. It wasn't in her anymore. You should have found me when I was twenty-one, she thought, you should have seen me. Standing in front of the mirror in a swimsuit. Riding my bicycle through the scent of orange blossoms, the dense subtropical night . . .

Marliss came out of the Senator's room, some instinct, the thing that guides the schools of fish when they all turn at once. She came to stand beside Justine at the window and, when she saw that Marvin was coming, she put her hand on Justine's forearm. In warning or in sympathy, Justine couldn't tell. Were they together in this?

"I wish he hadn't decided to come," Marliss said.

"You called him yourself."

"I know I did. It's what the Senator wants. That doesn't make it right."

"Don't," Justine said.

"What?"

"I'm happy to see him. I'm sorry, I know I shouldn't be. But I am happy, you know? My little ray of sunshine."

"What?"

"I don't know. I can't sort it out."

"He's going to get himself hurt," Marliss said.

Justine watched in dumb show: the black Ford pickup slowing as it passed the old home place down in the valley, the white buildings scattered among the leafless trees. Then it came toward them up the hill at not much more than a walking pace. There was something deliberate, sinister in his slow progress.

"Maybe that's what he wants," Justine said.

"What?"

"Nothing."

"There's my dad," said Marliss.

On cue, Lex came out of the shed nearest the house. Whatever it was he did in there. Justine had seen him in there lately, just sitting and smoking and looking off into the middle distance.

"Oh, Christ," said Marliss. "What's that in his hand?"

"I can't tell from here."

"Tell your Indian friend to get out of there," Marliss said. "Go down and tell him to get out. I don't want this kind of trouble."

"How could I tell him anything?"

"You go down to him and tell him to go," Marliss said. "Go on and hurry! Somebody's going to get hurt."

"Lex wouldn't do anything, would he?"

Marliss just looked at her as if she was a little baby, a little stupid baby, and Justine felt a thrill deep along her spine. This was trouble, this was real. She let go of the window molding and started to run toward the stairs, slowly, like a person under water.

Marvin finished the cold beer and crumpled the can and tossed it into the back of his truck, where it rattled around, breaking the quiet in Billy Lefthand's yard.

Then got in the truck and started it up and drove out, careful. A thousand ways to die, he thought: pinned under your own truck. They'd find you in the spring. Take a lot of pills and do some drinking, cross a biker in a bar one night. You could get killed by a bear. One of these deaths was waiting out there for him: liver cancer, railroad accident, drinking and driving. But right now he was somebody else's death.

It felt good to turn the tables for a change. Instead of waiting around for some anonymous fate to show up and claim him, now Marvin had a hand in it. He was taking charge.

He spent the slow drive down imagining what it would feel like, how he might try it. Marvin didn't know the first thing about killing somebody. In the movies, they just put the pillow over their faces but it seemed to Marvin that he could breathe through a pillow himself. And what if the old man fought back? He remembered the power in those big freckled forearms, power that had gone to sleep, true, power that had let itself go into weakness. But what if that strength came back? Marvin felt a prickling along his scalp, an inkling that this wasn't going to be as easy as it seemed when it was just an idea in his head.

Coming out of the woods, though, he thought: I am the angel of mercy. This is what I am supposed to be doing. Go and give a drink from the death cup. Give the old man his rest. And then he would be done with all of them and done with her and then he could move along. He felt like the woods, the fields and forests, were coming to take the old man back and Marvin was just their hand in it. As if he had a place, as if he meant something, as if the talk of the wind in the trees had suddenly become intelligible.

Talk to me, Marvin thought. Tell me what to do and I will do it.

Out of the woods and onto the blacktop again. He felt a sickness, back in the known world: fences, satellite dishes, passing Pepsi-Cola trucks. A growing suspicion that he had missed the point entirely, let himself get caught up in commercial crap, in wanting and buying and paying for the things he bought. At the same time knowing that he wasn't any good at it, really, that this mooning after something different had left him in between. If he was really in this everyday world he would have had a house and a wife by now and he would be the one to take the drift boat out with the bankers on a summer night. That's the life I want, Marvin thought. Forget the past, the possibilities that never quite materialized, the ghosts on the TV screen. Get my ass in gear and get out there and make some money.

Out of the Silver Creek Canyon again, and as he started out west toward the mountains and toward the Senator's place he started to realize again. A human life, he thought—a murder. A mercy killing. Marvin realized that he was not going to be able to do this. He didn't know or love the Senator. He didn't owe him enough to make this make sense. A simple roadside accident.

They can all go fuck themselves, Marvin thought: the woman, the husband, the Senator. They're the ones that owed *him* something. Instead he was driving out to do their dirty work for them and he knew he shouldn't be and he didn't stop driving. This is where I get in trouble, Marvin thought. Walking in with my eyes open.

Not until he was in the Senator's driveway did it turn real to him and by then it was too late to back out. He had a feeling like a gate was closing behind him, although he could have turned around and driven out any time. He had a feeling like there were eyes in the house watching him, eyes in the barn. Maybe he could get in and get out and do the Senator this favor—but even as he thought this, he knew it wasn't true. Her husband was there, and the hired man. It really would be much easier and more sensible for him to turn his ass around and get out and stay out.

But she had sent him the message and that was the deal. If she asked him, Marvin would do it. Another code he didn't make up, didn't actually know if he approved of it or not, but it didn't matter. You act like a man, he thought. High performance. Here I come.

He drove up to the gravel turnaround in front of the big house, the big disgraceful house, and cut the engine of his pickup and sat there a minute. But waiting wasn't going to make this better or easier. He got out, empty-handed, and started toward the front door, which swung open before he could get to it.

It was her husband, standing in the doorway.

"Can I help you?" asked the husband.

There was somebody behind Marvin, too, but he couldn't turn

to look—like a game of chicken, he thought. Whoever blinks loses. Whoever backs down.

"I came to see Jess," Marvin said. "She left a message."

"I don't think so," the husband said.

"Look," Marvin said. "Please, okay? She called me and she wanted to see me. That's all. I just want to tell her something, talk to her for a minute, and then I'll get out of here."

"I can give her a message."

"We're getting off on the wrong foot here," Marvin said. "I don't have anything against you."

"I don't have anything against you either. But she isn't well, and I can't let you see her."

Marvin stood silent, trying to think of a way through or a way out. The husband had a name but Marvin couldn't remember it. His face was a bureaucratic blank, like a man from the Motor Vehicle Department. Some kind of everyday concealed rage, and Marvin knew he was dangerous. Marvin was giving him permission to use whatever anger he had stored up inside him, whatever daily grievances and insults had accumulated over the years, the death of a child, Marvin remembered, the theft of his wife. Marvin didn't have the anger to match this. He felt quite suddenly calm and foolish. These things have a logic of their own, he thought. I shouldn't get caught up in them.

"Look out!" she said.

It was Justine, peering around her husband in the darkness of the doorway. He could see the pale oval of her face, felt the surge of happiness inside him, and then he understood why he had come: for her, for love.

"Lex, leave him alone!" she said.

She was talking to the man behind him. Marvin stepped sideways, twisting, trying to see the other man without turning his back on the husband. The husband stepped in front of Justine, edging himself out of the doorway. The man behind him was the ranch hand, the older one. Marvin didn't know his name. He was a short gnarled root of a man in denim from head to toe, carrying an ax handle in his hand.

"I don't want trouble," the little man said. "I think it's about time for you to pick up and go, all right?"

Here is the point, Marvin thought. Here is the moment we have all been waiting for. I can pick up my things and go home and this trouble will be over. Nothing good will come of this and I have no business here.

For a moment he thought that he would go, and the thought came as a relief. Whatever was going to happen next, he didn't want to know. Just walk.

But as soon as this thought formed in his mind, he knew it wasn't true. It was too late—whatever he meant to do, whatever evil thought or evil spirit had brought him here, it was too late. He couldn't back down now. Not with Justine watching. Not in the sight of these two men.

Marvin turned his back on the little man with the ax handle and started toward the door again. He could hear Justine say something but he couldn't make it out, like she was speaking a language he didn't know. One foot in front of the other, he thought, it doesn't matter what you feel. Here is the script and all you have to do is follow. He saw the husband looming in the doorway, suddenly surprised and maybe afraid. This fear in his eyes made some dark part of Marvin happy.

And then he saw the eyes glance away, behind him, and then away, and he heard the swishing of the ax handle in the air a moment before it cracked into his shoulder. He half collapsed, spun to face the small man and saw the handle raised again and ready to strike down at him. Marvin raised his hand to defend himself, the little man brought the ax handle down again on the hand that Marvin had raised to protect himself and smashed the upraised hand and Marvin felt the small bones breaking with a kind of wonder. One lucid moment—he stared at his hand—and then a pain like gasoline and then he turned, ready to kill him one-handed, and the ax handle landed on the side of his head and that was that.

She was praying when the medical techs came and slowly lifted Marvin away from her and left her there on the ground like the discarded shuck of something. He too was on the ground, center of attention, the rituals of medical life being performed on his body: pulse, respiration, blood pressure. And in that moment Justine felt the fear all alone, the familiar spirit. What if he was dying? What if Marvin was to be taken from her too? And there was no ground under her feet, no reason to hope. She had been here before with Will and she had hoped and she had prayed and she had wept until her eyes felt like burnt sockets, the holes where someone had put out a flaming stick. She had torn her clothes, literally, in the secrecy of her bedroom, and then hid the torn blouse so Neil wouldn't find it. She had done what she could and more, she had continued to hope and more, past the point of hope and still not giving up, until the blank indifference of the world finally wore her down.

"Holy Mother of God, pray for me, now and at the hour of my death. Hail Mary, full of grace, the Lord is with thee. Blessed art thou among women and blessed is the fruit of thy womb Jesus."

"He's okay," one of the medical technicians said to her. "He's messed up but his vitals are good. What happened, anyway?"

She opened her mouth to tell them but no sound came out. Marvin was alive. After that it didn't matter. She knew that she loved him and now she was sure of it and it felt strange, that she had never known this before or maybe never admitted it to herself. One more name to call herself. And in among her happiness that he was alive, twined around and inextricable, was the knowledge that it didn't matter, not for her. They were out of time. Even if he could forgive her for the things she had done, there wasn't a time or place to do it. Goodbye, she thought. Good luck. I love you.

"Could you come and take a look?" Marliss said.

They all stopped, and turned to look at her. She was standing in the doorway with tears running down her face.

"It's Henry," Justine said.

Marliss turned to look at her, a look of contempt. Not simply that Justine was stupid but she had always been stupid. Marliss had never liked her.

Then she turned back to the technicians, without answering Justine.

"It's the Senator," she said. "I think something might have happened."

Another siren. Everybody looked: a sheriff's car.

"Alvarez, go take a look," the ambulance driver said. "We can take care of this one."

This one, Justine thought. Mine.

Marliss stood aside and Lex and Neil and one of the technicians filed past her on the way upstairs, the technician with his black tool kit. Marliss stayed in the doorway, waiting for Justine. She didn't know which way to go. She wanted to go in and pay her respects to Henry but there was Marvin on the frozen ground, under a blanket, the two other technicians wheeling the gurney toward him and Marvin still not moving, a little sound coming out of the back of his throat, a humming.

Marliss walked over to where Justine stood. Her eyes were full of the same unexpected hatred and contempt and Justine felt it down in the center of her belly, the fear.

"What happened?" Justine asked.

"Never mind," Marliss said. She stared up into Justine's eyes, just so she got the message. This was her doing.

"You can go now," Marliss said. "All of you."

Justine stared at her, bewildered. This angry stranger.

"You did it," she said.

"Never mind," Marliss said. "You can just go."

And turned and went back into the house and left her there, alone. "One, two, three!" the ambulance technician said, and she turned and they had loaded Marvin onto the gurney and then they raised it and wheeled him over the lumpy frozen ground to the waiting ambulance. The cop pulled up, parked, got out and looked around, as if he was enjoying the scenery. The doors closed on the ambulance but it didn't move. Justine stood there, listening to the wind blow through the fence line and the bare trees. There was nobody to keep her company. The cop started to walk toward her. The dogs, in the kennel next to the barn, began to bark. She looked back over her shoulder at the house and there, in the second-story window, was the pale face of her husband like a moon, staring down at her, watching her every move.

"Fucking rich girls," Bob Champion said.

"She wasn't any kind of girl," Marvin said. "Thirty-eight years old. She wasn't all that rich, either."

"You know what I mean."

Marvin bobbed his head.

"I do," he said.

"Get in over your head. Doesn't take long, either."

He ripped the check out of the big brown vinyl book, handed it to Marvin, who fumbled with it. His left hand was in a cast to the elbow, his right hand bandaged, the outside two fingers splinted together.

They were in the kitchen of Bob's house, which was really Bob's wife's house—decorated in what Bob called French Provincial Whorehouse and smelling like several room deodorizers. Floral, Marvin thought: the difference between real cherries and cherry Life Savers.

"There's a little extra in there," Bob said. "A couple of hundred. I'd give you more but I haven't got it."

"That's all right," Marvin said. "I mean, thanks—I appreciate it."

"The other thing is," Bob said, and he looked around like he was embarrassed or scared. "Well," he said, "even if you get all healed up, you know, by the spring, you've got some people pretty well pissed off at you. I mean, I know it's not your doing."

"Some of it is."

Bob looked at him sharply, and Marvin saw that Bob was angry at him too—not angry like Marvin injured him or anything but pissed the way you get when somebody does a stupid thing. Marvin should have seen the consequences.

Bob said, "Yeah, you're right, it is. You could have done a little better for yourself. Doesn't matter much now."

"No."

"It's all water under the bridge, as they say. But it wouldn't make much sense for me to hire you back on."

"No, I understand that," Marvin said.

"I mean, there's a fucking carpenter behind every tree in this town. It's not like I've got anything personal against you, you know that. Just I can't afford to lose the work. You know what I'm saying."

"It's a small town."

"Smaller than you think," Bob said. "Apparently."

He grinned at Marvin, without humor and without affection.

"You fucked up," Bob said.

Marvin felt a flush of anger in his blood: Bob was right and he knew he was right and Marvin had no choice. He had to take it. Didn't mean he had to like it. I'll pop you one, Marvin thought, take that smile right off your face. Then remembered his hands. Then remembered this wasn't Bob's fault at all.

"Okay," Marvin said. "I fucked up."

"I'm not trying to rub it in."

Bob closed the checkbook and stood up from the kitchen table and then this was over too. He stretched out a hand and Marvin gave him the bandaged wreck of his right hand to shake and it was done.

"You got any ideas?" Bob asked. "You thinking about sticking around town?"

"Oh, you know. I've got a daughter down in California, I haven't seen her for a while. After that I don't know."

"California," Bob said. "You can have it."

"I don't mean to stay."

"Well, we'll see."

Bob edged him closer to the door, the proverbial bum's rush, Marvin thought. Here's your hat, what's your hurry? What was he supposed to do here? But it had already been done, everything had already happened that was going to happen here. One foot in front of the other, then. Keep moving. Something would happen next. His truck was waiting outside, idling, breathing exhaust into the still cold air. His guns, his father's records, his clothes were packed in the camper shell on the back. Marvin didn't want to let go of this moment, somehow. If he could just hold on. If he could slow things down.

"It's weird," he said.

"What?"

"Oh, just one thing leads to another and now here I am again, you know?"

"I guess I don't."

Bob was looking at him and they weren't close, they weren't really friends, and Marvin knew he didn't have any business telling Bob this. It was personal. But he couldn't seem to stop.

"This was just where I always thought I would end up," Marvin said. "You know, to come here and make a life. And now I'm all packed up again and heading out, I don't know."

"You should have taken better care," Bob said.

He was looking at Marvin, he was putting a judgment on him, and there was nothing Marvin could do.

"I don't mean anything personal," Bob said. "But, you know, you could see it coming."

"Maybe you could."

"Well, yeah," Bob said. "Well, okay. What are you going to do about your tools?"

"What do you mean?"

"I don't know," Bob said—and then they both looked at Marvin's hands. "There's a bunch of that stuff I could use," Bob said.

"I don't think so."

"I didn't mean anything by it."

"No," said Marvin. "I was wondering myself, you know, it all depends on how they heal up. But there isn't a hell of a lot else I know how to do. I could always go back to being an EMT, I guess."

"I always wondered why you quit."

"It gave me bad dreams," Marvin said. "Can you give me a hand loading up?"

"Sure thing. I think I got them all here."

He went back inside to fetch a sweatshirt and Marvin sat there hating it, all of it. Life in the goldfish bowl.

The garage door opened from inside and there were Marvin's tools: the circular saw and belt, the Makita power miter, the hole saw, the big 14.4 cordless drill and five-gallon mayonnaise buckets and files and fishing tackle boxes full of God knew what, Marvin couldn't remember. He lifted what he could but it was mostly Bob, tossing the stuff into the truck with no more care than he had to. The stuff in cases bounced off the bags of clothes. The practical life, Marvin thought. I could have learned it from you.

"I'm sure there's some shit I missed," Bob said.

"That looks like most of it."

"Well," Bob said—that awkward pause before moving on, nothing more to say or do but still . . . Their breath came in clouds in the cold morning. Finally Bob said, "Anything else I find, I'll set it aside for you here. There's always something."

"Thanks," Marvin said.

"No, thank *you*. Anyway."

"I'll see you."

"See you."

He stepped back into the garage, and then the motorized garage door closed in front of him—smiling all the time, insincere—and Bob disappeared and that was that.

A cold pearly morning of frost and ice fog was lifting, the sunlight somewhere inside, a few layers deep. Out, then, past the town and the edges of town and the mobile-home lot that was the last thing before the cows start: INSTANT QUALITY LIVING stuck in his head and rang there, a little circle of words for his mind to go around and around. INSTANT QUALITY LIVING INSTANT QUALITY LIVING. A rosary, Marvin thought. The magic words. The ice was lifting off the fence posts and the roadside weeds, jewels and beards of ice that melted into water as the sun emerged from the white sky and Marvin knew he might be seeing this for the last time. One of everything, he thought: that's all he had left in the bank. One morning, one road, one more thing to do and then he was gone. The future—anything past this morning—loomed in front of him like a blank place, a television between channels. The creek ran next to the road, half buried under ice. A magpie lit on a gopher corpse.

This place used to belong to him, all of it.

He drove to his house, he packed the last of his boxes and suitcases into the back of the pickup. The empty rooms called out to him. They wanted him to stay and feel sorry for himself, the gray morning light crawling across the bare floors. But it was almost noon by the time he got packed, time to go if he wanted to get anywhere that night. Though there was no hurry. The motels stayed open and the Denny's and the gas stations. He could drive all night if he wanted to. If he had to.

Anywhere, anybody.

He checked the thermometer outside the window for the last time: twenty-one degrees. He had bought it but it was screwed into the wall and he'd decided to leave it—a little souvenir of himself, of the person who lived in that house, the person who could still be living there.

Justine in firelight, at the old house.

But it was no use thinking about things. He turned the lights out, locked the door and slipped the key under the closed door and that was that. It was too cold to linger, and besides, there wasn't any point. Nothing Marvin thought now would keep him here. There were no more problems to solve.

"Closing time," he said aloud. You don't have to go home but you can't stay here.

His voice rang across the ice crust of the snow, out into the hard sky and was lost. The creek ran through ice, a constant chatter. He stared out at the snow-covered pastures, waiting for an explanation. He was looking for the words to explain himself but there was nobody listening. The sun was high overhead, bright but lifeless, and the sky was a beautiful transparent blue. A cowboy moon shone through the day. Marvin shuddered. There was something wrong with him, something damaged, he didn't even know what was missing. A magpie, messenger, flew onto the nearest fence post and stared at Marvin but he could only see the bright eyes and blue-black feathers and white. Beautiful, he thought, but he knew that wasn't the message. The world has never stopped speaking, Marvin thought. The world is alive.

He would take the back way down into Rivulet and then the

state road—two-lane—and then pick up the interstate, out into the big world. It was time to get moving. Marvin got into his pickup, fumbled the key into the ignition with his bandaged hand and started the Ford. Out into the big world again. I'm free again, he thought, and drove off slowly, never daring to look back. What had been left behind. The road opened up in front of him and took him in.

Printed in the United States
by Baker & Taylor Publisher Services